The Wedding Veil

"Masterfully woven . . . a literary homerun."
—*New York Journal of Books*

"A perfect blend of historical fiction and modern love.
I didn't want it to end." —Fiona Davis,
New York Times bestselling
author of *The Magnolia Palace*

"An awe-inspiring novel." —Brit & Co

"A delightful, glamorous fairy tale for those of us who
know that 'happily ever after' only arrives after we've
learned to stand on our own." —Kristin Harmel,
New York Times bestselling author
of *The Forest of Vanishing Stars*

"Like sweet tea, Woodson Harvey's writing coats your
soul with heart." —E! Online

"Through an exploration of love, family, and identity,
The Wedding Veil guided me on a heartfelt journey
brimming with endearing characters and delightful
twists. I absolutely loved it." —Kristina McMorris,
New York Times bestselling
author of *Sold on a Monday*

The Summer of Songbirds

"A warm, hopeful story of friendship, love, and second chances. Put this in your beach bag immediately."

—Emily Henry,
#1 *New York Times* bestselling
author of *Book Lovers*

"Harvey reminds us that sisterhood can take many forms . . . With a strong dose of nostalgia . . . [fans] will revel in the support the women demonstrate for one another."
—*Booklist*

Under the Southern Sky

"A heart-wrenching tale of love and loss . . . Fans of women's fiction will devour this."

—*Publishers Weekly* (starred review)

Feels Like Falling

"This is more than a novel about friendship; it is also a story for friendship: you will find yourself sharing it with everyone you love. Dive in; the storytelling is delicious!"
—Patti Callahan Henry,
New York Times bestselling
author of *Becoming Mrs. Lewis*

"Fans of Mary Kay Andrews and Mary Alice Monroe should add this to their beach read lists."   —*Booklist*

fervently, you'll forget they're not actually real. Another masterpiece."

—Kristin Harmel,
New York Times bestselling author
of *The Forest of Vanishing Stars*

"Harvey's growing fan base will find another great beach read in this second novel in her Peachtree Bluff trilogy. . . . Harvey is an up-and-coming Southern writer with staying power." —*Booklist*

Slightly South of Simple

"My prediction is that writers come and writers go, but Kristy Woodson Harvey is here to stay." —*HuffPost*

"Heartfelt . . . I look forward to getting to know this cast of strong Southern women even better."
—*Deep South Magazine*

Kristy Woodson Harvey

The
Wedding Veil

A Novel

POCKET BOOKS

New York   London   Toronto   Sydney   New Delhi

Pocket Books
An Imprint of Simon & Schuster, LLC
1230 Avenue of the Americas
New York, NY 10020

This book is a work of fiction. Any references to historical events, real people, or real places are used fictitiously. Other names, characters, places, and events are products of the author's imagination, and any resemblance to actual events or places or persons, living or dead, is entirely coincidental.

First Pocket Books paperback edition May 2024

POCKET and colophon are registered trademarks of Simon & Schuster, LLC

Simon & Schuster: Celebrating 100 Years of Publishing in 2024

For information about special discounts for bulk purchases, please contact Simon & Schuster Special Sales at 1-866-506-1949 or business@simonandschuster.com.

The Simon & Schuster Speakers Bureau can bring authors to your live event. For more information or to book an event, contact the Simon & Schuster Speakers Bureau at 1-866-248-3049 or visit our website at www.simonspeakers.com.

Manufactured in the United States of America

10 9 8 7 6 5 4 3 2 1

ISBN 978-1-6680-2530-7
ISBN 978-1-9821-8073-7 (ebook)

To my sister-in-law Dorothy Coleman,
my cousin Sidney Patton,
and all the women who have worn the wedding veil.
Each of you inspired this story of what it means to be a
part of something that has come before—and will
remain long after.

The
Wedding Veil

Magic

Six-year-old Edith Dresser's skates moved heavily, as if she were rolling through sand, across the patterned wool rug in her mother Susan's bedroom. She lived for moments like this, when she had her vivacious, beautiful mother all to herself while her three sisters continued their skating downstairs in the dining room. Usually, her mother's lady's maid would have helped Susan get ready for the party she was attending this evening, but she wasn't feeling well. So instead, Edith stood—her skates making her taller—admiring the rows of frocks for every occasion in her mother's closet.

"Do you think the pink for tonight, darling?" Susan asked. Edith tried to focus on her mother, but her child's eyes wandered to the back corner of the narrow closet. "I love pink, Mama," Edith said as she clomped ungracefully to a garment she knew well. With a tentative finger, she traced the lace on the edge of her favorite piece, the one she and her sisters loved to try on most: her mother's wedding veil.

Susan turned and smiled, watching her daughter study one of her most prized possessions. In a burst of energy, she moved behind Edith, swept the long veil off its hanger, and motioned for Edith to follow her. In the light and opulence of her bedroom, Susan placed the cherished Juliet cap on her small daughter's head, gently touching the rows of pearls at the bottom. She smiled.

"Just look at you, my girl," Susan said as she arranged the lace-edged tulle around her daughter's shoulders, the contrast great against her gray wool dress. Edith stood as still as one of the statues in the yard, holding her breath so she couldn't possibly damage the veil.

Staring into the mirror, Edith felt transformed. It was still her reflection looking back at her, in her usual outfit with her favorite roller skates. But, somehow, she was completely different.

Susan bent down until her eyes locked with her daughter's in the mirror. "One day," she said, "when you are quite grown up and find a man you love very much, you will wear this veil just like I did when I married Daddy."

Edith watched her own eyes go wide, imagining. Then she scrunched her nose. "But I want to stay with you, Mama." Edith knew that, in other houses like hers, little girls were supposed to be seen and not heard. They weren't allowed to roller skate inside and certainly weren't permitted to play dress-up in their mother's elegant clothes. Why would Edith ever want to leave a mother who let her keep a dozen pet turtles in the yard?

Susan laughed, moving in front of her daughter to

adjust the veil again. She wrapped her in a hug and said, "No, Edi. You are going to find a wonderful man and be the most beautiful bride. Daddy will be there to walk you down the aisle, your sisters will stand beside you as your bridesmaids, and I will sniffle into my handkerchief and wipe my eyes because I will be so proud and happy."

Edith was confused. "If you're happy, why would you cry?"

"Because that's what mothers do at their daughters' weddings."

Edith studied her mother, trying to think if she had ever seen her cry from happiness. She couldn't remember a time, but, then again, Mama had a whole life that didn't involve Edith, many hours that she would never see. And she figured that Mama liked living with Daddy, along with Edith and her sisters Susan, Pauline, and Natalie. So perhaps Edith would come to like having a family of her own as well. But she had conditions. Thinking of her favorite storybook, *Cinderella*, she said, "If I'm going to get married, I think I'd like to be a princess."

Susan laughed delightedly. "Yes, yes. You, most certainly, will be a princess. You will live in a castle with many acres to roam to stretch your legs and plenty of fresh air to fill your lungs. You will have your own lady's maid and a nursery full of lovely children. You will find a husband who will love you more than the stars, who will give you the earth and everything on it."

This gave Edith a wonderful idea. "Can I marry Daddy, Mama?"

Susan smiled indulgently. "Well, I'm married to Daddy. But you will find a man just like Daddy, who is kind and handsome and loves you very much. And he will take care of you like Daddy takes care of me."

Edith nodded. Becoming a bride suddenly seemed very, very important. She looked back at herself in the mirror, at how beautiful the veil was and, when she was wearing it, how beautiful she became. "Is this a magic wedding veil, Mama?" Edith asked.

Susan nodded enthusiastically. "Why yes, darling," she whispered. "You have discovered the secret. Once you wear it on your wedding day, you will be happy forever."

Edith, looking at herself one last time, wondered if she should share this life-changing news with her sisters. But no. That would ruin it somehow. She had a secret with her beloved mother, one to call her very own: The wedding veil was magic. And once she wore it, the fairy-tale life her mother had promised would be hers.

Follow the Rules

Present Day

M y mother had been telling me for months that an April wedding in Asheville was risky. *Snow isn't out of the question, Julia,* she'd reminded me over and over again.

But as I stood awestruck at the brick pathway that led to the conservatory at Biltmore Estate, admiring a field of tens of thousands of orange and yellow tulips, their faces turned toward the sun, it felt like snow was definitely out of the question. A long table sprawled in front of the brick and glass space, with a massive garland of roses, hydrangeas, and, of course, tulips running its entire length.

"It's perfect," Sarah, my best friend and maid of honor, whispered in this holy quiet. I nodded, not wanting to break the silence, not wanting to disrupt the overwhelming peace.

Sarah linked her arm through mine. "Are you ready?"

I nodded automatically, but what did that even mean? Could anyone ever be ready? My wedding wasn't until tomorrow, but this bridesmaids' luncheon was the start of the wedding weekend. While my fiancé, Hayes, and his friends shot skeet and drank bourbon and did whatever else a groom and his groomsmen did before a wedding, I would be here sipping champagne and eating tea sandwiches with my mother, my bridesmaids, my aunt, and the women in Hayes's family—including his mother. Their difficult relationship made my feelings about this event complicated. What made them simpler was the woman responsible for the splendor of this day: my grandmother Babs.

Maybe a person couldn't be responsible for the *day*—after all, no one could control the weather. But Babs was the kind of woman who seemed like she could. She—along with my aunt Alice, who was my wedding planner—hadn't just picked the brown Chiavari chairs that went around the table and had umpteen meetings with the florist and agonized over every detail of the menu for this luncheon. She had actually, somehow, made this day a perfect seventy-two degrees filled with beaming sunshine and fields of impeccable tulips because it was *my* day. Even if she didn't quite approve of the groom.

Babs never came out and *said* she didn't approve. But I felt it. I knew.

My mother on the other hand . . .

"It's here! It's here!" she practically sang from behind me. I turned to see Mom and her twin sister coming up the path.

"So getting here an hour early to have a glass of

champagne by ourselves didn't really pan out, did it?"
Sarah said under her breath.

"On the bright side, Mom *looks* like a glass of champagne," I said.

She was wearing the most perfect champagne-colored sheath with a tiny belt at the waist and chic tan pumps. Aunt Alice was clad in an eerily similar dress in pale blue, but with a wrap. I hadn't actually seen either of these outfits on my mom or aunt, but I had heard about them for months.

"They look gorgeous," Sarah said. "And very well coordinated." They had perfect matching blowouts, although Mom's hair was much lighter, verging on blond, while Alice still made the valiant attempt to keep hers dark, even though it meant that covering her grays was a constant battle.

"Did I tell you about the PowerPoint?" I asked.

Sarah furrowed her brow, which I took as a no.

"Babs took an iPad class at the senior center so she could better assist with all the wedding details. She made everyone in the family send photos of their outfits—complete with shoes, accessories, and purses—for each event. Then she made a presentation and distributed it to the entire family to serve as a packing list. Let's just say," I added, as Mom made her way to us, "some of the first outfits we sent to Babs didn't make the cut."

Sarah burst out laughing. When it came to important family events, Babs didn't leave anything to chance.

Mom smiled and leaned over to hug and kiss Sarah and me. "No, no," she said, picking up on what I'd just said and imitating Babs. "Don't think of them as cuts. Think of them as *edits*."

Alice wrapped her arm around me. "Well, girls, we

made it. It's here. We're all wearing the appropriate outfits. It isn't snowing."

"What is so wrong with snow?" I asked.

"It's a logistical nightmare," Aunt Alice said.

"Where is Babs?" I asked, finally realizing she wasn't
here. We had all gotten ready at the Asheville mountain
house that had been in her family for generations, and I
had assumed she would ride with Mom and Aunt Alice
since Sarah and I had left early.

At that same moment I heard, "Girls, come quickly!
You have to see this!" from behind me. One of the conservatory doors flung open and I saw Babs, all five foot
two of her, in a navy knit suit, pillbox hat, and kitten
heels, looking as though this estate belonged to her. She
waved us over and we hurried in.

I'd been told we were having this event outside in the
gardens, another point of panic for my poor mother and
her snow. But as I stepped through the door, I realized
that wasn't wholly true. Amid the palms and hydrangeas, orchids, and birds-of-paradise, and—best of all—
what must have been hundreds of butterflies, a small
table held a chiller bucket with an open bottle of champagne and five flutes. Quick as a wink, Babs began filling the glasses and handed one to each of us. "I thought
we'd toast our girl before we went outside for lunch," she
said.

I smiled, looking around at my four favorite women.
Sometimes my mom drove me batty, but I loved her dearly.
She and my aunt Alice seemed to be in a world-ending
spat as often as they were getting along, but they were always there for me. Sarah was my ride or die. She had been
since we were five years old, when she had stood up for
me after I was wrongly accused of talking in class. Her

job as a public defender was no surprise to anyone. And then there was Babs, who inspired me every day with her tenacity, her spunk, and, like any wonderful grandmother, her wisdom.

Now she raised her glass and said, "To my bright, beautiful Julia, who has always been poised to take on the world. May you find your eternal happiness, my darling girl."

Everyone raised their glasses gleefully, but as we all clinked, I felt a familiar panic welling up in my throat. Could I do this? Could I marry Hayes tomorrow? And, maybe more important, should I?

Follow the rules, I thought. *Follow the rules.* The other women might have been toasting to my wedding, but Babs was testing me. She was asking me why I had changed course so suddenly, why I hadn't stepped into the life I always thought I wanted. I stood taller, straighter, convincing myself that I *was* doing that. Hayes and our family were my future. The rest would work itself out.

My friends began filing inside the butterfly garden as well then, a man in a black-and-white uniform appearing to serve them champagne. Seeing all these women gathering to support me, to support my marriage to the man I loved, reminded me that my uneasy feelings were silly. Every woman felt nervous before her wedding. Right?

I looked up at the dozens of panes of glass—handmade, no doubt—that formed the roof of this historic building. I wondered what it would have been like to draw the plans for the massive arched windows inset in this beautiful brick. Realizing I was jealous of the architects who lived more than a century ago, I wondered if perhaps I had done the wrong thing, walking away from my dream career. I looked down to see that a butterfly had landed on the rim of my flute. Sarah snapped a picture with her phone, startling me out of my thoughts, as Babs clinked her glass with a fork. "Ladies, we have a quick surprise before lunch is served."

I moved over to Babs as the guests murmured excitedly. "Being inside the conservatory isn't enough of a surprise, Babs?" I whispered, so as not to scare off the butterfly.

"In life, and especially at a party, there can never be enough surprises, Jules." She raised her eyebrows. "It's the surprises that direct our path."

As if she'd heard, the monarch on my glass spread her orange-and-black wings and flew off into the orchids, back where she belonged.

A woman who looked to be in her midfifties, dressed in a black-and-white Biltmore guide uniform, appeared in the doorway with a stack of books. "I am delighted to introduce one of Biltmore's finest guides," Babs said to the group, "who is here to take us on a tour of the conservatory and gardens. And, in honor of Julia's wedding, we have a very special treat. With the help of the Biltmore staff, we have compiled a book of photos from Cornelia Vanderbilt's wedding day for each of you."

I put my hand to my heart. "Babs! You didn't!" I had visited Biltmore Estate with Babs many times while growing up, and over the years, I had developed quite a fascination with the house and maybe even more so with Cornelia Vanderbilt, the little girl—and later, woman— who grew up and lived here. I knew she had been the first bride of Biltmore, but I couldn't recall ever seeing any photographs from that day. As the guide handed me a book, my heart swelled. Babs was so thoughtful.

"Do you remember the first time I brought you here?" Babs asked. "You were the only six-year-old in the world who was as thrilled about the architectural details of Biltmore as you were about the candy shop."

I laughed. "And you were the best grandmother for getting me an annual pass every year for my birthday."

"Some kids like Disney World."

"I guess this was my Disney World." I smiled.

Babs put her arm around my waist and squeezed me to her side. "I love that we get to have yet another memory here at Biltmore, that this place we've always loved so much gets to be a part of the most special weekend of your life."

I opened my photo book to the first page and Babs clapped her hands with excitement at the photo of Cornelia Vanderbilt, standing by the grand staircase at Biltmore, exquisitely dressed in a satin gown and holding a streaming bouquet of orchids and lilies of the valley. The guide, smiling at the group, said, "If you look at the first photo in your book, you can see that Cornelia's veil included Brussels rose point lace." I really zeroed in on it. Babs and I leaned closer, gasping in unison.

"It is a sight to behold, isn't it, ladies?" the guide asked.

I could feel my heart racing, but that was silly, wasn't it? I was just so keyed up about the wedding, the excitement of this day. But then again . . .

Sarah glanced over my shoulder. "Whoa. That's crazy."

"Isn't it?" I replied. "Is Cornelia's wedding outfit on display somewhere?" I asked the guide.

She shook her head ruefully. "The gown has been lost to history, as has the heirloom veil worn by Cornelia Vanderbilt, her mother, Edith, and Edith's sisters and mother. Their whereabouts are a mystery. But a team from London re-created Cornelia's wedding outfit from photographs in painstaking detail and with some difficulty. It is part of the *Fashionable Romance* exhibit that will be opening here at Biltmore soon."

"Jules! We should go!" Sarah trilled.

I locked eyes with my grandmother. She had seen it too, hadn't she? "Babs?"

"What?" Her face was a blank canvas.

Turning away from the guide, I said in a low voice, "It's just that . . . don't you think this looks like *our* veil?"

"I think so," Sarah chimed in.

Babs smiled. "Oh, Jules, I think your love of Biltmore has gotten the best of you." She looked down at the picture. "Won't it be great that you get to wear something that looks kind of like the Vanderbilt veil on your special day?"

I peered at her, but she just smiled.

"All right, ladies!" Aunt Alice said. "It's time to celebrate our lovely bride!"

I laughed as my bridesmaids gathered around, champagne flutes in hand, to corral me to the table.

I looked down at the photo again. That veil just looked so similar. Then again, I was at Biltmore—the place where I had spent so many hours dreaming of finding my own happily ever after—the day before my wedding. Babs was probably right: my Vanderbilt obsession had finally gotten the best of me.

My Solemn Vow

June 2, 1898

O n her wedding day, a girl only wants her mother. *It is a bit unhinged to want one's mother when she has been dead for fifteen years,* Edith Stuyvesant Dresser thought, during those last minutes before her fate was sealed and she would bear a new last name. Even still, as her sister placed the family veil—the lace point heirloom—on her head, she couldn't help but wish that her mother was here to help her step into her high-necked satin gown, designed by her favorite French designer. It was a gown fit for a princess. A gown fit for an heiress. A gown fit for a Vanderbilt.

"You're breathtaking," Pauline said. "And you're going to be so happy," she added, squeezing her sister's hands as the other two Dresser girls, Susan and Natalie, looked on.

Edith glanced behind her, taking in the court train trimmed in the exact lace her grandmother had worn.

As the *New York Journal* had reported, "It is an admirable thing to have lace, and it is also an admirable thing to have ancestors, but when one can have both lace and ancestors it is most admirable."

But everyone had ancestors. Perhaps not ancestors with influence, with power, with importance like she did. But how could something as simple as a family name carry so much authority in the eyes of the world? Edith guessed that was for the best. If it weren't for her family name, she certainly wouldn't be here now, effectively removing the financial stress of her last several years.

Her mother would have told her not to worry so much, that her privilege was her birthright. And, she reasoned, she'd had more than her fair share of struggles in her twenty-five years.

"Do you remember how we used to play in this veil when we were little girls?" Pauline asked, her bright eyes sparkling wistfully. She was always the romantic.

"And Mother would talk about the wonderful men— men like Daddy—that we would marry one day," Natalie filled in for her. "That the veil would make us happy forever."

Edith smiled. Much to her delight, she did remember her mother's soft, pale hands affixing the veil just right on her daughters' heads and clapping in glee.

"Those were wonderful days, weren't they?" Edith asked. She paused. "I barely remember them now." Pain seared through her. Her parents had, after all, left her an orphan when she was only ten.

Her sister Susan, the oldest, the most serious, was the one to reach out to take her hand. "I feel them, though. Don't you?"

Edith nodded. She felt her parents' influence in her

life as though they were an invisible presence guiding her toward her next step. She nodded. "I do believe they would have wanted me to marry George."

Not because she loved him; nothing as frivolous as that. Polite society was abuzz with the truth: She needed his money to continue to live in the manner to which she was accustomed; he needed her prominent family name to continue to insert his family into the right circles. That was the way of the world. Edith told herself that her parents would have approved. She hoped it was true. And her sisters, who were always her strength, had reassured her every step of the way. When their grandmother died, she left behind a letter in which she reminded her family that *a house united can never fall.* Through all the trials and tribulations they had faced over the past fifteen years or so, Edith and her siblings had been by each other's sides, the anchors in each other's lives.

And now, here, today, they would celebrate.

Edith studied her reflection in the mirror, her shoulders slumped slightly, an unfortunate habit created from years of slouching to obscure her nearly six-foot frame. Women were supposed to be petite, pocket-sized—at least that was how it seemed to Edith. She often wished she could be smaller.

"Stand up straight," Pauline said, standing up straighter herself, pulling her sister's shoulders back. "Be proud. George Vanderbilt chose you, in all your statuesque glory."

Pauline's flair for the dramatic always made things more fun. And perhaps she was right. Their set had been quick to compliment Edith on her poise, her elegance, her beauty. They couldn't all be wrong, could they? Surely not. Edith kissed her sisters one by one as they prepared to leave for the church. Then she stood up tall, proud.

She stood up even straighter as she entered the vestibule of the American Church of the Holy Trinity in her beloved Paris. The Vanderbilts had all come from New York for the special day. And in minutes Edith would be one of them.

"You ready?" her brother LeRoy asked, breaking Edith out of her thoughts.

Edith smiled. In the wake of their parents' deaths, LeRoy had struggled. Edith knew it must have been difficult for him, the only boy among all those sisters. But now, today, he was a strong, dapper man, about to walk his sister down the aisle. "I think I am," she said, sounding surer than she felt.

"It isn't too late to change your mind," he joked.

"We both know it most certainly is," Edith whispered. But she knew she wouldn't have changed her mind even if she could have.

Marrying well was her only real job, her most important role in life. Today, she was fulfilling her purpose. Edith took a deep breath as she and LeRoy stepped out into the flower-covered aisle.

For months, friends, strangers, and reporters had wondered and watched to see the spectacle that would be Edith's wedding to one of the 400, the nickname given to the wealthiest families in America. George Vanderbilt cared little about being a part of that rarefied set, one of the chosen families who would fit in Mrs. Caroline Astor's ballroom, which, much to Edith's delight, George had never so much as darkened the door of. George didn't care for costumes and frivolity like his sisters or even business like his father and brothers. Instead, he chose books, scholarship, art, and design. He chose to focus his energy on building a home the likes of which the United States had never seen.

And then he picked Edith, despite the rumors that, at twenty-five, she was practically an old maid, and despite *Form* magazine's proclamation that she was much less pretty than her sister Pauline. But, she reminded herself the moment she caught the eye of her brother-in-law, Pauline's husband, the Reverend George Grenville Merrill, who would marry Edith and George, Pauline was prettier than everyone. She didn't hold it against her.

People had said that the thirty-five-year-old all but confirmed Vanderbilt bachelor had set his sights on another society mistress. But no one could argue that now, as he stood at the end of an aisle lined with orange blossoms, on a fragrant and splendid June day. George Washington Vanderbilt undeniably had his sights set on one Miss Edith Dresser.

As she and LeRoy made their way down the aisle, and George's twinkling eyes met hers, Edith knew for sure that he was going to be a wonderful husband. He had warmed her heart so the day before when, after the civil ceremony where they were pronounced man and wife, George had felt moved to donate to the Eighth Arrondissement on Rue d'Anjou where they had been united in matrimony. What warmed her heart more was when he had asked her, "To whom should we make the donation, my dear?"

We. He valued her opinion. He considered them one already. When George had suggested helping the orphans of the district, Edith had almost wept with happiness. Edith, herself an orphan—though, admittedly, not exactly of the sort they were helping—was touched beyond measure. It was her greatest wish to be of service to the world. She knew then that George wanted the same thing. At times, in their society, it had made them outsiders. Now, it made them the perfect fit. In the words of her grandmother, *a house united.*

As she reached George, Edith whispered, "I just abhor being the center of attention, all these people looking at me."

"You look lovely, dear," George said, taking Edith's hand in his. "They can't help but be dazzled. And just wait until Asheville meets my new bride." She wondered then if perhaps she should have worn the dazzling Boucheron ruby and diamond tiara and choker that George had gifted her. But as she fingered the lace of her handmade veil, she decided her sisters had been right: her simple, elegant wedding attire was best.

As Reverend Merrill began with "Dearly beloved, we have come together in the presence of God," Edith knew she should be focusing on the ceremony. But the thought of moving to Asheville, North Carolina, after the wedding—and to the United States' largest, most glorious, and most glamorous home—suddenly caused butterflies to form in her stomach.

Edith had maintained a sense of composure and even, at times, true joy, despite the tragic loss of her beloved parents and the struggles that befell her family after. Edith was a fighter. She was a survivor. And, more than all that, she was a woman who knew how to make the best of any situation. No matter what her life in North Carolina held, she would make do.

No, she decided. *I will thrive.*

Her breath caught as her sister's husband asked, "Will you have this man to be your husband?"

"I will."

As George agreed to have her as well, she smiled, thinking that, after this, before moving to North Carolina, they would be off to a place much less foreign to her: Vienna. Four months traveling Europe would certainly give them time to get to know each other better, to seal their fates more permanently so that, by the time she arrived at her new home, she would have a true best friend to share it with.

I am a Dresser. Always and forever, Edith thought as she recited her wedding vows: "I, Edith, take you, George, to be my husband." *Even though today is the day I become a Vanderbilt.* "To have and to hold from this day forward." *A Vanderbilt.* "This is my solemn vow."

Reverend Merrill bellowed, "Those whom God has joined together let no one put asunder!"

Edith Stuyvesant Dresser was now Edith Dresser Vanderbilt. A daughter of one of America's founding families had married a son of one of its wealthiest.

As the congregation recited the Lord's Prayer to conclude the service, Edith smiled at her husband. He smiled at her. And an unshakable bond took hold. Whatever the future brought, for better or worse, for richer or poorer, in sickness and in health, they were knit together for eternity.

Little did Edith know that, for her, *until death do us part* would only be the beginning.

Fractured Fairy Tale

Before I had time to ask Babs anything else about the beautiful image of Cornelia Vanderbilt we had just seen, Mom began herding us all to our seats at the table outside the conservatory. *During a wedding weekend, adhering to the schedule is the most important thing*, Aunt Alice had reminded me over and over again. I had thought my marriage to a man I loved was the most important thing. I had been wrong, apparently.

I was about to protest that Hayes's mother hadn't yet arrived, but before I could say so, she appeared in her pencil-thin, ultra-high stilettos and a fitted navy dress that hugged her in all the right places. I didn't see her much, so when I did, it always surprised me how stunning she was with her cascades of auburn hair. My mom and aunt were pretty, but Therese was a bombshell. And a CEO bombshell at that.

As she sashayed over to kiss my cheek, her signature scent, created by a famous perfumer in France, where she lived, lingered. She was the female version of Hayes. He had inherited her blue eyes, right down to the sparkle, along with her effortless, soft hair, her easy laugh, and her wide smile. Sometimes, in moments like this, I would forget, just for a minute, how tense things were between them. I would forget that the night I met Hayes, after a soccer game between our rival high schools, was also the day his mother left their family. Or, at least, that she left and they decided not to go with her.

"I am so thrilled this day is finally here," she said evenly but happily. Therese had this practiced, powerful calm about her that always made me feel like a bundle of untamed energy in comparison. "You look spectacular! I am so happy that you and Hayes are finally making it official."

"Ladies, if everyone could please find their seats," Aunt Alice called. I could hear the stress in her voice. We were already four minutes behind schedule. Later, I knew, she would say, *That Therese with those legs up to her neck thinks she's above the schedule. She is not.* No one *is above the schedule.*

As we all sat down, a slew of servers swept in with salads, and I noticed that the glasses on the table had already been filled with rosé. While I was chatting there had been, no doubt, a struggle ensuing around me. Babs would have given Alice the eye for having the wine poured before we sat, and Alice would have glared back, silently insisting that she knew it was improper but that it was the only way to save those precious minutes in her precise schedule, and it was, after all, almost noon. I could almost hear her saying: *I have to get everyone out of here by two o'clock, for heaven's sake, if we have any prayer of getting hair and makeup done before the rehearsal at five.*

I smiled just thinking about it. A movement caught my eye then, and I popped up out of my seat. *Sorry, Aunt Alice.* The most handsome man I'd ever known was striding across the lawn in a green hunting vest, shotgun case strapped across his chest. His hair was adorably disheveled from wearing a hat all morning, and he was grinning at me. Even now, after all we had been through, all the times we had broken up and gotten back together, he still made my heart race. And now, I knew he made every woman there swoon when he said, "I know I'm not supposed to be here, but I just had to see my girl." He kissed me quickly. Everyone was smiling at him, googly-eyed. Everyone except for Aunt Alice, who was glaring.

I was about to ask if he wanted to sit down when a combination of dings, beeps, buzzes, and chirps erupted at the table. Normally, I wouldn't have looked at my phone in the middle of a luncheon, but as concerned looks passed everyone's faces, I grabbed it by instinct. There must have been an AMBER Alert. Or a weather warning. Mom's snowstorm!

Hayes pulled his phone out too, and I watched his face register horror as he processed whatever message it contained. I slid my finger to open my phone screen. It wasn't a weather alert. It was a group text, from a number I didn't know, to everyone seated around the table, plus the man I was going to walk down the aisle to the next day. I pressed play on a video. And after a few seconds, before Hayes could grab my phone from my hand, I had seen quite enough.

Babs's proclamation from earlier flew through my mind. *It's the surprises that direct our path.* I couldn't breathe.

I looked at Therese, as panic washed over me. I thought about that first night I'd ever talked to Hayes, about the tears that stood in his eyes from more than a crushing soccer defeat. That night, as soon as I'd realized his mother had left her only son behind for a job opportunity in a different country, I felt deeply protective of him. I'd been there for him no matter what. But clearly, he didn't feel the same way about me.

I looked up at Hayes now, humiliation engulfing me. I felt lightheaded, like I might faint. My fiancé was on-screen making out with another girl on a dance floor.

All eyes around that table were on me, but it was Sarah who jumped up and put her hand on my back. That was when I came back into myself. The feel of her hand connected me to the real world again. And I ran so quickly she could scarcely keep up.

"Julia! It isn't what you think!" Hayes called behind me, running after us.

I ignored him, racing through the gardens toward the parking lot. What had previously felt like a magical meadow of tulips now felt like a field of doom.

Once I reached the asphalt, I finally stopped, realizing I had no idea where I was going to go. I had drunk too much champagne to drive. "I can't imagine where that video came from," Hayes said breathlessly as he reached me, suddenly looking like a stranger. "That was from years ago. I don't even know that person's name."

"Years ago?" I spat back at him. "We've been together for a decade, Hayes! You don't look sixteen there."

"Jules, you have to believe me," he said, stepping

closer, trying to take my hand, which I ripped away. "Seriously. It was ages ago. It was one mistake."

My face felt hot, not from the activity but from the shame. I hadn't just been humiliated. I'd been humiliated in front of all the women who meant the most to me. I wanted them to believe that I was going to have a perfect marriage and a happy life. If they couldn't believe it, how could I?

"You don't deserve her, and you never have," Sarah hissed, which is when I realized she was still standing beside me.

"Could you please leave, Sarah?" Hayes asked. "This is a private matter."

"Can I leave?" she asked sarcastically. "Um, no. I cannot leave. And once it's in a group text it is no longer a private matter, you asshole. People we've never even met will be talking about this by nightfall." I knew she was right. Videos like these spread like wildfire. And it seared through me because tomorrow was supposed to be the first day of the rest of our lives together.

Turning back to me, Hayes looked me straight in the eye. "Julesy, you are the love of my life. I can't live without you, and I swear to you that video was from so many years ago that I couldn't even tell you where it was from. I would never cheat on you. You're going to be my wife. I'm going to treat you like gold."

I wasn't crying anymore, but he was.

"I don't know who in the world would send a text like this, but they clearly don't know a thing about us. Please don't let something so stupid ruin our perfect day, Jules. You deserve this so much. We have dreamed of it for so long." I looked into his eyes and was surprised to find that they looked the same to me as they always had. And that was what made Hayes and me work. To the outside world, he was the cool, handsome, put-together guy. But I was the one he showed all the real stuff to, the one who saw his scars.

It was Sarah who finally spoke. "We'll consider what you're saying," she said as the rest of my bridesmaids started walking toward us. On the one hand, I didn't really want to see anyone. On the other, Hayes deserved to face the firing squad.

"You can't take her away from me," Hayes cried. "She's the love of my life."

"The video could have been from one of the times you were broken up," Ashley, one of my friends from college and ever the optimist, offered.

"What?!" Leah, the realist, practically spat. "Are you just going to stand there and pretend like we don't all know Hayes is a cheater?"

"I'm not a cheater!" I could hear him trying to protest, but I couldn't see him anymore from behind my friends, who had all gathered around me.

"This really concerns me, Jules," Catherine said, as if that was helpful. Hayes finally broke through the circle, taking my hands, looking me in the eye. He showed me his phone.

"Do you see how low-quality this is? No one has a phone old enough to take such a sucky video. It's clearly from a long time ago."

There wasn't a time stamp, and I couldn't exactly place where it was. It could have been any bar in any city.

"Babe, this happened when we were broken up." We *had* broken up kind of a lot. Once just a few months ago, in fact, when I'd heard a rumor about Hayes and a girl at work and called off our engagement. He had actually made her call me to disprove it, which had been pretty embarrassing for everyone. I hadn't taken him back right away, but then . . . I faced a major hurdle, and Hayes was always my safe place. It seemed silly to not get back together.

"I can't even remember which breakup it was. Everything from those awful times is just a blur. But it doesn't matter now. I love you. We're getting married."

He was so beautiful when he was sad. But no. *No*. We'd been through this before, and I wouldn't let him do this to me again. "We *were* getting married," I choked, taking my engagement ring off and throwing it at him. He actually caught it. I did feel a little regretful then. When Hayes had slipped that ring on my finger, I'd felt like my fate had finally been sealed.

He cautiously took a step closer, still holding the ring. "Jules, I promise you, this didn't happen when we were together. Plus, it was nothing. It was a onetime, stupid mistake. I felt awful about it after we got back together, and I never told you because it was so stupid that it didn't matter."

"It matters to me," I said sulkily.

"Haven't you ever made a single mistake in your life?" He paused and smiled down at me. "No, of course you haven't, because you're Julia Baxter, perfection roaming the earth."

He pulled me to him, and I let him, mostly because, okay, yes, there was that *one* time I made out with a guy at a party in college after Hayes and I had a huge fight. In my mind, I'd broken up with him. Even still . . . I had also made a mistake once. And it meant nothing to me. So maybe we were even.

I ignored the other voice in my head that told me this was a pattern. I had ignored it for years now. I ignored it because I never had proof. I ignored it because I loved him and his beautiful face and his starched shirts and how stunning we looked in pictures together and how he always said the right thing. I ignored it because the sixteen-year-old version of myself had vowed to take care of this hurt, sad boy, to put him back together, and even after a decade, I found it impossible to break that vow. In January, I ignored it because, maybe for the first time, I needed *him* to put *me* back together. I needed somewhere to turn, and Hayes was the easiest choice. No matter how many times we had tried to walk away from each other, we always found ourselves back together. And that was love, right?

Also, it was the day before my wedding. The venue was paid for, the food was prepped, the band was almost to the hotel. There was no way to alert two hundred guests to the fact that the wedding was canceled.

And so, when Hayes slipped the ring back on my finger, I let him. "Ladies," he said to my troop of brides-maids, "this video is old and irrelevant, and I'm sorry that any of you had to have your day ruined by it. But please know that I am going to be the best husband to Julia that anyone could possibly be." They smiled. Maybe a little warily. But they still smiled.

He kissed me again, and I breathed him in, let him pull me close. "Jules," he said. "Come on. How could you even think I would hurt you? You know me better than anyone."

I did know him better than anyone. And, as my heart raced uneasily, I realized that was precisely the problem.

Hayes was a wounded bird, *my* wounded bird. Mine to protect, mine to save, mine to *fix*. And it had taken me until right then to realize that many a fractured fairy tale began just like that.

A Lady

March 6, 1914

Edith once again adjusted the red bedspread around her husband, George, in his bedroom on K Street in Washington, D.C.

"Red is my favorite color," George said drowsily. "It's a color of power, isn't it?"

George's room at Biltmore House and the decadent Louis XV Room where Edith had delivered their daughter, Cornelia, were also red. Some days, Edith might have agreed with George, but today, after a series of terrible nightmares, it seemed too closely related to the color of blood.

George set his book down on the bed and patted beside him.

"I can't sit beside you," Edith said, horrified. "I'll hurt you."

"Edi, darling," George said, "it was a routine appendectomy. It went perfectly. Dr. Finney said so himself."

Edith knew what the doctor had said better than anyone. Maybe George's surgery was bringing back unpleasant memories of her parents' deaths. But she couldn't shake this unsettled feeling . . .

"I miss Biltmore," she said, changing the subject.

He nodded and winced as he sat up a little more. "So do I. It will be good to get back." He smiled and took her hand as she finally acquiesced, sitting down gingerly beside him on the bed. "Sometimes, when I'm feeling down, I think of that first day I took you there."

She smiled. There were few days she remembered quite so vividly. Those perfect newlywed moments were burned into her memory.

October 1, 1898

Butterflies fluttered in Edith's stomach as she sat in George's private train car, smoothing her gray traveling dress, more because of her nerves than any perceived lines or wrinkles, and fussed with her feather collar again. *A lady doesn't fidget*, she reminded herself. Edith had resided—and traveled—all over the world, and she would be fine wherever they lived. But even if she didn't like Biltmore House, she reminded herself, they could live elsewhere. George's Fifth Avenue mansion, maybe, or the Bar Harbor house. If she became terribly homesick for Paris, George, with his wandering nature, would surely agree to return. She would not be stuck here if she didn't love it like her new husband did.

She looked over at him, sitting beside her in the train that was so luxurious she felt that perhaps she could live here if Biltmore proved not to be to her liking. But the closer they got to the estate, the more excited George became. "Just wait until you see the grounds. And the view," he was saying. "Mount Pisgah is the reason I bought the land. She is the majestic warrior of the forest."

Edith had noticed throughout the course of her honeymoon that her husband read so much sometimes it seemed as though he was speaking in the languid prose of a novel. She felt such a surge of love for him then that she reached over to take his hand.

He squeezed her hand back, winked, and said, "We'll have to christen her, you know."

Edith blushed. And though it wasn't necessarily lady-like, she wasn't all together unhappy about that fact.

"Isn't it wonderful how fate works?" George asked, gazing at Edith as if she were a crown jewel. "Before the honeymoon, I knew you would be the perfect mistress for a home like Biltmore, a polished and well-bred society woman who was capable of handling the social affairs that I would rather not. But, after these months, I have to say, my dear, that I have grown quite fond of you."

Maybe it had been the views of the Borromean Islands from the terrace or the ancient gardens they'd visited while on their honeymoon abroad, but after four months of travel, when Edith boarded the *Augusta Victoria* to return home with her new husband, she was his, body and soul. The fact that he'd insisted on making stops in Lenox, Massachusetts, and Shelburne, Vermont, to show her off to his sisters Emily and Lila made her think that George felt the same way. This confirmed it.

"And my family has certainly taken a shine to you," he said, echoing her thoughts.

Edith beamed with pride because that was the idea.

His sister had confided in Edith that they had always babied George and expected very little from him. He wasn't a businessman like his father or brothers. He was a scholar—one who, quite frankly, his male relatives didn't understand. Biltmore, and, specifically, its less-than-fashionable location, was just another example of his preferences differing from theirs.

"Yes, the magical inner workings of fate," George said, contentedly.

Fate. Edith had to control her laugh at her husband's mention of the word. But she had to ask, "Do you mean in regard to us?"

"Why, yes, of course." He took his wife's hand. "To think we both happened to board the *St. Paul* and had our paths cross in such a way that we knew we were meant for each other."

Edith laughed. "I think everyone we've ever known was aboard the *St. Paul,*" she teased.

"Well, you were the one my meddling sisters set their sights on for me, so that has to mean something," he teased back.

She laughed. George's sisters had, she had later learned, known Edith would be aboard the ship and enticed George's friend William B. Osgood Field to play matchmaker. If George wanted to call "fate" Field putting so much effort into the union that the papers had pronounced *them* engaged—well, then, yes, fate was wonderful indeed.

"Darling," she said, "I do have to ask . . ."

His face lit up, and she sensed that he was expecting a question about Biltmore, which he would not be receiving. "Were my Christmas gifts to you unforgivably forward?"

The pair burst into laughter. After many intertwinements on the *St. Paul*—a few where Edith had to will herself not to be terribly seasick—and much time spent together in Paris, Edith had brazenly declared that if George Vanderbilt were the one for her, he had best decide quickly. As such, she had gifted him a copy of *Quo Vadis*, a love story in which George, a discerning reader, wouldn't be able to help but see vestiges of his own love story—or potential love story, as it were—with Edith. Tucked beside it? A small book on patience. Even Susan, who was less than thrilled about her sister taking up with a *Vanderbilt*, had found the gesture terribly funny.

"I think they were appropriately forward, daughter of the Gods."

"A genuine daughter of the Gods" was one of the many, many titles—some flattering, some less so—that the papers and magazines had pronounced her. George had found this particular proclamation from the *Washington Times* so appropriate that he had taken it for Edith's nickname. It was, Edith had to admit, quite a bit more flattering than, say, the publication that mentioned she had America's bluest blood but no actual money. After months of the papers talking perhaps as much about the Vanderbilt wedding plans as the Spanish-American War, Edith had had quite enough of everyone's comments about her personal attributes, including but not limited to her height, proportions, facial features, hair, breeding, and intelligence.

It had reached the point that, one day, George had exclaimed to Edith, "You are my fiancée, not livestock!"

The papers had been slightly kinder to George—but only slightly. Speculation as to why he had never married ran wild and it seemed that all were in disbelief that the thirty-five-year-old confirmed bachelor was settling down.

"Particularly swarthy," Edith replied, using her favorite nickname the papers had given her new husband, "I'm just glad I was able to catch your eye."

"You caught it and it is yours." George smiled warmly as the train car pulled into the station.

Edith's nerves returned.

There was no doubt, as she exited the car, smile pinned to her face, that all eyes were on the new Mrs. Vanderbilt. She couldn't blame people, really. For years, George—and Biltmore, for that matter—had been theirs. And now, at least in part, they were hers. She would simply have to convince the people of Asheville that she was worthy of their love. Her warm smile would be a better start than she could have ever imagined.

For three glorious, breathtaking miles, Edith tried to keep her mounting anticipation at bay as George explained that Mr. Frederick Law Olmsted, the famed landscape architect who had also created Central Park, had designed the approach to create that anticipation in all who traveled it. George had fretted about his bride not being introduced to Biltmore in the summer. But this October day seemed, to her, just right.

"Aren't the leaves spectacular?" her husband asked, interrupting her thoughts.

"How could you not fall in love?" she asked, truly spellbound by the burnt orange, vibrant yellow, and deep amber hues that surrounded her; the fall burst into a firestorm of color as though it was as happy to welcome Mrs. Vanderbilt as the staff who lined the road to greet them.

Looking at her pointedly, George replied, "How could I not?"

Edith looked away to avoid the blush creeping up her cheeks. Roses and carnations filled the air along with cheers from the seemingly endless estate workers they passed. She waved and smiled at all of them, gasping with delight at the sight of the adorable Jersey calves brought in by dairy workers to greet their new mistress. "I will learn each of the estate workers' names," she said confidently.

George raised his eyebrows. "There are three hundred of them, Edi. I think simply learning the names of the dozens of house staff members will be task enough."

She shook her head and smiled at him. "I am a part of Biltmore now. We're in this together. I want them to know that they are important to us."

George squeezed her knee and kept his eyes fixed on her face, as if waiting for something.

Edith gasped as they reached their destination. She had never seen anything like it, the way that, suddenly and without warning, Biltmore House sprang into view in all its glory. Just like that, something she had all but forgotten—her mother's voice—flooded her mind: *You will live in a castle with many acres to roam.* Edith could practically feel that veil atop her head, smell her mother's flowery scent. Perhaps Edith had become a princess after all.

The leaves, the cheers, and the view of America's largest, most spectacular home all collided in a mere moment underneath the horseshoe made of flowers that read, almost unbelievably, "Welcome home."

Welcome home, Edith thought. *Home.*

"Is it to your liking, Edi?" George asked, without a hint of irony.

Edith only laughed.

After years of being an orphan, of then losing her grandmother, of scrimping and saving and moving from one fashionable yet inexpensive locale to the next, what she thought she found most to her liking was the idea of really, truly, being home.

Edith turned to George and said, "Does it offend you if I say that wherever you are is to my liking now?"

What shocked Edith most is that she truly meant it.

———

Now, almost sixteen years later, in a very different house in a very different place, Edith still felt most at home wherever she was with George. She hadn't meant to fall in love with him so handily, but he had made it impossible not to.

"That was a magical day, George. One of the best of my life."

"You know, my dearest, I think the entire time I was building Biltmore, I was creating it for you. I was thinking of you, and maybe even our Cornelia too. I didn't even know you yet, but I wanted you to have everything."

Edith controlled her sigh. Biltmore had, over the last few years, become more and more of an albatross. They had nearly lost it on more than one occasion. She was certainly made of strong stuff, but the stress of its upkeep had taken its toll. But when she closed her eyes, when she imagined their daughter playing in the fresh mountain air, the beauty of the cool limestone walls, and the sprawling sitting rooms—and, maybe most of all, George's beloved library—she knew it was a place worth fighting for.

"And I think if we continue its full transformation into a working estate—"

Edith looked at George's pale, tired face and decided this was a conversation that could wait. Instead, she finished, "When I think of Biltmore, I think of you. Biltmore is the essence of you, the essence of Cornelia, the representation of all I love most in this life." In rare moments like these, Edith could put away the worry and simply feel grateful for her family, both her biological one and the one she had made in Asheville, the people from all walks of life and every station.

George smiled at Edith and took her hand. "Second only to our daughter, Biltmore is my life's greatest work. It makes me so happy to know that no matter what happens, I have created a legacy that future generations of Vanderbilts can look on with pride."

A warmth crept over Edith, thinking of her part in that legacy. She knew, in fact, that it might not continue without her. George was a kind, caring man, but perhaps he hadn't known enough strife and hard work in his life. They could agree on what would make Biltmore sustainable—the dairy, Biltmore Industries, selling some of the forest land, among other things—but Edith had learned quickly that when it came to matters of their business, she couldn't wait for him to lead her. George had a bit of a tendency toward distraction and wanderlust and could hardly be pinned down long enough to transform an idea into action. It was how he was raised, the precious baby of the family, the apple of his doting mother's eye until the day she died.

In contrast, Edith already had Cornelia out on the

land, learning how the dairy operated, the ins and outs of Biltmore Industries—the thriving weaving and woodworking business they had created—committing to memory the names of every family member that lived on the vast estate, learning their specific role in the running of America's largest home. No, George wasn't one for hard work. But Edith was, and Cornelia would be. Edith would see to that.

"Edi, could you fetch me the papers please?" George asked. "They should be here by now. And where is that lovely daughter of ours? I'd like to talk to her."

Edith smiled warmly, putting aside her worries about the estate. "I will find her. The newspapers too. But please, for me, close your eyes and rest for just a moment."

George sighed. "I'm so tired of resting. Resting, as you know, doesn't come easily."

She leaned over and kissed her husband lightly on the lips. "I know, George. I know."

She stood up and he grabbed her hand. "I love you, Edith," he said. "I truly do. You and Cornelia are the best thing I've ever done with my life."

"And Biltmore," she joked. "Now quit procrastinating on that nap."

He smiled.

As Edith walked down the steps, she touched her lips. When she was younger, she used to worry that marriage devolved over the years, that the person she was when she married George would barely resemble who she became inside her marriage. It was true—Edith *had* changed. But she had become a woman she was proud to be.

She grabbed George's papers from the kitchen and fixed him a glass of water. She could have asked one of the servants, but she liked taking care of him. When Cornelia entered the room, Edith looked up. "Oh, good. You're here. Make sure you say goodbye to Daddy before you go out with Bunchy." Rachel Strong—or "Bunchy," as everyone called her—and Cornelia had become fast friends at Miss Madeira's, where they went to school. Both American heiresses—Bunchy because of a string of Cleveland department stores; Cornelia because of the railroad—they had quite a lot in common.

Cornelia smiled. "He seems almost like his old self, doesn't he?"

Edith nodded, a tremendous weight lifted off her shoulders. He was going to be okay. Her George was going to be fine.

It struck Edith in moments like this, when her daughter was relaxed and casual, bathed in morning light, how lovely she truly was. And the days Cornelia would be Edith's were fleeting. She would find a proper man. She would marry. It would happen before Edith could turn around, she knew. While she had friends who were endlessly fascinated already with making the perfect match for their daughters, Edith was most interested in keeping Cornelia young as long as she could. "When Daddy gets well, you should take him for a swim in the fountain. He always gets a kick out of that."

Cornelia smiled brightly. "Or maybe the swimming pool." After all these years, Cornelia had never given up the idea that her father would learn to swim. But she didn't know that George had nearly drowned in Rhode Island as a child and, had a teenage girl not come to his rescue, neither of them would be standing in this kitchen right now. Edith found the fountain, where he could comfortably stand, more of a realistic prospect.

Edith looped her arm around her daughter's as they made their way back up the stairs. Cornelia was George's greatest work. *Well her, and Biltmore*, she thought, chuckling to herself. George loved Biltmore and she loved him. And that was why she was working so hard— had already worked so hard—to save his dream.

JULIA

Getaway Car

After being blown out, airbrushed, and Spanxed into my fitted lace wedding gown, even I had to admit that I looked amazing. I didn't really look like *me* per se. But the woman in front of the mirror looked like she belonged on Hayes's arm.

Last night, at our rehearsal dinner, I had been that woman. I had laughed at our friends' toasts, cried at my father's, and sobbed as Hayes made a speech in my honor so beautiful that I felt as though he didn't even need to say his wedding vows. I knew he loved me. I was sure of it. And wasn't that what really mattered?

Now, Sarah, in her maid of honor dress, caught my eye in the mirror. "You look too good in that," I said. "You aren't letting me shine."

She rolled her eyes. "You are practically the cover of *Marie Claire Weddings*."

I bit my lip.

"What?" she whispered.

"Do you think he's telling the truth?"

She held up her phone again and, for what had to have been the fiftieth time, we played that grainy video. I'd watched it so many times I could now pinpoint the exact moment Hayes would lean down to the girl he was dancing with—a girl who wasn't me—and start making out with her like she was his last meal. *Oh my God*, I thought. *She* was *his last meal.*

I started to feel nauseous, the horror of the day before washing over me again. In the mauve and green back room of the church I whispered to Sarah, "Am I an idiot? Do you think he's lying to me?"

Sarah sighed. "You know, Jules, it's hard for me because I've known Hayes almost as long as I've known you. I can't even imagine a world where you two aren't together." She paused. "When you used to walk into parties holding hands, it was like time stopped. The way he would skip class to get you peanut butter M&M's . . ."

I smiled and bit my lip. "And remember when he had flowers delivered to AP Bio?"

Sarah smiled. "Oh, I remember. Everyone remembers. He worshipped you, Jules, even then."

Before I could say anything else, Aunt Alice, in a breathtaking navy gown, burst through the door with Mom and Babs on her heels. "All right!" Aunt Alice trilled. Evidently, the MOB, GOB, and AOB hair and makeup portion of the day was over. I had, in the interest of pretending to be a low-maintenance bride, told my bridesmaids not to come to the church until an hour before the ceremony. But really, I just couldn't face my friends after yesterday. I knew they were all talking about this, debating whether I was making a mistake. And I knew it came from a good place. Mostly. But I couldn't handle it.

"It's time for the first look!" Alice said excitedly.

With their pinned-on fake smiles and particularly high-pitched voices this morning, the effort Alice and Babs were putting into pretending they weren't horrified I was still going through with this was truly heroic.

"It's happening!" Mom said, clutching her hands over her heart.

She wasn't pretending. This was definitely the best day of her life. She loved Hayes. *Loved* him.

"Do you believe him?" I had asked my mother the day before. Despite the cool mountain air and her sleeveless silk sheath, she had looked uncomfortably close to sweating.

That was when I realized how desperately *I* wanted to believe him.

"One hundred percent," Mom had said so firmly I was almost convinced. "There isn't a woman in the world who wouldn't kill for a man who loved her like Hayes loves you."

Those words rang in my head now as I was about to make what was either the best or worst decision of my life.

Mom always took Hayes's side. She loved him. Who didn't? He was gorgeous and cool; he was brilliant. He smelled like Irish Spring and Old Spice and had rows of straight white teeth. He had a great job, impeccable manners, and while his choice in friends left a little to be desired, we could not keep away from each other. We had a sort of electric spark that, even after all these years, made it impossible to walk away. We had tried.

I turned to Alice, who was shifting anxiously from one foot to the other, the photographer by her side. "Could you give me just a second alone with Hayes before the pictures?" I asked.

Alice and the photographer looked puzzled. "But that's kind of the point," the photographer said. "I'm supposed to capture the first moment you see each other."

I smiled sweetly. "We can reenact it."

"But then . . ." Alice said.

"It's all right. If Julia wants to see her fiancé alone, she should be allowed to do so," Babs said, stepping beside the photographer. "It's *her* wedding day," she added tersely.

The photographer looked lost, and Alice took a deep breath. I was certain she was counting backward from ten in her head.

I hadn't been sure about a first look, but Hayes had insisted. He didn't want to be too emotional when he saw me walk down the aisle. I had agreed under one condition: I would wear the dress, but I wouldn't wear my veil. That was the part that carried all the good luck anyway.

I walked out of the back room and entered the long, outdoor, stone-covered breezeway that connected the church with the Parish Hall and Sunday school rooms. The tap of my high heels echoed in the space. When I saw Hayes, my heart caught in my chest. Forget finance. That man could have been in movies.

There were tears in his eyes as he reached me and pulled me to him, kissing me. "You are breathtaking." He kissed me again. "And I love you." He stood back to admire me. "You are even more beautiful than you were at nineteen in your deb gown."

That made me laugh. "What I mostly remember about my deb ball was *someone* being late because he drank too much at a Bid Day party and lost track of time."

He laughed now too. "Yeah, but you tying my bow tie in the elevator while I changed into my tux pants . . ." He looked off wistfully, as though this was a story for the ages.

I raised my eyebrow. "With Babs, Pops, Mom, and Dad waiting because we were late for pictures?"

He kissed me again. I could say one thing for Hayes: he made things memorable.

I pulled back a little. "You haven't even seen me with my veil yet," I said playfully. That was when my stomach wrenched again. The veil . . . That long-standing symbol of love and happiness in my family, the good-luck charm that practically guaranteed a perfect life and marriage, was about to go on *my* head. Could I uphold its reputation?

"Tell me again," I whispered. "Tell me I'm the only one for you."

He looked at me sadly. "Julia, don't do this; don't ruin this perfect day. You are the only woman in the world for me. You are all I dream about, all I see. And I promise I will be the best husband you could possibly imagine."

"All right, lovebirds!" the photographer called, appearing through one of the stone archways, Aunt Alice by her side.

"We only have six minutes of our allotted first-look time left," Alice added in that same high-pitched tone from earlier.

As Hayes leaned down to kiss me, to reassure me that all was right with the world, the photographer began snapping. And Hayes whispered in my ear, "Don't ever leave me. Please don't ever leave me."

Every nurturing instinct I had stood at attention. I had to protect him. I had to fix him. I *had* fixed him. If I wasn't there, he would fall apart.

When we finished a few minutes later and I walked back into the bridal room, Sarah was there to meet me. She looked a little green.

"What?" I whispered, panicking that something else had happened.

"I might have new information. But I don't have to tell you—"

"Tell me!" I cut her off.

"This is awful . . . But I guess the video has gone public because someone DM'd Catherine about it last night."

When people were messaging my bridesmaids on Instagram, it *was* bad. My heart was beating out of my chest.

"So, when Hayes was in Charlotte and you were in Raleigh . . ." She bit her lip guiltily. "Remember, this information is coming from a total stranger—"

"Who has no reason to lie," I interrupted, my heart now beating so loudly I could hear it in my ears.

Sarah shrugged. "Well, I don't know. But she claims that this girl is someone named Chrissy Matthews. Apparently, she and Hayes had a little thing on and off for . . . well, a few months anyway, while you were in school in Raleigh. The day Chrissy found out about you, she vowed to tell you."

I felt like I couldn't breathe because all the pieces started to fall into place. "That must have been why Hayes proposed to me." I said it more to myself than to Sarah.

Hayes had graduated the year before I had and moved to New York while I finished my architecture undergrad at NC State. Then, not six weeks after I graduated and we were reunited in the City That Never Sleeps, where I would be doing my internship before going back for my professional degree, he got a job offer he couldn't refuse in Charlotte. A large bank was looking to hire a new managing director of investments, a job which, quite frankly, he was terribly underqualified for. But Hayes being Hayes, he didn't let that deter him. We wanted to end up in North Carolina, and a job like that was unlikely to come along again. He had to take it.

But I had just started my internship at Abrams Architecture, one of the country's most prestigious firms, in New York, and it was an opportunity I couldn't pass up. If I was going to become a world-renowned architect, like I had always dreamed, I needed to learn from them. Then I would have enough experience under my belt that I could go back to State, complete my one-year professional degree, and sit for my licensure exam. So Hayes would move to Charlotte while I finished my degree. The plan was set.

But right after I completed my internship and moved back to Raleigh to start my last year of school, Hayes had turned up unannounced on my doorstep. He was uncharacteristically disheveled.

"Jules, I can't spend another moment apart," he'd said before I even let him in the door. "I need you. I can't live without you. Please marry me. I want to start our lives together now."

Honestly, I had expected something grand and intricately orchestrated, so in some ways, a simple proposal like this made it easier for me to say yes. That the proposal came from his downtrodden, miserable heart, that it originated from a place of missing me so desperately that he couldn't breathe without me, made it more charming somehow.

He looked so hopeful down on his knee.

"Of course I'll marry you, Hayes," I'd said. After he had given me the ring and come inside, I'd added, "But you know I have to finish school. It's only nine more months."

He had seemed distressed. "Do you really have to finish? I'm on the fast track now, babe. You don't have to work."

I guess that should have been a red flag, but we had been apart for so long—I was tired of the separation too. Even though I told him there was no way I wouldn't finish my degree, I have to wonder if that conversation paved the way for what happened six months later when, even though I was almost to the finish line, I did drop out of school. If I hadn't known I could run to Hayes, would I have let that one humiliating incident define the rest of my life? Had I ignored my better judgment because I knew marrying Hayes was a ticket out of a tough time?

Now, thinking of how happy I had been working toward my degree, how sure I was that everything in my life was falling into place, made me realize how quickly everything had fallen apart. My dream of being an architect had come crumbling down all around me.

I steeled myself. I had let my dream go. I wouldn't let Hayes go, too. But had he even left me any other choice?

"Maybe Hayes did propose the same night Chrissy found out about you. I don't know." Sarah looked uncomfortable. "I have no idea if this is even true." She was studying my face. "But now you have all the information I have."

Chrissy Matthews. "So that video was of her," I said. "And it definitely wasn't from years ago."

Sarah didn't try to argue with me. We both knew it was true.

I tried to wipe the stunned expression off my face as my parents walked into the bridal room. Fortunately, it was so chaotic, no one was really paying attention to me anyway. "MOB and FOB, you're up!" Alice called as she followed them in. "Photo time!"

Dad smiled at me and put his hand over his heart. "My little girl is all grown up and getting married."

"There will be time for all that later!" Alice said, practically shoving him out the door.

"I'm going to go meet the bridesmaids trolley," Sarah said, giving me an encouraging smile. Then she whispered, "You're okay. You've got this."

Then there were two. Babs was waiting, smiling, holding the veil. The wedding veil. The heirloom that had given three generations of women in my family happy marriages—and would potentially make me the fourth generation.

"It's time, my love," she said softly. I could barely look at her. Last night, lying in bed, all I could think about was the fact that Babs had seen Hayes making out with another girl on video. She was the last person I'd ever want to see that.

I leaned down so that she could reach me, my heart still pounding. But before she put the veil on my head, she paused.

"Jules, may I say something?"

I smiled tersely. "You're going to even if I say no."

"I am. I just need you to know something."

I studied her face, thinking she was going to share an eloquent pearl of wisdom, the secret to her success with my grandfather for all those years. Instead, she said, "Sweetheart, it is not your role in life to fix another woman's mistakes."

My eyebrows rose. She didn't have to elaborate. But how did she know the pressure I felt to take care of Hayes? I had been so humiliated the day before that I didn't have any choice now but to look strong and act proud, so, to save face, I pretended to be nonplussed. "Babs, I know that." But inside, I started freaking out. *What if it's up to Therese to fix her mistakes, not me?*

Babs didn't seem to pick up on my anxiety, and simply nodded. "I just wanted to be sure."

She started to raise the veil to my head, with its yards of lace and tulle, but then pulled it down to her chest again. "I can't even count the number of times I stood in your mother's bedroom while you climbed in the back of the closet to pull out your great-grandmother's lucky veil and try it on, the number of times we talked about the day you would wear it, how it would symbolize all the joy your marriage would bring." As tears filled her eyes, the weight of this hit me. I loved Hayes, but hadn't that voice in my head, that gut feeling, been telling me all along that I didn't fully trust him?

As that veil—with all its family history and symbolism—nearly reached my head, I suddenly *knew*: Hayes and I would never make it. And if I went through with this, then I would be the one to sully the family wedding veil, to bring an end to its streak of long and happy marriages.

"Stop," I whispered, then repeated louder, "Stop!"

Babs looked alarmed.

"Babs, I'm not sure," I said.

She nodded very seriously. "Then let's get the hell out of here," she whispered.

I put my hand to my mouth. I'd never heard Babs cuss. "But Mom will kill me."

"Better an unhappy day than an unhappy life."

I stopped, feeling stuck to the floor, the train of my gown suddenly so heavy it was in danger of pulling me down.

"Come on," Babs hissed. "She'll recover. You might not." She shook her head. "I have an idea."

"Sarah!" Babs exclaimed just as Mom and Sarah walked back into the room.

"The trolley is running a few minutes late," Sarah said. Under her breath, she added, "Because Laney got drunk and lost her shoes."

Babs smiled tightly. "I'd like a picture of you and Julia in the courtyard, please."

Everyone followed Babs outside, including Mom. "Meredith, sugar, your hair needs a little touch-up in the back," Babs said.

Mom rolled her eyes. "Goodness gracious. I knew it!"

Sarah and I locked eyes, and without a word, I knew she understood what was about to happen. Mom turned back into the church, and Babs turned to me. "Run!"

With no further instruction, the three of us took off through the parking lot, running toward Babs's Cadillac. Sarah helped me stuff my giant dress in the back seat of the getaway car while Babs leaped in front. And though I'd been conflicted, the moment we pulled out I felt like I'd dodged a bullet.

It was only then that something hit me. I said: "Who in the world could have sent that video?"

Maybe they did it out of malice. Maybe they did it out of kindness. Either way, whoever sent that video might have just saved me from making the biggest mistake of my life.

Cattle Prod

Present Day

I can't explain exactly when or how it happens, only that it does. At some point over the years, our children suddenly decide that they have free rein to parent *us*. It starts slowly. A comment here, a suggestion there. And then they take over, fully and completely, as though you didn't do a perfectly fine job raising them in the first place.

So here I was, in my own living room with its stunning view of the ocean, among my inherited furniture and knickknacks and whatnots, sipping tea that my daughter had made me not as a peace offering but as a trap. I would never walk away and leave a perfectly good cup of tea, which she well knew. She stopped pacing by the fireplace and glared at me. "What were you *thinking*?"

It had only been two days since my granddaughter

had become a runaway bride, so maybe I should have been easier on my daughter. Even still, I didn't want to play into the ruse that I was the child and she was the mother here, but I couldn't quite help myself from saying, with the attitude and intention of a teenager, "I don't know, Meredith, perhaps I didn't want my grand-daughter to be unhappy for the rest of her natural life?"

It couldn't help but make me think of my late hus-band, Reid. And thinking of him, as I did no less than a thousand times a day, sent a shot right through my heart. It had been nearly fourteen months since he'd passed. And, yes, I could get out of bed now—not our bed, obviously, where I was certain I would never sleep again—but the guest bedroom bed, anyway. I could go to bridge club or book club, sit in the living room with the latest *Reader's Digest*, even though Reid wasn't sit-ting in his hideous recliner, reading a book a few feet from me. But I would not stop loving him until my dying breath. He was my one and only, my true love, so I meant it when I said, "Meredith, I think my grand-daughter deserves eternal happiness. Forgive me for being so selfish."

She sighed. "Mother, I know that you and Daddy had a fairy tale, okay? I get it. I understand. But not everyone is whisked away by the love of her life and spends sixty years swooning. Not everyone gets that."

"Well, they *should*," I said.

My daughter was pacing again now, her shoulder-length hair tied back with a ribbon, elegant and grace-ful in a pair of cigarette-legged black pants that made her seem slightly taller than her five feet five inches. She was a pretty little girl who had grown into a lovely woman. Both my girls had. They had the same long, slender neck and womanly figure. Meredith and Alice, my green-eyed beauties. They had brought Reid and me so much joy.

"Sweetheart, don't take this the wrong way," I said, knowing she was guaranteed to take what I said next the wrong way. "But it has broken my heart to see you so unhappy. It has nearly undone me."

"I'm not unhappy," she spat, stopping her pacing.

I put my hands up in defense. "Far be it from me to tell you what you are, but Meredith, you have been separated twice in the last decade. You certainly aren't blissful."

She sighed and looked at me wearily. "But we're together now. I guess that's what I'm saying. Yes, Allen and I have had our share of problems. But we love each other, and we have worked them out."

I nodded. "I respect you for that more than words can say. But I will be very clear in that I do not wish that same fate for your daughter."

Surely she didn't, did she?

Meredith finally sat down beside me on the long sofa, upholstered in a seashell print that she hated. She wouldn't have to hate it much longer. "Mother, you drove the getaway car? What message does that send?"

I set my teacup down on the end table and crossed my arms. I tried to look indignant even though I knew some of the culpability for this *was* mine. Just not in exactly the way Meredith believed. "It sends the message that I love my granddaughter more than I love my reputation. It sends the message that I prioritize her happiness over everything else. What message does it send that you told her she would never find anyone as good as Hayes?"

She rolled her eyes. "You know how she is, Mother. That girl is flakier than a biscuit. Hayes is strong and steady. She can't take care of herself. She needs him."

It wasn't wholly untrue that my granddaughter relied on her fiancé quite a bit. Especially once she, with no explanation, had left architecture school. That little girl who had been carrying around graph paper notebooks and sketching since she was six years old had suddenly quit. Just like that. When she was only months away from finishing her fifth-year professional degree, from sitting for her licensure exam, from achieving her dreams.

"Meredith, you have to know what happened. You *have* to," I said. I picked my teacup back up, the china still smooth and delicate after all these years, and took a sip, inhaling the scent of spicy cinnamon as I did.

She rolled her eyes again. Ah, now we were back to mother and child. "If I knew, don't you think I would have fixed it? Do you know what it took for Allen and me to scrimp and save and get her through college? And I cringe to think that she's paying student loans for two semesters of graduate school that she didn't even finish. And now that she isn't going to be living with Hayes, that he isn't going to be there to support her—what in the world will she do?"

I guessed that was the silver lining. "Well, she'll have to learn how to take care of herself. It's a lesson we all must learn, and believe you me, the older you get, the harder it is."

I'd like to say that I could have taken care of myself long before now, long before I was this woman of eighty who felt afraid living alone in her own home. I wrapped my hands around the cup, the warmth feeling good on my tired fingers.

"But she always goes back to him, Mom. Always. And, yes, it's no secret that I have been happy about that in the past. I love Hayes. So sue me. But at this point, she's dug a hole so deep that it isn't only that she loves him. She *needs* him, in the most practical way."

I was from a different time. I was a woman who had raised her children and relied on her husband for the rest, so I wouldn't necessarily disparage Julia's choice if I had believed it was what she wanted—which I did not. But the problem was much larger. "He cheated on her, Meredith. They aren't even married."

She pointed at me decisively. "Exactly. That's what I'm saying. They weren't even married. If they were married, he wouldn't have done that."

Meredith and I had always had different logic on this particular matter, so we would agree to disagree.

She sighed. "And it's more than that. She will take him back. She always does. And he will go after her. Because he always does. This is their pattern, falling apart and being flung back together. They love the drama of it all, the romance. They can't live together, but they can't be apart. In a week I'll be getting a phone call that they're getting married after all, and I'll have to call everyone back and put this whole thing together again."

It wasn't particularly untrue what Meredith was saying. I had received more sobbing and gleeful phone calls from my granddaughter about this particular boy than I would like to say. I suppose I always assumed she would eventually get out from under his spell, that she would see that she deserved something steady, someone who would bring her peace. But I had to consider that maybe peace wasn't what she wanted. Maybe peace wasn't ever a part of the plan. The idea of those two getting together again was beginning to give me a headache. "It will all work out, one way or another" was all I could say. But even I didn't know if that was true.

Then I had a thought that made me chuckle.

Meredith glared at me. "What could possibly be funny about this?"

I composed myself enough to say, "Just the thought of poor Alice trying to put this wedding back together again."

"What if Alice decides Hayes and Julia need to release those ridiculous doves at the ceremony and one gets loose in the church again?" Now Meredith began to chuckle.

"Can you imagine if they had gotten married?" Tears were coming out of the corners of my eyes now. "Bird droppings were *everywhere*!"

When we had laughed away all our sorrow, I looked around the room, noticed how unthreatening it seemed in the light of day. It was only at night that the fear started. I'd tried to convince myself that it was ridiculous. This had been my home with the man I loved for decades. I had raised my children here, hosted Easter egg hunts for my grandchildren, laughed as they slid down the banister. I had held Julia's engagement tea here, for heaven's sake.

But it wasn't my home anymore. Not with Reid gone. Alone in the dark of night, I felt terrified, panicked. Every creak of the floor, groan of the wind, chime of the grandfather clock, sent my heart racing into my throat. And I decided that now was as good a time as any.

"Meredith, I need to talk to you about something else."

She looked tired, which I guessed was a suitable way for a woman whose child just left her fiancé at the altar to look.

"Is it serious? Because I can't handle anything else today."

I nodded. "Then it can wait."

She sighed and got up, starting her pacing again. But after a few moments, she stopped. "No. Now I have to know."

"You know how my friends Judy, Annie, and Fred have all moved into those lovely little apartments?"

Those lovely little apartments were part of a graduated senior living facility where one could buy an apartment or town home, then move to assisted living when the time called for it. Many of my friends' children had practically driven them there with a cattle prod. I was having the exact opposite experience—I wanted to go. Meredith and her sister, Alice, might not agree on much. But they were united in the fact that this was our family home, I was only eighty and in great shape, and I should not give up my house.

"Yes, Mother," Meredith sighed. "I know your friends have enjoyed Summer Acres. But Judy has Parkinson's, Annie is nearly ninety, and Fred's children were practically flinging him out the front door so they could have the house."

All of that was true. But what was also true was that once their spouses were gone, my friends' homes held heartache instead of happiness.

"Well, would you and Alice not like to have my house?" I asked, amused.

Alice had made no bones about wanting this house for her family someday, and I had to think the extra money Meredith would receive when her sister bought her out would lighten the financial burdens that she and Allen faced—especially now that they had paid for the wedding that wasn't. She never confided much in me about the causes of their separations, but she swore it wasn't someone else for either of them. Meredith loved her position with the city, but Allen had had difficulty maintaining a job over the last decade, and they certainly led a two-income lifestyle. I couldn't think of anything much more stressful than that.

"Why do you always give her what she wants, Mother? Why? She's so conniving and you just keep bowing down to her."

"She isn't conniving. She's just high-strung." I knew Meredith was hurting over her daughter's pain, so I gave her some grace. But Alice had worked herself to death to create a perfect wedding weekend for Meredith and Julia, and I didn't think that should be discarded. I also knew she knew what was coming next, and it was breaking her heart. "Sweetheart, please come sit down beside me."

She sat reluctantly. "I know what you're going to say," she said. "You're moving. I just don't quite understand it."

She didn't need to understand it. Only I did.

"And I suppose Alice will be moving in here?"

"I suppose she will."

She nodded. "Fine. That's fine."

Later that evening, I hugged my daughter goodbye and went back to my bedroom to make a plan on how to organize my things to move. As I was going through my dresser drawers, sorting through items to keep, toss, and donate, I imagined what Reid would say if he were here now, what he would think about me giving up the home we had shared for so long. But he wasn't here. And, like my granddaughter, I had a responsibility to do what I thought was best, no matter what Meredith said.

I smiled as I pulled a worn fraternity pin from the top drawer, cold and heavy in my hand. Much of the gold plate had chipped to reveal dull, dark metal standing in its place. In some ways, it reminded me of myself. Different, changed, faded. But, underneath, that pin still held every magical feeling that it had the night I had received it, the week before my wedding—albeit from a man I did not marry. It still held the promise of something that couldn't be seen with the eye but could be remembered by every cell. It was a pin that made me think; a pin that made me wonder what might have been. Not what could be. No. It was too late for that now.

Holding that pin was a tangible reminder of a hard-won lesson: There comes a time in every woman's life where she must put her own happiness first. I was learning that lesson a little late. I would make sure my granddaughter didn't suffer the same fate.

JULIA

Off Schedule

A getaway-car scene *is* dramatic, and I liked the statement it made, something I wasn't brave enough or bold enough to actually say out loud: I wasn't coming back. But as I looked out the backseat window, I remembered how devastated Hayes had looked the first night I met him, the night his mother had left him. I couldn't just run away with no explanation, could I?

"Oh no," I groaned.

"No second thoughts now," Babs said.

"Jules!" Sarah scolded.

"No second thoughts," I said. "But I forgot my purse."

"No problem," Sarah said. "Babs, you pull up to the church. I'll sneak around to the side entrance to get it."

But as we pulled up, I could see Hayes standing at the edge of the lawn looking for . . . Well, me, I assumed. I knew I had to talk to him.

Hayes's face lit up when he saw me get out of the car. "Oh, thank God," he said. "For a minute I thought we had a runaway bride situation on our hands."

He was trying to maintain his usual upbeat attitude, but I could see in his face that he knew what was happening.

I shook my head, tears filling my eyes.

"Jules," he said softly. "It's okay. We still have five minutes before the service starts. We can pretend this never happened."

I was swamped with guilt. I had sworn I would never leave him. "I can't marry you, Hayes. I'm sorry."

"Jules, come on. We've been through all this."

"I love you," I whispered. "But I can't live my life like this."

"But—"

I put my hand up. "I can't marry someone I don't trust."

"After all this time, after all these years, after all this *love*, you trust an old video more than you trust me?"

That was the root of the problem—I trusted an anonymous video more than I trusted the man I was supposed to marry. Even still, I let him pull me to him one last time; I let him kiss me. Even after all these years, he made me melt; because of all these years, we fit together seamlessly. I felt breathless in his arms. Just as I was about to change my mind about leaving him, though, I thought of Chrissy Matthews. Had he made her feel breathless too? Did he have what we had with someone else? My heart shattered all over again.

"I can't go through with it, Hayes. I'm sorry."

He just shook his head, staring at the ground. Then he looked back up at me. "Go on our honeymoon."

"What?"

"Right now. Change your ticket on your Delta app. Get your bags out of my trunk. Take some time. Clear your head." He rubbed my arms. "You'll come back to me after you do some thinking. I know you will."

That was when I knew, for sure, that he had cheated on me. Jilted men do not offer free honeymoons if they don't feel guilty about something. They just don't.

As I climbed back into Babs's car to leave the church for the second time that day, Alice ran out, clipboard in hand. "Where have you been? We're off schedule!"

Hayes almost looked amused when he put his arm around her and said, "I think you can throw the schedule out, Alice."

Now, three hours later, on a tiny commuter flight, "What can I get you, shug?" rang out, making me jump. The flight attendant in her blue Delta uniform was wearing tons of makeup, and she looked tired. I guessed she could have said the same about me.

"Alcohol," I replied.

She raised her eyebrow. "Uh oh." She scooped ice into a plastic cup and poured vodka over the top of it. "That bad, huh?"

I nodded as she splashed Dasani Lime over the vodka. "I'm going on my honeymoon."

She looked around and, obviously not identifying anyone who could be my brand-new husband, said simply, "This one is on the house."

I took a swig that burned as it went down as she handed me a pack of cookies and moved down the aisle.

The few sips of vodka must have done the trick because the next thing I heard was the captain's voice over the loudspeaker: *Flight attendants, please prepare the cabin for landing.*

I blinked a few times, and it all came flooding back. Today was supposed to be the happiest day of my life. I was supposed to be married. But just a few hours ago, I had changed out of my wedding gown in the airport bathroom and given Sarah my dress. As she'd left the airport lobby, she turned to me and said, "You deserve to find the love of your life, Julia. You deserve someone who sends you flowers and writes you love letters." I hugged her, my tears wetting her shoulder. As she walked away, still in her bridesmaid's dress, I felt fiercely alone. I almost didn't get on the plane. But somewhere deep inside I knew I should. Tears pricked my eyes.

I probably could have slept all the way to St. Thomas had it not been for the plane change in Charlotte. Charlotte. Chrissy Matthews. I was furious all over again. How could Hayes have done this to me? Just like that, my tears dried, and righteous indignation took their seat at the table.

I deplaned and waited around in the Jetway for my valet-tagged bag. I could see my nondescript black suitcase out the small window of the door as a man in an orange vest unloaded it. I grabbed it practically as it touched the floor and was off, suddenly needing some air. I also realized I was positively starving.

Even still, as I walked, I savored the light in the airport atrium. The elegant glass wall rolled and arched into the ceiling, creating a moment of modern splendor in an unlikely place. I wondered how many passengers bustled through this airport every day, never noticing the beauty surrounding them, never considering the hours of brainstorming and drafting, planning and constructing, that went into something like this. I won-

dered how many people spent their lives missing what
was right in front of them.

The line at Chick-fil-A was punishing, but I *needed*
Chick-fil-A. The buttery bun, the two pickles, the crisp,
never soggy chicken skin—nothing else would do. As I
stood in what was more a massive conglomeration of
people than a line, considering the number one with
half unsweet tea, half lemonade I'd order, the wedding
that wasn't—and my mother's furious voice over Babs's
Bluetooth when she told her we had fled—felt so far
away. No, not far away. Impossible.

With only three people in front of me, I unzipped the
top pocket of my suitcase and reached in. When I didn't
feel my wallet, I rummaged around, grabbing what I
thought was a rolled-up T-shirt and instead yanking out
a pair of men's boxers for the entire line to see. But they
weren't Hayes's brand. And I *knew* I had put my wallet
there.

My heart racing, I unzipped the main compartment
of the bag enough so I could see inside. I gasped. I could
make out a rolled-up needlepoint belt, a pair of loafers,
and a dopp kit, none of which belonged to me. And, ew,
I had just touched a *stranger's* underwear!

As panicked as I was, I briefly considered staying
to get my Chick-fil-A, but remembering I didn't have
any money, I turned to race back to the gate. My heart
pounded as I formulated a plan. Fortunately, I had
zipped my license into the inside pocket of the jacket I
was wearing, so I *could* get my furious parents to wire
me money to get home if I needed it. But how did one
even get wired money? It was a phrase that had no actual
application to my life. Were there money-wiring places?

And, if so, would there be one in an airport? And, furthermore, after I had run out on my wedding, would my parents even send me money?

Before I could catastrophize further, I realized that I was only in Charlotte. Sarah could come pick me up in like two hours if, worst-case scenario, my bag really *was* gone.

As I raced down the hallway, swerving among the throngs of people, I made a mental list: My glasses were in that bag. My expensive new bikini. My computer with the CAD files of my final project drawings from architecture school. Well, I certainly never wanted to see *those* again. If they were lost, that would be the silver lining. But I wanted everything else back. And maybe, just maybe, the person who took my bag had realized the mistake.

I was like the desperate lover in a Hallmark movie: out of breath, chest burning and hair disheveled. And I realized two things as I reached my last gate. One, if I was this winded from what couldn't have been more than a half-mile run, I needed to seriously examine my fitness level. Two, my bag! The handle was up and a man was leaning casually against it in front of the gate agent's counter. Well, he was pretending to, at least. If he had actually leaned on it, the four spinner wheels that worked so incredibly well would most certainly have slid out from underneath him. He grinned at me. That was when I noticed something I hadn't noticed about a man—at least a man who wasn't Hayes—in a long, long time: He was kind of cute. Actually, he was more than kind of cute. He was seriously, amazingly cute, with a head of short, dark hair. His shirttail hung loosely over a pair of jeans that were fitted but not so tight that they looked forced.

"My bag!" I exclaimed, so relieved I could have melted into a puddle on the floor. As I reached the man and unzipped the top pocket, I pulled out my wallet and hugged it.

"I figured you'd come back for the bomb you have in there," he said, grinning.

I gasped. "You can't say *bomb* in an airport," I whispered.

"You're right," he whispered back. "And I'm glad you came back, because I have a kilo of cocaine in my bag."

Now I rolled my eyes. "Can you even fit a kilo of cocaine in a carry-on bag?"

He shrugged. "I don't know. I've always been a little sketchy on the finer points of pounds versus kilograms."

I nodded. "Same."

I finally remembered that we weren't out for drinks. He had my bag and I had a plane to catch for, depressingly, my honeymoon.

My suitcase buddy exhaled deeply. "I was almost hoping my bag was lost."

I needed to go but now I was intrigued. "Why in the world would you want your bag to be lost?"

"It has my shitty CAD drawings in it."

I felt my chest go tight. "Are you an architect?" I asked hesitantly.

"That's kind of debatable. I mean, technically, yeah. In the way that I did all the school and graduated and stuff. But do I deserve the title? Don't know."

I could certainly relate. Been there, failed that. "Okay, well, thanks again. I've got to get to Terminal C."

I scooted his suitcase to him, but strangely, he didn't return the gesture. Instead, he started walking, pulling them both behind him. "I'm going to Terminal C too," he said, by way of explanation.

"Well, you're going to get our bags mixed up again," I huffed.

He stopped and looked at me, amused. "Oh, *I* am, huh? So this is all my fault?"

I smiled, remembering how anxious I had been to grab that bag before it had even touched the ground. Okay. So maybe it wasn't *all* his fault.

He started walking again. "You know what, you're right. I didn't take your bag on purpose last time, but I might very well do it on purpose this time."

I squinted at him.

"So I can see you again," he said slowly, emphasizing each syllable.

God, was I this out of practice? I was, I knew. I hadn't even considered that another man could be interested in me in so many years that I didn't recognize his flirting.

"Well," he said, as we reached the huge sign for Terminal C, "this is where I leave you."

"Okay." I smiled. "Off to St. Thomas."

He laughed. "*You're* going to St. Thomas? *I'm* going to St. Thomas. Well, no. Not St. Thomas. The BVIs by way of St. Thomas."

"Me too!" Suddenly things were looking up. But then I remembered. "I'm going on my honeymoon."

He looked around. Then, understanding, said, "Oh, no . . ."

I nodded.

"You can't fly to your honeymoon alone." He walked to the desk at our gate, and I followed him for a reason I couldn't explain.

"Excuse me," he said, "my wife and I are on our

honeymoon, but we weren't able to book seats together." He winked at me. "Is there any way you could help?"

The gate agent took our passports and typed for what seemed like an absurd amount of time for a simple seat change.

"All right, love birds," she finally said. "I managed to get you seats together and a first-class upgrade too."

"Wow! Thank you so much." I took the few steps to the small waiting area and sat down in the navy seat that looked like it had the least amount of crumbs on it.

"I'm Julia Baxter, by the way," I said as my "husband" sat down next to me. "Probably good to know your fake wife's name in case we're questioned."

"I'm Conner Howard." He leaned over. "I would shake your hand, but the gate agent might find that weird."

I stopped, my mouth gaping and my mind racing, putting the pieces of what I knew about this man together frantically. "*You're* Conner Howard. Like *the* Conner Howard?"

The man complaining about his shitty CAD drawings was the up-and-comer in the architectural world that everyone was watching, that was making every who's who and big voice in the industry feel threatened and thrilled all at the same time. He'd been the youngest member of *Architectural Digest*'s AD100 this year. He was, like, my age.

I was on the verge of gushing as the voice on the loudspeaker announced, "Priority, you may board now."

Conner, looking amused, stood and led me through the line.

"Garrison Towers is my favorite building. I mean, seriously, my favorite," I gushed as I stepped over the metal threshold and onto the plane.

"Okay, wifey, let's take it down a notch." I barely noticed how nice it was of him to put our matching bags in the overhead compartment, I was so taken.

"I mean, the lines and the symmetry . . . The way you implemented those half floors." I gasped.

We sat down side by side and got situated. Then he placed his hand on mine. "Are you joking?" He looked around. "Did someone put you up to this? Because there is no way anyone in the world is nerdy enough to have a favorite building, especially not one designed by me."

"Um, no. No one put me up to this. I'm honestly just that nerdy."

"So, are you an architect too?"

As his question seared through me, I felt the detestable scrunch between my eyes that my mom said was going to give me wrinkles. Maybe technically I was. Or, at least, could be. But I wasn't in the habit of sharing my failures with cute plane strangers, so I just said, "You could say I'm an architecture enthusiast." There. That was true.

"May I get you something to sip on before we take off, Mr. and Mrs. . . . " she trailed off.

Conner smiled at the flight attendant with the grin that had changed for me in the past few minutes. Where I had been interested in but a little annoyed by this stranger, now I was completely starstruck.

"Have you decided yet whether you're going to take my name?" he asked.

Earlier I would have said no, but now . . . "Um, yes." I looked up at the flight attendant. "Julia Howard has a nice ring, doesn't it?"

Conner laughed and squeezed my hand. "I'll have an IPA and Julia here would love—"

He turned to look at me. "Oh, honey, you know," I said playfully, suddenly feeling giddy. "I always have a rosé before takeoff."

He looked back at the flight attendant. "You know what? We're celebrating. How about some champagne?"

My mind raced with questions for one of the foremost architects in the country who had also proven himself to be funny and kind. So, no, today had not gone exactly the way I had planned. But, even still, I was going to end it by drinking champagne with a cute guy. As the plane took off for its four-hour flight, my problems started to seem so far away—and, for the first time in a long time, I felt like anything was possible.

CORNELIA

Laid to Rest

March 6, 1914

Thirteen-year-old Cornelia Vanderbilt had always preferred Asheville to Washington, D.C., but, even still, this house on K Street had felt like home. Now, her heart racing in her chest, she knew it would never feel like home again.

"Daddy!" Cornelia screamed breathlessly, shaking her father's arm. "Daddy!"

"George!" Edith yelled, uselessly, putting her hand to her husband's face.

Cornelia and Edith had returned upstairs after getting George's glass of water and newspapers and found him slumped over, lifeless.

"Emma!" Edith screamed to her lady's maid. "Get Dr. Mitchell immediately!"

"Dr. Finney said you were fine, Daddy!" Cornelia screamed. "Wake up!" Her shouts turned to sobs.

Cornelia's and Edith's eyes met over George, Cornelia's hot panic turning into a deep, silent dread. She noticed her mother was breathing hard as they shared a look, a knowledge: they had lost him.

Just the night before George had seemed almost well to Cornelia, joking about keeping the boys in D.C. away from his daughter, who was attending an all-girls school but who still had plenty of opportunity to come in contact with suitable young men. George had had nothing more than a routine appendectomy. He had been to one of the finest surgeons in the country. He *had* to be okay. He just *had* to.

Time seemed to stand still as Edith wrapped her arms around Cornelia, her own tears choking her. Minutes later, Dr. Mitchell, the family's physician, arrived to confirm what they already knew: George was gone.

It was as if Cornelia could feel a part of herself slipping away too. Who would read to her now? Talk to her about art and music, study the globe and imagine all the places they would visit next? And, one day, when she was quite grown up, who would walk her down the aisle at her wedding? Cornelia began to feel faint. If it weren't for her mother's strong arms holding her up, she felt certain she would have collapsed onto the floor.

It wasn't until days later, when Edith and Cornelia were on a train for New York to bury George, that Cornelia finally asked, "If you go too, Mother, what shall become of me?"

Edith took Cornelia's hand sympathetically. "I'm not going anywhere, darling. It's you and me against the world now."

"But *what if*, Mother?" Cornelia could feel the heat rising in her face. Did her mother not even have a plan?

"You have Aunt Pauline, Aunt Natalie, and Aunt Susan to look after you, sweetheart. But I promise, nothing's going to happen to me."

Somewhat pacified by the thought that she did, indeed, have plenty of family and that they wouldn't leave her alone on a street corner to rot if the worst happened, Cornelia then asked, "Why isn't Daddy being buried at Biltmore? It was the place he loved most. It's the place where we will be."

Edith smiled sadly at her daughter. "Because the Vanderbilts are all buried in the family mausoleum at the bottom of Todt Hill."

"Where the Commodore grew up," Cornelia confirmed, hesitantly. She had heard so many stories about her larger-than-life great-grandfather, the railroad tycoon and purveyor of the Vanderbilt fortune. How different he seemed from her own kind and caring daddy. "But we can't go see him there, Mother."

"I know, Nelly. But Daddy spent so much time, money, and energy designing the mausoleum that I know it's what he would have wanted. His family is in the mausoleum, and he should be too."

"*We* are his family, Mother."

Indeed they were. "When you get back to school—" she started.

"No!" Cornelia interrupted. "No, Mother, please don't make me go back. I want to go to Biltmore. That's where I can be with Daddy." Feeling absolutely overcome with despair, she added, "It would have been better if we had all died on the *Titanic*."

"Cornelia!" Edith scolded. "Don't say such a thing. Your father would never have wanted something so awful to happen. He would be grateful that we are safe."

Not two years earlier, in 1912, the family was slated to be aboard the maiden voyage of the unsinkable ship. At the last minute, Edith had felt such a nagging need to avoid the world's most glamorous and exciting boat that she persuaded George that it would be more fun to go home on the *Olympic* with George's niece and her husband instead; they could all dine together at night. It would be grand. George had been sulky that they wouldn't be on the prestigious maiden voyage that everyone was talking about—until news of the *Titanic* broke.

"Your mother saved us," he had told Cornelia. "You must listen to her because she always knows best."

Cornelia leaned back against the seat and closed her eyes, picturing herself singing and laughing with her father, reading on the loggia beside him, losing herself in his vast library with him by her side, instructing her on what to read next. More than K Street, more than New York, Biltmore was home; Biltmore was him. The thought of going back to school, even with all her friends there, felt terribly lonely. At Biltmore, she could ride mules with her friend Rose, take Cedric and Snow, the giant St. Bernards who were as gentle as lambs, for walks in Biltmore Village. There were fewer parties and politics, fundraisers and teas. She could have her mother all to herself. Tears slid down her cheeks, escaping from beneath her closed lids. She wasn't sure if that was what convinced her mother or perhaps something else, but Edith finally said, "All right. If it means that much to you, we will return to Biltmore as soon as Daddy is laid to rest."

Laid to rest. Laid to rest. The words pinged around in

Cornelia's head for the rest of the train ride and then on the ferryboat that took her and Edith past the southern tip of the city to Todt Hill. She still couldn't understand how her father could be buried in New York when the place he had created to rest was hundreds of miles away, in a magical forest of his own creation.

Buy a Ticket

As the morning sun streamed through the thatch-roofed dining hut where I was having my coffee and bagel, one of the resort cats tiptoed to a sliver of warmth, arched her back, stretched, and curled up in the triangle of light. I looked out over the white sand, toward the glittering sea, and smiled as a group of children tipped their kayak over, squealing with delight. Their mother, who popped up directly after them, looked less thrilled.

The sun, waves, and gently swaying palm trees had lured me into a sense of contentment so deep that I could almost forget what a complete mess I had made of my life. And it had only been two days. I glanced at the clock in the dining hut and realized it was almost ten. I would have just enough time to scurry down the crushed-shell path to my treehouse room and slip on my bikini before paddleboard yoga began. Paddleboard yoga was my new favorite thing. I had paddleboarded before, sure. And one of the aftershocks of my architecture school dropout flail was undertaking my 250-hour yoga certification. But the brilliance of combining yoga and paddleboarding had never occurred to me—until yesterday. And now I was hooked.

The phone in my room was blinking red with a message when I got there, but I didn't think much of it. Who would possibly be leaving me a message *here*? Then again, it wasn't like I had cell reception. It could be my mother or Babs. I almost let it go so I could get to paddleboard yoga a little early like I was planning. But something in that urgent blinking light wouldn't let me off the hook. What if it was Hayes? Would I call him back?

Deciding I could cross that bridge if I came to it, I picked up the phone and hit zero for the resort operator.

"Yes, Ms. Baxter?" Yesterday, the hotel staff had greeted me as "Mrs. Mitchell"—something that, later, made me dissolve into a sobbing puddle, certain I'd made a mistake, horrified at what everyone might be saying about me back home. I hadn't been able to get myself together the entire night. But today, somehow, I was too relaxed to worry about it.

"Do I have a message?" I asked.

The receptionist read: "I'm holding a private reception aboard *Sea Suite* tomorrow morning for architecture enthusiasts before the boat leaves for Anegada and our brief time as fake husband and wife ends. Please RSVP. Yours, Conner."

I laughed. "Would you like me to place the call for you?" she asked.

I hesitated. I almost said no. But even though I wasn't going to go, I had to at least respond, didn't I? I mean, sure, I was a world away and owed nothing to a perfect stranger. But then again . . .

"Yes," I said. "Put me through."

I heard her click off as the phone began to ring. I almost hoped Conner wouldn't answer. Then I would have legitimately done my due diligence, but I wouldn't actually have to talk to him. I could let him down easy via voice mail.

"Hello?" a deep voice on the other end of the line said.

"Conner?"

I could hear him smile. "So you got my message."

"I did but . . ." I bit my lip. I was going to tell him I couldn't go sailing with him this soon after I had broken up with my fiancé, that I had a bit of soul-searching to do. But what if he didn't mean it like that? What if he was only trying to be friendly? And then I would have made a fool of myself in front of one of my idols.

"So, what do you say?" he asked. "Sailboat, wine, cheese, me?"

I laughed. Okay. So he *probably* meant it like that. "Conner, at the risk of embarrassing myself and mis-reading your intentions, I just broke up with my fiancé two days ago."

"Mmhmm. I hear that. I totally do. But we're in the British Virgin Islands. You can't sit in your room the whole time. Let me show you around."

I looked out the window, past the bamboo porch, at the endless blue sea dotted with islands. Yeah, who would want to sit here for days on end? "So this isn't a date?"

He laughed. "Oh, no. It's definitely a date. For sure."

"Conner!" I scolded.

"Fine, fine. We'll talk about your weird obsession with architects, and I'll pretend I'm simply attempting to be friendly, not trying to embark upon a steamy vacation fling that we'll both think of wistfully for the rest of our lives."

The laugh in my throat escaped. That did sound kind of nice. Who wouldn't want to have a vacation fling? I'd just left Hayes at the altar, sure. But I wasn't his grieving widow.

At any rate, I heard myself saying, "Well, when you put it that way, who could possibly say no?"

"That's what I was hoping!" he exclaimed cheerily. "My dinghy will be at the dock to pick you up at ten tomorrow morning."

It was only when we hung up that I wondered who in her right mind would entertain passing up a sailing adventure in the BVIs with one of America's biggest up-and-coming architects. But then I remembered that the majority of Americans probably weren't all that interested in architects. I glanced at the clock on the nightstand and grabbed my phone. Then I realized that no one could text me on it anyway and, reluctantly, I put it back. I hadn't thought of myself as a person who was attached to her phone, but it was occurring to me on this trip that maybe I was. Walking down the steps without it felt oddly vulnerable.

But the closer I got to the paddleboard dock, the freer I felt.

Yesterday's class had been taught by a strong and stable woman. I looked like Bambi learning to walk. Today, a chiseled man with shoulder-length white-blond hair, no shirt, and a killer island tan wearing red swim trunks handed me my paddleboard. I looked around. I didn't see any other students, and yesterday's teacher was nowhere in sight. "Where's Dana?"

He shrugged. "How should I know?"

I laughed, his flippancy catching me off guard. "Well, isn't she teaching?"

He shook his head. "Nope. She's gone. I'm teaching today." He looked around, checked his watch, and grinned. "Looks like it's just you and me."

"Oh, gosh," I said. "Well, then, that's okay. We don't have to do it." One-on-ones were always so awkward.

He didn't respond but instead grabbed my board and put it in the water for me, helping me stay steady as I climbed aboard. "We need to paddle out far enough so that if you fall, it won't be tragic. I'm Trav, by the way," he said as our paddles sliced through the water, which was so clear and still I almost hated to disturb it.

"Julia," I replied.

"Have you done this before?" he asked. I turned to glimpse his smile.

"I'm an old pro," I said breezily, losing my balance and regaining it, hoping he didn't notice.

"So, just yesterday then?"

Yeah. He definitely noticed.

I laughed. "Okay. So paddleboards might not be my forte, but I am a certified yoga instructor."

"Well, that's half the battle."

Twenty minutes later, as Trav stepped from his board to mine to adjust my downward-facing dog, I realized that, despite the lunacy of the past seventy-two hours, I was enjoying myself immensely.

An Island Company sticker slapped to a power pole I

had seen the day before ran through my mind: *Quit your job. Buy a ticket. Get a tan. Fall in love. Never return.*

Hayes flashed through my mind. Then Conner.

"Trav?"

"Julia?"

"Do you think that everyone who comes to the islands has fantasies of staying forever?"

"I don't know. I came for spring break." He cleared his throat. "Spring Break 2012."

We both laughed. I'd never considered myself to be the kind of person who would just flee her life and escape to the islands. But, as was becoming abundantly clear, maybe I wasn't sure what kind of person I was at all. As I attempted to shift into Warrior Pose, I realized it was high time I found out.

EDITH

All Men Are Ghosts

April 11, 1914

The first night back at Biltmore after George's death
felt impossible. Every creak in the stairwell, every
plant in the winter garden, every work of art in the tapestry gallery was George. Every inch of it was a reminder
of the man Edith had loved wholeheartedly. The man
who was not coming back to save her. In these weeks
after his death, the blows had kept coming when Edith,
swamped by her grief, had learned that the money—at
least the money she had access to—had all but run out.
There was a large trust for Cornelia, which she would
receive when she became the rightful owner of Biltmore
on her twenty-fifth birthday, but, until that day, there
wasn't even enough left to cover the bequests George
had made in his will—and he had taken out a mortgage,
unbeknownst to Edith, on their K Street house in Washington. There was so much to do, to save, to figure. But,

for now, there was so much to mourn she couldn't face it, not yet.

Edith curled up in bed beside her frazzled, exhausted daughter underneath the thick, heavy linens that George had procured before he had even met Edith, and held Cornelia's tired hand. "I feel him here, Mother. Don't you?" Cornelia asked hopefully.

"I do, Nelly. Of course I do." Edith paused. "I feel him everywhere."

But it was a lie. That was what hurt her heart the very most. Biltmore *reminded* her of George, sure. But she couldn't hear George; she couldn't feel him. She didn't know what existed on the other side of this life, but over the past few years, her fate had become so intertwined with her husband's that she thought for sure he would be with her even now that he was gone. But he had just vanished, suddenly and fiercely. He had left her when she needed him most.

Cedric, their giant St. Bernard, jumped into bed with his two mistresses—something that was normally strictly forbidden. Edith laughed. "Did I ever tell you that your father's friend Henry James described the hair left behind by Cedric and Snow as something akin to piles of polar bear fluff?"

Cornelia laughed too. A welcome sound. Edith usually found dog fur highly unsuitable for bedrooms. But now, tonight, the women of Biltmore needed another warm body.

When Cornelia and Cedric were breathing heavily, taken away by their dreams to somewhere kinder than here, Edith made her way down the grand staircase and buzzed for a cup of tea in the library. George's library exemplified a dark, heavy rococo style with deep red furnishings, a stunning ceiling painting of *The Chariot of Aurora*, and Karl Bitter's "Venus and Vulcan" and-irons, chiseled of gilt bronze. Noble, George's favorite footman, delivered the tea as Edith sank into George's chair, close to the roaring fire. It occurred to Edith how very young Noble looked. He had been in service at this house since he was fifteen years old and was now maybe in his midtwenties. He was bright and calm, and the other servants had an undeniable respect for him.

"It's different without him, isn't it, Noble?"

He nodded slowly. "But we'll get through it together, Mrs. Vanderbilt. We are here for you, for whatever you need." He cleared his throat, trying to hide his emotions. "Mr. Vanderbilt will be sorely missed."

"Noble?" Edith wondered if she was oversharing, but, then again, Noble was practically family. "My only real qualm about interring George in New York was that so many of you who have been faithfully by his side for even longer than I have weren't able to pay your final respects."

"It's okay, ma'am. The service here will do well to put our hearts to rest."

But Edith was barely listening now, her eyes scanning the rows and rows of George's books, which, to her, all contained a small part of her husband. Or, perhaps, more aptly, he contained a small part of them.

"Noble," Edith said, not wanting to talk but also not quite ready to be alone. "Did you know that George was considered one of the best-read men in the country?"

She took a sip of her tea, the thin bone china warming her chilled hands.

"Yes ma'am. I had heard that. And he was generous with his books, too, always sharing them."

Edith nodded, setting the cup back on the end table and gesturing to the carving of the oil lamp above the tapestry hanging over the fireplace. "Do you know what the oil lamp in the carvings and in George's bookplates symbolizes?"

"I don't believe I do, ma'am," he said.

And that was what made Noble the best of the best in the service industry. Noble knew every inch of Biltmore far better than Edith. But he knew she needed a listening ear and so he lent it.

"The eternal quest for knowledge," she said. "That's why each bookplate is engraved *Quaero ex libris Biltmoris*. Inquire in the books of Biltmore."

"Mr. Vanderbilt certainly knew how to do that," Noble said, smiling.

Edith finally looked up at him, taking in his sandy hair and expressive eyes, the way his fitted waistcoat— one brass button, one silver, as was the custom here at Biltmore—was so neat and orderly even at this late hour. It struck her how tired he must be after a day not only full of work but also emotion.

"Thank you, Noble," Edith said quietly, releasing him, leaning back and closing her eyes. As she heard his footsteps reach the door, the full weight, peace, and comfort of home washed over her. Something cold on her hand jolted her eyes back open. But it was only Cedric's nose. She fluffed the fur on his head. "Hello, dear boy. You miss him too, don't you?" He lay down beside her, faithful as ever.

Edith sighed, soaking in the feeling. She was finally back in George's library, where she could rest, where she could grieve. Not only was her husband gone but she couldn't even visit his grave. At least, not practically. Going to New York to sit with him wouldn't happen often. But surely he was here, among his most prized possessions: his books. This was, after all, where the ghosts lived, wasn't it? Honoré de Balzac, Charles Dickens, Sir Walter Scott. Their cherished friend Paul Leicester Ford would forever remain here, his devotion to George and Biltmore immortalized in the dedication of his novel *Janice Meredith*. Edith wished that George had written a book in his life, that she had something in his voice. In lieu of his memoirs, she picked up what he had left behind: one of three leather-bound volumes of the darkest green embossed in gold. *Books I Have Read, G.W.V.*

"A man is created by stories," George had told Edith once. Was that true? And, if so, could she find him in the pages of the books he loved so much? Could they bring him back?

What had George been reading before he died? Edith turned to the very last page, to the very last entry, running her finger over her husband's distinctive, scrawling cursive. It was so distinguished, she always thought. Especially now, when it was all she had left of him. The last entry: *3159 History of the U.S. by Henry Adams Vol 3rd*.

Her astonishing, studious husband had read 3,159 books in his too-short life. And those were only the ones he had recorded. What a feat. But still, Edith thought that she would probably not want something so dry to be the last book she ever read. It struck her that she should choose more wisely from now on, treat every book as though it could be her grand reading finale. The previous entry: *3158 History of the U.S. by Henry Adams Vol 2nd*.

Her finger moved up a line and she stopped, her hand suddenly shaking: *3157 All Men Are Ghosts by L. P. Jacks.*

All Men Are Ghosts. The words sent chills down her spine. Maybe she was reading too much into this. But could it be a sign? From her beloved George? Did he know that he was leaving soon and wanted to tell Edith he would come back to her? But he hadn't come back to her. At least, not yet.

Edith took a deep breath and tried to calm herself. She hadn't read the book. Perhaps it wasn't about ghosts at all, but a lovely metaphor. Maybe it expounded upon the idea that all men were simply shells of themselves. Yes. That's what it had to be. With a shaking hand, Edith located the volume and slid it off the shelf. She took a moment, as she sometimes did, to pretend that she was an outsider looking in on the situation. Did it make the least amount of sense that her dead husband had left her some sort of message in his reading journal, that she was supposed to read this book and he would come back to her?

No. It made no sense at all. But she was a widow now. A bona fide, alone-in-the-world, parentless widow at that. She was entitled to go a bit crazy, if only for a little while.

She opened the first page of the book, and, as if to bring George back to her, took a whiff of the pages. They smelled like leather and maybe a hint of smoke from the fire that was always burning in the library hearth. Edith felt hesitant as she began to read. Her breath caught in her throat when she came to: *No genuine ghost ever recognized itself as what you suppose it to be. . . . In short, the attitude of mankind towards the realm of ghosts is regarded by them as a continual affront to the majesty of the spiritual world, perpetrated by beings who stand on a low level of intelligence; and for that reason they seldom appear or make any attempt at open communication, doing their work in secret and disclosing their identity only to selected souls.*

She couldn't go on. Would she be one of those selected souls? If George could come back to her, if he could appear to her, would she even want him to? Would it terrify her beyond imagination? She decided that it would. She felt determined to put the book back where it belonged, back in its proper place, to leave the tempting of fate and ghosts alone—even if it was the ghost of one she loved.

But before she did so, Edith turned to the small end table, removed a cigarette and, with a shaking hand and several attempts, lit it. As she inhaled, she heard, plain as day, "You know I don't allow smoking in the library, darling."

Fear pierced through her, and she jolted. Cedric shot out of the room as quickly as if he'd seen a bird, and the leather-bound volume in her hand landed with a decisive thud on the herringbone wood floor. She looked around and, seeing nothing, decided she was losing her mind. But hadn't the dog heard it too? He had bolted before the book fell, hadn't he? Or was she simply overtired? "It's okay to hear me, Edi." The voice again. "I want to stay with you."

Taking another long inhale of her cigarette, Edith decided she was delirious and needed to go to bed at once. Or that the voice she was hearing inside her head was just her imagination conjuring what she wanted to hear. But, then again, if the book was to be believed . . .

"George," she whispered.

"I'm here, Edi. I'm here. Don't worry. I'll help you take care of everything."

For the first time since she had heard the news of George's true financial standing at his death, Edith felt calm, soothed. The entire time they had known each other, Edith and George had been in this life together. That wasn't going to change just because her husband was gone. She still had a partner, even if he was a silent one. As George had taught her, sometimes a silent partner was the very best kind.

The Finest Places

I had been taught what to wear to a noon wedding versus a 6 p.m. one, a funeral, a church service, a graduation, and a baby shower. But no one had ever instructed me on what the heck I was supposed to wear on a gorgeous day on a fabulous boat, in the British Virgin Islands, on the first date since I'd broken my engagement and fled the country.

It sounded pretty damn glamorous when I thought about it. I rifled through my bag, finally deciding on my white bikini, which, due to my spray tan, would contrast against my skin wonderfully. I had bought new cover-ups for my honeymoon, but what if Conner wasn't wearing a bathing suit?

I grabbed a long white linen maxi dress, deciding it would be the perfect compromise. It was enough like a cover-up but dressier. I realized then that I hadn't picked out an outfit to go on a first date in ten years, which seemed ludicrous. And this wasn't just a regular date. This was a date with a man of substance, of reputation.

I was so busy focusing on my hair and outfit and lip gloss that I almost forgot to be nervous. I slipped my feet into gold sandals and rushed down the path to the dock. When I saw Conner in a navy pair of swim shorts and a white T-shirt, my heart flip-flopped. *It doesn't have to be a date; it can just be a meeting of the minds,* I told the butterflies in my stomach. Where the minds find each other very attractive and are tan and relaxed and likely to get a tiny bit tipsy.

Conner appeared to be admiring me as I walked toward him, and he stood still, as if stuck to his spot on the dock. When I reached him, he leaned down to kiss me on both cheeks. "You are as beautiful as I remembered."

I rolled my eyes. When he had met me my face had been covered in so much wedding makeup it felt like shellac.

He reached his hand out, leading me down the dock to a small, inflatable rubber dinghy that would take us to where the large boats were safely moored in deeper water.

Helping me in, he said, "Okay. Here's my ship. Magnificent, right?"

We both laughed, but I'd be happy as a clam to spend the day in this tiny boat with this handsome man. Conner pulled the cord on the engine, and with a loud crank and a whiff of diesel, we puttered off.

"I was going to wow you with my sailing abilities," he said as I put my hand down to touch the water, "but the crew thinks it's best if they take over so that I can really enjoy the day with you." I was kind of disappointed. I had pictured us out on the open seas alone, Conner teaching me the difference between a jib and a mast, standing behind me, showing me how to steer. I mean, clearly no one needs to be taught how to steer. But I was trying to live out my romantic comedy dream date here, and that would obviously be a part of it.

I admired the sailboats in the water, wondering which we would go to. The most beautiful, for sure, was a huge one with a shining silver hull and masts that looked like they reached all the way to heaven. When Conner turned the handle on the engine to steer us toward the boat, my eyes widened. "For real?" I definitely hadn't wanted to be an architect for the money, but maybe Conner was even more successful than I'd thought. "Is this *yours*?"

He laughed. "Oh, God no. You know how I built Garrison Towers?"

I obviously knew that.

"This is the Garrisons' boat. They're letting me use it as a bit of a thank-you gift."

I'm sure my mouth was gaping. "So what you're saying is that the crew won't let you show off because it takes an entire crew to get this thing going?"

He nodded. "Exactly."

Two men in white polo shirts and black shorts helped me aboard, and right away, a woman in the same outfit appeared with two spot-free martini glasses. (I noticed because spot-free in the islands, especially aboard a boat, is quite the feat.)

"May I offer you a Sea Suiteini?" she asked.

I smiled. "Thank you." I took one and then whispered to her, "What in the world is a Sea Suiteini?" I didn't want Conner to hear in case it was something incredibly common that I should have heard of.

"This boat is the *Sea Suite*, and it's our signature drink, but made weak for brunch."

Well, when in Rome, right? I held the glass up in a cheers motion and took a sip. I felt Conner's hand on my back as he took a glass too.

As the stewardess stepped aside, I saw that the large outdoor table was set with a pair of matching white plates trimmed in navy, bearing the initials *SS* in the middle. A bouquet of what I now knew, after months of wedding planning, were pink ranunculus sat in the center of the table.

"Hungry?" Conner asked.

I raised my eyebrows. "Not a date," I replied.

"When would brunch ever be a date?" He grinned. Brunch was basically always a date.

We sat down and one of the men who had helped me into the boat appeared. "Brunch will be served as soon as we get underway."

I eyed Conner. "Is this your life?"

He burst out laughing. "You're joking, right?"

I shrugged. I didn't know him. The engines roared to life.

"I literally had to get my passport to come here. This is the first time I've left the country. But I haven't taken a vacation since . . ." He paused, thinking. "Well, ever. I have never taken a vacation since I started work. When the Garrisons said I could stay on their boat I wasn't exactly expecting this, to be honest."

I felt myself relax as we began to pull away from the shore.

"May I say, though, that I'm glad you're here to share this foray into luxury with me?"

"May I say I'm glad too?" I could already tell these islands were going to look completely different from the water than they did from my treehouse room. I was instantly glad I had come.

"So, overall," Conner asked, "has this been the honeymoon you were expecting?"

I laughed so hard I almost spit out my drink.

"Oh, good," he said. "I took a risk there. I was afraid it was too soon."

It *was* too soon. Even still, I smiled as a plate of eggs Benedict appeared before me.

"Miss, we also have vegan and gluten-free options if you prefer," the stewardess said.

I smiled. "I will eat pretty much anything that doesn't eat me first."

She laughed.

Savoring my first bite I said, "So this is the glamorous life of an architect, huh? Hundred-foot sailboats, crews calling you sir, jet-setting around the globe?"

Conner nodded. "Absolutely. Or maybe paralyzing self-doubt tempered by tiny glimpses of glory, which are then tempered again by negative reviews from random passersby about your buildings that make you reconsider your entire life and everything in it."

I laughed but I was also realizing how strange it was that he had come out here alone. "It seems unfair," I said, wiping my mouth, "that you know my whole sad backstory and I don't know any of yours." Well, that wasn't entirely true. He didn't know *all* my sad backstory.

"I don't really have one. I have a super-normal life."

"No one has a normal life," I interjected.

"True. But, I mean, my parents have been married

for forty years and still hold hands, and my sister married the guy she's been dating since high school and just had her first kid."

"Those guys you've been dating since high school don't always turn out the way you think."

Conner raised his glass. "Lucky for me."

I smirked. "But happy parents are underrated, I think."

"Yours aren't?"

I shrugged. "Together, yes. Happy?" I looked out over the water and thought about this. "Sometimes, yeah. Often, actually. But you know how some people have those relationships where they can't live with each other and can't live without each other?"

He shrugged. "In theory, yeah. With friends, totally. I'm just lucky enough not to have any firsthand experience."

I nodded. "Well, that's good. Because I have and it is no picnic." The thought of Hayes was like a shard of glass. I looked down into my martini, realizing I was drinking it too quickly. I was rambling. "And what about you?" I asked, eager to get off the subject. "Do you have a girlfriend?"

"Yes. And she finds it perfectly acceptable for me to shepherd beautiful young women around on yachts in the Caribbean. She wouldn't have wanted to come with me to this shithole anyway."

"Who would? These eggs Benedict are barely edible." They were divine. "So, is it inappropriate of me to ask why you're here all alone?"

He laughed. "No. Not inappropriate. We're in international waters so anything goes." He took a sip of his martini. "Two of my best friends are meeting me in a couple days to spend some time in Anegada, and then we're going to pick my parents up in Saint Thomas to go to Jost Van Dyke for a bit before I finish my vacation in Tortola. But believe it or not, no one could take three weeks off to come with me the whole time." He lifted his glass. "So I'm lucky I met you."

I lifted my glass. "Cheers to that!"

He put his napkin on the table. "Let's go to the front of the boat, pretend it's ours, and laugh snidely at the unwashed masses cruising by on their fifty-foot yachts." He took off his T-shirt, crumpling it on the chair.

I took off my dress so I could start working on my tan and followed him.

We stretched out on the loungers on the front deck. The sun felt warm and perfect.

"Do you mind if we cruise a little?" he asked. "I thought we'd go to Soggy Dollar for lunch."

I lit up. I had read all about the famous local beach-front bar. "Yes, please!"

It occurred to me then that maybe it wasn't the best idea to be in another country with a man I barely knew on a boat that wasn't even his. But I was lulled into contentment by the drink and the sun and the gentle water, so I let the worry pass by and focused, instead, on how great my tan was going to be.

———

Three hours later, waves crashed over the dinghy, threatening to capsize our little boat as we made our way to shore again. "I should have had Axle bring us in," Conner said, laughing as the spray drenched us again.

Axle. The first mate. I wondered how many people actually worked on this boat.

"But then what kind of adventurers would we be?" I

practically shouted over the noise of the angry surf. The water farther out was calm, but the breakers were huge despite the clear skies.

Once we—somehow—made it to shore, I helped him pull the boat up onto the sand.

The white maxi dress that had seemed so chic this morning now clung to my skin, feeling disgusting. I wasn't sure if I could go to the bar in just my bathing suit, but even still, this would never do. I peeled my dress off and spread it on the side of the dinghy to dry. "Can I go in like this?" I asked Conner, peering up at the open-air space to see what other people were wearing.

"Can you go to the Soggy Dollar Bar in your bikini?" he asked. "I believe that's the dress code."

He reached out to take my hand and led me to an open table where he plopped down in a plastic chair. I wished I had brought a towel, but it probably would have gotten drenched too. I looked at the chair warily.

As I sat down, a goat—an actual goat—jumped up on top of the low table and peered at me curiously.

I burst out laughing. "I only take you to the finest places," Conner said.

But *this* was what I had really imagined when I dreamed of the islands—laid-back bars, random livestock, colorful, open-air settings.

Conner pulled the goat by the collar he was wearing—which, I noted, bore the insignia of my rival university, UNC—but he stood firm, bleating sorrowfully at him.

We both dissolved into hysterics. "He wins," Conner said, sitting back down.

"A goat isn't the worst dining companion I've ever had," I said.

At that moment, I had the most distinct urge to write

a letter to my grandmother—something I did very, very often. I wanted to tell her that I was having so much fun that I had forgotten all about the wedding drama and home and work. Everything, really, except for Conner and this magical day. And I knew I would do it all over again if he asked me.

Higher Ground

July 16, 1916

Edith could barely see, the rain was coming down so hard. She was soaked through her clothes, her poor horse so wet that she could hardly balance atop his saturated skin. *Dear Lord, please let it stop*, she prayed. The storm the week before had caused Asheville's French Broad River to rise considerably. But after just four dry days, here they were again, drowning in rain just as fierce. Noble, who'd insisted on riding beside Edith, called over the noise of the driving rain, "The paper said yesterday brought more rain to the Blue Ridge than had ever been reported in a single twenty-four-hour period in all of the United States! Can you believe that?"

As the drops pelted Edith's face, she called back, with a hint of irony, "Well, Noble, I really can."

No one knew what would come next. But what they could say with certainty was that the water was rising. In addition to Edith and Noble, more than a dozen men on the estate had ridden out on horseback to help relocate families away from potential flooding.

Cornelia, the head housekeeper, and Edith's lady's maid had stayed at the house to get organized, much to Cornelia's consternation.

"I need to get Rose!" Cornelia had protested when Edith had told her she was to stay home. She was very concerned about her closest friend from the village.

"Her family is coming, my dear. I talked to them yesterday. You need to be here as families come in search of higher ground."

Cornelia hadn't been thrilled but she had relented and, with the house staff, was now rushing about gathering cots, making pallets, and utilizing all available beds to house as many estate workers—who mostly resided in Biltmore Village—as possible. Women and children in some rooms, men in others.

Edith and Noble had already spent two days riding from house to house, knocking on doors, sending those with no place to go—including Rose and her family—to Biltmore. Edith was exhausted, proud, devastated, and terrified all at once. She couldn't bear to think of those who refused to leave their homes. What would become of them?

She stayed atop her horse as Noble banged furiously on the last door on their route. Once. Twice. Three times. "I think we've done all we can," Edith called to him when they received no answer. "Let's go home!"

He nodded and mounted his horse again, following Edith. She felt terribly unsettled as she made her way back to the main house. If the skies closed and the

floodwaters receded, they might be okay. But if not . . .
Well, Edith was no stranger to tragedy.

Emma met Edith at the front door of Biltmore. "Hurry,
ma'am," she said. "Let's get you out of these wet clothes
and into a warm bath before you catch your death of cold."

The thought made Edith shiver. Cornelia had already
lost one parent. Edith really must be more careful. But
she knew that her presence made some of the more
reluctant families relent and come to stay in what was,
she hoped and prayed, the safest structure in the Blue
Ridge Mountains.

The sounds of activity from the dozens of Biltmore's
guests made Edith smile despite her fear. Children's feet,
little voices, adults talking, planning, strategizing—there
was an electric hum in the air, a vibration of nerves and
anxiety. But, also, the mere fact of everyone being together made them all a little stronger.

Edith took a deep breath. She must be brave. For her
people.

"Mama!" Cornelia called, bursting into her room.
"Emma wants to know if there's anything we want to
take up top with us."

What could she not replace? "Daddy's reading journals and my wedding veil!" Edith said suddenly.

She finished dressing as her daughter took off like a
shot.

She and Cornelia took up their post in the observatory. Not only did Edith decide it was the safest place in
Biltmore for her daughter, as it was the highest point,
but it also had a view of the entire property. The French
Broad was one of the most beautiful parts of the Asheville landscape, but beauty could be a fickle friend, and,

in this instance, a dangerous one. Biltmore's distance from the river would keep them safe. It had to.

Every few minutes Cornelia peered out the window. "The water is over the front step," she reported. Then, "It's almost to the base of the lions," she said a few hours later, referring to the Italian rose marble beasts that protected the house.

Maybe it was the knowledge that she had helped as many people as possible stay safe, but Edith felt eerily calm in spite of looming disaster.

"Nothing to do now but wait, darling," she said. "And no matter what, I have you, you have me, and it will all be okay."

Cornelia nodded bravely. The sound of the rain pounding on the roof was almost deafening as she and her mother perched side by side on George's sofa. Edith looked at her veil, draped over a chair, thinking of not only her wedding day but also of her mother and sisters, the strong women who had also worn this veil, the women who had made her who she was.

She gathered the yards of lace and tulle in her arms and sat back down. "Have I ever showed you the secret inside the Juliet cap?"

Her daughter shook her head, wide-eyed.

"You see this piece of silk?" she asked, pulling it up. "Underneath are the initials of all the women who have worn this veil."

"Wow," Cornelia said, tracing her fingers over her ancestry, her birthright. "Will my initials go in there one day?"

Edith nodded. "One day when you're quite grown up and find the perfect man who adores you for all the magnificent things you are, then you can wear the veil too." It wouldn't be long now, Edith knew, looking at her beautiful nearly sixteen-year-old who was growing more quickly by the day.

Running a length of tulle through her fingers, Cornelia asked, "Is that how it was between you and Daddy?"

"Oh, yes," Edith said without hesitation. But she knew it was all more complicated than that. While certainly they had married out of family obligation, she had come to love him so truly. "I miss him every day," she said.

"Me too," Cornelia responded as a gust of wind sent rain pelting into the window. She nestled closer to her mother.

"Daddy made sure this house could withstand anything," Edith said to soothe Cornelia, but also herself. She thought now of the sandbags lining every door and window frame downstairs. She almost laughed at the idea that they could hold rushing floodwaters back. It was like imagining caging a deer in a trap meant for a field mouse.

"Are you nervous, Mother?" Cornelia asked.

"Maybe a little," Edith answered honestly.

"Would you like me to tell you a story?"

Edith smiled. "I would like that so very much."

Wind howled and debris flew, children wailed and toilets flushed. But over the noise of it all, the ping of the water on the slate and copper roof, combined with the slow cadence of Cornelia's voice, had a tranquilizing effect. And as the floodwaters reached the paws of the massive lions that kept watch at the front steps of Biltmore, Edith, who hadn't slept properly in days, drifted off, if only for a moment.

She dreamed of being that brave bride again, that magical veil atop her head, the man she would come to love smiling at her warmly, keeping her safe. Then she saw herself placing that same veil atop her beautiful daughter's head. It felt like a symbol of what she hoped to give her, a passing of the torch. When Cornelia, in Edith's dream, handed the veil back to her, Edith startled awake, her heart racing. As she reoriented herself, remembering where she was, she saw the smallest sliver of late-afternoon light peeking through the window. The weather had broken; the storm was over.

Slowing her breathing, steadying herself, she felt like maybe it had all been a bad dream. Either way, once again, they had made it through. And that was something to be grateful for.

Soggy Dollar

I had told myself I wouldn't stay with Conner all day. But really, when was I ever going to get the chance to go to Soggy Dollar Bar again? There was no rush, was there? And they *did* have the best Painkillers in the entire world. (The rum drink, not the prescriptions.) Plus, the waiter had finally removed the goat when he brought our lobster rolls, so I could actually see Conner across the low table.

Nothing makes you dive right into a date and forget that the man you're with is one of your heroes quite like when said man drops sauce-covered lobster out of the bottom of his bun right onto his white T-shirt, glops it up with his finger, and doesn't seem to notice the massive stain he leaves behind. He was still about the cutest thing I'd ever seen. And, what's more, he was easy to be with. We'd been sitting at this bar for over an hour talking about everything—friends, life, funny stories. Like we'd known each other forever.

When Conner asked "What's next for you?" I didn't even feel panicky.

"Is it weird that my line of sight doesn't extend beyond the next week?"

"We could always steal the yacht," he said seriously.

I nodded, taking a sip of my drink. "Totally. We'd be completely inconspicuous in a hundred-foot yacht and the crew would *never* think to radio us in."

"Right," he agreed. "I'm sure they wouldn't. But we'd have some provisioning issues pretty quickly, and I can't go a day without caviar, so . . ."

We both smiled.

"What are you working on now?" I asked.

"At this particular moment, I'm working on a short story, not a building."

"Do you write?"

He took the last bite of his lobster roll and swallowed. "I haven't written anything yet, but in this story there's this devilishly handsome architect who escapes to the British Virgin Islands where he meets a stunning, mysterious woman who has just left her fiancé at the altar. He only has a few days to convince her to keep this thing going when they return home." He paused. "Okay. Now you fill in the holes of how he helps her do that."

It was nonsense. We'd known each other about a minute, and there was no future here. But, God, it was flattering. After the heaviness of Hayes and the breakup and, really, just the last few years of feeling like I'd been stuck in a glass elevator that I couldn't break out of, I was finally having fun.

"The heroine of that story sounds amazing," I teased.

"Brilliant, unassuming, gorgeous without being too caught up in her looks."

He nodded earnestly. "She is. She really is."

"Seriously, though, my grandmother has a really cool little cabin in Asheville, and I'm thinking maybe I'll go there for a while."

"And do what?"

I shrugged.

"Forgive me if I'm overstepping," he said, "but if you love architecture so much, you know you could *be* an architect . . ."

"Well, I technically have a degree in architecture."

He furrowed his brow. "And you don't want to be an architect anymore, but you acted like I was Bradley Cooper when you met me?"

I felt my face redden with embarrassment. "Was it that bad?"

"Well . . ."

Conner was studying me now. "Have you taken the ARE?"

The Architect Registration Exam was an essential part of becoming licensed. I shook my head. "But I have done my supervised hours."

Confusion was written all over his face. "I'm sorry. I solve problems and put things together for a living, but I can't quite get this to add up."

Suddenly, I didn't want to be here anymore. I didn't want to talk about this, about the humiliating day that caused me to walk away from fulfilling my dream. But it wasn't like I could just run off now like I had then. I was on an island—and not the one my resort was on. So, I had to stay with my ride, whether I liked it or not.

I stood up, hoping I didn't look as flustered as I felt.

"Should we face the stalwart sea again, hope that we aren't washed away by her unforgiving hand?"

He just sat, looking at me curiously.

I pointed. "I'm kidding. We're only like fifty yards away."

"You don't say 'yards' about water distances. When we steal the boat and you're being questioned, that will be a dead giveaway that you're a rookie."

I nodded, relieved he hadn't noticed my anxiety, that our repartee was back. And maybe, most of all, that we could avoid the very unfun subject that was killing my vibe. "Good to know."

We shoved the dinghy back into the water, and I realized right away, as the first spray of water hit me in the face, that my mission to dry my dress had been fruitless.

"Okay," Conner said calmly. "Ariel is making us a delicious five-course dinner at eight."

"The Little Mermaid?"

He nodded. "Yes. The evil sea witch still has her voice, so we'll play charades to figure out what we're eating."

"I'm not staying for dinner, Conner. This has been great, but I need to get back to the resort."

"To your empty hotel room by yourself?"

That was kind of harsh. But it was also totally true.

"Well, yes. I don't want to overstay my welcome."

"You can't go back," he continued, "because we have to go to Foxy's after dinner."

Foxy's was one of the most famous bars in the BVIs. A can't-miss. Even I knew that.

"And then," Conner continued, "have you ever seen Mars?"

I gasped sarcastically. "You have a boat *and* a space-ship?"

I tried to stay serious, but we both laughed. "Noooo. But Mars is rising at 4:03 a.m., and I think it would be irresponsible—nay, reckless—for us to not sleep on the bow, under the stars, to see it rising."

"I don't have an overnight bag," I said lamely. It was only partly true—I had packed a change of clothes and a few makeup essentials in my beach bag. I didn't have everything, but I had enough. I thought of Babs always saying she never went anywhere without her passport. *You have to be ready for adventure when adventure calls*, she always said. I would usually agree with her. So why, lately, did I feel so afraid of everything?

"Would Amelia Earhart have said she couldn't complete another flight because she didn't have the right clothes?"

I cocked my head. "I hardly see how that relates."

"She's an adventurer. You're an adventurer."

Babs would *love* this guy.

The trip back to the boat was much less eventful than the trip out—still wet, but less bumpy. All the while, I had to shake the feeling that I was doing something wrong, that I was cheating on Hayes. But I had to remind myself that wasn't the case; I was free to do as I pleased. Hayes wasn't the one for me because I couldn't trust him. No one could pull me back in, make me forget myself and my self-worth, better than he could. And I deserved better than that.

Once we reached the boat, Conner helped me up, and then, grabbing a huge plush, black-and-white-striped towel from a basket on the stern, wrapped it around my shoulders like no one had done since I was a child.

He ran his hands up and down over my arms to warm me. But he was still standing there, towel-less, looking so adorable—and a little cold. So I spread my arms out to open the towel. He stepped toward me, and as he wrapped his arms around me, I wrapped mine—and my towel—around him.

I felt the unexpected heat of being so close to him rise in me.

"You're so warm," I whispered.

"Am I?" he whispered back, just inches from my face, leaning in to kiss me.

My entire body felt tingly. This was fun and exciting and, best of all, *new*. No backstories, no old wounds. Just an intensely passionate kiss on the back of a gorgeous yacht on a day drowsy with rum and full of expectation. I knew I would never see him again, but that was maybe what I liked best of all about this. I didn't have to think or plan. I could just kiss.

I kissed Conner over candlelight on the stern of the boat eating shrimp and fillet. I kissed him on the crowded sandy dance floor of Foxy's. I kissed him as I lay on his chest at 2 a.m. on the bow of the boat. I kissed him at 4:03 when I opened my eyes to see the Red Planet in plain view and again at seven when the sun was too bright to allow us more sleep.

And now, on the dock in front of my resort, I was kissing him again.

"I have to go," I said flirtatiously as he grabbed my arm, pulling me back in.

"Just one more kiss," he said.

The rum had long worn off, but I felt drunk on Conner, on fresh feelings, on butterflies in my stomach and a type of desire I hadn't felt maybe ever.

"I need to go shower," I protested.

"Here on the islands they strongly suggest showering

with a friend to conserve water," he said, his cheek on mine, his scruff feeling masculine and right.

I know I shocked him when I said, "Anything for Mother Nature."

I turned and started walking. A few seconds later, I glanced back over my shoulder. "Well, are you coming or what?"

His face looked like I'd just told him he'd won a Pritzker, architecture's most coveted prize. He caught up and took my hand, our arms swinging like we were children on the playground, the crushed shells crunching under our feet. What had been so light between us was now heavy with the promise of what would come next.

At the bottom of the stairs to my treehouse room, Conner folded me into his arms and kissed me again, and I could scarcely believe how natural it felt to be with him. I didn't delude myself that this would be more than a onetime thing. But maybe I'd be able to take it for what it was: the fling that reminded me I could open my heart.

Conner put his hand on my back to let me go up the stairs first. I turned to smile at him halfway up. I was almost to the top when I stopped so abruptly that Conner ran into me.

My eyes went wide as the man sitting on my porch turned to look at me. "Hayes?" I whispered.

I had no reason to feel guilty, and yet, here I was, bathing in shame. Conner hooked his finger through the back belt loop of my jean shorts in a gesture that was oddly comforting. He could have run off. But he stayed. Maybe it would have been better if he had run. But knowing that he would be by my side as I faced the music soothed me. And I couldn't help but wonder if maybe this was more than a vacation fling after all.

Swept Away

Five days later, it was official: Biltmore had been spared. But it was, perhaps, the only thing that had. The floodwaters had begun to recede in large part, but even still, they were up to Edith's knees as she made the slow and deliberate walk from her home to her beloved Biltmore Village, which housed hundreds of the estate's workers and most of the shops they frequented. She wanted to check on each and every building, but first she needed to make a stop at the hospital. It was all she could do not to sit down and positively weep. The time for that would come later, she knew. For now, there was too much to do.

Eighteen years ago, arriving at Biltmore had felt hopeful, charmed even. Edith had felt that all her worries were behind her, the struggles of the life her family had been leading swept away by George and his outrageous fortune. *Swept away*, Edith thought again as she sloshed through the water filling her boots.

After days of rain and two huge storms, the Swannanoa's banks could no longer hold the majestic river, and the dams at Kanuga and Osceola had burst. Walls of water had smashed into Biltmore Village and downtown Asheville, nearly fifteen feet high in some parts. The water at Biltmore's gates had reached nine feet. But she had held it back.

Edith had just begun to believe that finally, two years after George's death, things were starting to get back to normal. Edith and Cornelia spent the school year in Washington and long vacations and glorious summers at Biltmore, riding horses together, fishing in the streams, playing tennis. Cornelia had become the ultimate comfort for her mother, and staying strong for her daughter was what allowed Edith to move forward, to rebuild, to get creative about saving her beloved home.

But now this. The flood of the century. The paper had reported twenty-nine deaths just yesterday, all people Edith knew. Edith recalled four of them as she placed her hand on a huge maple tree, feeling a sense of sadness wash over her as she thought of those who'd clung to it days earlier, these limbs their only hope against the rushing floodwaters.

"I wouldn't touch that, Mrs. Vanderbilt," a man with a rake in his hand called. Edith assumed he'd come hoping to clean up, but the water hadn't receded enough yet. "All those people who died. That there's the death tree."

"Or the life tree," she said, thinking of the survivor she was going to visit. "It all depends on how you think about it."

He tipped his hat.

Edith turned to look out over the vast, ruinous land-scape. Biltmore Village had been George's dream and hers. A place where people could come for work, for education, and to better their lives. George had presented that charming community to Edith in its completion as a birthday gift, a sign of happy times, an investment in the community they so desperately wanted to serve. The charming shops and cafés had become the central hub, providing everything the estate workers—most of whom lived in the village chateaus—needed.

Now, the village—like George—was gone. And all the good seemed to be gone right along with it. Homes had been replaced by piles of debris. The nursery—a major source of income for the estate—was at least eighty-five percent destroyed, including Edith's cherished herbarium, her collection of almost 500,000 preserved plant species. It broke Edith's heart. But that was, perhaps, the least of it. People had drowned, and livestock too. Edith could not make peace with it, this senseless loss of life.

As she sloshed her way through what had only days earlier been a vibrant example of goodwill and even better ideas, her heart stopped. The remains of a house— *the* house, in fact, of the very girl she was going to see in the hospital—that had been no match for the raging waters. Another loss for a family that had already lost so much. Edith's heart raced with panic. She felt sick, nauseous, and looked around frantically for a place where she could sit to reclaim her composure, but as everything was covered in water, she pressed on.

Edith allowed herself to feel the full weight of her self-pity. If Biltmore—that great and shining beacon that Edith had saved from financial ruin on more than one occasion as of late—had been destroyed, would it have been better?

But on his deathbed, George had proclaimed to her that Biltmore was his legacy, *their* legacy, a sign that his family, which had struggled so to find their rightful place amid American royalty, had persevered. And she would fight for it at all costs.

"Dear George, please help me," she said as she opened the door to the village's hospital, its red roof and stone façade making it look more like a charming mountain home than a place for the sick and injured. The interior of the hospital was light, bright, and airy, with plenty of room between beds so patients didn't feel cramped or crowded. She was grateful that this building, at least, had been spared.

A nurse in a white uniform—Mrs. Hartwell—stopped her bustling. "Mrs. Vanderbilt!" she exclaimed. "What a nice surprise!" Her perkiness astonished Edith, especially considering she was holding a tray of bloody gauze and instruments.

"I'm so sorry for the loss of Miss Foister and Miss Walker," Edith said, thinking of two of the women—nurses in this very hospital—who had lost their lives after hours of clinging to that maple tree.

Mrs. Hartwell nodded sadly. "Any news on Captain Lipe?" she whispered.

Edith nodded gravely, suddenly immune to the uncomfortable wetness soaking through her riding boots. "I'm here to see Miss Lipe," she said.

Mrs. Hartwell, understanding, led Edith into an open room of beds. She and Cornelia often spent days here talking and cross-stitching with patients, reading to them, offering a friendly smile. Edith spotted Kathleen Lipe right away. She was lying still on her back, serene, her short hair matted to her head. Even with her eyes closed, Edith could see the dark circles underneath them. What an ordeal she must have been through. What an ordeal she would continue to relive for the rest of her life. At eighteen, she was no longer a child, but Edith suspected that the daughter of Biltmore's head carpenter and skilled-labor overseer would grow up today if she hadn't already.

As Edith sat down on the stool beside her bed, she couldn't bear to wake her. But Kathleen opened her large, round eyes to the light and blinked, perhaps in disbelief, to see who was sitting beside her.

"Mrs. Vanderbilt," she whispered.

"Shhh," Edith said. "Don't feel like you need to talk, sweet Kathleen. I know this has been an unfathomable ordeal for you."

"Papa," she managed to eke out. "Have they found Papa?"

Edith's stomach turned. She had declared that no expense would be spared to find Captain Lipe, one of George's first hires on the property. She had wished and hoped that he would be found alive, clinging to a tree or a roof. But no. The fate of Captain Lipe was, unfortunately, what they all had feared.

"He was so brave, Mrs. Vanderbilt," Kathleen said weakly. "Papa held me to that tree for hours. We kept climbing higher and higher as the water rose."

Edith's eyes were filled with tears, her stomach sick and knotted at the thought of those poor souls, those *people* clinging to the very tree she touched earlier.

"Lifeguards kept trying to rescue us, but they

couldn't reach us. After a while, his arms finally just . . . slipped away. The last thing I remember him saying is 'Shucks! Shucks!' Have you seen him, Mrs. Vanderbilt? Is he okay?"

The hope in her eyes broke Edith's heart as she took Kathleen's hand, which was wrapped in bandages. "Darling," she said gently, "I'm afraid your brave and valiant father didn't make it." Captain Lipe's body had been found less than half a mile from the gate of Biltmore Estate, a proud hero of a man reduced to a bloated, contorted shell. Edith hated being the one to share this news, but she had felt, somehow, that it should be her. The Lipe family was one of their own. They had celebrated Christmases and May Days together, sewn garments for the less fortunate, spent many a cold winter night talking around the fire. Mrs. Lipe had fled to higher ground with their disabled daughter and her aging mother when the rains came, and Edith felt she had enough on her plate without having to wade through floodwaters to deliver the terrible news to her child. Kathleen had lost a father, but by the sheer grace of God, she still had a family to go home to.

Kathleen started to weep. "If only we had evacuated with Mama!" She looked up at Edith earnestly. "But then who would have stayed behind to tie the chickens to the porch?"

Edith knew that that porch—and that house—no longer existed. But Kathleen had faced enough loss this week. The news about her destroyed home could wait.

"I lost my parents when I was a young girl," she said, wondering if the child could even hear through her sobs. "And that sort of loss is terrible. But I am a parent, and I can tell you for certain that if your daddy had the choice of saving his life or yours—if he had to lose his life instead of face the world without you—he would make that sacrifice again and again."

Kathleen wiped her eyes. "But what is to become of us now?" she asked. "What shall we do without Papa here to keep us safe?"

Edith stroked the girl's bedraggled hair, wanting to soothe her, knowing that her arms and legs, torn and bruised from hours spent clinging to tree bark, were the least of her wounds now.

"We are Asheville women," Edith said to Kathleen, putting on a brave face. "We are strong; we are resilient. We are smart and savvy. We will rebuild our town. We will get through this. Together."

"We will get through this together," Kathleen repeated.

Hearing the girl repeat her words of solidarity almost made Edith believe them.

———

That night, after Cornelia had gone to sleep, Edith returned to the library, as she so often did now, to talk to George. Even when they had been gone for months, Edith could come here to find him again. Edith and Cornelia, when they were at Biltmore, lived in the renovated bachelors' quarters to save money on heating and other bills, so uncovering her chair and table in the oft-closed library had become a part of her ritual. She would talk to George about Cornelia and Biltmore, about the trees and the estate, about the dairy and the future. And as long as she was sitting in the library, he talked back.

She had never told anyone this, of course, for fear she would be placed in a sanitarium and Cornelia would be, as she had once feared, all alone. But by the time the flood happened, this practice of speaking to George in the library was as commonplace to her as breathing. She had forgotten it was something to be ashamed of.

As Edith flopped down in the red chair near the fire and lit a cigarette, she could hear George's scolding. This was how it always began. Her smoking; him scolding her.

"After today, even you might need a cigarette, George," she said. "It feels insurmountable. I think we have to let the village go."

"You have to rebuild it, Edith," the response came immediately. "It was your dream. Don't let it die."

The village, that place to house and help the estate workers, *had* been her dream. Now, as they did in all her unfilled moments, figures began to fill Edith's head: 86,700 Biltmore acres that she had sold to the United States Forest Service. Five dollars per acre. A $65,000 mortgage on her K Street home. Edith remembered George's family ridiculing him, teasing him for spending all his money in a place where property values were next to nothing. George's Folly. But he wanted to make his family proud. The thought steeled something inside her.

Saving Biltmore seemed impossible. But they had done it before.

When the Panic of 1907 had arrived, the market crashed, and they lost all that money, but they figured it out. When they hadn't been able to pay the property tax bill in 1909—and, in turn, the county hadn't been able to pay its teachers—Edith and George had figured it out. And when they had bailed Edith's brother LeRoy out of his railroad debacle and lost, they had figured it out then, too. But could she really bail them out again? And without George by her side?

Edith, feeling hopeless, spoke again. "I'm too tired to

start over. I'm too tired from the work and the stress of holding on to this ship that, quite literally, if the last few days are any indication, is sinking."

The reply was simple. "If not you, then who?"

She sighed and leaned back in the chair, taking another drag of the cigarette. "I'd love to be the one to put it all back together, but I'm tired. How can I fix this when I can barely handle things as they are now?"

"Mama?" a voice questioned. Cornelia stepped into the library, the low light making the defined angular features of her face even lovelier than usual. "Who are you talking to?" She looked around, questioning.

"Oh, no one," Edith said, waving it away. What would her daughter think if she told the truth? What would anyone think? "I was just thinking out loud." She couldn't deny that maybe that was true. Maybe it wasn't George's voice she was hearing. Maybe it was her own. But, while it stuck around, she would savor it all the same.

Cornelia sat down on the couch across from her mother. "What are all those people going to do?" she asked, a worried look on her face.

That was when Edith decided. Alone, she could fall apart. But for her daughter she had to be strong. "What do you think Daddy would do?" Edith asked.

Cornelia thought and then said, "He would rebuild. He would help all those people."

"Then that's what we shall do." She nodded resolutely. "So let's go up and get a good night's sleep. Tomorrow we'll don our boots and gather all the men we can find, and we'll lead the clean-up efforts. We'll make the plans. We'll gather the troops and go into battle."

Cornelia smiled. "You're thinking about Daddy, aren't you?"

"What gave me away?"

"That's what he would have said. 'Gather the troops and go into battle.' " She paused. "Mama? Are you ever afraid?"

Edith thought before she answered. There was value in telling the truth. But, looking into her daughter's face, she knew that now was not the time to confess to her fear. Now was a time to buoy Cornelia's spirits.

"Did I ever tell you about the letter my grandmother left behind when she died?"

Cornelia shook her head.

"In it, she reminded our family that a house united can never fall." Edith paused. "What about us. Are we united?"

"Of course we are, Mother." She smiled. "So we cannot fall."

"Exactly, my dearest darling. Plus, Daddy is always with us. What is there to possibly fear?" Edith tried to ignore it when the voice—maybe George's, maybe her own, answered, "Quite a bit, I'm afraid."

Even still, she pinned on her most confident smile. Edith's greatest strength was that she had learned how to be a survivor. Now it was her job to make sure Cornelia did, too.

The One and Only

I didn't blame Hayes for being upset. I could only imagine how I would have felt if I had showed up to our honeymoon to surprise him and found him with another woman. But after watching that video, it seemed in character for him.

"What the hell, Julia?" he said. "I get here last night for a romantic reunion and you aren't even here. And then you show up with . . ." He looked Conner up and down like he was rotten meat. "*Him.*"

I stepped up onto the porch and Conner followed me. I turned back to look at him and he seemed relatively unruffled. I was *very* ruffled. But it made me like him more.

"What are you doing here?" I asked Hayes dumbly.

My ex-fiancé stood up now, stepping close to me. I had forgotten how handsome he was. The man practically smoldered. "This isn't how this was supposed to go, Julia. You were supposed to feel sad and wistful after a few days and realize that some stupid video didn't matter." His voice was soft, low, and familiar. "Then I would come here and we would talk. You would forgive me. We would remember what we've always known: we're meant for each other."

"I'm sorry," Conner said. "If you're meant for each other, why did you cheat on her in the first place?"

Right, I thought, steeling myself. *Yes. Excellent question.*

Hayes's eyes locked on mine, and I could tell he was furious. "Who the hell is this?"

"Oh, um," I stumbled, "this is Conner Howard."

"Look, man, Julia and I have some things to discuss, so you need to move along."

Conner stepped closer to Hayes. "I'm staying until Julia tells me it's time to leave."

Uh oh. This wasn't exactly how I was expecting my morning to go. Conner had given me the best day yesterday. We had laughed, we had joked. For the first time in a while, I had had *fun*.

But then there was Hayes. When I got away from him, I could see our relationship was dysfunctional. But when he was here, so hot and focused on me, it felt like maybe that was my cross to bear, a part of the story of our lives that was playing out. I had loved him for so long sometimes it felt more like a habit than an actual choice.

I looked from Conner to Hayes. It wasn't like I was choosing between them. I mean, I had only known Conner for a few days. I'd known Hayes for ten years. Didn't I owe it to him to hash this out?

"Julia," Hayes said. "Can you please tell this person to leave so we can talk?"

I turned back to Conner. He was so darn cute. Not five minutes ago, I had wanted nothing more than to vacation fling my heart out with him. I sighed. It wasn't like I could tell the fiancé I had left at the altar to hit the road, right? "I guess you should probably go."

Hayes smiled victoriously. I rolled my eyes. "You didn't win a competition, Hayes. I'm not taking you back. But I don't want Conner to have to be in the middle of our drama."

Conner squeezed my wrist. "I'll call you tomorrow."

"You will *not* call her tomorrow," Hayes said sternly.

Conner turned to look back at him, icily. "Oh, I assure you, I will."

"Okay," I said, sensing that this was going to get heated if I didn't intervene. "Thank you, Conner. I will talk to you then."

Hayes looked furious. As Conner's footsteps started down the stairs, I said, "So what did you think, Hayes? You'd just come here, I'd fall into your arms, and we'd get married beneath the stars?"

He was instantly sheepish. "Maybe not married right away . . ."

"I don't trust you," I said. "That's it. Breaking off our wedding wasn't a dramatic stunt so we could have amazing makeup sex. It was a true and honest breakup, a declaration that this isn't the right path for me."

The hurt was all over his face. But I had to make things clear once and for all.

"But this is what we do," he said, his voice smooth and overly calm, as if trying to hide his shock. "We break up, we realize we can't be apart, and we get back together.

We're between steps two and three now, although I hope we're closer to three so we can enjoy our vacation." He stepped closer to me, putting his hand on my hip. "Babe, I love you. We're meant to be."

I knew what was coming next because he had done it to me so many times I couldn't even count.

"That night I saw you in the parking lot after we lost State to you guys . . ."

This was where I was supposed to say, *I saw you leaning against your open tailgate, tears in your eyes, and I had to comfort you.*

But I didn't say it. Nope. Not this time.

Hayes, noticing my hesitation, filled in my part. "And you said, 'But Hayes, if we never lose, we don't know how good it can feel to win.' "

This was usually when my heart softened, when I reasoned that, sure, maybe we had lost for a minute, but we had found our way back to each other. This was the part when he would kiss me and the heat between us took over. But as he leaned in this time, something happened. Something different. *You deserve better*, ran through my mind.

I pushed him away. "No," I said. "Nope. Not happening."

Hayes threw his hands up in the air. "Julia, you're being so unreasonable. Everyone knows we're supposed to be together."

"Everyone except me," I said resolutely. "We've broken up and gotten back together too many times for this to be right. After junior homecoming, when you flirted with April Moore instead of dancing with me during Senior Beach Week, when you were wasted for five days straight, and then again during my junior year of college, when you kept ignoring my calls. Don't forget my first work Christmas party, when you acted like an ass to my boss. And then last January, when I thought you were sleeping with a coworker. We're not doing this again."

He shook his head and sat down in one of the rocking chairs on the small porch. I looked into his face and saw what I loved most about him: his vulnerability. He didn't show this side of himself to anyone else, and I think that was what usually made me ignore his indiscretions, pretend not to know what was going on when I wasn't around. I was the only one who could fix him. But I couldn't do that anymore.

I sat down in the rocking chair beside him. "I've thought about this a lot. I really have. Call me old-fashioned, but I want my husband to be all mine."

"But I will be!" he interjected. "Why can't you understand that? Yeah, I'm not perfect, but Jules, I swear to God, I have only ever loved you. And I promise you that once we're married I will never even *look* at another woman. Don't you believe that?"

"I want to," I said. "But I don't think it's your nature. And that's okay. You'll find your person. But I'm not going to trap you in this box when I know I'm setting us both up for failure." I paused. It didn't matter now, did it? But I had to know. "How long were you sleeping with Chrissy Matthews?"

He exhaled sharply, stood up, and started pacing. I knew I had shocked him because he was right: this *was* our pattern. I was embarrassed that it had taken me this long to realize it—and to recognize that it was destructive. When Babs or Sarah, who were the only real insiders, would point out their concerns, I reasoned that they'd never known love like this. It was only now that I could see they had been right all along: this wasn't love; it was a vicious cycle.

He paused, obviously debating whether he should tell the truth about Chrissy. Finally, he spoke. "Okay, so I slept with her a couple times," he said sheepishly. "I'm not proud of it, and I never wanted to hurt you."

I knew it. But hearing him say it still hurt. "A couple times?"

He waved his hand. "A few. But it was stupid and I'm sorry. I'm so, so sorry." He got down on his knees in front of me. "You're my family, Jules. Your family is my family. Your mom was the one who took me to get my wisdom teeth out and your dad coached my travel basketball team. We've been on every family vacation together for years. Remember when we went to Key West and the streets flooded and we ran around barefoot for days in the rain?" He was talking fast now, almost frantically.

I remembered. And it hurt to let it go. "Surely you don't want to live the rest of your life like this. Do you want to be eighty and relying on some stories from when we were sixteen to keep us together?"

He got up and started pacing again, glaring at me. "Is this about him? Is this about *Conner*?"

I rolled my eyes. "Yes. It is. I'm throwing away a decade because of an architect I met in the airport. Come on, Hayes."

"Well, is it about that rumor with Selena because—"

I put my hand up. I might not always trust this man, but after she called, I was absolutely certain that Selena from HR was not interested in Hayes from Investments.

"No, Hayes. If this is about anyone it's Chrissy Matthews, but that isn't even really it. And you know it."

"Let's go get a drink, hang out on the beach, sleep on it," he said, sounding desperate.

He wasn't hearing me. But we couldn't fix this. I couldn't fix Hayes, no matter how many times I tried. And it was time for me to accept that.

"Not this time, Hayes," I said softly. "I love you, and I don't want to hurt you. But we're done."

He looked at me blankly, as if not comprehending. So I walked through the sliding glass door of my room, rustled around in my suitcase, and, back on the porch, attempted to place my diamond solitaire in his palm. He put his hands up. "I don't want that back," he said. "I bought it for you. And I want you to keep it."

I thought it was another ploy, but the way he looked at me, I knew that he finally understood. He leaned down and kissed my forehead, and I let him, tears flowing. This was goodbye. As he left my room, I felt like practically half of my life was walking away down the stairs.

I watched him step onto the path. He stopped, standing still. Then he looked up and called, "Jules, I was trying to do a dramatic leaving scene, but I seriously don't have anywhere to go. The hotel is full, and there aren't any flights until tomorrow."

I sighed. We *were* pretty remote here. It wasn't like he could run over to the closest Comfort Suites. I called down to him: "You can stay on a rollaway tonight. And then I want you gone."

He nodded sadly.

I looked at him seriously.

"I hear you. I swear. We're through." He paused. "But

don't you think it shows growth that I didn't try to pick up a girl on the beach and stay with her instead?"

I picked up one of the flowers in the vase between the two rocking chairs and threw it at him.

I would miss him. I knew I would. But I had decided my fate. One more night wouldn't change a thing.

Infatuation

I think the two-bedroom is going to suit you nicely, Mrs. Carlisle," Anna, the perky woman showing me around Summer Acres, was saying. Her background led me to believe she was in her midforties, but her shiny ponytail, light dusting of freckles, and shorts made her seem much younger. I couldn't help but think that "Summer Acres" sounded like the name of a farm where people sent their lame horses and biting dogs. But Summer Acres was absolutely lovely, more like one of those charming planned communities than an over-sixty retirement village.

As Anna opened the door to a beautifully built town home on a street of beautifully built town homes, I felt myself relax. It was small and bright with neighbors very close by.

"We can change the countertops to your liking," she

said as we entered the kitchen, despite the fact that the white Corian was clean, versatile, and perfect for me. "And the units on this street come with a screened porch—and, of course, a view of the lagoon."

No, it wasn't the ocean, and waking up and falling to sleep without the crash of the waves on the shore was going to take some getting used to. But the community's "main house," as they called it—which included assisted living in its wings but was essentially a huge, oceanfront beach club otherwise—was a two-minute walk and always full of people.

That was the thing I couldn't explain to my daughters. I was lonely. I still had bridge club and book club and plenty of friends to visit, regular Wednesday night dinners and Saturday lunches with my girls. But it was more than that. After spending fifty-five years living with the same man and twenty-two years raising our children together, the house full of their friends and laughter, I felt so terribly alone.

I was certain I would spend many a day on this screened-in porch with my coffee and a book. But knowing I could pop up for a meal if I wished, that I could take up golf or join in on nightly happy hours, that I could learn to knit, take Zumba, and participate in daily devotionals, made me feel so joyful I could burst.

Anna smiled. "Mrs. Carlisle, do your children want to tour the unit?"

I controlled my eye roll. There it was again, that assumption that I was now the child, and my children were in charge of my goings-on. Maybe that would happen one day. But not yet.

"My children don't actually know I'm here," I said.

"They aren't thrilled about the idea of my downsizing, so I want to be extremely sure before I tell them."

She nodded. "A woman who knows her own mind. I love it."

I did know my own mind. But listening to myself instead of them was hard. Opening the door to the master suite, which was situated to also have a lovely lagoon view, Anna continued the tour. "And the bathrooms, of course, have walk-in tubs."

I wanted to tell her—obstinately—that I was still perfectly capable of getting in and out of my own bathtub. But it was getting difficult. How many more years did I have of that, really? A walk-in tub might be a perfectly splendid contraption as I got older.

"Would you care to see the apartment options as well?" she asked, smiling.

I shook my head. "I don't believe so."

"Well then let's go tour the rest of the facility!" she said excitedly.

We climbed into the yellow-and-white-striped Summer Acres golf cart waiting out front, which, if the brochure was to be believed, matched the umbrellas on the beach that I would be all too thrilled to sit under on summer days.

As we drove past the tennis and pickleball courts, a bocce area and basketball court, Anna said, "In the town-home area, we handle all medication delivery, and housekeeping visits for an hour each day to help with daily chores. On Fridays, they come for two hours to get you spic and span for the next week and change your sheets."

"Really?" I asked, noting that I felt more excited

about not having to change my sheets than I did about the main house's ocean views.

I hadn't yet been inside the clubhouse, so it made me a little nervous. But as I opened the large glass door and stepped onto the wide-plank hardwood floors, I found it even more beautiful than its pictures. A young man waved at me from the activities desk, where Anna led me. She handed me a glossy magazine that looked more like *Town & Country* than a brochure. "You will receive one of these each week with all the available activities. Of course, golf, tennis, the beach, the pool, and athletic club facilities are available anytime, but we love to see our residents at theme nights, band parties, mixers, dances . . ." She took a breath and continued. "We're actually revamping our lifelong learning program to include not only more speakers but also six-week dedicated classes on everything from the French Revolution to Indian cuisine."

"I feel like I'm back in college!" I said. Back in college with one glaring exception: I was very much without my Reid. I felt weepy at the thought. But, then again, Reid would not have been terribly fond of Summer Acres, so that was a small consolation.

"You're going to love it here, Mrs. Carlisle," the man behind the desk said. "There's everything to do, and nothing if you prefer it."

I smiled warmly at him. "What about dining?" I asked Anna.

"If you'll follow me, I'll show you," she said.

She led me toward the full dining room, which had vaulted ceilings, huge windows, and French doors that took advantage of the peerless views of the sand dunes and the ocean beyond. "You'll see here that there are many, many options. We don't want residents to feel like they are being assigned a table, but we also don't want anyone to feel alone before they have the chance to make friends, so we have a bit of a buddy system at the beginning while you're getting acclimated. Afterward, you are welcome to sit with anyone you like, no one at all, or at the communal table."

It felt more like a club than a nursing home, and for that, I was glad. I thought the girls would love it as much as I did.

"Shall we go check out the casual dining area and coffee bar?"

I raised my eyebrow. "Am I going to become a woman who can't get going in the morning without her latte?"

She winked at me. "I believe you are."

After the tour, Anna urged me to bring my family back, to think it over with them before making such a huge decision. But Summer Acres was perfect—and, most important, I could move through levels of care here that would carry me through the rest of my life. I prayed that I would never have to endure years of treatments or hundreds of doctor's appointments, but old age required a lot of maintenance even for those of us in good health. Having someone to drive me to and from appointments, take me to the grocery store if I could no longer drive, and many other conveniences was almost as appealing as having three meals a day cooked for me and bingo on Thursday nights against the backdrop of live music and signature cocktails.

I knew how in-demand this facility was. I had been waiting for six months for a two-bedroom town home to become available. I didn't want to wait six more. I felt in my very being that moving here was the right thing.

"I'd like to put my deposit down," I said, practically feeling my late husband in the room with me as I did. I think he would have approved of this decision, would have wanted me to be well taken care of and surrounded by friends during my autumn years. I was always grateful for him, for the life we had together. And, at this moment, when I opened my checkbook, confident that I could afford to take care of myself, I was more grateful for him still. Reid was always scrimping and saving to put more away—something that I could now see was for my benefit.

Getting to come here and be taken care of in my old age was a luxury. I figured after the first time I hosted bridge here, I'd bring in quite a few more converts.

"Well, that is good news, Mrs. Carlisle," Anna said. "We are so happy to welcome you to Summer Acres. Would you like me to schedule our moving crew to help you transition out of your old home and into your new town house?"

I nodded. "How splendid! I will barely have to bother my family at all. And I'm leaving quite a lot of my furniture at the beach house, so it shouldn't be too much trouble."

"You could never be trouble," Anna responded. "Let's grab your paperwork and get everything processed for you. Do you have another hour?"

I smiled. "Darling girl, I have all the time in the world." After a lifetime of raising children—of being Brownie leader and class mom, PTA president and dinner cooker, boo-boo kisser and hair braider, I was used to my days being too full. Now I could finally rest.

While I waited for Anna to get back, I pulled out the

postcard that had arrived the day before from Julia in the islands. I had been saving it for a time I could savor it slowly. I had collected postcards for years, and wherever she went she sent me additions for my collection.

Dear Babs,

You will never believe this, but I met one of my architectural heroes on the plane today. He was charming and humble, smart and interesting. (And, well, so cute!) For the first time in a long time I realized that Hayes isn't the only man in the world. I had forgotten that, but I suppose love is complicated. Infatuation, on the other hand, is so simple. Maybe if I'd realized that a little sooner, I wouldn't have made it so hard on all of us.

All my love,
Julia

That girl. What I wouldn't give to go back in time, to have a crush on a boy again. Those days were long over for me.

"Mrs. Carlisle," Anna said, breaking me out of my thoughts. "Would you like to meet your new liaison?"

I looked up at her from my chair. "My liaison?"

"Your buddy," she whispered. "They think it sounds too much like summer camp, so when others can hear me, I use the proper term."

I laughed. "My dear, at eighty years old, I can't think of anything better than summer camp."

She smiled.

"How can I already have a buddy?"

"We had one of our favorite residents approved for the program this morning, and we thought why not go ahead and introduce you two, let you get acclimated?"

"Wonderful," I said.

I followed Anna out to the terrace where a man with his back to me, in a suit, stood overlooking the ocean.

As he turned, Anna said, "I'd like you to meet—"

"Miles?" I gasped, breathless.

"Barbara," he said, putting his hand to his heart. "Oh, Barbara." He took both my hands in his.

"So, I presume you two have met?" Anna asked curiously, looking from Miles to me.

"At summer camp," Miles said, to which Anna laughed delightedly.

"*You're* my buddy?"

"Haven't I always been?" he responded, smiling at me, revealing that same grin he'd worn sixty years earlier when we were head counselors at Camp Holly Ridge in the North Carolina mountains.

"How long has it been?" I asked, thrilled that someone from my past had popped up here.

"Well, we haven't seen each other since we were, what, twenty-one?"

I nodded. "Let's leave it at that. Math can be a touch frightening at our age."

He laughed.

"How long have you been here?" I asked. "How did you even recognize me?"

"Barbara, you haven't changed one bit," Miles said. "I would know you anywhere."

Was that a *blush* I felt coming to my cheeks?

I thought of Julia and her postcard.

Infatuation indeed . . .

Called to Serve

November 21, 1918

I don't know why you want to go to college anyway," Bunchy—Cornelia's best friend from Miss Madeira's— said, her head leaning off the side of Cornelia's bed.

"Because I want to learn things. I want to fill beakers and study history and read great books." Cornelia wrapped the familiar Red Cross armband around the blue sleeve of her uniform.

"Well, I hate to tell you this, but if you want to read great books you have the finest library in all the world right here in your own home. I suspect anything else would be a disappointment."

Noticing her friend's voice sounded strange, Cornelia turned and, crossing her arms, studied the way Bunchy's dark hair streamed down the side of the bed as she hung upside-down off it. "Rachel Strong, whatever are you doing?"

At that, Bunchy sat up. "I read an article about how blood rushing to your head is good for your skin."

Cornelia rolled her eyes, but silently vowed to try it later. "But, really," she said. "Do you have no interest whatsoever in going to college?"

"Certainly not a girls' school," Bunchy said. "I've had enough of that at Miss Madeira's."

"Well, I don't want to go to a girls' school either," Cornelia said. "I want to go to the University of North Carolina, but they won't let me in until I've had two years of college elsewhere, and I don't want to go anywhere else." Wasn't that how it always was? Cornelia was a woman who had positively everything, but she still wanted the few things she couldn't have. She was convinced that the next impossible thing she got would fix this unholy restlessness inside her. That thing, she felt sure, was college.

"Having to wait two years doesn't seem very fair," Bunchy said.

Cornelia considered that for a moment. It didn't when you got right down to it.

"But anyway," her friend added, "who would want to go to college when all the men are off at war?"

Cornelia laughed. Her friend did have a point. Plus, there had just been that awful business about university president Edward Graham dying of the Spanish flu. Her stomach gripped. What a senseless loss. The UNC campus had been quarantined for months and, from what her mother had gleaned, had essentially turned into a military training camp and research facility. She shuddered at the idea of being trapped on campus, of being one of the dozens of students hospitalized. Or, perhaps, being one of the five who would never go home again.

It was certainly very different when she and Edith took a tour of the campus—it was hard to believe that had been more than a year ago now, right before the US had entered the war—and Cornelia had been one of the many people enchanted by its huge, lazy oak trees. President Graham himself had led their tour, and he'd regaled them with stories about Old East, the oldest building on campus.

As they stood in front of it, President Graham explained its history. "The plaque on the original cornerstone of Old East," he said in an authoritative tone—one Cornelia assumed he had earned—"was lost during renovations." He turned and smiled at Cornelia. "It just recently turned up in a Tennessee metalsmith shop of all places. The owner just happens to be a UNC graduate and, knowing the significance of the piece to the university, returned it."

Cornelia smiled politely as her mother exclaimed, "Well, imagine that!"

There was no doubt that Edith could charm any person, any time, a product of her upbringing where a young lady's communication skills were key. *Being pretty is fine, being smart is nice, but being gracious will get you everywhere*, she always told Cornelia. Watching her mother now, Cornelia had to admit that it seemed true. Boring but true.

A girl who looked to be a little older than her walked past and, catching Cornelia's eye, motioned with her head for her to come toward her. "And what are your plans for the future of the campus, President Graham?" Edith was asking. As the president launched into another story, Cornelia, seeing her chance, snuck away.

"Hi," the girl said as Cornelia joined her on the campus path, reaching out her hand. "I'm Ruth McKend-rick."

"I'm Cornelia."

Ruth eyed her. "Have you ever noticed how women introduce themselves with just their first name or, worse, as Mrs. So-and-So? A man would never do that."

Cornelia laughed, liking this Ruth right away. "All right, then. I'm Cornelia Vanderbilt."

A wave of recognition washed over Ruth's face. "Ah. I see. First name is just fine then."

The pair laughed, and Cornelia was surprised that this stranger, without an explanation, seemed to under-stand her need for anonymity. Noticing the perfect stitching of the pin tucks on Ruth's blouse and the smart pleating on her skirt, Cornelia had to assume that Ruth was from a family with means—that perhaps, in some small way, she was here to escape her family name as well.

"Are you thinking of enrolling here?"

"Yes, one day," Cornelia said. "I'm graduating high school next year and then, of course, I have to attend two years elsewhere. But I hope so. Are the classes very hard?"

Ruth nodded. "They are challenging. And with only twenty-five girls here we have to prove ourselves. But we're certainly never without a date on a Saturday night." They both laughed again, and Cornelia found herself wishing that she could start college right now, that this Ruth could be the one to walk her through her first days and weeks on campus, show her the ropes. "But I think working harder only serves us in the future, right?" Ruth paused, taking Cornelia in. "Although, I suppose a Van-derbilt doesn't have to do much work . . ."

Cornelia shook her head. She'd never made her own bed or cooked her own breakfast. That was true. But she had spent her whole life helping around Biltmore Village and copious amounts of time making bandages for the war effort overseas. After the flood, especially, Edith and Cornelia had put every ounce of time and energy into rebuilding and revitalizing, re-creating what George had envisioned while also giving back to those families whose husbands and sons had gone off to fight. It was exhausting, but Cornelia had learned that serving the greater good was perhaps the most rewarding experience of her life. She was no stranger to hard work.

Now, in her bedroom with Bunchy, thinking of that day, Cornelia realized that if she hadn't known what hard work was then, she certainly knew it now. With so many of the men off at war, the women had picked up considerable slack around the house and on the farm. And everything else had changed too. Edith and Cornelia had stood side by side with the cooks and kitchen maids, canning tomatoes and okra from the farm, preserving peaches and making applesauce. Their ten-course meals with decadent desserts had turned to salads so the meat, sugar, and fats could be sent overseas to the soldiers.

"Maybe you'll meet a very eligible bachelor on our rounds today," Cornelia joked.

"Just what I've always wanted," Bunchy said, placing her hand over her heart—and her Red Cross patch. "A man with a fatal fever—or perhaps on the verge of consumption."

Cornelia groaned at the macabre joke. The girls were planning to head into Biltmore Village on horseback that morning to deliver soup to ill estate workers. Cornelia was the tiniest bit fearful about going out in the midst of a flu outbreak, but at their young age and in such good health, she and Bunchy had a good chance of recovery if they did—God forbid—contract the vile illness that had taken so many lives. They made their way down the vast flight of stairs and into the banquet hall where dozens of women, all dressed like them, were drinking tea and eating breakfast before embarking on their morning duties.

Cornelia stopped as she did every morning to look at the Service flag, where it hung right in front of the Latin carving that translated to *Grant us peace, O Lord, in our day*. The flag honored Biltmore men—including her mother's dear Noble—who had been called to serve. Some of the men had even been excited to go off to war. But Cornelia had to think that, when they arrived on those battlefields, it must have felt decidedly less thrilling.

As they studied the flag, she noticed it had thirty-five blue stars now—symbolizing the men who had returned home safely—and three for those who had lost their lives. That meant the fate of twelve souls was still in God's hands. Bunchy asked suddenly, "What would you give your life for?"

"What?" Cornelia asked.

"Well, I just mean, all these men went overseas to fight a war to protect our country—the world's freedom, really. They went knowing they were risking their lives."

"Yes, but many didn't have a choice. They were called up. They had to make the best of it."

Before they could continue their conversation, Edith appeared, putting an arm around each of them. Hordes of women were bustling around the house, making preparations for the day.

"Girls, after you deliver the soup, could you please go down to the country club and make sure everything is ready for tonight?"

Cornelia nodded and caught Bunchy's eye. Her friend was smiling. Planning a glamorous charity event was second nature to them. They had leaned on their well-heeled friends to raise money for dozens of causes in their young lives. Tonight, they would raise money for the war. "Of course we can, Mrs. Vanderbilt," Bunchy said. "Do you need us to taste the champagne? Make sure all is in order there?"

Edith smiled and squeezed her daughter's friend's shoulder. "Why, yes, Rachel. What a help you would be to me."

"Mother, I have to say," said Cornelia, "putting the finishing touches on the party sounds a lot more pleasant than standing on the streets in Washington selling flowers."

"Buy a forget-me-not and save a Belgian baby," Bunchy chimed in.

"It's shocking how many more flowers a pair of beautiful teenagers can sell for the food shortage in Belgium than an old mother," Edith mused.

Cornelia gave her mother a once-over, noting how, even in her uniform, her slim figure was prominent, her strong cheekbones and pronounced nose looking regal and proud underneath the Red Cross hat that seemed to sit almost too jauntily on the top of her head. It reminded Cornelia of Edith's wedding photos, of the way her beautiful veil with its dainty cap had perched so perfectly atop her lovely, well-proportioned face. But she was far from a bride today. No, Edith was a warrior.

And no one could deny that, here, Edith Vanderbilt was in her element. Cornelia had seen how it had crushed her when the government training camp hadn't been placed on Biltmore grounds, on the land she had offered for the cause. Edith needed to have purpose; she needed to *help*. It was what Cornelia admired most about her. And, in charge of a cadre of women who were tending the wounded and nursing the sick, Edith had found her place in the war effort.

Edith winked at Cornelia now. "I'm going to spend the day at the hospital seeing what more we can do there."

"You're a wonder, Mother," Cornelia said, meaning it.

"Mrs. Vanderbilt," Bunchy said, sincerely this time, "the hospital—and the whole village, really—is a marvel. You would hardly know the flood happened two years ago."

Edith nodded. "We have already won a few wars of our own, haven't we, girls?"

Cornelia's heart swelled with pride as she watched her mother walk away to speak with a group of nurses, ready to plan the day.

As Cornelia and her friend walked out the front door of Biltmore, into a chilly morning that would soon give way to a warm afternoon, she took a deep breath, savoring the feel of the sun on her face, the vibrant leaves molting into a red-gold sea, the color of a fiery sunset. She smiled to see her friend Rose, her first school friend from Asheville, walking up the drive. My, how their lives had diverged. Rose had already married. Cornelia couldn't imagine being married yet. But, then again, Rose and Andy had always had eyes for each other, even in grade school.

"What are you doing here?" she called to her friend.

"Did you think I was going to let all of Asheville rally for our troops and our sick and simply stay at home on the sidelines?" Rose said, smiling.

Cornelia noticed the glimmer in her friend's brown eyes. Rose had always had a quiet confidence about her. When Cornelia met her, on the first day of second grade, Rose had been standing by herself on the playground, singing as if no one could hear her. Cornelia wondered at the girl, at her ability to simply be herself. She wanted to know what that would feel like. And so, she went up beside Rose and joined in. "Oh! Susanna, don't you cry for me!" Rose had smiled at her. She'd smiled back. They had been friends ever since.

Now, Rose stepped between Cornelia and Bunchy and linked arms with them. Three different women from three different upbringings united in the pursuit of a common goal. It was poetry in motion. It was what would make the world a better place. Cornelia felt sure of it.

What would you give your life for? rang through her mind.

And suddenly, that eternal restlessness inside of Cornelia settled. The sum of her life became clear: her father's legacy, her mother's spirit, and the preservation of a world with days just like this, full of beauty, filled with purpose and, for the moment, brimming with hope.

JULIA

Two Halves of a Whole

One last night with Hayes might not have been the best idea. It felt sadder than I'd imagined. But, in some ways, it also felt right. People spent their whole lives chasing that elusive closure. Now, here we were, getting that very thing. We got to spend an entire dinner together, highlighting all the reasons why we didn't belong with each other after all.

Sitting at a table under the stars by the beach, I asked, "Do you think something like this should become common practice after a breakup? Everyone should sit down with a bottle of wine and rehash what went wrong?"

Hayes laughed. "Or we could pretend it's our first date."

I smiled sadly. "I almost wish we were meeting for the first time so we could have a future, not a past." But as I looked at this man I'd spent so many years with, I wondered how much we even had in common anymore; if this were a first date, it might also have been the last.

"Do you think my mother will ever forgive me?" I asked. The sound of the waves on the shore was romantic and lovely and, with a belly full of pineapple chicken and a glass of wine in my hand, I had been lulled into relaxation despite the awkwardness. No doubt about it, this would have been a perfect honeymoon—if I had married the guy, of course.

"I'll talk to her," Hayes said. "I'll see if I can make her understand."

"She has always liked you better than me."

Hayes grinned at me with that megawatt smile that had been impossible to resist for most of my life. "Sorry, babe. Nothing I can do to turn off my inherent charms."

"Are you going to date Chrissy Matthews?" I asked, casually, like I didn't care. But I cared so much. Just because I didn't want to marry Hayes didn't mean I wanted someone else to. In fact, I think every girl secretly wishes for a man to pine for her and comforts herself in the knowledge that—maybe forever—he still loves her most.

"I'm not going to date anyone for a long, long time, Jules," he said, wiping his mouth and setting down his fork. "In fact, I'm going to wait a while to make sure you don't change your mind."

"This is a weird breakup," I said.

"We've been best friends for a decade. I can't just slink off into the night and never see you again. We're not getting married, but we're still two halves of the same whole."

Two halves of a whole. What a beautiful thought.

"My turn," he said.

I nodded.

"Is it my fault you aren't an architect?"

I wondered if I looked as surprised as I felt. "I'm the only person whose fault it is that I'm not an architect." I was the one who hadn't had the courage to stand up for myself. Hayes had simply been a safe place to run.

"I wish I had pushed you to finish school," he said. "But it seemed like whatever happened made you change your mind about calling off the engagement, and I was scared that if I pushed you on it, you'd leave me again . . ."

God, I was pathetic. Hayes was right. I had finally gotten up the nerve to break up with him for what I thought was the final time. Then I'd hit a bump in the road, and I didn't crawl back. I ran. Sprinted. To his house, his arms, and his protection. He'd asked me what happened, I didn't want to talk about it, and that had been that.

I don't care what you do as long as we're together, he'd said. After that, I fast-tracked the process of becoming a yoga instructor and then taught enough to support my small student loan payment, shoe-buying, and Netflix, and he'd let me skate along. He never even complained. And if I ever mentioned it, he'd just say, *You're going to be my wife. I'll worry about our bills, and you worry about what you want to do next.*

"Do you want to talk about it now?" Hayes asked.

I shook my head.

"Well, for what it's worth, if I had it to do over again, I would have been the man you deserve. I would have pushed you to finish, to face whatever was holding you back. I do feel somewhat responsible."

I took a big sip of wine, feeling a little ill, realizing

that this breakup was only part of how my life was changing. I had to find a place to live now. I had to get a real job that would pay my real bills. Suddenly, I felt very overwhelmed.

After dinner we walked along the shore back to my room, which, for the night, had become Hayes's room too. In a moment of guilt and weakness I said, "I'll take the rollaway." He was, after all, the one paying for the plush, king-size bed I had been sleeping in—and, I remembered with a tinge of shame, had almost brought someone else into it.

"Nah," Hayes said. "I'll take the rollaway. You're on your honeymoon."

We both laughed as that huge man climbed on top of the tiny rollaway, his feet nearly hanging off the edge. "Don't worry one bit about me," he said. "Don't feel the least bit guilty that tiny you is in that huge bed while I'm over here swallowing the rollaway whole."

I stretched out, making myself as big as possible. "This will do for now."

Hayes rolled over and looked at me. "I do love you, Julesy. I wish you would change your mind."

"I love you too, Hayes. I swear I do. But I can't go through it anymore. I have to walk away."

His tired eyes locked on mine. Then he turned over on his other side, away from me—I assumed so I wouldn't see his sadness. I didn't want him to see mine either. My heart felt heavy as my tears fell silently on my pillow. For ten years, Hayes's hand had been the one I had held, his phone number the one I had memorized, his arms the place that kept me safe. Maybe it had been a false sense of security but, all the same, it had helped me through the hardest times of my life: my parents' separations, Pops's death, fights with friends. Suddenly, I felt intensely vulnerable.

A few hours later, still unable to sleep, I snuck out of bed and stepped out onto the small porch. I opened the email from Babs that I had downloaded earlier while connected to the spotty hotel Wi-Fi. It had a header of the Carolina shore with pink flamingos saying, Wish You Were Here, and was perhaps the tackiest thing I had ever seen. It made me smile, which I assumed was its intention.

My dear Julia,

They say that love is grand, but I'm with you: Infatuation is the ticket. Well, for me, maybe. An old lady who has parted with the love of her life, who knows that there is neither the time nor the inclination to find again what she has lost. But you, my dear, have so much time, all the time in the world, for infatuation to turn into deep, true love. I know you are afraid of separating from Hayes. What a huge part of your heart he has! But I promise you, Julia darling, there are other loves out there for you. When you are ready, you'll find the right man. When it's time, you'll know.

All my love,
Babs

I couldn't help but think of Conner and the way he made me feel on that boat, so swept away and breathless. It was, of course, a way that Hayes had made me feel a million times too. Was any of it real? And how would I know? I sat down to write back.

Dear Babs,

I think it is finished. Actually finished this time.
H leaves in the morning and I know it's right. So
how is it then that he is taking such a huge part of
my heart with him? Why does it still hurt so much?
I do wish that love was easier. I don't know how
you have managed to breathe after the loss of Pops.
Have you found a way to be happy without him? I
hope you have. If so, can you tell me the secret? See
you soon!

All my love,
Julia

I tiptoed back into the room and placed the postcard on the end table. Suddenly, that big, comfortable
bed looked so vast, so empty, so foreboding. Hayes was
breathing softly, the light bathing him. I kissed my hand
and put it to his cheek. A part of me wanted to crawl
in bed beside him. I had always felt so small, so safe in
his arms. But if the last year had taught me anything,
it's that sometimes safety can be deceiving. Sometimes
safety is the disease, not the cure.

———

The next morning, I could hardly eat my breakfast. I
was trying to be brave and strong as I sipped my coffee
and looked out over the water, and then back at Hayes.
Our little two-top table underneath the porch overhang
held so many emotions that I thought it might break in
two—like my heart.

"Well, I guess this is it," Hayes said after we finished,
setting his napkin down and looking forlorn. "Ten years

of love swept out to sea in a moment." We both laughed, albeit a little sadly.

Out of the corner of my eye, I saw a figure walking up the dock. I glanced over and did a double take, hoping it wasn't obvious. I didn't want Hayes to see Conner, in his white bathing suit and polo shirt, locking eyes with me. He put his hands over his heart and shrugged.

What could I do? I couldn't run after him with Hayes right there. Maybe he didn't deserve those last moments of just the two of us together, but I believed that I did. This was my last chance to say goodbye to us, to our life together. But I wanted to signal that Conner wasn't seeing what he thought he was seeing. I wasn't taking Hayes back; I was seeing him off.

How did I encapsulate all of that in an unnoticeable movement? I shrugged, hoping he'd get the message. But when I did, Conner hung his head, turned, and walked back down the dock, which is when I knew I'd made the wrong movement. Shit. And that was it. I couldn't call him. I couldn't exactly google the boat's satt phone number. As he had told me when we were together, his boat would be leaving today, heading off to new adventures with his friends and parents. I felt strongly, as I watched him walk away, that I would never see Conner again.

I focused back on Hayes, my sadness compounding. "I am always here for you, Julia," he said. "I promise. You are my first and only love, and there's nothing I wouldn't do for you. Ever."

I smiled. "I feel the same."

He stood up, and I stood too. He wrapped me in a hug, and I lingered there, my head on his chest, knowing it would be the last time, praying that I was making the right decision. He kissed me, and I let him. It was goodbye. It was forever. Then I watched as he made his way down the dock, walking with that distinguishable swagger that was his and his alone the entire way. He stepped onto a boat that would take him to the ferry. He turned, blew me a kiss. I didn't catch it. I didn't need it anymore.

I waved, watching as the boat pulled away from the dock, getting smaller and smaller and then disappearing into the blue horizon, the sky meeting the sea and obscuring everything—even this great big love that, like a river swallowed up by the ocean, had finally run its course.

BABS

Young Life

I kept telling myself, as the Summer Acres movers put the last box in their truck, that this was going to be a lovely surprise for my daughters. Although they might not exactly be thrilled that I had decided to move with practically no notice, wouldn't they at least be impressed I had managed to get all my possessions packed for the new town house without their help? Although I knew that not bothering them was perhaps what they were upset about most of the time.

Summer Acres had sent over a team of three ladies for three days to help me pack. I was paying them handily, but it was worth every penny to make decisions with unemotional bystanders who, for some reason, kept asking, "But does it bring you *joy*?" I didn't know. Could a person get true joy from an inanimate object? Plus, joy was a relative term. Easy Spirits were never going to bring me joy. Jimmy Choos brought me joy. But my feet would probably answer that question differently.

I was leaving almost all my furniture and larger possessions behind, but it was shocking how much I'd accumulated over the years. I had imagined leaving my house with a suitcase and a rack of hanging clothes. Instead, I was taking a rack of hanging clothes, a few pieces of special furniture, and nineteen boxes, six of them filled with books I positively could not leave behind.

I had promised myself I wouldn't have a dramatic parting with my home. I would still be here often to visit, after all. But the night before the move, unable to sleep, I had walked from room to room taking in every detail, as though, after eighty years of this being my family beach house, I might forget something. Sure, the bathrooms had been updated, the kitchen redone, furniture moved in and out. But the wood paneling and original floors remained. The peerless view was the same, although the beach shrank or expanded from year to year depending on the storms. The wide front porch was as it had always been. It was only I who had really changed.

When had this place that had felt as natural to me as my own hands become frightening? When had the quiet become scary?

Deep down, I knew the answer.

I tried to remember the warm, cozy parts of that terrible night, the ones that reminded me of a crackling fire and a fresh vase of flowers, both of which had been part of the scenery.

I was sitting in my white upholstered club chair, across from Reid's recliner, catching up on my reading for the Friends & Fiction Book Club, while Reid, ever consistent, was engrossed in a *Reader's Digest* issue.

He broke the silence when he asked, "Do you think we should get a dog? It's quiet around here."

I slammed my book shut and gasped. "Reid! I've been thinking the exact same thing! I didn't want to say it out loud because it's so impractical at our age."

"I was thinking maybe we should get a rescue dog, a little older and calmer."

"Really? I'd prefer a puppy. We can still rescue one." I stood up and started pacing around the room because I was so excited. "We could put his bed right here." I gestured to the spot between our chairs. "And we could take him for walks every morning."

"And potty train him." Reid groaned. Well, yes, perhaps we had done enough of that in our lives. But still. You must take the good with the bad.

"But that warm puppy nose and those ecstatic tail wags!"

Reid closed his magazine now and looked at me, amused. "You really want a puppy?"

"I think it would brighten things up. We could use some new, young life around here!"

I never could have imagined the irony of that statement.

Later that night I'd stood in the bathroom, brushing my teeth in my silk pajamas. Reid had wrapped his arms around me from behind and nuzzled my neck, kissing the spot where it met my chin. I had smiled at him through my toothpaste foam. We held hands as we fell asleep.

That was what I wanted to remember.

When I woke up early the next morning, I was surprised that the sun was already shining through our bedroom windows, radiating off the crashing waves.

I hadn't gotten up once to use the bathroom? A miracle! I looked over to see if Reid was stirring, to decide if I should let him sleep or if I should get up and make coffee.

His face looked pale, his lips a little blue. Dread washed over me. "Reid!" I squealed in a pitch I thought only schoolgirls were capable of. "Reid!"

I touched his neck, frantically searching for a pulse, my hands shaking. That spot where his pulse should be, that spot on me where his lips had been not eight hours earlier, was cold.

Unable to still my hands enough to dial, I hit the side button on my phone and said, "Siri, call 911." She did. I remember saying my address and then walking around to Reid's side of the bed, pumping his chest with all my might—a useless feat considering the give of the mattress—breathing my breath into him. Isn't that what we had done for each other for all these years? Breathed the same air until we had become one?

I sobbed as they put him in the ambulance, stood screaming in my front yard as they drove him away. I don't know who called my daughters, but Meredith was suddenly there, guiding me back into the house. I was, after all, still in my pajamas.

I had heard friends say that watching their spouses or parents leave this world was a peaceful experience. Why hadn't I gotten that? Mine had been terror. Trauma, really. And I knew that day I would never, ever be able to get back in that bed without him.

Now, I waved out the front door at the moving truck, the one that held my curlers and socks, soap, and beloved high heels that I could still wear for short stints of time.

I turned to do one more check of the house. That's when I noticed I had forgotten something too important to trust the movers with. My black-and-white wedding photo in the sterling Tiffany frame Reid's parents had given us as a wedding gift. Holding it, I sat down, allowing myself to feel the familiar sadness that sometimes overwhelmed me. Even still, it was all worth it. I would do it again in a heartbeat.

In the house we had shared for more than fifty years since that photo was taken, I looked at that picture, studied that wedding veil, and thought about my granddaughter.

I walked back into my bedroom and opened the closet door, the yards of lace and tulle puddling on the floor, the only thing still hanging, resplendent, in the empty space. I would have Meredith come get it and have it resealed in an heirloom box, so it could be preserved for another generation.

That wedding veil was mine. It was my mother's. It was a part of our family history, one of the most important parts, in fact. I held that picture to my chest.

I checked the ancient stove once more to make sure I'd turned it off, walked out on the porch, and took a deep, salty breath. Sea oats danced in the rolling dunes, and the ocean beyond was plaintive and contemplative, just like I was.

As I locked the door for the last time and got in the car, I reveled in the thought that this would be a new chapter for me. I looked down at my watch. I wanted to be settled into the town house in time to get to the five-thirty Stretch and Sculpt followed by a group beach walk, cocktails, and dinner. I had a highlight appointment tomorrow, and I thought I'd punch my color up a bit, make it a kickier blond. I had Botox scheduled the following day, and though my daughters proclaimed it silly at my age, I felt strongly that looking and feeling one's best were paramount. *Why could everyone else get fillers and plasma facials while I had to grow old gracefully?* I wondered as I pulled out of the driveaway and onto the road that would take me to my new home. I wouldn't stand for it.

When I reached Summer Acres, flashing my pass at the man in the gatehouse, an extreme sense of calm washed over me. My phone rang. Alice. Well, there went my calm.

"Good morning!" I trilled.

"Mom? Where are you? The doors are locked and it's so dark in here." She paused and gasped. "And some of your stuff is gone!"

"How about you get Meredith on the line?" I asked, pulling over into the fitness center parking lot so I wasn't talking while driving. I wasn't taking any chances. At eighty years old, they will take your license if you so much as sneeze behind the wheel.

Alice sighed. "Mom, you're scaring me."

"Honey, everything is just fine. Can you add your sister to this call so I can tell you what's going on?"

A few silent seconds passed. "Mom?" Alice asked.

"I'm here."

"Meredith?"

"Present and accounted for!"

"Oh, good. Well, girls, I have some news I didn't want to share until it was all settled, but you should know . . . I've moved to Summer Acres. Today."

"What?" they shouted in perfect unison.

"It felt like the right time, and I didn't want to bother either of you with the decision."

Dead silence.

"Okay, sweethearts. I hope you'll come visit soon, but I need to go direct the movers."

"How could you move and not even consult us?" Alice interrupted.

Always needing to one-up her twin, Meredith said, "I knew you were *thinking* about moving, but Mom, this is a hair brash."

"Mom, are you feeling okay?" Alice asked.

They constantly thought I had dementia. My leg hurt: dementia. I had a new cavity: dementia. I didn't want to go to church with them: dementia.

"I told you she looked tired last week," Meredith said.

"Well, you might have said that, Meredith," Alice snapped, "but tired isn't going off the deep end and moving without telling your children."

Since I was basically out of the conversation now, I just hung up the phone, started the car, and resumed driving. If prior experience had taught me anything, it would take them a good ten minutes to realize I wasn't on the line. I whistled as I drove.

Although by the time they realized I had hung up, they would, no doubt, question whether I had dementia.

As I approached the front porch of my new home, I noticed a man sitting in one of the rockers. *These movers are slackers*, I thought. But then I realized the man had on khakis and a blue checked oxford shirt, not the Summer Acres T-shirt the movers wore, and he wasn't a mover at all—instead, he was my liaison and long-lost camp buddy. My heart raced at the sight of him, and I wondered at my good fortune. I had pictured my Summer Acres buddy to be an old woman with a walker who bossed everyone around, not the beautiful boy I had met decades earlier at summer camp. I shook my head, getting myself back together. I couldn't be daydreaming about having a *boyfriend*, for heaven's sake. How pathetic and cliché. Old woman moves to a nursing home and takes up with someone who isn't her husband? Nope. Not for me. I would never complicate my children's lives or disregard my husband's memory in that way.

As he opened my car door, though, helped me out and gave me a hug, he smelled so nice, so familiar. His arms felt so strong. I didn't have to play by the rules all the time, did I? And what was wrong with being friends with a member of the opposite sex?

"Are all the liaisons this attentive to their charges?" I quipped, raising an eyebrow.

"I'd venture to say that not all liaisons have spent the past fifty-plus years pining for their charges, so I'd say that's highly doubtful."

"Miles!" I scolded as I took his arm.

Well, maybe not *friends*, exactly.

"You sure travel light these days," he said.

I shrugged. "With the wonders of the internet I figured why not have everything delivered right here? It's time for a fresh start."

"You can say that again," he said, squeezing my hand, which I'd placed in the crook of his arm as he helped me inside.

I looked up into his hazel eyes and that face that time had changed but also made more the same. When we were camp counselors—Miles at the boys' camp, me at the girls'—we saw each other in the mess hall every day. We had a few opportunities to sneak off together for walks, but between sessions when the campers were gone, we'd make ourselves comfortable on the riverbank for our nightly talks, my left knee touching his right.

I was with Reid then. I had met him my junior year of high school. He was the senior basketball star for our rival team, and I, in my skirt and curls, was the cheer captain. Before every free throw and after every basket, he'd turned to look at me, as if he were playing just for me. And, little by little, we began seeing each other. We were all but engaged. But in my day a woman didn't go steady until there was a ring on her finger. So I saw other boys. My camaraderie with Miles wasn't a betrayal in so many words: we never did much more than talk. Even still, I knew it wouldn't have thrilled Reid.

But now, standing in the foyer of my new town home, I realized that Miles and I had a second chance to be friends . . . or, as we might have been many years ago, something more. But I knew I couldn't explore that. I could never be disloyal to my husband. "Miles, how in the world did fate conspire to bring us here, to let you be my buddy?"

He smiled. "Well, it was a little bit fate. And a little bit my seeing your name as a prospective new member on the board meeting roster. I wasn't sure if it was you, but I had to know."

I laughed. "You knew?"

He nodded. "Barbara, the thought of seeing your pretty smile again was the only thing in the world that could make me actually sign up to be a liaison." He paused. "All these years, we weren't that far apart, you know. I've spent the last twenty-five years, since my wife died, just up the road in New Bern."

"Oh, Miles," I said, truly sorry for him. "Twenty-five years alone?"

He nodded. I led him out to the tiny screened-in back porch where the day was beginning to warm. We each sat in one of the standard-issue plastic rocking chairs that I would soon be replacing.

"What about you? How long has Reid been gone?"

"Fourteen months," I whispered. Then I looked up at him and said what I had never revealed to anyone else. "After he died beside me in bed, my house terrified me. I didn't know how I was ever going to be able to live there again without being afraid."

He nodded. "I've lived with Myra's ghost for all these years. She follows me wherever I go."

"What happened?" I whispered.

He looked down at his feet, ashamed. "Suicide," he said quietly. Then he looked back over at me, his eyes full of pain. "Barbara, I didn't even know anything was wrong. I've been living with the guilt a long time."

I took his hand and looked out at the lagoon, rocking slightly. It was almost as if we were back on that river-bank at camp all those years ago.

Sitting on the back porch of my new life, holding the hand of a man who wasn't new to me at all, I realized that, even after all these years, there was still something there. I was too old to play games, too old not to take a second chance if I had one available to me. I turned toward Miles and smiled. He smiled back. "Oh, Barbara."

That was all it took for me to know that he felt exactly the same.

JULIA

A Part of the Sky

It took a day or two for it to sink in: Hayes was gone. Conner, who had been my brief distraction, wasn't coming back. And I had to fly home to reality, face the music.

I tossed and turned that night, filled with dread. My dream of being an architect was gone. I had no job, little money, and plenty of bills. What was I going to do?

As the sun began to stream through the windows, I started to feel the slightest bit better. I needed a plan. That was all.

I glanced at the alarm clock to see that it was nearly seven. I felt like I could sleep all day or, at the very least, lie in bed all day and cry. But a guided hike was leaving at eight, and even though it was going to take all the effort in my body to get up, put on a brave face, and view the world through this new Hayes-free lens, I was going to go.

I rubbed on my sunscreen, assessing my tan in the mirror of the bathroom, which was made entirely of teak and felt more appropriate for a yacht than a resort, slipped on a pair of shorts and a jogging top and grabbed a water bottle, a hat, and sunglasses. The sun was low and lovely, as if it was lazily making its way out of bed too. Only a handful of people stood at the base of the mountain trail when I got there. Usually, I would have made small talk, but this morning I just couldn't.

"Jules!" Trav exclaimed when he saw me. "I've missed you at paddleboard yoga!"

"Yes, well, I've missed you too. My life crisis got in the way."

He made a terrified face, and we both laughed.

"Last hike," I said sadly.

"Of your whole life?" he asked sarcastically.

I smirked at him. "Ha-ha. I have to go home tomorrow—and I'm dreading it."

"You should just stay," he said.

I laughed, thinking that the balance in my bank account was roughly the same as one night in this pricey resort. "I wish. I have had a recent reversal of fortune in the financial department."

"Reversal of fortune. How very Shakespearean of you." He waved at our small group. "We're heading up the trail in three minutes! Make sure you have water and sunscreen, please." Then he turned back to me. "Is this because of the calling off the wedding thing?"

I shrugged. "Well, yeah. That and the dropping out of architecture school thing. Which I'm still paying for, by the way."

Trav winced, rubbing his chin. "Tell you what. I'm short a yoga teacher the next two weeks. I can't pay you, but I can house you with us and get you free meals if you could use a couple more weeks to languish in your existential crisis. Would that help you out?"

I gasped, thinking it over quickly. I had enough in my bank account to cover my student loans and health insurance for a little while. It would be tight, but I could stay here two more weeks, soak up paradise, and fig-ure out my next steps in the meantime. And, if I stayed, there was always the chance I might bump into Con-ner. After island hopping with his friends and parents, would he come back here looking for me?

When I didn't answer immediately, Trav said, "Just let me know after the hike."

"Spring Break 2012?"

He grinned. "Never looked back."

I followed him up the trail, the others behind me. "I know it's warm this morning," he called to us, "but when you see the view from the top, it will all be worth it."

This was, perhaps, my favorite thing about the BVIs: the clearest Caribbean water juxtaposed against the most majestic mountain peaks. It was geographic per-fection.

As I hiked, focusing on the flora and fauna of one of the world's most beautiful places, my head cleared from the drama surrounding me. I thought of Babs and how I couldn't wait to see her when I got back—and maybe delve a little deeper into my thoughts about our wed-ding veil. I smiled when I pictured her seeing me. *You look so sun-kissed, darlin'*, she would say.

Yeah, we all knew that a tan wasn't healthy, but Babs sure did love it.

As we reached the vista, I climbed up to stand on a mud-colored rock and took a deep breath. Up here, with the sparkling water far below, it felt like I was a part of the sky, like the real world didn't exist anymore. The clear blue ocean dotted with the green of islands, surrounded by mountains, looked like a movie set. Could something this beautiful actually be real?

"This is my best thinking rock," Trav said, startling me.

I smiled, noticing his vintage HUGS NOT DRUGS T-shirt. Trav was practically a caricature; he fit every stereotype I'd ever known about a disgruntled American who left behind the rat race for the good life.

"When I have a big decision to make," he continued, "I come up here and sit on this rock."

"For real?" I couldn't imagine that Trav was making a lot of tough decisions, but I liked the idea of it.

He nodded. "For real. You should try it." He gestured toward the group. "I'm going to take them back. You know the way if you want to stay behind for a few minutes?"

I nodded.

"If you aren't back in an hour, I'll come make sure you haven't been eaten by a mountain lion."

"Well, that inspires a lot of confidence."

As the group made its way down the mountain, I sat on the rock, which felt cool and mossy against my bare legs, closed my eyes, and breathed in deeply. I'd meditated before. I wasn't *good* at it. Being good took real focus on clearing your mind, and that wasn't my favorite thing. But in the stillness of the moment, it seemed more effortless than usual. Or maybe my sleepless night had me all thought out.

I figured that, once I got quiet, I would think about Hayes. But instead, I thought about the moment Babs had been about to put the wedding veil on my head and how panicked I'd felt. My entire life that veil had been a symbol of happiness, but I realized that, for me, its significance wasn't even really about marriage. It was about the connection that touching it, wearing it, seeing it, made me feel to Babs and Mom, to my great-grandmother, and Aunt Alice.

I would love to bring them here someday. I smiled, looking out over the mountains, thinking of Asheville, of that bridesmaids' luncheon, of Cornelia Vanderbilt and *her* wedding veil. I knew Babs thought it was crazy, but there was just something about seeing it in that photo, a hum, a *feeling*. I had to investigate more when I got home.

Home. What did that even mean now? The idea of going back to my parents' house filled me with dread. But with no money, it wasn't like I could just get a place of my own. I could stay with Sarah for a while if I went back to Raleigh . . . And if I was in Raleigh, I should probably finish school. For the first time in a while, the thought of that seemed sort of appealing. Or, at least, necessary.

A small lizard scurried up beside me, completely unafraid. The mere idea of facing my failure terrified me. But being an architect was what I had always wanted. And now I had to start taking care of myself. Even if I did decide to go back—assuming they would take me back—I couldn't start the summer session for a couple months. So, if I stayed two weeks here, I was getting closer to filling my time. I thought then of Babs, of that mountain house that sat empty and alone so very often. I was sure she would let me stay there for a bit while I got my ducks in a row.

I wondered if maybe my failure wasn't that big a deal after all. People stumble. *I will get back up*, I decided, as I, literally, got back up.

As the sun glinted on the water, I felt lighter somehow. Walking down the mountain, I felt better than I had in a while. I was going through a transition phase in my life, but wasn't that normal? I could salvage things; I could get back on track.

Back at the resort, Trav had pulled his hair into a bun and was wiping his face with a towel. He was sitting at the end of the dock, and I sat down beside him. He didn't say anything. Didn't even look at me.

"I'll do it," I said. "If it's really okay, I'll stay for two more weeks."

Trav smiled. "Excellent. It's just two classes a day. I'll send over the schedule." He turned back toward the water and said, "Then what?"

I smiled because, for the first time, I was finally okay with not knowing.

Back in my room a few minutes later, I sat down at the dark-stained mahogany desk by the window and pulled out a postcard that had a picture of the sun setting behind the mountain I had just climbed that morning. I wrote:

Dear Babs,

 I'm staying for two more weeks. Can you believe it? Teaching paddleboard yoga, clearing my head, figuring out my next steps. But I'd also really love your advice . . . Speaking of, how would you feel

about a trip to Asheville? We could eat at all our
favorite restaurants and visit our favorite place?
And maybe . . . I could stay for a bit? Either way,
see you soon!

Xs and Os,
Julia

If Babs would let me stay at her house for a while, I could figure out the future. I would need to call the school, first, of course, see if going back was even a possibility. Get in touch with financial aid. Reapply to the program . . . It suddenly felt overwhelming. But then again, I had plenty of time to make a decision and still be back for the fall semester.

I looked out the open window at the dozens of sailboats dotting the water with their grace and majesty. I wondered if Conner was still on one. It would be, quite frankly, hard to miss.

That old insecurity that I wouldn't make it as an architect—the one that constantly drove me back to the familiarity of Hayes—set in. But that part of my life was over. Finally. I got up, stretched, and walked out onto the porch, leaning on the rail. I had two choices: I could dwell on what I should have done differently, or I could move forward.

I liked the idea of that.

Queen of the Nile

March 24, 1923

Cornelia leaned toward the mirror in her bedroom on K Street in Washington, took a pencil to her eye with a quick flourish, and leaned back again, examining her appearance. At twenty-two years old, everything about her was vibrant, fresh, and vivid.

"You are the picture of Cleopatra," Edith said, sitting on the edge of the bed, wrapping her arm around one of its four posters. "Perhaps even more beautiful."

When Cornelia had asked her mother what her costume should be for the fancy dress ball being hosted by Commissioner Rudolph—president of the governing body of Washington—and his wife, Edith's answer had been almost immediate: "A strong, beautiful woman who is a bit mysterious. Cleopatra!" Edith was the queen of the fancy dress ball, having hosted some of the most lavish ones of the past few years, and she *always* knew what the best outfit would be.

Cleopatra—the queen of Egypt, the inheritor of Greece's vast cultural gifts, and, perhaps best of all, a woman who had lived out one of the world's greatest love stories . . . Yes, Cornelia couldn't think of any woman quite so fabulous or fantastical to portray, especially now that, she had to admit, finding a love of her own was on her mind. The war was over, the men were home, and the country's spirits were as gay and heady as she could remember. The parties were glorious and there was so much fun to be had. This was Cornelia's time to shine.

As Edith lowered the bronze headdress, adorned with snakes and jewels, onto Cornelia's head, Cornelia examined herself in the mirror once again. She wore a flowing gold gown cinched at the waist, and a bejeweled collar hung heavy on her neck. She looked quite star-tlingly like the Queen of the Nile.

Edith sighed wistfully as Cornelia stood. "Ah, to be young and in the prime of life again, with everyone and everything out there waiting for you."

Cornelia gave her mother a once-over. "Mother, you might not be as young as you once were, but I'd daresay you are *certainly* in your prime, and every eligible man your age seems to be jockeying for the position by your side."

Edith *had* been connected in the papers to more than one man, even though she very, very seldom talked to Cornelia about her romantic pursuits. They were all perfectly nice men. Some were powerful, and very rich, and Cornelia knew that if Edith had been a different woman, she would have married one of them to offset some of the financial difficulties they had endured since

George's death. But she was a devout widow, and even after all these years, she felt it inappropriate to choose a second husband when her daughter had yet to choose a first. Who Cornelia would marry was more an object of fascination in the papers than who Edith would marry, if that was even possible.

"Your father was the man by my side, Cornelia," Edith said simply. "And, since then, you have been the woman by it. I need nothing more."

"You don't even need Governor Morrison?" Cornelia asked playfully. Her mother was trying to be coy, but she was missing tonight's party to have dinner with the North Carolina governor, who was in D.C. on business. And she must like him, because fancy dress balls were Edith's favorite.

Edith rolled her eyes. "What about you, dear? Are any of the interested parties catching your eye lately?" Cornelia had begun to feel a vague sense of unease, of longing for something she couldn't quite place. In her set, that longing usually led in short order to an engagement. She assumed she needed to choose a person to spend her life with. That would settle what felt so very unsettled within her. She thought of her friend Rose, of how happy and content she was in her pretty little house in Biltmore Village, with her husband, Andy. Then again, hadn't Rose always seemed happy and content? Bunchy, on the other hand, ran from the very idea of marriage like it might drown her. Her wildest and freest friend seemed to gain all her joy from nights out on the town, raucous parties, and flirtations with men she had no intentions of getting serious with. Cornelia didn't quite feel like she fit in either of her best friends' categories.

Cornelia sighed and slinked down in her vanity chair. "I'm just grateful you're not forcing me into one of those horrible arranged marriages to a foreigner," she said, shuddering. "I simply cannot understand why all these American women marry men from abroad, only to use their family fortune to restore a rotting castle without proper plumbing and electricity." More than a few of Cornelia's contemporaries—and even her own family members—had left the US with their broke-but-titled husbands, as was all the rage among their set.

Edith laughed. "Yes, Nelly. You have made your feelings quite clear—and quite public, I might add."

Cornelia rolled her eyes. Seemingly every paper in the country ran ridiculous spreads declaring that she and Edith would keep their money in the United States.

"Some women are wooed by titles," Edith said, holding a pair of Cornelia's earrings up to her ears.

"You should wear those tonight," Cornelia said. Then, back to the matter at hand, "I am not interested in any man's second-rate title."

"But finding true love?" Edith asked.

Cornelia laughed and said, sneakily, "That situation is of high interest."

"Darling, you must keep an open mind," Edith said. "I would never force you into anything, but you simply cannot predict who you will fall in love with."

You simply cannot predict who you will fall in love with played on repeat in Cornelia's mind several hours later. The car had stopped by Bunchy's house to pick her up and the two had gone together to the party, unaccompanied by a chaperone. My, how the world had changed in the past few years. Cornelia loved it.

Light danced in every window of the commissioner's imposing brick home, which stood right around the corner from the vice president's house. Tall luminaries lined the path, which was crowded with ladies and gentlemen dressed in their finest costumes, waiting to be received by the commissioner, his wife, and whatever other dignitaries they had deemed suitable for the receiving line.

Mrs. Rudolph, dressed as a charming Marie Antoinette, curtsied deeply to Cornelia and Bunchy, and they all giggled. How she managed to balance that enormous wig on her head, Cornelia would never know. "Thank you for inviting us into your lovely palace, Miss Antoinette," Cornelia said.

"It's my pleasure," she said with a wink.

Excited chatter, punctuated by laughter, rose and fell with the beautiful music playing in the distance. The country's nobility had been transformed for the evening into Elizabethan pages, corpulent kings, storybook characters, and daring knights.

As Cornelia and Bunchy entered the house and made their way into the ballroom, they stopped to look around. "This is positively glorious," Bunchy whispered. Three massive crystal chandeliers hanging from the ceiling created a romantic atmosphere, and each of the dozen or so tables around the perimeter were bedecked with huge candelabras holding dripping wax candles and surrounded by flowers. A twelve-piece band entertained the very full dance floor.

Cornelia smiled as Bunchy took two champagne coupes from a tray and handed one to her friend. The bubbles tingled in her mouth as she took a sip, a precursor of the fun they were about to have. As she took her second swig, Cornelia caught the eye of a tall, handsome man from across the crowded room of costumed socialites. His gaze was locked on her, and when her eyes caught his, he smiled, and she swore she could see a mischievous glimmer in them. But maybe it was the candlelight. As he began walking toward her, she stood straighter.

"What is he wearing?" Bunchy asked in awe as the striking stranger strode toward them.

His golden armor and large helmet, which was bedecked with a massive plume of red feathers, couldn't help but turn the heads of every person in the room.

Once he reached Cornelia, he smiled. "Why, there she is. The woman I've been waiting for."

Cornelia generally felt very strong and very in control. But at the sight of this man, she reddened—and found herself quite out of words.

"The Cleopatra to my Mark Antony," he clarified, which was when she noticed that his accent was decidedly British. She wanted to use it as a black mark against him—he was a foreigner, after all—but found that she could not. It was as if lightning had struck her. "John Cecil," he said, taking her hand. "But my friends call me Jack."

"Cornelia," she replied breathlessly. Then she thought of her brief encounter with Ruth, the lucky coed in Chapel Hill, the one whose ranks she had never joined, and added, "Vanderbilt."

She broke her trance long enough to glance at Bunchy, who was dressed as a garden nymph and wearing a bemused expression on her face. Cornelia knew that she was finding this all terribly funny, as Cornelia was not the type of woman to be befuddled. Not when teachers at Miss Madeira's tried to stump her. And certainly not now by something as common as a man. She gathered herself enough to say, "So, are you telling me this so that I will call you Jack, or so that I won't?"

He smiled. "Cornelia Vanderbilt, Cleopatra, you may call me anything you see fit. Anything at all."

She held her glass up to him, and he clinked it with hers. "Are we beginning our own Society of Inimitable Livers?" she asked, referring to the name Antony and Cleopatra had given their club of drinking friends. Instead of responding, he asked, "Would you do me the very distinct honor of a dance?"

She felt a touch disappointed. He hadn't gotten the joke. But a man couldn't have everything, right?

Regaining her composure, she said, "Why, of course. For the good of Egypt, I mean."

They both laughed. For a split second, she had a horrifying thought. It was her mother who had told her to dress up as Cleopatra. What if she had sent this British aristocrat dressed as Mark Antony to woo her? What if this was a trap?

But as Jack pulled her close and led her around the dance floor, that thought drifted away. If her mother *had* sent him, maybe it was because she knew something Cornelia didn't. Perhaps it was because she knew this man was right for her. Or perhaps this was simply fate.

"So what's it like?" he asked as the music played.

"What's what like?"

"Being a Vanderbilt, of course."

"What's it like being a duke or a lord or whatever ridiculous thing I assume you are?" she asked snappily.

He laughed. "I am none of those things, unfortunately. I am nothing more than a grandson of a marquess."

A marquess. In spite of herself, Cornelia was the slightest bit impressed. He was being honest with her. She was rarely honest with anyone. People seemed to have all sorts of preconceived notions about her. It was the price she paid for her family name. Bunchy, her mother, and Rose were the three people in her life she truly let see into her heart.

She looked up at Jack. Usually she changed the subject when people asked how it was to be a Vanderbilt. Or she extolled its glorious virtues, because who wanted to hear one of the richest women in America complain about her life? But there was something in his eyes, something that made her feel uncharacteristically unguarded.

"I don't know what it's like to be the grandson of a marquess, but being a Vanderbilt can be lonely," Cornelia admitted.

"Lonely?" Jack questioned, meeting her eye. The music stopped and she went to pull away, but he held fast— much to her delight. "With all those servants around? All those friends to entertain?"

She shrugged. "I hate being in the spotlight, the papers talking about everything I've eaten that day and what I wore, who I sat with, what occasion I celebrated. And sometimes I'm afraid to bare my soul to anyone at all for fear that my innermost thoughts will end up on the AP wire the next day."

"Hmmm." He nodded knowingly. "I'm actually going to phone all this in momentarily."

Before she could formulate a witty response, another man Cornelia didn't recognize tapped Jack on the shoulder. "May I cut in?"

Jack obliged, but Cornelia noticed—or maybe hoped—

that he looked reluctant as he did so. Or perhaps she shouldn't have been quite so honest.

As the night continued, Cornelia noticed herself making eye contact with Jack as she danced with other potential suitors. She felt dismayed if she looked over at him and he wasn't looking back at her. She longed for him to cut in and struggled to make conversation with anyone else. But perhaps he hadn't felt the spark that she had. Maybe it was all in her head.

At the end of the night, Jack crossed her path again. "Miss Vanderbilt," he said quietly with a wink as he passed, placing something in her hand so discreetly that even she wasn't sure it had happened.

She nodded and smiled as he walked off. It took every ounce of self-control she had to wait to open the note until she was home, back in the safety of her lavishly appointed room on K Street.

> *To the enchanting Miss Vanderbilt:*
> *I must see you again. Might I meet you tomorrow night at 5 p.m. for a walk? Away from the prying eyes of the press and the whispers of society matrons, you should feel free to be your true and lovely self, who has captivated me at first breath.*
>
> *Ever yours,*
> *Jack Cecil*
>
> *P.S. I'd prefer that our drinking society bear its later name, one that I feel quite certain already is better suited to our fate: Companions to the Death.*

Cornelia held the note to her chest, feeling giddy and girlish as she did, and not wanting to hide or deny either feeling. He got the joke! He knew! It felt, in a way, as if this simple exchange of Antony and Cleopatra trivia had sealed their fate.

"Well, do tell, my dear," Edith said with a bemused expression, entering the room in her pearls and fur from her own night out. "It appears your night might have been slightly more fruitful than mine."

Cornelia's cheeks glowed; her countenance sparkled. She had left with round, sad eyes and returned positively radiant.

"Mother," she said breathlessly, "I think I'm in love."

Swingers

O ut!" I called, putting my finger up. Ah, tennis. How glad I was that I had continued playing all these years. Even when Alice and Meredith had asked me not to, for fear that I would break a hip or blow out a knee or some other offensive old lady concern, I refused to do any such thing. Although I had succumbed to the dreaded tennis elbow brace.

We were playing mixed doubles this morning, just one set. It seemed to take longer now that we were older. My partner, David, and I were winning 4–2 over our opponents, Miles and . . . *Linda.* No. I shouldn't think of her like that. Linda had truly taken an interest in my acclimation to Summer Acres this past week or so. She was lovely. She wore her fawn hair pulled back with a clip on each side and had the kindest smile. And it wasn't her fault that she had pulled Miles's name out of the hat when we drew partners for the game—like pre-school children—or swingers. *Swingers*. The mere idea made me chuckle out loud.

"What's so funny?" David asked.

David was a short, muscular man who was dread-fully serious but, as I had heard, delightfully brilliant once you got to know him. But I didn't need to get to know him now. Now, I needed to win. As a girl, my competitive side was deemed unfeminine, a character-istic I should bury at all costs. Now, as a woman of a new millennium, it was part of my charm.

"Nothing's funny," I answered David's question, draw-ing close to him. "Your serve is beautiful today. One more of those beauties, and we'll be up five–two."

David nodded.

"If you can possibly serve to Linda's backhand, she's almost guaranteed to hit it down the line right to me, where I can cram it all the way to the baseline behind her."

David smiled now. "You're my favorite partner," he said. "Most of these women are just out here to pick up men. You're a real player, Barbara."

I chuckled again, but my face went dark when I heard Linda say, flirtatiously, "Miles, your strokes are so pol-ished. Could you give me a lesson after?"

I controlled my eye roll, but Miles must have noticed my agitation because he winked at me, producing the type of butterflies I had assumed I was no longer capa-ble of. "You're going down, Bullock," I said, pointing my racket at him.

"Am I?" he said. "Avenging your great Camp Holly Ridge loss?"

I laughed delightedly. The camp tournament had

come down to Miles and me in a singles match for all the marbles. He had beaten me handily.

"Please serve," I called to David. "This has just gotten personal."

David, fortunately, was a great player. He dropped the ball right where I asked, and as expected, Linda delivered a clean backhand almost directly into my racket. I smashed a forehand volley to the baseline. Game.

Linda started the next game. It was her serve, and while she wasn't a bad player, she was certainly the weakest on the court. What I hoped would be the quick last game in the set became a case of Keep Away from Miles. I hit the final shot, a risky lob that paid off, sailing way over Miles's head all the way to the baseline behind him. Linda couldn't get there in time. It wasn't pretty, but it did the trick.

David and I tapped rackets before walking to the net and shaking hands with Miles and Linda.

"Good game," I said to them, and they responded in kind.

I walked underneath the cabana, toweling myself off. The morning humidity had finally caught up with us. I ran my fingers through my short, damp hair, missing the ponytails of my youth. As Miles approached, I said, reminiscing, "I don't care if I win or lose as long as I get to be on the court with you."

He laughed. "That's what I said to you when I won the Camp Holly Ridge tournament, isn't it?"

I nodded. "It was terribly sweet, if not slightly condescending."

"I don't want to beat you or lose to you anymore, Barbara. I want to be your partner, if you'll let me." Fortunately, I was already warm enough from the exercise that

I knew he couldn't see the blush rising up my cheeks. Goodness, the man was coming on strong. It pained me to admit that I had thought of him often these past sixty years, had wondered more than once what we could have had. But it made me feel unfaithful, ungrateful to my beloved husband. Reid had been a sure thing back then. Miles, with his big dreams, was new and exciting, which scared me a little. Or maybe the woman I became when I was with him all those years ago was what scared me. I couldn't be sure.

"Such a flirt," I said playfully.

"Not a flirt," he said back. "Most sincere. And at the risk of sounding like a high schooler, would you accompany me to the dance tonight?"

My heart fluttered dangerously, but then I remembered I already had plans. "Unfortunately, my girls are coming out here for dinner tonight."

"Unfortunately?"

I laughed. "Oh, that sounds awful. I positively adore them. It's not unfortunate, except that I know they're only coming to scold me for making this big decision without them—and that I can't go to the dance with you."

"Don't most people want their parents in places like this?" Miles asked. "Where they don't have to worry about them?"

"Exactly," I agreed. "That's what I said."

He stepped closer. Oh, my heart. It baffled me how feelings of nearly sixty years could just flood back like this. Maybe that's just what these were: memories of feelings. But, at my age, maybe memories were enough. "Tell you what. I'll meet you there early so we can get in a dance or two before the girls arrive."

"It would be an honor," he said. "Now, may I escort you home?"

I nodded, following Miles to his Carolina-blue golf cart.

"Did you feel like I do when you lost your wife, Miles?" I asked as I slid in the front seat beside him. "Like enjoying anyone's company, smiling, having a bright day is wrong? I want to dance with you tonight, and I already feel guilty about that."

Miles smiled sadly at me. "Oh, Barbara. You were in a loving, committed marriage. Of course it's going to be hard to take a step forward. But I know that Reid must have been a wonderful man for you to have chosen him over me." He winked and I laughed, feeling those butterflies again. "I think he would have wanted you to have a second act."

No one would ever be to me what my Reid was. He was the love of my life, now, then, and forever. But I know he would want me to be happy. "We talked about it every now and then, how we wanted each other to find happiness again if one of us left before the other," I said, voicing my thoughts. I paused. "But it's hard when you're the one left behind."

Miles took one hand off the wheel and reached over and squeezed my hand. I looked down, expecting to see the same soft, unlined hands I had had when he first held them. Instead, I saw two hands that were wrinkled, with pronounced veins and dark age spots. But they were hands that remembered. Hands that, maybe, could find solace in each other.

"Did you ever think of me over the years?" Miles asked, putting his eyes back on the road. "Not to be too forward, but I always wondered. I'd catch myself in these moments remembering you—your laugh, something you said—and I'd wonder if you ever thought of me too."

"All these years, Miles, I have always had a soft spot for you."

At eighty, when one has had and lost her great love, even the thought of a man that makes her come alive again is perhaps more than a woman should hope for. But hadn't it always been like this with Miles? Isn't this part of what had scared me about him?

"You still have one of the prettiest forehands I have ever seen," I said, trying to lighten the mood.

"And that serve of yours . . ." he replied.

We both laughed. Miles pulled in front of my house and walked around to my side of the cart to escort me to my door. "I'll see you tonight," he said, grinning broadly, making me feel like a kid again.

"I look forward to it."

He leaned down to kiss my cheek goodbye. "I'm so sweaty!" I protested. But I secretly loved every moment of his affection and attention toward me.

"You're perfect," he replied, taking me in. "I'll see you at six."

That evening, showered and fresh from the on-site beauty parlor, I hummed as I spritzed my neck with my favorite perfume, smiling at my reflection in the mirror. I mused that age had brought such perspective. In my youth, I would have lamented every line, scrutinized my waist, my legs, any spots I found. Now, sure, my face was wrinkled, my lovely figure long gone. But I was alive. I had lived eighty years on this earth, and even though my knees hurt, my elbow ached, and it took me a little longer to get around, I was still proud and grateful for every day. As I fastened a belt around the waistline of my favorite blue dress, I felt happy for a second chance.

I grabbed my small purse from the dresser after I slipped on my kitten heels, noticing the postcard I had received that morning. Sweet Julia. What grandmother worth her salt wouldn't jump at the opportunity to go on a trip with her beloved granddaughter? It was silly, but even though I was excited at the prospect of a getaway, part of me couldn't bear the thought of leaving Miles for what would be at least a weeklong trip, if not two. And it was certainly entirely too soon to ask him to go with me. Wasn't it?

Although, with Miles and me, hadn't these feelings always been hidden away like a set of fine china that you only pulled out every now and again? Were we simply making the decision to start using the fine china every day?

I walked into my small garage, opened the door, and backed out my pink golf cart. Yes, pink. When in her life does a woman get to have a pink golf cart? Miles and I had decided—via text—that I would meet him at the clubhouse so as not to raise any eyebrows with my girls about how I'd gotten there should they want to ride back to the town house with me after dinner.

When I pulled up to the clubhouse where the valet took my cart, Miles was waiting for me in a seersucker suit holding a single pink rose, which he handed to me. I smiled. "What a lovely gesture," I said.

"What a lovely woman," he replied.

I waved him away, but I couldn't have felt better.

The band was just cranking up, the dance floor empty, as we entered the building. I had forty minutes until the girls would arrive, and I planned to savor each of them in the arms of the man who made me feel so happy.

The first chords of "The Way You Look Tonight" began, and Miles took my hand, leading me to the dance floor. "But we'll be the only ones dancing," I whispered.

"Which is exactly how I want it," he responded, a glimmer in his eye.

As he led me around the dance floor, I couldn't help but feel like I had been transported back in time to the camp dance we'd gone to together all those years ago. It was nothing short of a miracle the way we still seemed to fit together.

"Has it really been sixty years since we've done this?" I asked in disbelief, as other couples followed our lead and joined us on the floor.

"Don't age us," Miles scolded.

We both laughed, and I realized I hadn't felt this happy in quite some time.

"How can this be?" I asked Miles. "How can it be that I can fall right back into the same feelings?" For the briefest of moments, I felt embarrassed I had said that out loud.

But then Miles said, "I think this is how it works. When you see someone you once had a connection with, you might have aged, but the connection hasn't. Some people simply belong together. As friends, or mentor and mentee, parent and child." He paused. "Or great loves."

I laughed. "Were we, Miles? Were we great loves?"

He smiled sadly. Miles and I had spent only that one summer together. Just three months as camp counselors. And, yes, we had written letters and had phone calls until I got engaged that winter. But I always knew we couldn't truly be together.

"It nearly broke me that you married Reid," Miles said after a moment of silence. "I think that's great love."

He squeezed my hand, and I sighed. "But marrying Reid was always the plan, Miles. I had dated him for years. I had feelings for you, sure—"

"But they weren't as strong as your feelings for Reid?"

How to answer his very complicated question. I was so lost in his arms, in the music, in this dance, in the feeling of what used to be between us, that a shocked "Mother! What *are* you doing?" made me jump.

I wanted to pretend that sentence was directed at someone else. But, alas, I'd know that voice anywhere. I turned to see Meredith and Alice, looking every bit the identical twins they were, arms crossed, glaring at me—identically.

"Girls, I'd like you to meet my friend Miles," I said sheepishly. "Miles, these are my daughters, Meredith and Alice."

"Twins," he said, shaking their hands warmly. "How delightful."

"How do you do?" Alice asked. Meredith smiled icily.

"You're early," I said dumbly, bracing myself for the smart response that might follow.

But Meredith only said, "We wanted to meet with the staff for a bit, but now that we're all here, we might as well eat."

"*All* of us?" Alice questioned.

"Well, we have a reservation for three," Meredith said stonily.

I could see Miles's face fall.

"I guess I could see if they could accommodate an

extra," Meredith said in a tone that *dared* Miles to take her up on that.

"No, no," he said. "I would never impose on a mother-daughter dinner. I know how important those are."

I'm sorry, I mouthed to him.

He smiled bravely. That was just like him, always trying to bolster my spirits even if it meant crushing his. We hadn't discussed any of this yet—meeting the family, what we were. For heaven's sake, we hadn't even had a proper kiss. I was making too big a thing of all this in my mind. But as I walked to the edge of the large room, to our table overlooking the ocean, I glanced back at Miles. I saw his pain and—what's more—his fear. Maybe I *was* jumping in too quickly; maybe I was diving in too deep. But when I saw his face, I realized I wasn't the only one.

JULIA

A Professional

I woke up to my phone beeping beside me and, as I sat up quickly, almost hit my head on the ceiling. It took me a second to come out of my dream (where I was rebuilding the Empire State Building) and back into the reality of being here, in the BVIs. What the guest rooms had in spades—elegance, light, air-conditioning—the screened bunkhouses did not. If I redesigned them, I would remove the faux ceilings and expose the wooden rafters, take down the outdoor awnings that blocked the light from coming in, and replace the old, torn screens. Easy, inexpensive fixes would make the whole place more appealing.

I looked down from my top bunk to see that Elise, who led "Sunrise Paddles," was gone. But Jackie and Nina, who were on lunch and dinner service today, were still sleeping. I felt sorry for Elise, who had to get up before all of us. I think we had gone to bed around two after a night of tons of laughter . . . and even more rum. Although it might have been three. But whatever time it was, these girls were fun. The guys too. It wasn't only the scenery that was pulling me out of my funk.

I lay back down on my mattress, which was roughly the thickness of a city phone book. I had to admit that, given my current conditions, I was partially glad I had only two more nights here. The resort was a place I never wanted to leave, but the cabins were far from idyllic.

What they lacked in amenities, though, they made up for in something the resort didn't have: Wi-Fi. It was spotty and slow but it existed, hence my ability to send and receive text messages. Although I was usually grateful for this, it also meant I got messages I'd rather not see.

Hayes: Where the hell are you?

I sighed. Why did he care? I thought I had washed my hands of him when we said our last goodbyes. But, as his text indicated, if he wanted to know where I was, perhaps Hayes still had some hope. I thought about not responding but decided that was immature.

Still in the islands. Never return, remember?

For real? You're staying there?

I looked down at the concrete floor below my bunk. Just a few more days.

Ah. Good luck with it, Jules. I just wanted to make sure you were okay since I hadn't heard from you.

Was I okay? I was a little hungover. But otherwise, yup. I felt pretty okay.

Are you okay? I asked.

Sure. Just need to talk to you, but I know you don't have service there. I'd rather it be in person, but if it can't, call me when you can.

I sighed heavily again. Did he want me back? Had our breakup been less final on his end? Well, if that was the case, I'd deal with that when I left. For now, two more days in paradise. I sat up again, scrunching my neck so as not to hit the low ceiling. Well, okay . . . Paradise-ish.

I laughed as a text from Sarah came in. I hate how tan you are.

I haven't posted any pictures.

Sarah: But I just KNOW.

I missed her so much. We'd been texting like crazy, but I couldn't wait to actually talk to her in person and give her a big hug.

I climbed down the rough ladder, my feet hitting the polished concrete floor. The warm breeze blew through the screens. The weather here generally seemed to be a perfect 84 degrees with blue skies as far as the eye could see.

I rinsed off quickly in the shower with the plastic floor grate and moldy curtain that smelled vaguely of mildew. It gave me the creeps and, not knowing that I'd be staying here so long, I hadn't packed shower shoes. I had to push away thoughts of foot fungus at least twice a day. I brushed my teeth in the small sink, which had rust around the drain, and hastily pulled my hair back to complete my morning routine. Makeup felt like something from my old life, where I wasn't savagely tan and my day didn't revolve around how many times I could dive into the surf.

The walk down to the beach was about three times as long as it was from the resort, but that certainly wasn't something to complain about. It was an island paradise, and it gave me time to think. Only, what I had been thinking about seemed too big, too scary to actually put into action. So maybe that thinking time wasn't so great after all.

As the thatch-roofed water center came into view, I saw Trav. I waved and he waved back, pulling paddleboards out of their storage cubbies. It was really my job. But I got the feeling that Trav thought I was too prissy for manual labor. Let's just say I didn't give him any cause to think otherwise.

"Thank you so much for getting those," I said as I reached him.

He rolled his eyes. "Little thing like you. I don't know how you'd lift them."

I just smiled wordlessly. He knew I could lift them.

"You have a private lesson today," he said.

"No class?" I asked.

He shook his head. "And since tomorrow's your day off, this is it for you, kid."

"Do I get paid more for my private lesson?" I teased, since I was getting paid nothing.

"You could practically max out your 401k," he teased back.

I was kind of surprised that Trav knew what a 401k was. "Are you going to miss me when I leave?" I asked.

He grinned at me. "The islands bring us when we need them, and they send us home when we are ready to go."

"I don't feel ready to go," I said, pouting.

"You can't argue with the islands." He cupped my chin in his hand. "I bet you're more ready than you think."

Out of the corner of my eye, I saw a familiar figure walking up the dock. It couldn't be. But it was. My entire body tensed. Conner.

"Who's that good-looking yoga instructor?" he asked as he got closer.

Trav looked at me protectively with a questioning eye. I nodded inconspicuously. This wasn't some creepy guest he needed to intervene with on my behalf. This was adorable Conner. I felt a little nervous at seeing him for the first time in a couple weeks.

"I want to ignore the fiancé in the room but . . ." he said as he reached us. I could tell he was nervous too, which, strangely, made me feel better.

I laughed. "He's gone," I said. "I was actually having a closure breakfast with him that morning when you saw us. I sort of thought I'd never see you again."

He scoffed. "Conner Howard doesn't walk away from a challenge." He smiled at me.

"Don't talk about yourself in third person, please. It's super creepy."

He nodded. "Duly noted."

I could feel both our nerves melting away. "How has the rest of your trip been?"

He shrugged. "Good. Fun. Less fun than when you were with me?" he said hesitantly.

That was when I finally relaxed. Our dynamic was back. "Same," I said. Then I paused. "Wait. How did you know I was here?"

He smiled. "Well, my parents stayed here for a couple nights before they went home, and my mom was going on and on about this paddleboard yoga instructor she thought was so cute and who was going to finish architecture school." He raised his eyebrow.

I laughed, remembering the petite lady with the kind eyes who had really wowed me with her balance. "That was your mom?"

"It sure was. You're going to finish your professional degree?"

"I like trying things out on strangers, but, yeah, I'm thinking about it."

He grinned proudly. "I took a leap of faith that maybe it was you, that maybe you hadn't gotten back with that guy, and that maybe, just maybe, you were still here."

I nodded. "That's a lot of leaps."

He locked his eyes on mine. "You are worth it." He paused. "Hey, want to go have an opening breakfast?"

"An opening breakfast?"

"Yeah, you know. Like the opposite of your breakfast with Hayes."

I laughed. "I wish I could, but I have a private lesson."

He pointed at himself. "Me. I'm your private lesson."

I smiled. I had hoped that was the case. "Well then, let's get out there."

"I'd really rather just go eat breakfast if it's all the same to you."

I leaned down and struggled to pick up one of the paddleboards under my arm. "Can't sneak off on the job. Grab a board and an anchor and follow me!"

Trav looked amused.

I began paddling off into a secluded spot that was deep enough that if Conner fell—which, let's face it, he was going to—he wouldn't hit the bottom.

I looked back to see him following me, shakily. I smiled and dropped my anchor, motioning for him to come up beside me. He knocked his board into mine. "Conner, we can't do yoga this close together," I laughed as he dropped his anchor.

"No?" he asked innocently, turning to square up his body with mine and running his free hand down my cheek. He put his hand on my waist, tentatively, and suddenly, my butterflies had butterflies. I moved to wrap my paddle-free arm around his neck, and when I did, my board tipped, knocking us both off our precarious balance and into the cold water.

"You're supposed to be a professional," Conner said, laughing, as he came back to the surface. Our paddles were floating nearby, and I swam to Conner and held on. This time, I wrapped my arms around him and kissed him. He brushed my wet hair off my forehead and kissed me a second time. "Hi," he whispered.

"Hi." I smiled.

"How about you come back to my boat with me?"

I nodded, climbing back on top of my paddleboard. "We can take these over. Trav won't mind."

I let Conner get up ahead. I was so surprised to see him again that I was practically floating on air. But I was also already dreading having to say goodbye. I adored him.

He helped me onto the boat, and I kneeled to lift my paddleboard onto the deck. Conner pulled me up, and wrapping me in his warm embrace, kissed me again. It felt so good to have his skin on mine. He tasted of seawater and smelled just a little bit earthy and real, which I found intoxicating.

As we kissed, I felt him pull the ties on my bikini top with a practiced hand. "Oops," he whispered as it fell.

"Conner," I scolded.

"The staff has the morning off," he said.

"Someone will see!" I protested.

He took a step back to admire my toplessness and said, "Well, then, we'd better get you inside."

He pressed the button to open the sealed door and we stepped inside, the door closing behind us. In a matter of seconds, my body was pressed against the glass, his hands in my hair, and suddenly, any proclamation of

not seeing him again felt impossible, silly. As the string
on my bikini bottom gave way, I forgot that Hayes was
the only person I had ever slept with, and that maybe I
should be nervous about what that meant. I forgot about
the girl I had been with him for all those years. Today,
right now, I was a woman.

CORNELIA

A Vanderbilt

April 29, 1924

If Cornelia was honest with herself, she knew she'd fallen in love with Jack partly because of his English accent. But was that so wrong, really? She knew plenty of girls who had fallen in love with a man because of his money or his title, his family or his connections. Although Jack did have all those other bright, shining qualities, everyone knew that Cornelia, who was widely regarded as America's wealthiest woman, didn't need any of them.

Cornelia had never thought of herself as the type of woman to be caught up in a whirlwind romance. But Jack had changed everything. He understood her. He took care of her but also knew when she needed to take care of herself. Not a month ago, he had announced, on one of their daily long and rambling walks, "Connie, I've decided to leave my post."

Jack was the first secretary of the British Embassy in Washington, D.C.

Cornelia was shocked. In their strolls around Washington—solving the world's problems, as it were— they had daydreamed about leaving it all behind, about trading newspapers and political functions for the serenity of Asheville. She hadn't believed it would actually happen.

"Jack," she argued, "you love your post. You can't give that up."

"I can't be happy without you, my dear," he replied. "And you cannot be happy without Biltmore."

She slipped her hand in his. How true it was. Biltmore was Cornelia's playground, her birthplace, her birthright. It had always been her safe haven from the insatiable eyes of the press that, whether she was in New York or Washington, Newport or Maine, seemed determined to eat her alive. Most of all, it was her remaining connection to the father who had loved her above anyone or anything else—even the dream home he had created in the Blue Ridge Mountains.

"What will you do there?" Cornelia asked hesitantly.

Jack looked over at her, never slowing his pace, matching her step for step as they kept their heart rates up, warming themselves against the chilly March air. "I'll manage the farm, oversee the dairy. I'll work with your mother and the lawyers and the estate managers and superintendents to ensure that Biltmore lives to see another generation." He paused. "And what about you? What do you dream of when you think of our lives at Biltmore?"

"Art, maybe. Motherhood, perhaps?"

Jack stopped walking and pulled his future bride close, kissing her for all the world to see.

"Motherhood will suit you quite nicely," he said. "I am sure of it."

Looking at her reflection now, on her wedding day, Cornelia smiled, thinking about what a wonderful father Jack would be. She believed in her heart that he would be almost as good as her own father.

"He would have loved to walk you down the aisle," Edith said, appearing behind her in the large gilt Louis XV mirror, speaking almost as if she could hear what her daughter was thinking. Edith and Cornelia had spent months renovating many of Biltmore's spaces in preparation for the wedding, ensuring their family and more prominent guests would have places to stay. On Cornelia's wedding day, there were certainly plenty of spaces to choose from to dress. But Edith's lushly appointed room was large enough to hold both the bridesmaids and her aunts. Plus, Cornelia loved imagining her father having this room outfitted for her mother, George seeing Edith in every marble-topped commode, plush chaise, and the Pierre-Philippe Barat clock on the mantel. She only hoped that Jack thought of her in the same way.

Her father was so prominent and so present in her thoughts that Cornelia felt as if he *could* see her now. Plus, he was in all the details here. Darling Jack had proposed to her on the anniversary of her father's death, hoping to give her a happy memory of that day to help balance the devastatingly sad one. Last night, her mother had presented her a gift, a framed photograph of her father that sat on the dressing room table now. He was wearing his dinner jacket and black tie, hold-

ing an infant Cornelia swathed in her long white christening gown. They were on the loggia at Biltmore, and
her father's ink-black hair, slightly askew, indicated a
windy day.

He was looking at Cornelia in the photo like she was
the only person on earth who mattered, looking at her
in the way that every father—even one with everything
in the world at his fingertips—should look at his baby
girl.

"No man has ever loved a little girl the way that
George loved you, Nell," her aunt Pauline interjected.

"What?" Aunt Susan protested. "I believe Daddy loved
us as much as George loved our Cornelia."

Edith rolled her eyes good-naturedly at Cornelia.
The Dresser girls, as they would always and forever be
known, were Cornelia's favorite relatives.

"I don't know . . ." Natalie chimed in, her tone light.

"Isn't it strange that none of us had our wonderful
fathers with us on our wedding days?" Pauline asked her
family.

The morning sun streamed through Edith's bedroom
window, and it was only as Cornelia caught the eye of
Bunchy, her maid of honor—who was lounging on a
gold-and-purple-covered chaise—that she realized she
was a little tired. The pair had stayed up entirely too
late the night before. Among the topics of conversation?
How Cornelia should use the marabou throw her friend
had given her as a wedding gift, along with a crepe de
chine negligee and lace sheets and pillowcases.

"Lady Cecil," Bunchy teased, standing now. "How do
I look?"

Cornelia grinned broadly at her friend. "You know
Jack is the third son. I'll never have a silly title." She

rotated her finger, indicating that Bunchy, in her white organdy gown with full sleeves, should turn. She did so, giggling merrily. She was lovely. But not as lovely as Cornelia, in her simple straight gown of white satin and lace, her cropped hair perfectly styled. But the outfit mattered little. It would be covered by the pièce de résistance: her family wedding veil.

The door opened and Emma, Edith's lady's maid, entered. When she saw Cornelia, she put her hands to her mouth. "You are beautiful." She paused. "But Mrs. Donahue is going to have a coronary if you don't go down and have your picture made."

They all laughed. Mrs. Donahue was the head housekeeper and in charge of, well, everything. There was no doubt she had been the one to orchestrate the unforgettable serenade that the workers had arranged for Cornelia and Jack the evening before. They had gathered on the lawn with lights and lanterns, noisemakers and whistles. Cornelia ran out the door gaily to greet the terrific noise. She couldn't think of a better way to celebrate her impending nuptials.

As Cornelia stood to head downstairs, her mother protested, "No, darling! Not yet!"

"You are forgetting the most important thing!" Pauline added.

"Isn't the groom the most important thing?" Bunchy quipped.

"Not when you have a wedding veil like this," Susan said.

Cornelia was quite tall, but her mother was taller. She placed the four yards of tulle and Brussels rose point lace, adorned with Florida orange blossoms for the occasion—a nod to Edith's own wedding—on her daughter's hair. Cornelia smiled down at her satin wedding slippers, which were also each adorned with a single orange blossom. Her father's close friend and trusted advisor Chauncey Beadle, who had brought so much of Biltmore to life, had gifted them to her from his own supply for the occasion.

Bunchy handed the bride her bouquet of orchids and lilies of the valley, from local Middlemount Gardens. Cornelia had insisted that everything be from Asheville, or, barring that option, as near Asheville as possible. The one point on which her mother had not conceded was the wedding cake, which was brought in from Washington, D.C. Upon seeing the layers of perfectly white, fluffy frosting, Cornelia had to admit that this was a case of mother knowing best.

"You have never been lovelier," Edith said, adjusting the veil around her daughter's shoulders and face.

"You have never been lovelier either," Cornelia said. And she meant it. Her mother, in her gown of pale green and gold crepe de chine, was known as much for her kind heart, brilliance, and generosity, as for her impeccable sense of style. Her mother really could put together an outfit, choose an accessory, or place a hat in the way that was most flattering. It didn't hurt that, with her tall and slender build, everything looked particularly spectacular on her. Cornelia was grateful to have inherited her mother's figure, especially since she loved sweets so much.

In a bustle of tulle and silk, the bridal party made their way down the grand staircase. Bunchy held Cornelia's arm, her mother holding the train of her dress and length of the veil behind her so as not to wrinkle them. As the party moved out of the way Cornelia paused at the bottom of the steps, veil arranged all around her, bouquet cascading nearly to her knees, for the photographer to snap and snap.

"Smile, lovely bride!" the photographer called as Cornelia leaned against the wall at the bottom of the grand limestone stairs.

"Just imagine All Souls draped in flowers and bathed in candlelight," her mother said from where she stood behind the photographer, taking in her beautiful daughter. All Souls Church was as near to George's heart as any project he had ever undertaken. Designed by close family friend Richard Morris Hunt out of the same red brick, pebble dash stucco, and timber trim as so many of his other buildings, it was truly a work of George's heart, aptly named since it was his wish to bring all the souls in the Asheville community together. But if it was George who had begun that mission, it was his wife and daughter who had truly carried it out.

"Imagine the church? Just think of your handsome groom smiling from the end of the aisle!" Bunchy chimed in.

Cornelia smiled, thinking of her fiancé. "Oh, he'll look handsome," Edith said as the photographer snapped away. "But you, my dear, are simply breathtaking."

After a dozen or so more photos, Mrs. Donahue appeared at the top of the stairs. "All right, all right," she said, scolding. "That's enough or we are going to be late." Cornelia, for one, was relieved. But before she could get out the door, she wondered what it would be like to return to this house—which some would say was too large to ever be a home but was, undoubtedly, for Cornelia—as a Cecil.

A lump formed in her throat at the thought. Before

the lump could turn to tears, her mother helped her out the door, and Cornelia gasped at the sight of Old Frank, Biltmore's longtime gatekeeper, on the esplanade, in a brand-new coat—a wedding gift from her mother—and a jaunty top hat. "Frank!" she declared. "You are more than dashing! Aren't you every bit the gentleman?" As he reached her, she leaned down to kiss him on the cheek, much to his delight.

Frank dabbed his eyes with a handkerchief. "Our little Nell is all grown up." Frank had been on the estate even longer than Cornelia and doted on her like a kind uncle or close family friend; he had played games in the garden with her when she was a child. Remembering the jacks he always kept in his pocket for days that seemed to stretch too long, she squeezed his arm just as Mrs. Donahue began shooing her to the car.

"That car is for you and *your* bride, Frank," Edith said, pointing to the fifth car in line.

"For us?" Frank gasped.

Dear Frank was overcome with joy.

Bunchy and Edith squeezed in beside Cornelia in the back seat, taking care not to crush her dress or veil. Cornelia regretted that her friend Rose wouldn't be beside her as she stood at the altar. But Rose was pregnant and couldn't very well be expected to stand. Still, she would be sitting in a reserved seat near the front where her friend could see her, and in some ways, that was almost better. Mr. Plemmons, the driver and family friend, turned and winked at the bride. "Am I getting you to the church on time or driving the getaway car?"

Bunchy laughed delightedly. "Bite your tongue!" Edith exclaimed.

Cornelia smiled at Mr. Plemmons, thinking that this

had almost been the perfect day so far. She had never expected something like this, something so wonderful, to happen to her. She had fallen head over heels in love with Jack Cecil. She might even go so far as to call it love at first sight. But, in spite of her joy, a part of her was nervous about the changes marriage might bring.

All she could think about as they drove away was that, yes, she was destined to become the next mistress of Biltmore. But, in a matter of hours, never again would she walk through the door of her home as a Vanderbilt.

JULIA

Permission

After a day of sunning on the deck, swimming in the sea, and laughing together, I told Conner that I needed to get back to the bunk room. He rolled over on top of me. "There is absolutely no way I'm letting you go, Julia. No way."

I sighed and lay back, the sand feeling warm against my neck and upper back, the water cool on my feet. We were lying in the shallows of a nearby, unnamed island, and truthfully, I couldn't imagine going back to my dank, spartan bunk room when the luxury of the yacht was a possibility. "Tomorrow is technically my day off," I said sleepily.

"Your last day is your day off?" He laughed. "Then you must stay with me," Conner said, kissing my neck, burying his face in my hair.

I nodded. I would have said yes to anything he wanted from me at that moment.

He propped himself up on his elbows and looked down at me. "I want to picture what you'll be doing when you get back home. What are your plans? Will you really go back to school?"

I smiled. He was so sweet. "Well, my grandmother has this charming stone mountain cabin that looks like it came out of 'Hansel and Gretel.' I'm going to go there to get my ducks in a row." I paused and bit my lip. Saying this next part was going to make it real. "And after that, I've decided: if they'll let me, I'm going to go back and finish."

Conner smiled. "That's fantastic news!"

"Yes, but . . ."

"But what?"

I sighed. "What if they won't let me back in?"

He peered down at me intently. "I'm not sure I can help you unpack that problem unless you tell me why you quit in the first place."

I had never told the whole story to anyone but Sarah because, in my heart, it felt so heavy, so big. But here, on the sand with the sun streaming down, I realized that maybe it wasn't. There were trillions of grains of sand on this little stretch of beach. My little problem suddenly seemed small, insignificant.

"I feel really dumb because it isn't going to sound like a big deal," I began. "But when it happened, it felt like it was the end of the world." I paused. Conner was quiet, waiting. I knew I wasn't getting out of telling him this time.

He rolled back over, lying next to me on the sand. "I won't look at you while you say it. That will help."

"I guess," I said, looking up at the sky. "I was working on my final project for my second semester of my professional degree. I had already had my site plan approved, so I wasn't even really that worried about it."

"Okay. I'm tracking."

"Do you know who Alex Winchester is?"

Conner laughed. "Um, yeah. Obviously. Basically the master of small-space living as we know it."

"It is really something to find someone who is the same kind of super nerd as you."

He laughed and turned on his side, rubbing his thumb down my cheek. "It is. I just never imagined that she would be quite so beautiful and captivating."

I could feel myself blushing as he leaned forward to kiss me.

"So, Alex Winchester." Conner turned back to face the sky.

I nodded. "I really wanted to challenge myself on the project—and, honestly, I wanted to impress Professor Winchester—so I decided to go way above and beyond. I talked to my grandmother for inspiration, and after doing a lot of research, I eventually drew this graduated living community that was very different from anything else I'd seen. It was green and sustainable and arranged in these sort of pods . . ." I trailed off, feeling sick just thinking about it. "It's kind of hard to explain, but I was so proud of it. I'm embarrassed to say that I daydreamed about the praise, how excited everyone would be by my innovative idea."

"And?"

"And, evidently, the idea was impractical, expensive, and if I was ever going to make it as an architect, I was going to have to learn to follow the rules. Professor

Winchester told me that, if that project was any indication, I would never make it as an architect." I said this
part fast, so the pain couldn't touch me, so I couldn't feel
the sheer humiliation of being told by one of my heroes
that I wasn't good enough.

Maybe other people's opinions shouldn't matter that
much. But Professor Winchester's, who was not only an
expert but also the one signing off on my thesis project,
mattered quite a lot.

Conner put his hand on my bare stomach and, still
not looking at me, said, "Damn, that's harsh."

"I had dreamed of this one thing my entire life, and I
let one person's opinion break me. I was going to fail the
class because I didn't have time to start over on a new
project. I couldn't stand the thought of having to repeat
it, of not graduating on time."

"So you just left?"

I put my hands under my head. "Yeah. And want to
know the craziest part?"

"There's more?"

"The day before I had been feeling so confident, so
sure of myself, that I had finally freed myself of Hayes. I
had called off our engagement. And then this happened,
and I was so freaked out, I ran right back to him." I
paused. "I think you know the rest of the story."

We lay there in silence for a moment, gazing into the
impossibly blue sky before Conner asked, "Can I look
at you now?"

"Yeah." My voice seemed small. I felt small. I wanted
to be tough and brave and the kind of woman that Professor Winchester couldn't intimidate. But it was hard,
and I was soft inside.

"I'm not an expert or anything, but I can tell you, one

hundred percent for sure, that not only is breaking the rules a big part of architecture but so is criticism."

I was expecting something warmer, fuzzier. Something like, *That professor is an idiot and you are amazing.*

"Architecture is invention, it's collaborative," Conner continued. "Sometimes it works. Sometimes it doesn't. And if you're going to be inside of it, you are going to have to be willing to fail and fail and fail, to know that for every win there are going to be a dozen losses."

He sat up now and turned to me. "Jules, I hate to say it, but that professor prepared you for this job in a way that an easy A never could have." He paused. "If I had to guess, this was a test. And I hate to tell you, my friend, but you failed."

I was a girl who had been raised to win, to succeed. Hearing Conner's proclamation now that failure was just a part of the process was a perspective I'd never considered before.

"You need to go back, Julia. You need to finish. You're a great paddleboard yoga teacher"—he winked at me—"but I think you have a bigger mark to make on the world."

I laughed then. Because I obviously knew I had been wasting time all these months. I knew that I had been ignoring the feeling deep in my heart about wanting to go back to school. And maybe, now, I was finally at a point where I didn't have anything to lose. I needed to try again, and, if I had to, fail again. I knew I shouldn't need anyone's permission, but well, I couldn't be expected to learn the hard lessons all at once, could I? Conner's guidance felt like the permission I needed.

He smiled. "If anyone ever tells you again that architecture is about rules, send them to Garrison Towers."

He looked over at me. "Tell you what: I'll help you. We'll get those plans up to snuff, and you'll roar back into that school. They won't be able to tell you no."

Was this what a real relationship was? Did grown-up couples push each other to be their best, not just let each other sink into what was comfortable? It made me realize that what I had had with Hayes wasn't grown-up.

And now, against all odds, I didn't want to delete my CAD drawings anymore. In fact, I couldn't wait to share them with Conner. I looked around at the perfect cerulean stillness surrounding me. I would miss the sun and waves, but I had a bigger purpose. I had more to do. And it shocked me to realize that I couldn't wait to get home.

A Line in the Sand

July 27, 1925

E dith's fishing line made a satisfying hiss as she cast it way out into the river, her fly landing with barely a ripple. She looked over at her daughter's placid, lovely face.

"Are you sure, Mother?" Cornelia asked again, her line hissing as well. "Positively sure? Being the first female president has meant so much to you."

Being the first female president of the North Carolina Agricultural Society for the past five years *had* meant so much to Edith, more than she could ever convey to her daughter. "I have truly savored and enjoyed every moment I have held the position," Edith said. "But it's time to move on."

She didn't want to sound conceited, but being the president of the association meant she had become a successful farmer—that she had, at least in part, been able to salvage her late husband's legacy. With the help of her beloved son-in-law, Jack, and her friend and confidant Judge Junius Adams, she had managed to turn the thousands of acres surrounding Biltmore into a working farm that, if it didn't completely sustain the property, certainly helped.

Edith looked over at her daughter, her fishing pants tucked into waders and a belted jacket over her crisp white shirt. It was like looking in the mirror. The only thing that could have made this quiet morning better would be if George was there. But, then again, Edith was feeling particularly nostalgic today. "Do you know I would never have done any of this without your father? Even in his death, he helped me grow into the woman I was meant to be."

Cornelia smiled.

Edith, the little girl who had grown up in Newport surrounded by pets, was now the mistress of champion dairy cows, award-winning Berkshire hogs, and blue-ribbon sheep. She had spent years revamping the North Carolina State Fair, attending county fairs, creating agricultural clubs for boys and girls, and making speeches both in person and over the radio.

Many who had heard that Edith was retiring from her post simply believed she was tired. Those people were wrong. On the contrary, Edith had her eye on a bigger political prize. She would be taking to the campaign trail with Senator Peter Gerry as his most important aide and confidante: his wife.

Whenever she felt afraid of this new step she was taking, Edith would remember what the *Charlotte Observer* said about her first speech as president, the one she had feared so violently that her hands shook and her voice wavered. She had walked off the podium feeling exhausted but proud—and not altogether sure of how she had done. But it had been deemed "the smartest 15-minute speech to a joint session of the general assembly heard within the historic walls of the state house in a long time."

She had faced her fear then; she would face her fear now—even if it was of a slightly different kind.

"Darling," Edith said, turning to her daughter. "I need to talk to you."

Edith had wondered if she would ever be ready to move forward, to let another man take the place that had once been occupied by George. But, on Cornelia's wedding day, something had happened to Edith, something shifted. As she'd placed the family veil on her daughter's head, Edith felt as strongly and truly as she ever had that she was passing the torch. For so many years, the care and keeping of Cornelia had been Edith's responsibility. But now, with the passing of an heirloom, she felt she could pull back from that. Cornelia was a grown woman with her own family now. Next month, on her twenty-fifth birthday, Cornelia would inherit Biltmore and receive the money that would make its upkeep in its original fashion possible. Edith knew that it was time for her to think about what would make *her* happy again.

"Are you all right, Mother?" Cornelia asked, a hint of nervousness in her voice.

"I am wonderful, my dear. Positively wonderful. I am a *grandmother*, for heaven's sake, the greatest of all rites of passage." She paused, casting the line again with a practiced flick of the wrist.

She smiled, thinking of her news, of Peter Gerry,

of how he had asked so many questions about her life here at Biltmore. Edith had known Peter and his wife, Mathilde, for many, many years, their paths crossing often during her life in Washington. They were a dynamic duo, a Washington power couple. Peter, the handsome senator, was the great-grandson of Elbridge Gerry, a signer of the Declaration of Independence, and Mathilde had inherited one of America's most outrageous railroad fortunes—and, if the rumors were to be believed, tempers.

Edith had never seen that side of Mathilde, but she knew she could be quite competitive. She tried to stay out of society gossip, but even Edith couldn't help but be amused when the word around town was that Mathilde had purchased a strand of black pearls belonging to the Prince of Russia to supposedly keep up with her friend and competitor Evalyn McLean, who had purchased the Hope Diamond. The pearls were said to be ill-fated, and Edith had heard whispers that the marriage of Mathilde and Peter was no more. Because of the pearls, many said. Others believed the split was due to the arguing. Edith had seen enough in her life to believe that perhaps both were true.

She hadn't expected to get more information as close to the source as she did that January. Edith had been anticipating this particular speech in Memorial Continental Hall for days. Helen Keller was set to address a benefit for the American Foundation for the Blind, a worthy cause in which Edith was quite interested. She walked inside the beautiful building, noting that its embellished balconies were already full of well-heeled society women—and a few men. She pulled her fur-trimmed coat tighter around her to stave off the chill of the evening and, looking around to find her group, felt a touch on her arm.

She turned and found herself, an instant later, embracing her friend Peter Gerry.

"Edith!" he said, pulling back from her. "It has been too long. You look sensational."

She smiled demurely. "You too. I'm so glad to see you." Then she remembered her friend's recent misfortune. "I'm so sorry, Peter," she said. "Are the rumors true?"

He smiled. "They are. But why should you be sorry? I'm certainly not."

She put a gloved hand to her mouth to cover her laugh. "Mathilde is a perfectly lovely woman."

"Yes, yes. Perfectly lovely until she doesn't get her way . . . But I wish her well and all of the appropriate things."

Edith smiled. "Well, I should be off to find my friends—"

"Shall we sit together?" Peter interrupted.

She glanced over his shoulder, spotting her usual group, but decided her companions would be all right without her. Besides, Peter had always been a good friend and she hated the idea of him being there alone. Although, as handsome as he was in his three-piece suit, she couldn't imagine his being alone for long.

"Does the town know?" he whispered as they sat down among the throngs of other participants. Even at six feet tall, Edith had to adjust her position to see over the hat of the woman in front of her.

"Know what?"

"That Mathilde is Sumner Welles's problem now?"

Edith gasped.

"Then I take that as a no."

Sumner was Caroline Astor's grandnephew, a well-heeled member of the State Department who ran in their circles. Peter was being flippant, but Edith knew the betrayal must have stung. "Oh, you know those Astors. Always up to no good," she joked, hoping to lessen the blow he must have been feeling.

"President Coolidge reportedly is very unhappy about the match," Peter said. "There is even talk of Sumner being stripped of his diplomatic career, so perhaps all's well that ends well." He winked.

Edith studied him, deciding whether this could be true, but he only nodded. She had no reason to doubt him. It was only then that she added, "On that note, I hope us sitting together doesn't cause any rumors."

He smiled at her and clasped her hand. "Oh, I certainly hope it does." He paused. "Better yet, let's make the rumors true!"

Edith smirked. She had plenty of wealthy, handsome suitors, that was for certain. But none quite so young. Peter was, after all, almost seven years her junior. She was certain that the mere sight of her here with Peter would cause a flurry of gossip column stories in the following days. "Peter. Be serious."

"I am serious. Why not let me take you to dinner?"

She shook her head.

"I have some difficult decisions coming up in the Senate, and I'd love your opinion."

She was warming to this idea.

"Who do you have a better time discussing politics with than me?" he added.

She smiled. That was true. And things with Peter were easy. They were comfortable. She trusted him.

"What's your take on allowing Count Károlyi to make speeches while he's in the US?" she asked. It was a small but contentious matter of debate whether the former president of the Hungarian Republic should be able to speak freely about his controversial politics while on US soil.

Peter put his finger up. "I'll tell you tomorrow. At dinner."

Truly, deep in her heart, Edith had not imagined then that this simple interaction would be the start of something so important. But Peter was not only a brilliant man, he was a kind one. She adored him, and he reciprocated. They had the same goals. They could make a difference in the world. And, after Mathilde married Sumner in June, she was out of excuses to push him away. Her other suitors were wonderful. But Peter Gerry wowed her.

Even still, she couldn't help but feel slightly conflicted when she confessed to her daughter, "I, Nelly, am getting married."

She had meant to say "am in love." But she couldn't quite bring herself to. Did she love Senator Peter Gerry? She felt quite certain she did. She loved his political views. And his social graces. She loved how he loved her, how he leaned on her and valued her opinion. The other men she had dated since the death of George—Governor Morrison, General Pershing, General Carr—certainly noticed that she was a political and financial asset, despite large fortunes of their own. But they didn't value her opinion. Not really. Peter, on the other hand, was her true equal in every sense of the word, and he praised her for her finely tuned intellect and political instincts, for the way she could relate to women from all backgrounds. If that wasn't love—at least the type she wanted in her second marriage—she wasn't sure what was.

Cornelia laughed. "Well, this is quite a surprise." She paused. "But you know how I've always loved Peter." Cornelia had known the senator for years, a fact that Edith hoped would help ease this transition for her daughter.

She nodded. "The wedding won't be for a little while. So please, please don't breathe a word of it. We're planning to do it in London, out of the eyes of the press, with just our families and close friends." Edith looked her daughter in the eye, her nerves catching up to her. "I need you there, Nell. Please say you'll be there."

Cornelia smiled sympathetically. "Of *course* I'll be there, Mother. I adore Peter. You know I think he is a perfect match for you." She reached over and squeezed Edith's hand. "Albeit a little young," she added, under her breath.

Edith cried out in consternation and Cornelia laughed. Her mother had been overly worried about the few-year age gap between herself and the senator. Cornelia began reeling in her line. "We should get a move on. We have work to do!"

"The wedding isn't for a time, dear girl. Didn't you hear? And it's barely an event. No plans needed."

"We need to dedicate a new room at Biltmore to you and Peter. We'll spruce it up a little, make it fresh."

"No, no. Peter and I have plans to build a new home in Biltmore Forest." The very idea of moving into Biltmore with a new man made Edith queasy. The house was George's first love, and when she was inside it, she was his wife. Edith couldn't abide the thought of sharing a bedroom with another man under that roof. When she had told Peter, he had been supportive, agreeing to build a new house so they could start fresh in a new place. The creation of Biltmore Forest, the sale of the tract of land on what had become Vanderbilt Road, had been yet one more way in which Edith had managed to keep Biltmore House running.

Cornelia balked. "Mother, we have two hundred and fifty rooms, many of which are falling apart and in desperate need of an infusion of capital, and you want to put your money into something new? I thought we were on the same team here. I thought we wanted to save Biltmore at all costs."

"Not at the cost of your father's memory and dignity," Edith snapped.

"You're being hysterical. It's the 1920s, for God's sake. Women remarry all the time. You aren't dancing on his grave about it."

Edith peered at her daughter. "How can you not see that moving into Biltmore is precisely what that would be?"

———

Hours later, when the house was silent and all were asleep, after the anger had worn off and mother and daughter had made up, agreeing that the process of building a new Mediterranean stucco mansion would be quite the project, Edith did the thing she had been dreading most: She ventured to the library. She had to tell George.

Her rational mind found this exercise inane and potentially crazy. But her heart found it necessary. She had been trying mightily to quit smoking as of late. Peter didn't like it, and she had to admit that, sometimes, her lungs felt a little full. But, back in the library, she couldn't help herself. She removed the cloth covering her usual chair and end table, sat down by the fireplace, and rested her sterling cigarette case on the end table. The bachelors' wing had been the real living space of Biltmore for so long now that she could scarcely remember what it was like for the main house to be her home. She removed a cigarette and lit it, inhaling deeply, her frazzled nerves calming.

"Ah, my dear, will you never learn?" The voice came almost immediately.

"Hello, George," she whispered, exhaling the smoke that felt smooth and calming after an entire day without it. She looked around the library. "George, can you believe it? Can you imagine that our baby girl is going to be the rightful owner of Biltmore in just a few weeks?"

The voice—which she could still never be quite sure was George's or her own—replied, "I remember holding her for the first time like it was yesterday."

Edith smiled and felt herself relax. Cornelia would be twenty-five. The house would be hers. The money George had left would be hers. Their troubles would finally be over. But that wasn't why she was here. Edith cleared her throat.

"My dear George, I've come to give you some news," Edith said quietly.

There was no reply so she responded quickly, before she lost her nerve. "You know you are my great love, the father of my girl, my one and only. But the time has come for me, George. With Cornelia married and Biltmore's fate all but sealed, I need to move forward. I want to make changes in the world."

Edith paused, tears coming to her eyes. She whispered, "I want to get married."

"Then I wish you well" was the instant response. She wasn't sure what she had expected. An argument? An insult?

"You were the best husband a woman could ever ask for, George. Kind and loving, warm and generous, brilliant and thoughtful. I will never, ever forget you. Not for a day, not for a moment." It was true. Eleven years had passed since she had lost George and, for Edith, he was still the one who made her heart happiest.

"I loved you wholeheartedly, Edi. But I see that the time has come for us to part ways. I wish you well and send you all the love and luck in my heart." There was a long pause. And then came the end. "Goodbye, dearest wife."

Just like that, the silence was so thick, so deafening, that Edith wondered if she'd lost her hearing. Only the sound of her puff on the cigarette in her hand let her know that her senses were still intact. She snubbed the cigarette forcefully into the ashtray. She knew that it was her last one. And good riddance.

Tears filled her eyes again as she realized that it was the only good riddance that night. A knowledge washed over her: This library had gone quiet. She had made her decision, drawn her line in the sand. And she was certain she would never hear the voice of George Vanderbilt, her great love, ever again.

JULIA

Until We Meet Again

There is something almost indescribable about the way time passes when you are completely engrossed in the person that you know you might be falling for. The hours on the clock don't matter. A rumbling stomach is the only indicator of mealtime, and exhaustion so pure that you fall asleep in the other person's arms is the only sign that it's time to sleep. That was what happened to Conner and me. Waking up in his arms on his borrowed boat—the light streaming through the windows overlooking the glorious sea, making love before breakfast—beat the pants off waking up to a bumped head in the bunkhouse.

But I had to face reality. My flight to Asheville left the next morning. I had to go back to a world where I had no safety net.

"Tomorrow," I said, my face buried in Conner's chest.

"Tomorrow isn't real," he said. "Tomorrow is a construct of someone else's time, and I think we should live in ours." I looked up to see if he was serious. He was not. He sighed. "I know. Tomorrow. Then Monday, it's back to the real world. Back to schedules and meetings and client pitches."

I felt a rush of excitement. "I'm suddenly jealous of all those things."

He sat up. "You don't need to be jealous. You'll be doing all that soon."

I rubbed my eyes. "I hope so."

"Hey," he said. "You should come to New York. Transfer to Cornell or Columbia or Pratt."

I laughed. "Come on, Conner. I can't do that."

"Why not? You have to finish school somewhere. Why not New York?" He took my hands in his. "We can see what we're like. Outside of paradise."

God, it sounded magical. But I couldn't do that. "Conner, I don't have some huge nest egg to fall back on. I'll be taking out student loans and teaching yoga to support myself if I go back to school. I can't afford a place in New York." My face fell. "Reality is super unsexy." I sat up cross-legged across from Conner. "Plus, don't you see?"

He shook his head.

I sighed. "If I do that—move to New York—I'm just relying on you to save me like I did Hayes. I have to see if I can make it on my own. I just broke up with my boyfriend of ten years. I don't even know who I am without him."

He nodded. "And you can't run straight into another relationship or you won't know who you are without me."

"Is that okay?"

He laughed. "Jules, that's more than okay. I knew it was a long shot." He shrugged. "But a guy's gotta ask."

It was so supportive; it made me wonder if I would ever find anyone else that good.

He pulled me to him. "So maybe someday?"

I nodded. This conversation was the exact opposite of the last decade of my life with Hayes. Instead of guilting or manipulating, Conner understood I had to choose what was best for me. And what's more, he respected that.

"One day," he said, his eyes bright with laughter, "we'll be walking down the street, and our paths will cross again."

"My heart will race because it's you—and I'll be ready for this then," I said back, putting my hand over my heart dramatically, continuing the game of writing our fairy tale.

He pulled away from me. "I won't be able to take my eyes off you, not just because you're so beautiful but because you'll be so in your element. You'll be so alive, living your purpose. And I'll know that we were right to wait, that you couldn't be with me until you really knew yourself."

"Our eyes will lock," I continued. "And I'll wink."

"And, without a word between us, that's how I'll know you're ready."

We both laughed, but, despite the corny exchange, I had the feeling that Conner did hope our paths crossed again. I hoped so too. I leaned over and kissed him. "Thank you for understanding."

"Breakfast?" he said.

"Breakfast," I agreed.

"And then," he said, "let's pretend that tomorrow doesn't exist. Let's make this last day as perfect as it can be and when we go our separate ways, we'll always have this memory to hold on to."

I nodded in agreement. "Until we meet again."

"Until we meet again."

Mistress of Biltmore

August 22, 1925

The sun had yet to rise, but Cornelia couldn't sleep. On Friday, her twenty-fifth birthday, she had become the true and rightful owner of Biltmore House, and the weight of that felt so heavy yet so exciting that she couldn't seem to shut off the chatter in her mind even two days after the event had taken place. And so, before the rest of the house woke up, she stood at a canvas in the wood-paneled room that had once been her father's observatory, attempting to paint the way the sunrise hit the garden to the left of the house, one of her favorite spaces on the entire property. She was so engrossed in what she was doing she failed to notice that each time she dipped her brush, the lace trim on the sleeve of her pink silk robe picked up a speck of whatever hue she was using.

As the sun began to shine on Biltmore, she stood

back to study the painting. She wasn't Monet, but she was improving, slowly but surely. She felt certain of it. Cornelia stepped toward the small sink she had had installed in what was now her art studio to wash her hands.

The installation had been an unpopular choice. "You'll ruin the wood, Connie," Jack had protested.

"Your father picked this beautiful wood himself, darling," her mother had chimed in.

But, in the end, Cornelia had made the winning argument: "What is the point of having this massive house if we aren't allowed to *use* any of it?"

To that end, Cornelia turned toward the black, steel spiral staircase that led to the roof, losing herself in her memories as she made her way up and opened the door to the landing. She couldn't have been more than four or five the first time her father brought her up here—far past her bedtime—to look for shooting stars.

He had been in a particularly contemplative mood that crisp, cloudless October night as he smoothed a blanket out and they lay on their backs, looking up into the night sky. They were high enough in the air that Cornelia felt as if she, too, were a part of the sky, just another celestial object floating through time and space. "No matter what," her father had said as they gazed at the full moon, "no matter where we are, we'll always be under the same moon, Nelly."

He showed her the Big Dipper, the Little Dipper, and Orion's Belt. "Astronomers use math to determine how much light the stars are emitting, their distance from each other. Writing and art are what we use to make sense of our lives. But it is science and math that truly govern them. The words might lead you astray, but the numbers are fixed, unchanging. It is the numbers that hold the stars' places in the universe."

Cornelia had never had much interest in numbers until that night.

Now, as she scrubbed the paint from underneath her fingernails, she realized something: Maybe it was her father's proclamation that the numbers would never lead her astray that had so thoroughly enmeshed her in her fascination with numerology. The art she was creating wasn't fixed or unchanging. But the numbers were. And twenty-five—her age now—was the number of introspection. So perhaps that was the reason why she had felt so contemplative and restless lately. But Cornelia knew that introspection often led to transformation. Was she ready for that? She had hoped that being in this place connected her to her father would help her find the answers she was looking for. But, instead, Cornelia felt she had only found more questions.

As the sun continued to rise, she made her way through the house, down the main house stairs, and up the bachelors' wing steps to her room. She didn't need to get dressed for this post-birthday ritual, but she did comb her hair at least. Then she opened the newspaper on top of the stack that was left for Jack each morning.

She didn't have to read long before she felt the anger rising in her. She made her way downstairs to the banquet hall, still seething even when she saw her mother and husband already seated at the table, waiting for her. Cornelia slammed the newspaper down on the breakfast table.

"Cornelia Vanderbilt Gets $15,000,000," the *Evening News* blared up at them.

She watched Edith and Jack share a glance.

"It's very déclassé," Edith said.

"It's like when they printed that you didn't get your fortune if we didn't live at Biltmore," Jack agreed. "Untrue and absurd."

"Nelly," Edith said. "Sit down, please. You love your birthday breakfast. Let's not ruin it."

Cornelia, remembering again that it was indeed her special weekend—not to mention that she would receive her fortune, even if it wasn't all of $15,000,000—softened.

"Why is this a tradition again?" Jack asked.

"Ah, well," Edith started, "the morning after Cornelia's birthday party when she was growing up, breakfast would be served right here in the banquet hall even though the big table was usually reserved for large fetes and important guests." She smiled. "At the request of the birthday girl, of course."

Cornelia smiled as she sat down. "My legs didn't even touch the floor when we started these breakfasts," she said, laughing, remembering swinging her feet as her pancakes were served. "It was the only day of the year that all of us—Daddy included—dined in our night-clothes."

Jack pointed to his robe, as though making a statement about how he was following protocol.

"We would talk about the birthday party we'd had the day before, who was there, what they'd worn. Even Daddy would joke about who had the prettiest bow or party dress."

The year George died, Cornelia figured the tradition would die too. But she had woken up the morning of her fourteenth birthday and, for old times' sake, ventured down into the banquet hall just to stand there, to feel small in the massive room with its lofty ceilings, grand organ pipes, intricate hanging tapestries and game mounts. She wanted to, like when she was little, tiptoe on the herringbone floor to see if she could cross the room without stepping on a single crack. She wanted to stand there for just a few moments and think about her father. She had been surprised—and truly delighted—to see her mother sitting at the set table, in her usual spot, waiting for her. Her father's place was set, too, though it was empty, of course. Her mother gestured to the place setting. "In case he wants to come," she'd said. Cornelia had smiled.

Cornelia grew contemplative now as she looked over at the set but conspicuously empty spot at the head of the table. Cornelia had had moments since George's death where she was sure he was there with her. She knew her mother had too.

Jack squeezed Cornelia's hand. "Well, according to tradition, let's talk about your birthday party."

"Everyone else is," Mr. Noble said, as he entered the dining room, handing Cornelia the Asheville newspaper.

She rolled her eyes. "Not again."

When she was younger, the prying eyes of the press had felt normal, ordinary. Lately, however, it had begun to drive her crazy. Perhaps it had started when she and Jack were courting, and more than one argument had begun because of some false speculation presented by one of the papers. It had created a life where, everywhere she went, she was convinced someone was talking about her. And now that she was the official mistress of Biltmore, she knew it was only going to get worse.

"I can't even have a simple birthday party without it making headlines?" she asked.

"Well, my love, at the risk of further angering you, 'simple' might be a bit of an understatement," Jack said.

Edith hid her laugh behind her hand.

Cornelia, even in her annoyed state, had to smile. Perhaps her pair of birthday parties weren't simple exactly.

Two days before, Edith had stood behind Cornelia, draping a strand of pearls around her daughter's elegant neck to help her get ready for perhaps the most important birthday of her life. Because this birthday, she was becoming mistress of Biltmore. It would all be hers. She loved that her father had left the house to her, even though she wasn't a son. She thought of her own tiny son, who was sleeping in the nursery, having this same honor one day.

Cornelia took a deep breath. "I can't decide which party I'm more excited about. The one with the estate workers this afternoon or the ball tomorrow."

Edith smiled. "I'm so thrilled that the Charles Freicher Orchestra will be able to join us."

Cornelia always loved when her mother said things like that, as though the orchestra had simply taken it upon themselves to attend the party, not that they had been paid handily to be a part of the celebration.

"I think Guthrie's Orchestra at this afternoon's celebration will be lovely as well," Cornelia countered. She still felt a bit strange about having one party with the employees and one with her society friends. But, with six hundred total guests, there wasn't much choice but to spread the celebration over two affairs, and even though she felt equally comfortable in both worlds, she knew the same wasn't true for her friends.

"I still wish we were having a fancy dress ball," Edith said.

"That's because you wear costumes so well, Mother," Cornelia said, smiling.

But she didn't want that kind of pageantry. She simply wanted to celebrate her birthday with the people she loved. Jack had asked her over and over what she might want for a gift. But she had already received the best gift this year: a son. And her true birthday gift was this magnificent estate. Asking for more seemed absurd.

The ice-cream cake the workers at Biltmore Dairy had presented her with at her first party was positively extravagant. Four feet tall and two feet wide, it took twenty-six gallons of ice cream to create the work of art, which was studded with roses, lilies, and the proclamation "May your joys be as many as the sands of the sea."

It was a truly marvelous gift, and while the Cartier cigarette holders and carved figurines presented to her by her society friends were lovely, she had a special place in her heart for that cake.

What she did not have a special place for was it being written about, her outfits being commented on and guest lists being scrutinized. She didn't mind so much when the *Asheville Gazette* did it. But then all the other papers picked it up, meaning that everyone in the country would be reading about her birthday by nightfall.

Now, at Cornelia's birthday breakfast, Edith read the *Gazette* aloud. " 'The beautiful array of summer gowns of the many dancers made a scene as beautiful as that of gay moths and fireflies in a fairy garden.' " She paused and put the paper down. "Well, how positively lovely. I can't think of a better description of a birthday party."

Cornelia sighed. "It is lovely. But it still feels like an invasion of privacy."

Edith nodded. "I understand. I very much do. But why now? This has been our whole lives, hasn't it?"

Cornelia was glad that a pair of servers swept in then with silver trays of pastries and fruit right at that moment. She was grateful that this was a light breakfast. She felt as if she couldn't eat another bite after the midnight buffet, but even still, she politely took a pastry and a few pieces of melon.

"I'm certain it's one of your 'friends' on the estate who's leaking these stories," Jack said.

Mr. Noble silently refilled their coffee cups. Cornelia had grown used to the way his coat sleeve hung empty, dangling by his side—he had lost his arm in the Great War. Because of his sacrifice, the true cost of the battle was always top of mind. It made Cornelia proud that her mother, upon seeing Noble's condition when he came home, had rehired him on the spot—and as head butler at that—without a second thought. And it astounded her that he was still, with one arm, the most talented and dedicated servant at Biltmore. He had relearned how to do everything, and maybe even do it better than he did before.

"Mr. Noble," Jack asked. "Tell me, do you think one of the staff leaked the story to the press?" Jack and Noble had bonded instantly over their English heritage. They had a similar accent—and a similar distaste for anyone and everyone they believed had betrayed Cornelia.

Mr. Noble cleared his throat. "That is not for me to say, Mr. Cecil." He paused, then continued, "But if I had to say . . ."

Jack smiled at Cornelia victoriously. Besides her

smallest love, George Henry Vanderbilt Cecil, and the man for whom he was named, Cornelia perhaps loved Jack and Mr. Noble as much as any two men in the world. She knew they were trying to protect her. Even still, she wasn't ready to concede this fight.

"No one on the estate would betray me. They are my friends, Jack. My real, true ones."

He looked at her sadly. Jack believed that these people were kind to Cornelia because being in her good graces got them to the places they wanted to go. She resented him for feeling that way. But it did put a shadow of a doubt in her mind. Were the estate workers her friends for her, or for what she could offer them? It was a lonely thought.

Edith waved her hand, taking a sip of coffee. "It doesn't matter how they get the stories. Much like charity balls and dress fittings, this is simply a part of our lives."

"I don't know how you handle it so well," Cornelia replied.

Edith laughed. "My darling, when I was your age, the press was debating everything from my appearance to my assets, my suitability for Daddy to my wardrobe. They mostly talk about how wonderful you are. I do wish you would just accept it as fact and move on. They talk about you because they love you."

Cornelia had never quite been able to put it into words, but right now, at her birthday breakfast, feeling the weight of her twenty-five years, it occurred to her: *What have I done with my life?* Perhaps it wasn't the papers writing about her that she minded. Maybe it was what they were writing *about*, what they had no choice to write about. They wrote of her outfits and parties because that was the fodder she gave them. Now that she was really, truly an adult, what was she going to do moving forward? Now was the time to take her place as a woman amid a cultural revolution.

Changing the subject, Edith asked, "Well, my girl, how does it feel, having your first birthday breakfast in the banquet hall as the true and rightful owner of Biltmore?"

Cornelia smiled and, on impulse, took a bite of pastry. Even though she wasn't hungry, it was warm and sweet and flaky, and she thoroughly enjoyed the feel of it on her tongue.

"It's quite thrilling," she said, feeling cheered. "This is my purpose now, the preservation of this place that my son will call home."

Cornelia knew that every new owner of anything comes into it with fresh eyes and bright ideas, and she hoped that some of hers would pay off. The estate was slightly more stable these days, but it was still far from self-sufficient. She would have her work cut out for her if she wanted to continue to sustain the home where she had lived and played since childhood. For the first time since her father died, she had the funds to do so. Cornelia felt up to the challenge.

Jack raised his orange juice glass, and Cornelia couldn't help but smile. "To Cornelia," he said, "new mistress of Biltmore."

"Hear, hear!" Edith responded.

Cornelia raised her own glass. "To new adventures and making Daddy proud!"

As they clinked glasses, Cornelia had to hope that maybe now, maybe this, would be the thing to cure the lost and listless feeling that, for years, through her smiles and manners, grace and graciousness, had taken hold of her heart. If not, she'd keep searching until she found it. She had to; she must. On this, her twenty-fifth birthday, Cornelia felt more assured than ever that a life without passion wasn't worth living at all.

BABS

Lease on Life

I held up a pink tweed jacket and a blue one, debating which would go better with the skirt I had just packed. I figured Julia and I would go out to at least a couple nice dinners while we were in Asheville.

Dinners. I had been avoiding Miles since the dinner incident the week before. It wasn't just that it was awkward; it was that, all of a sudden, accidentally bringing my daughters into the picture had made me realize how incredibly real this was. I was like a teenager again, diving headfirst into whatever felt good *because* it felt good. And now I had to back away, be an adult and think it through.

I chose the blue jacket, hung it beside the other clothes I was taking, and zipped my hanging bag. Who was that woman I had been those few days? Who did she think she was to attempt to move into a new phase of her life? My daughters certainly thought my behavior was outlandish and were asking me to separate myself from Miles.

They had scolded me like a child. "We're only thinking of you," Meredith said in a pleading voice across the table from me. When it got down to it, she tended to be sweeter than her twin. "We don't want you to get up with some man who is going to take your money and run."

I laughed in disbelief.

"That's a thing, Mom," Alice had chimed in.

"I know that's a *thing*, Alice. But, for one, I would never get my money entangled with a man at my age, and for another, I have known Miles since I was in college. He neither wants nor needs my money."

They shared a glance over the table. It was a glance that said, *Poor Mother is senile. She thinks a man could be interested in her for herself at her age.* It infuriated me, but despite my frustration, I chose the route of motherly compassion.

"Girls, look. I should have been honest with you about how difficult things have been for me without your father, how lonely I have been, how afraid."

"But now *Miles* is here to make you feel safe," Alice said sarcastically into her drink. I ignored her.

"Moving to Summer Acres has given me a new lease on life. I have people to eat with, things to do, a home that isn't full of memories, both good and bad. I don't wake up from night terrors about your father dead beside me. This is what I needed. It was the right choice for me."

"Did you move here for *Miles*?" Alice asked. "Was Summer Acres a part of your plan to be together, to forget Daddy?"

She had pushed me one time too many. I stood up angrily from the table and walked around to her chair. "Don't come back here until you can show your mother some respect," I whispered so no one else would hear—although, heaven knows, most of them couldn't have heard over the music even if I was shouting.

I walked out the door, Meredith on my heels. "She didn't mean it, Mother."

I waved for the valet to grab my golf cart. I just wanted to get out of there as quickly and nondramatically as possible.

"You know how she gets," Meredith continued. "We just worry about you."

I turned to her. "That's just the thing. I don't need you to worry about me. Your father was my great love, and I will ache for his loss every day. For her to insinuate that—"

"She didn't mean it, Mom. She knows you loved Daddy. But, come on, dating another man? At your age?"

I had been starting to warm to this one daughter, but now I was exasperated all over again. And Alice, true to form, hadn't even ventured out to apologize.

She had called me since to make amends, but, even still, the subtext from my daughters hung on every call: stop seeing Miles.

My daughters disagreed quite often. They were twins in looks and DNA, but they were usually opposite in thought. This, though? Their mother moving forward being an apocalyptic event? That was one point on which they agreed.

But, then again, I'd thought when I got home that maybe they were right. Maybe I was being hasty. And maybe I needed some time away from Miles to assess

that. Their little outburst had convinced me to sit down
at my desk and write my granddaughter.

> *Darling Julia,*
>   *I will meet you in Asheville on the day you tell*
> *me. It will be a much-needed breather for both of*
> *us, and please feel free to use the house for as long*
> *as you like. No one else does. You might as well.*
> *Life is short, dear one. We must make the most*
> *of it. Follow your heart. It can lead you to some*
> *outstanding places.*
>
> *All my love,*
> *Babs*

But now, as I finished packing my tote bag, I had to
consider that maybe it wasn't my daughters' outburst
that made me want to leave town. Maybe it was my
heart, my conflicted, troubled heart.

As I lifted my tote onto my shoulder and draped the
hanging bag over my arm, I had to admit that those
yoga classes I'd taken up recently were doing absolute
wonders for my joints. *Use it or lose it* was the mantra
around here. With the help of Summer Acres' marvelous programs, I was discovering that I could regain
things I thought I'd lost—flexibility, speed, mobility—
even at my age.

I opened the front door and startled at the figure
of Miles sitting on my front porch. Seeing him begged
the question: *What else could I regain?* He stood up and
walked over to me carefully, as if I were a horse he was
trying not to spook.

I cringed thinking of the way Miles's face had looked

that night at dinner, and the way it looked now: hurt. I knew there were things for us to discuss. But I wasn't ready to make a decision about all of this. Not yet.

"Hi," I said as sunnily as I could manage.

He sat back down and patted the chair beside him. "Barbara," he said, smiling.

I felt the awkwardness between us, the things we weren't saying, the questions we weren't asking. We had been inseparable and then, with no explanation at all, I had separated us. "I'm sorry," I said.

He squeezed my forearm. "For what?"

"For taking a step back. I needed some time to think." But I hadn't come to any real conclusions. All I had done was miss Miles. He smiled now, and my heart fluttered. There is no logical explanation for the ways in which people enter our lives and we know they will always be a part of our hearts. Miles was one of those people. He had been a part of my heart for all these years. And now here he was.

"May I ask you something?"

"Anything," I said warmly.

"Why wasn't it me, Barbara?" he asked, his voice impassioned. "Why didn't you choose me all those years ago? I know you wanted to. I saw the way you looked that night, when I came to you to ask you to choose me instead of Reid. Why couldn't I change your mind?"

He didn't have to elaborate. It was so easy for me to remember.

It was the week before graduation. The week before my wedding. The week before real life began. Miles had written me a letter, one of only a few he had written since I had told him of my engagement. He had asked to meet me at my college campus, had given me the time and place. I almost didn't go. I knew it was wrong. But I couldn't shake the feeling that this would be the last time I ever saw him.

I remember arranging my skirt, musing at the place Miles had picked for us to meet: the marble bench beneath Davie Poplar, the university's beloved, centuries-old tree.

As if carried in on the gentle breeze blowing through the UNC campus, there he was, strolling across the lush green toward this bench where, it was said, if you kissed, you would stay together forever. Wishful thinking, perhaps. But I was charmed nonetheless. I stood when Miles reached me, couldn't help but hug him, the fresh starch of his shirt scratchy on my face.

"Barbara," he said simply. That's when I could tell he was nervous. That's when I realized I was nervous too, my breath short.

We sat down on the bench. He tried to take my hands, but I pulled them away—gently, not harshly. He shook his head. "Barbara, I just want you to know . . ." He trailed off and started again, seeming uncharacteristically agitated. "Are you sure about marrying him? Are you positive? Because I can't help but think that . . ."

I knew what he couldn't help but think. "Miles, my marrying Reid has always been a part of the plan. This is just the plan coming to fruition."

"But what about your summer with me? What about the secrets we've shared, the letters we've written?" I could feel him getting bolder. He looked me straight in the eye. "What about the way you kissed me?"

"Miles, I . . ." I couldn't answer. Because I had kissed him. And it had taken my breath away. I knew then that

I was breaking his heart. And, what's worse, I also knew I was breaking my own.

When I couldn't answer, he said, "I'm sorry. I think I must have felt things that you didn't."

I should have left it at that. It was the proper thing to do. But I shook my head and, looking down at my hands, said softly, "I felt them too, Miles."

I looked up at him then.

"So marry me," he said. "Make a life with me."

I couldn't tell him then because I didn't understand what I was feeling. But Miles had big dreams that I knew would fling him far and wide. I had seen my parents chase dreams and take chances, buy things they could barely afford, go on trips on a whim, disregard responsibility. They were happy. But I felt untethered. I needed to feel secure. At that time in my life, I couldn't bear the thought of moving away, of pursuing a different path outside my hometown. I needed my future children to know what their lives were going to look like, my mother there to help me raise them. I needed to know what *my* life was going to look like. I had said yes to Reid because I knew he would be a wonderful husband, a great father. He would take over his father's business and we would live on the beach not ten minutes from where I grew up. He was settled, stable, sure. Safe. Miles, on the other hand, was not.

"I can't stop thinking about you, Barbara. And I have to think that if you could stop thinking about me, you wouldn't have met me today. You wouldn't have returned my letters these past few months. You know we have something special."

I did know. I knew exactly. It was the reason I had

cried to my mother over Christmas break, when I should have been celebrating my engagement. I had seen Miles only twice since our summer at camp. And each time, I had promised myself it would be to say goodbye. Only I couldn't. Once Reid proposed, I finally told Miles I couldn't see him anymore. But we still wrote letters. What harm could letters do?

"How can I love two men at once?" I had sobbed to my mother.

I remember the way she'd wrapped me in her arms on the couch, smelling of Shalimar and cigarette smoke, the way her rouge had left a stain on my wet cheek. "My Barbara," she had said. "I have been at this same place. I was terribly unsure about marrying your father. But the night he proposed, when that perfect stranger handed me a wedding veil on a train, I knew. I had been looking for a sign and that was the most obvious one I could imagine." She had looked me straight in the eye. "What you need is a sign."

A sign. Four months later, I couldn't deny that I had most certainly received mine. If I had been searching for a concrete reason to marry Reid over Miles, I had found it. My sign was permanent, steadfast, and unwavering.

As I sat under Davie Poplar in front of a wounded and pleading Miles, I knew there was no backing out of my wedding even if I wanted to. My future was set, my story written. There was a small part of me that wished I could call the whole thing off, to see what a different future looked like. But I didn't have that choice.

I couldn't tell him then. I couldn't explain. I looked down at my feet. "Miles, I adore you," I'd said. "I truly do. And in another time, in another place, maybe it could have been you and me. But I *am* marrying Reid."

I looked up at him again. "I will never forget you, Miles. I will maybe even always wonder what could have been. But this is how it has to be."

His face fell. "If you're sure, Barbara, then I know I cannot change your mind. But I wish it had been me." Despite his sadness, he still took my hand. I let him this time. He placed something precious, something meaningful, something he could only give once, into it.

"To remember me by," he had said.

And I had. I had remembered.

Now, on my porch, it was finally time to make amends. "There were so many times after that night that I wanted to write to you, that I wanted to explain," I said softly.

He smiled. "So you weren't placating me? I truly meant something to you?"

"Of course you did, Miles."

"And I still do?" The fear in his eyes gave away how hard this was for him.

Miles was not a man of subtlety. He was a man of action, of wearing his heart on his sleeve, consequences be damned. I touched his hand gently. Was I letting him down for myself? Or for the girls? Did it matter?

"Miles, you have been such a surprise. You have been alone for so many years now, but Reid hasn't even been gone a year and a half. I have so much to think about."

He nodded sadly and squeezed my hand. "I understand."

My heart felt heavy with pain and longing. But it was too hard; it was too complicated. I was too old to start over again. I was letting him down easy. It was kinder this way.

"Barbara," Miles said, not even turning to look at me. "All those years ago, you said that maybe in another time, in another place, it could have been you and me. Maybe that time and place is here and now." And then he was gone, as if our conversation had never even happened. And I was left, my heart beating through my chest, remembering, feeling, wondering if maybe he was right.

I never would have imagined that I would be standing face-to-face with the difficult and confusing inner workings of love again at my age—and certainly not with a man who had vanished from my life only to reappear decades later. But here we were. I needed to step away from this, gain some perspective. Lucky for me, there was nothing like the crisp, cool mountain air of Asheville to help a woman feel like her largest problems could be carried away on a white cloud. As I dropped my bags into the open trunk of my car, I let my biggest fear sink in: *Was I trying to use this new relationship to forget Reid?*

No. Of course not. Reid was the single best decision I ever made. But things change. Reid was gone. Julia hadn't gotten married. I didn't know what to say to Miles. And then there was that wedding veil . . .

A Leap of Faith

October 22, 1925

Edith felt like the combination of her nerves and excitement could fill up her room at Brown's Hotel in London. Well, room was an understatement. Just as Eleanor Roosevelt had said, the royal suite was so vast that Edith could scarcely find herself, much less her possessions. It seemed a shame to have such a large space for just herself. The bridegroom, in accordance with tradition, had stayed at Claridge's so they wouldn't see each other until the day of the wedding.

"Did you know that Rudyard Kipling wrote *The Jungle Book* here?" Cornelia asked.

Edith searched her mind, which was racing. "I don't think I did."

Cornelia caught her mother's eye in the mirror. "Are you nervous?"

Edith laughed. Did women in their early fifties still

get nervous? She supposed so. "I don't think nervous is the word for it. Anticipatory, maybe?"

"Tired is probably more like it," Cornelia said, yawning. "I don't know why you two insisted on getting married so frightfully early in the morning when we're all still adjusting to the time change."

Edith smiled sarcastically. Her daughter knew full well they were getting married so early this morning in an attempt to dodge the press. "I simply could not wait one more moment to become a Gerry," she said.

"While I," Cornelia responded, "would have loved nothing more than to have remained a Vanderbilt forever."

Edith rolled her eyes.

"It's a shame you aren't going to wear the family veil," Cornelia quipped, lounging on her mother's bed as Edith stood in front of the mirror, fussing with her collar. They both laughed, as that would have been terribly inappropriate for a second wedding.

"Can you imagine the headlines?" Edith asked, rolling her eyes.

Edith smiled, sweet memories of her first wedding day washing over her. She cleared her throat and Cornelia sat up, alarmed at the tears that had come to her mother's eyes. "Oh, Mother, I'm sorry. I didn't mean to be insensitive. I know how special the veil is to you."

Edith smiled through her tears, thinking of the veil that linked her to her mother, sisters, and daughter. All of a sudden, going into a new marriage without it made her feel terribly alone. "This was always going to be a difficult day, but I will try to make it a happy one, too," she said.

Cornelia got up off the bed and opened her mother's

generous traveling trunk, which Emma hadn't completely unpacked. She ran her fingers across the paint that spelled out the initials *E.S.D.* Her mother's original traveling trunk, from her days as a Dresser girl, was still perfectly intact. Cornelia selected a chic felt hat from atop the purple velvet–lined shelf. Then, just as her mother had done for her only last year, she placed the final touch for the day on her head.

"Ten-twenty-two is the most perfect wedding date I can imagine," Cornelia said. "It is a date that can't help but manifest dreams into reality. And here we are."

Edith tried to stop the alarm bells in her head from clanging—she was none too thrilled with this numerology nonsense Cornelia had found an interest in. It wasn't uncommon for women of their set to travel often, to set up homes in multiple places, but Edith didn't feel that Cornelia's New York friends—her artist set—were the best influence. Still, could a little silliness with numbers be harmful? Well, Reverend Swope, Edith's—and George's at one point—most trusted spiritual advisor was concerned. But, wanting to keep the peace, and knowing Cornelia would do what she wanted regardless, Edith took the bait. "And why is that?"

"The combination of one, zero, and a pair of twos means that you are going to be very happy in love. And twenty-two is a powerful indicator of cooperation and balance in a relationship," Cornelia said as she adjusted the hat on her mother's head.

In spite of herself, Edith smiled. It *did* make her feel a little better that the numbers were on her side, whatever that meant.

"There," Cornelia said, admiring her mother. "All set for *me* to walk *you* down the aisle."

When mother and daughter pulled up to the register office less than half an hour later, Peter looked every bit the senator in his refined derby hat and overcoat. "I'm not going to waste time taking my coat off, you know," he said as he kissed his bride hello. "I'm not living one more minute not married to you."

Sweet words from a man whom she truly adored. Edith had waited all morning for thoughts of George to flood her mind, for her sadness to throw her happiness off track. She had even warned Peter of the possibility. And, in true Peter form, he had said the most perfect thing in response: "Dearest Edi, if you weren't sad for the first man you shared a name with on the day you took mine, I wouldn't be marrying you. Your kind heart, your willing spirit, and your unfailing empathy are your best qualities. I will gladly share you with the one who came before me if that means that I get to have your hand and at least half your heart."

Part of the allure of Peter was that Edith had no reason to doubt his motives for their partnership other than pure, unadulterated love. He was vastly wealthier than she, cared little to ever step foot on the Biltmore property unless it was for her pleasure, and was several years her junior. She couldn't say the same for any of her previous suitors.

And now, he was going to be all hers for the rest of their lives. A few minutes later, at 8:50 a.m. on October 22, 1925, they pulled it off: Edith Dresser Vanderbilt became Edith Dresser Vanderbilt Gerry. She might have a new last name, but she would remain a Vanderbilt, always. And, as Peter and Edith stepped outside for the first time as spouses, Edith felt more grateful and blessed than she had in some time.

She felt happy on the ride to the Chapel of the Savoy, where she and Peter, now that they were married in the eyes of the government, would be joined together in the eyes of God. Edith had changed into a velvet coat trimmed in sable for the occasion, and after reaching her destination, was now holding her eight-month-old grandson, George, who was gleefully grasping at the fur. Standing in the doorway of the church, studying the vivid blue quatrefoil ceiling and black-and-white-tiled floor, Edith smiled at her beautiful daughter.

"Can you imagine that men and women have stood in this same spot taking these very vows since the 1500s?" she asked Cornelia.

She looked proudly at the beautiful daughter who would walk her down the aisle, the daughter that she adored so fully, that George had understood so well. Edith and Cornelia looked alike and dressed alike, rode horses and fished alike. But it was George who had understood her creative side, her artistic whims, her penchant for wanderlust.

"It boggles the mind, doesn't it?" Cornelia asked. "It makes me realize how very new America truly is."

George cooed, and Edith kissed his sweet, fragrant head. Looking into his wide eyes, she was surprised to find that it wasn't her husband, their wedding day, or even the wedding veil of her ancestors that she suddenly felt nostalgic for. It was her daughter, or, at least, the baby she had been, the girl she used to be.

Edith smiled at her grandson, his cherubic face, for a moment, morphing into her daughter's on August 22, 1900, the warm and lovely day on which Cornelia arrived. It was said that the world had a new richest baby. Cornelia had usurped the position from her own cousin, John Nicholas Brown II. Edith had prayed briefly that that wasn't the headline the newspapers chose and had said so to her husband.

"No, no," George reassured his wife, sitting at the end of the bed in the red and gold Louis XV suite. He gazed adoringly at his perfect new daughter, who was swaddled in his protective, fatherly arms. "With Cornelia's beauty, grace, and health, no one will even be thinking about money. They will proclaim her the world's brightest baby, the most beautiful—"

"The most adored?" Edith chimed in, smiling at her husband, who broke his gaze with his new daughter long enough to smile back at her.

"You have outdone yourself, Edi," George said.

She felt the slightest pang for her parents. Even now, even all these years later, she wished that they could be there to meet her baby daughter inside this intricately designed room with a view of the esplanade unrivaled anywhere in the house. She wanted them to see how she had grown up, where she had ended up and, most of all, that she was okay.

"What do you think she'll be like, George?"

He stroked his daughter's small cheek. "I think she will be headstrong yet kind, willful yet wise, strong and energetic but with a true soft spot for the less fortunate and aggrieved." George turned to smile at his wife. "In short, my darling, I think she will be quite like her mother."

It warmed Edith's heart, as George handed the tiny child back to her, that her husband thought those things of her. More than anything during her time at Biltmore she hoped to show her husband—and the whole world, really—that her soft spot was not only for Biltmore

Estate but also for its people. Building a lasting legacy had meant everything to George; now it meant everything to her, too. And she had to think that this new baby was another step toward that goal.

It was clear, from the moment she was born, that Cornelia was not only the child of Edith and George Vanderbilt but also a daughter of Asheville, North Carolina. The people of the town had claimed her from conception, and there was something incredibly calming in that fact. They would watch out for her and love her always. The *Charlotte Observer* had already gone so far as to publish a poem about "Tarheel Nell's" beauty, charm, and grace.

George kissed his wife. "I'll call Nanny in. You need your rest."

"Not yet," she whispered, almost uncertainly, as though she were a child asking a parent for more time to play before dinner.

George patted Edith's leg and simply said, "Whatever you'd like."

When he had left, closing the door behind him, Edith looked down at her new little girl. "See all that out there, outside that window?"

The tiny infant yawned, which Edith took as a yes. "That is your home. More than inside this house, more than your bedroom or the great hall or the banquet hall, these woods, this land, these mountains are yours. They will become a part of you, just as they did your father, just as they have me, and no matter where you go or what you do, they will always beckon you back home."

As Edith stared down into the face of her daughter, she already understood that she would never have another worriless day, that she would never stop want-

ing the best life had to offer for Cornelia. She prayed
quickly, silently, that this place, this house, this land,
would always call her daughter home, back where she
belonged.

George must have held the same prayer in his heart.
Because, some two months after Cornelia's christening, George arranged another special ceremony for his
daughter, a baptism of a different kind entirely. Whereas
she had been baptized in the church by holy water, now
it was time for her to be washed in mountain air and
soil and foliage, to not only be marked as Christ's own
forever but also Asheville's. George erected stained glass
windows at All Souls for many of the people he wanted
to honor, but for Cornelia, he instead planted a tree.

The mountain magnolia, with its broad, flat leaves,
seemed quite a good fit. It was a hearty tree, one that
would take root in the soil and, though twelve feet tall
now, likely reach five times that height in its lifetime. It
grew quickly and gracefully, as George and Edith hoped
Cornelia would. Its blooms, while fragrant, possessed a
more down-to-earth beauty than the full and flowing
perfection of its southern magnolia counterpart—a fitting symbol, it seemed to George, of the luxury and rug-
gedness that would form Cornelia's childhood.

When the tree was in the ground, Edith reached
out her hand, adorned with the large opal pinky ring
George had given her to denote Cornelia's baptism, and
touched the tree that would stand forever by the bass
pond, commemorating her daughter's life long after all
of them were gone. The ring was an estate piece that,
curiously, held Edith's original initials of *E.D.* and a setting that was, as legend had it, the same as the one Jose-

phine wore as a gift from her husband, Napoléon. As Edith held her tiny baby in a single arm, she thought of Napoléon and his now-famous proclamation: "Let her sleep, for when she wakes, she will move mountains."

Edith and George had had many talks about Cornelia's future and what it would hold. Would she move mountains? Would they move her? Looking down at her little girl, her heart so filled with joy, it seemed that both would most certainly come to be true.

Now, twenty-five years later, in a church across an ocean, Edith looked into the eyes of her grandson. George's legacy. She thought again about that day, about that tall, broad mountain magnolia. The tree, which was hearty and vibrant, was more an embodiment of Cornelia than any stained glass window. It was a fitting tribute to a little girl who refused to be contained in glass, whose wild and wondrous spirit would cause her to fling farther, to climb higher than they could have ever imagined.

Edith looked at her daughter again, no longer the tiny child she had once been but the mistress of Biltmore with a baby of her own. It took Edith's breath away, all they had been through, all they had lost. But some things remained. Today, she still wore that pinky ring George had given her the day of their daughter's christening. A new George Vanderbilt was here and poised to take on the world, though he would know a different man as his grandfather. And Biltmore still stood, tall and proud amid the mountains that had witnessed centuries of stories, the mountains that would remember them long after they were gone.

Edith took a deep breath and vowed to put the past

behind her. Peter was her husband now. Together, they would change the world. As she began her walk down the aisle, that tiny motion became the crossing of a chasm, a leap of faith. Edith was walking toward her future.

JULIA

The Vanderbilt Veil

Leaving paradise had been difficult, but I knew I was ready. I wasn't like Trav; I couldn't leave the real world behind for a life of island relaxation. In fact, after three weeks, the laid-back feel and lack of schedule were starting to stress me out.

I called Babs the night before I left, sitting on a stained wooden bench in the terra-cotta-tiled hut that served as the resort's lobby. The long phone cord of the landline stretched from the reception desk to the bench, and the attendant who had told me I had only three minutes eyed me warily.

"Babs!" I practically shouted into the phone.

"Jules, I thought you were never coming home!" Babs exclaimed when she answered. "How I have missed you!"

"I've missed you too, Babs. And I can't wait to see you in a couple days. I have so much to tell you."

"Oh! Tell me now!"

I gave my winningest grin to the woman in her resort-issued polo shirt. In return, she started tapping her pencil on the desk impatiently. "Sorry, Babs. I only have a minute. But I wanted to see if you would meet me at that *Fashionable Romance* exhibit at Biltmore. You know, the one with all the famous wedding outfits they mentioned during my *spectacular* bridesmaids' luncheon?"

We both laughed.

"Including Cornelia's?" she asked, a smile in her voice.

I wrapped the phone cord around my finger, a childhood habit I'd all but forgotten in the age of cell phones. I had thought about that veil we had seen at my bridesmaids' luncheon so many times on this trip. We might never know the truth about our wedding veil, but if we were going to try, this exhibit might be our only chance. How else would we ever see Cornelia Vanderbilt's wedding veil up close?

"Well, the reproduction of Cornelia's veil will be there anyway."

"Your vivid imagination is one of your best traits, my dear. But if it will put your mind at ease to know that our veil is all ours, I am happy to facilitate that."

I smiled. Maybe I *was* being silly. "But it'll be fun anyway, right?"

She laughed. "The most! I love you, sweetheart. I'll be counting down the days."

"I love you too, Babs. The most."

The woman behind the counter now had her arms crossed. I handed her the phone and smiled sweetly. "Thank you *so* much."

She said nothing.

I thought about Babs as I walked back to pack, about her life without Pops, more than a year since his passing. I wondered how a future without him felt to her. Much different and much bigger than a future without Hayes felt to me, certainly. But it did occur to me that we were both moving forward into a new and different world, where we didn't have a partner to fall back on. I was glad we had each other.

In a matter of a couple days, I was marveling at how quickly life could change. In a matter of hours, I had gone from an island paradise with the bluest water to a hilly mountain oasis. I stood outside Biltmore for a moment, admiring the perfectly manicured rows of emerald-green grass and the home that was certainly from another time, but whose scale and architecture made it seem as if it also belonged to another world. Maybe that's what had always intrigued me about it most. I could step inside and be transported.

Inside the entrance hall of Biltmore, my meeting spot with my grandmother, I practically ran as I saw her, all ready for walking in her Easy Spirits paired with a skirt suit and pearls. Babs's idea of casual wear, I guess.

"Let me look at you," Babs said. "Tan, rested, blonder. You look wonderful in every way."

I smiled. "So do you, Babs."

I filled her in on the details of my trip—and the man I'd met—and then, as I looked around, remembered where we were. "It never gets less astonishing, Babs," I said, taking it all in. "Over all these years of visits, the sheer size, the perfect details . . . it amazes me every single time."

Babs nodded. "I just can't imagine walking up and down those stairs every day."

I admired the cantilevered feat of construction. "They're a marvel, aren't they?"

"Oh, yes," she said ethereally. And then, "How so?"

I laughed. "The weight of each of these supremely heavy slabs of limestone is counterbalanced by the wall bearing down on it."

She cocked her head, and I could tell I was losing her. So I just said, "There was an elevator. And they probably had a servant get their things, anyway."

Babs nodded, and then she struck a pose so regal I could only image she was pretending to be one of the Vanderbilt women. "James, darling, can you fetch my scarf?" she said with an affected accent. "Oh, oops, I forgot my glasses too. At least you're getting your steps in!"

I smiled at Babs. My grandmother had a joie de vivre that made everyone want to be around her. When Pops died, I was afraid that spark would die too. But, slowly but surely, the spunky woman I had admired my entire life was returning.

We had both been here about a million times, so we forwent the audio guides, choosing instead to simply admire the house—and the wedding gowns of famous movie characters, part of the *Fashionable Romance* exhibit, that were displayed throughout. Of course, what I really wanted to see was Cornelia's wedding outfit. But I knew it was here somewhere.

I looked up the staircase again, at the monstrous light fixture that hung down three floors. "Do you know that this chandelier weighs seventeen hundred pounds? That it's held by a single bolt, which can only be accessed under the roof's copper dome?" I asked. It made me prickly with excitement. Not that I would ever plan a building remotely like this. No, houses like this were beautiful, but they were impractical and inefficient at best. That was part of being an architect—creating structures that fit the times. This was from a decidedly different one.

Babs raised her eyebrows. "Are these architectural things I hear coming out of your mouth?"

I had spent the entire day before on the phone with guidance counselors, admissions, and even the dean of the NC State School of Architecture. I was bursting to tell someone. "Babs," I said seriously. "I'm trying to go back to school."

Babs gasped and put her hand on her heart. "I love seeing you impassioned again," she said. "It makes me feel so hopeful and happy."

I was hopeful and happy, too. But then there was that nagging tug of doubt. What if I went back and failed again? Or, worse yet, couldn't go back at all? The dean had made it very clear that I was going to have to ask Professor Winchester's permission if I wanted to resume my degree. I had to be prepared that the answer might not be the one I wanted.

My phone beeped with a text, breaking me from my thoughts.

I sighed and held my phone up to Babs. "Hayes again."

When you get back, please give me a call. Really need to talk to you.

She shook her head. "Just call him, Julesy. Rip off the Band-Aid. You're sure in your decision, and there's nothing he can say to change your mind." When I didn't respond she repeated, more sternly, eyebrow raised, "There's nothing he can say to change your mind."

I laughed. "Yes. Right. Nothing. I have to admit, though," I whispered—you never knew who could hear you—"that a small part of my moving on has to do with Conner. Well, no. Not Conner. The *idea* of Conner. I felt like it was too soon for me to start something new."

She turned to me. "Sweetheart, take it from an eighty-year-old. There is no such thing as too soon."

"I think I could have loved him," I admitted. "But I just wasn't sure it was the right time. I didn't want to hurt Hayes. And I really do need to find my footing all on my own."

Babs smiled at me. "Don't we all, darling. Don't we all."

I raised my eyebrow at her. "Are you thinking of Miles?" I stretched his name out in a singsong voice. Last night, Mom had told me all about him and their awkward dinnertime meetup. She was less than thrilled about the idea of Babs moving forward with someone new. I understood Mom's feelings, and I couldn't imagine anyone ever trying to fill Pops's shoes. But I also wanted my grandmother to be happy.

Babs shrugged but I saw the smile she tried to hide. "Your meddling mother . . . It is nothing, really. An old friend and I were dancing, and your mother and aunt nearly had a coronary. The first ambulance of the day was for the fifty-eight-year-olds. It seems a little wrong, doesn't it?"

I wondered if Miles did the same thing to her heart that Conner did to mine, even at her age.

We stopped to admire the stunning indoor winter garden, one of my favorite places at Biltmore. The round, sunken room off the entrance hall, held up by columns, was filled with flowers and swathed in greenery.

"Babs, you don't have to placate me. You can tell me the truth about Miles. I won't say anything to Mom and Aunt Alice."

She rolled her eyes, and I had to laugh at the role reversal, my interrogating her about *her* boyfriend. "Well, if you must know, he was a beau of mine in our early twenties. We adored each other, but he wasn't the one. But now he's come back, and I, like you, am torn as to what I should do about it."

I tucked her hand in the crook of my arm.

"I think your new relationship is wonderful, Babs. I want you to find love again. As a very wise woman once told me, 'Life is short, dear one. We must make the absolute most of it.' "

"So you don't feel as though I'm betraying your grandfather?"

I laughed. "Babs, what you and Pops had was . . . poetry. It was a love sonnet in motion. But just because you might not have poetry again doesn't mean you can't have frothy prose."

Babs squeezed my arm and we smiled knowingly at each other. That mischievous glimmer—the one I hadn't seen since Pops died—was back. And I had to think that maybe this Miles person had something to do with that.

I studied the motion and balance of the *Boy Stealing Geese* statue in the center of the winter garden. "The Karl Bitter statues have always been one of my favorite things about Biltmore. And surrounded with wedding flowers . . ."

Babs and I skipped the music room, hustled through the loggia, and stopped in the library, where we both gasped at the full, bustled gown worn by Helena Bonham Carter in *Frankenstein*. Every space, it seemed, had at least a costume or two from the fashion exhibit.

"That embroidery is breathtaking," Babs said.

It was. But I was only interested in one wedding

gown. "Ma'am?" I asked the uniformed Biltmore guide behind the velvet ropes. "Where is Cornelia Vanderbilt's wedding outfit?"

She smiled. "Oh, all the Vanderbilt reproductions and heirlooms are on display at Antler Hill Village."

That meant getting back in the car and driving, but Antler Hill—which originally housed Antler Hall, where all the estate families would gather for celebrations—was one of my favorite places on-site.

"Thank you!" I said, turning on my heels.

"Wait," Babs said. "We aren't going to finish the tour? I want to see the dresses!"

"After," I said. "But the anticipation of seeing Cornelia's is killing me!" I couldn't wait to see that wedding veil.

Babs grumbled. "Fine. I will go. I will look at the veil. I will show you that it is strikingly different from *our* wedding veil. And then we will finish the tour and drink wine."

"Don't have to tell me twice," I said.

"What I don't understand," Babs said, as we made our way back to the car, "is where this crazy notion came from in the first place. I think I brought you here a time too many when you were a little girl."

I laughed, opening the car door. "Well, it *looks* exactly like our wedding veil. And our wedding veil was gifted to my great-grandmother—your mother—under odd circumstances. I mean, you just never know."

Babs laughed. "Honey, that's a bit of a stretch."

"Fine," I said. "Maybe it is. But I just have this *feeling*. Isn't that enough?"

I drove us through the lush green mountainous miles to the village. Whereas Biltmore House was extravagant and gorgeous—and original—Antler Hill was fairly new, more of an ode to George Vanderbilt's farming roots, so it had a very rustic-chic, barnyard-at-its-best kind of feel.

We made our way down the pebbled concrete path to the front door of the Biltmore Legacy building. With a stone foundation, wood accents, and a mansard roof-line, it very much had the feel of a converted barn and silo. We paused at the pair of wooden front doors. "Are you ready?"

Babs crossed her arms. "For what? For you to realize how wrong you are? Yes. Yes, I am. For heaven's sake, Julia. My mother was gifted that veil by a Russian woman."

"How in the world would she have gotten it from a Russian woman?" I asked as I held the door open for her and followed her inside.

"Sweetheart, do you remember Gran? I wouldn't put anything at all past her."

As if by instinct, we both walked straight to the display of the reproduction of Cornelia's wedding outfit, ensconced in glass. We walked around the side of the case to get as good a look at the veil as we could.

"It's the Juliet cap that really gets me," I whispered. "The two rows of pearls at the bottom, one at the top, that intricate lace in the middle." Spotlights shone on the delicate piece of tulle and lace that spread behind the Cornelia mannequin. Just seeing it made me feel nervous, like I was in the presence of greatness.

"And the embroidery around the trim of the veil," I said. "I've never seen it anywhere else. Except—"

"Yes, but I would imagine it was a popular style at the time," Babs said.

"Aha!" I whisper-exclaimed. "So you agree they look similar!"

Babs said, "It's a wedding veil, Julia. There are millions of them. The chances that two of them look the same are pretty good."

"Yes. Because I'm certain Cornelia and Edith just grabbed any old thing off the rack." I crossed my arms and gave her my serious, police-interrogator look. "Don't you remember *anything* else about how Gran got the wedding veil?"

She just shrugged. "Julia, I am nearly eighty-one years old. I'm grateful I remember my own name."

And that's how I knew that Babs remembered more of the story than she was letting on.

A Place for Strangers

November 30, 1929

Cornelia had put off this difficult conversation for as long as she could, but as much as she didn't want to have it, she knew she needed to. Four years ago, her twenty-fifth birthday had felt like an answered prayer. Her fortune was finally hers. The house—and their family—would be saved. But then, a month ago, the unthinkable happened: the stock market crashed. Of course, it went without saying that Cornelia's family found itself in a vastly better position than most. But, after years of fun and freedom, they found themselves needing to tighten their belts once again to keep Biltmore afloat.

As she walked in the direction of the back stairs, determined to go down to the butler's pantry before she lost her nerve, she stopped in the doorway of the oak-paneled drawing room when she saw the man she was in search of: Mr. Noble. She paused to watch him, empty sleeve dangling as he methodically dusted the etchings over the fireplace, one after the other.

"That really isn't your job, you know," she said, causing him to turn abruptly and smile. "These days everything is my job, ma'am. We must all work together."

His proclamation made what she was about to do all the more difficult. Cornelia sat down on the off-white settee perpendicular to the fireplace and motioned for Mr. Noble to sit in the chair flanking it.

"I really shouldn't, ma'am," he said.

"Please," she practically whispered.

Her friend and most faithful servant acquiesced.

"I wish I were here to tell you that the tide has turned, that our troubles are behind us and we can rehire those we have let go."

"I presume that is not the news," Mr. Noble said gently.

Cornelia noticed how his jacket, which had once been thick and new, was starting to show signs of wear. The brass and silver buttons, however, still gleamed due to his precise daily polishing.

Cornelia shook her head and was embarrassed to find that tears sprung to her eyes. "We are either going to need to let another member of the staff go or dock everyone's wages accordingly." She looked down as she said, hoarsely, "Even yours."

Shame washed over her as she thought about the great lengths Mr. Noble had gone to keep Biltmore in as good a shape as possible. She looked up at him again. "I do understand if you need to go elsewhere, Mr. Noble. I truly do. It is unfair of me to ask you to continue to do the massive amount of work you do here for even less—"

Mr. Noble cut her off. "With all due respect, ma'am, I am aware of the world and my current lot in it. I know the service industry is dying. I know that men and women have no food, no coal, no work. So please accept my great gratitude. Room, board, and reduced wages are far superior to no room, no board, and no wages at all."

Cornelia was embarrassed by the tears now running down her face and, wiping them away, said hastily, "It would break my heart if you left."

"Leave you?" he said, smiling. "After all your family has done for me? I would never."

Cornelia sniffed. "I will make it right one day. I promise you." She paused. "It is dying, though, isn't it? Our way of life?"

He nodded. "I'm afraid so, ma'am."

She bit her lip to hold back more tears. "When did it change, Mr. Noble? Our customs and traditions, parties and trappings used to dazzle the outside world. Now they only despise us."

He shook his head and smiled at her kindly. "People don't know you, Mrs. Cecil. They don't understand how truly good your heart is. They are only hungry. That is all." He paused. "They can't understand that, in your own way, you have lost quite a bit too."

It seemed so silly now, how much Cornelia felt that she had lost. When had she ever gone hungry or slept without a roof over her head? "Thank you, Mr. Noble. Truly. I cannot express what you mean to my family, what you mean to me."

Clearing his throat, Mr. Noble said, "If you'll excuse me, ma'am, I'll get back to work now."

She nodded. With that unpleasantness behind her, Cornelia walked out to the loggia to tackle the next part of her day. She sat down in a wicker chair, pulled her shawl tighter around her shoulders to hold off the chill, and opened the notebook she had left here earlier. It made her smile—but it also made her head swim. For years, she had watched her mother take on this very task, planning Christmas gifts for each man, woman, and child who played a part in Biltmore House, organizing a grand celebration for all of them, and, of course, ensuring that Biltmore was decorated to the nines for the holidays. Even with the reduction in staff, even with the toll of the stock market crash, she was determined to make this a merry Christmas for everyone on the estate. Her family's personal celebrations would take a hit, but that was okay. Yes, in spite of their troubles, this would be a Christmas to remember.

She heard the door open and turned to see Jack, tall, handsome Jack, dressed in his riding clothes, striding across the loggia toward her.

"Oh, lovely," she sighed. "Have you come to whisk me away for a ride? My head is already spinning, and I haven't even begun to plan the Christmas celebrations."

"Well, you know I plan to dress as Santa again," Jack said. "That is for certain."

Cornelia couldn't help but laugh. Jack was the best Santa of all Santas. One of the most glorious parts of Biltmore was that the giant fireplaces inside its banquet hall were complete with interior ledges—which, as it turns out, were perfect for standing on. "Darling, when you jumped off that shelf and onto the hearth last year, I thought all the children would die of happiness."

Jack raised his eyebrow. "When Mr. Noble discovered that he could hoist a tray with a martini up to me while I was inside, I thought *I* might die of happiness."

Cornelia laughed and Jack sat down beside her and smiled. But there was something in that smile that Cornelia didn't quite like. It was a smile that meant bad news.

"Your mother and I have been talking . . ." he started.

"No good sentence ever began that way," Cornelia said, more snappily than she meant to. She knew she had been snappier than she should with Jack quite often lately. The stock market crashing certainly wasn't Jack's fault. But things had been strained between them all the same.

Jack, as if he hadn't even heard Cornelia, continued. "Your mother mentioned that the Chamber of Commerce and Judge Adams had an idea . . ."

Judge Adams was Edith's most trusted advisor. Cornelia trusted him even if she had never particularly *warmed* to him. He was cold and abrupt to absolutely everyone—well, to everyone except Edith. Even still, Judge Adams never missed a thing when it came to the estate, and his solutions were generally good even if Cornelia didn't like them. She had a feeling deep in her gut that this might be one such idea.

"With tourism down since the crash and the town struggling—and well, us struggling right along with it, they thought that Biltmore might be a draw."

She took a deep breath. "Please tell me you aren't suggesting what I think you're suggesting."

Jack turned to look her in the eye. "Neely, we live in the bachelors' wing anyway. If we open the house to the public, it will bring considerable revenue into the estate. We would only have to put a few of the main rooms downstairs on display. We'd hardly even notice a few people walking in and out."

Cornelia felt her jaw drop. "You can't be serious! What about Biltmore Forest?" The creation of the Biltmore Forest neighborhood out of a parcel of land on the property had been another of Judge Adams's ideas— and it had been going well the past few years. "I thought that was going to be the solution to all our problems. A grand neighborhood where people could have their own piece of the Vanderbilt lifestyle."

Jack shrugged. "No one has the funds to invest or build right now."

Cornelia felt her stomach turn. Increasingly, the bad news, the struggle to maintain Biltmore, felt impossible. She tried one more tactic. "But I thought the dairy was doing so well!"

"It is, Neely, but the taxes on the house alone are fifty thousand a year. It was hard before the crash, and now . . ."

She wanted to say that she knew damn well what the taxes were because she was the one who paid them. But that seemed overly unkind, so she bit her tongue. "What about the appraisals?" she asked. "What if we sell off the art and furnishings from some of the rooms we never use anyway?"

Jack nodded. "That might buy us a few months, a year. But then this beautiful house will be forever altered. It will be dismantled piecemeal, sold off for parts. You don't want that, do you?"

The sadness of this moment overwhelming her, Cornelia said, "Jack, this is my *home*." She didn't say that this felt like the final nail in the coffin, the last step toward her childhood oasis not being hers anymore. And she ignored the truth that was impossible to ignore now: the fabrics were tattered, the curtains faded, the carpets worn, the leathers dry and cracking. Everything needed to be updated and refreshed. And updating 250 rooms was staggering, a monumental feat. In their current financial state, it was impossible. It was such a tremendous responsibility that Cornelia could feel herself shrinking under the weight of it.

"It will always be your home, Connie. I'm trying to keep it your home for a long, long time."

Cornelia thought of her family lunching at the small table set up in front of the fireplaces in the banquet hall, the grand Christmas tree lording over them. She remembered laughing with her parents when she was young, so happy and carefree as they fished in the bass pond and the river. This home was theirs, was *hers*. How could she possibly give it away? The thought of people traipsing through her sanctuary tore at her soul. She could practically feel her father, the father whose memory she had tried so desperately to hold on to, rolling over in his grave.

She shook her head, feeling her dangling earrings hit her neck. "There has to be another way." Jack took her hand so gently it made the tears she was holding back spring to her eyes. She didn't *want* any of this. "Jack, Biltmore is a place for dignitaries, for nobility, for family, for friends. It isn't a place for strangers, anyone with a dollar bill in his or her back pocket to gape and gawk. It's such a violation of our privacy."

Biltmore wasn't the place of her youth. Living in the bachelors' wing wasn't ideal. But *this*? It was more than she imagined, even in those moments when she felt this massive home crushing her.

As if he could read her mind, Jack said, "Connie, Biltmore has already changed for you. We only open the largest rooms for parties now, and we've already had to let go of most of the staff and cut the wages of those left. This is just one more small piece."

She put her head in her hands. "Maybe it is just one more small piece for *you*. But this was my father's dream, Jack. And we have ruined it."

It was an ending. She knew it. Cornelia could feel Biltmore slipping from her grasp, her memories crumbling all around her.

"Things will turn around," Jack said, soothingly. "They always do. But, for now, we have to do what we must to save your father's dream. Don't you see?"

She looked down at the book in her lap and took a deep breath, steeled herself, felt her heart rate calm. Jack was right, as usual. This would just be a temporary solution until the economy recovered. It wouldn't be long now. It couldn't. She could do this. It was the only option.

She nodded up at her husband. "Maybe if we do this I can reinstate Mr. Noble and his charges' wages—maybe even give them the raises they deserve."

Jack only nodded and squeezed her shoulder.

Either way, Cornelia knew for sure now that she had to make this the best Christmas Biltmore had ever seen. It had been a trying time, but there was nothing like sitting around a warm fire by a fragrant tree counting your blessings. She would savor all of it this year. Her children, her husband, her friends, this house. Because, if she had learned anything, it was that life was full of lasts. And you never knew when yours might be.

Fugitives

B ack in my small living room at the Asheville mountain house that had been my parents' since I was a little girl, the wood-paneled walls and roaring fireplace making it cozy and warm, I sank down into the comfortable couch and studied Julia's face.

"Have I ever told you how much you look like my mother?"

She turned and smiled at me. "No, but I love that."

"I think you might just have a little of her gumption too," I said. "I'm so proud of you for going back to school, for finishing what you started." I slipped my shoes off, much to my tired feet's relief, and Julia followed suit.

She grimaced. "As long as Professor Winchester says it's okay," she said. "And that's a big if."

"Chin up. Your great-grandmother never took no for an answer. Neither will you."

She laughed. "Channel your inner Gladys."

"Exactly!"

The light flickered off her calm face then, and I said, "Julia, is that what's bothering you? Facing Professor Winchester? Or is it the veil?"

She just shrugged, and I realized then that this absurd obsession was more about Julia's ruined wedding day than it would ever be about the veil.

To bolster her spirits, I said, "We might be in possession of the Vanderbilt veil! What's more marvelous than that? Old ladies don't get that many adventures. We have to capitalize on each of them."

"Babs! We might be fugitives! We could be in possession of a priceless family heirloom that doesn't belong to us!"

I blew air from between my lips. "Julia, yes, the veils sort of look alike, but so what?"

"I just have this . . . feeling." She tucked her legs up under her and turned to face me. "What else do you remember about the veil, Babs? What else did Gran say about how she got it?"

I closed my eyes and squinted, trying to remember. That's usually not a great tactic. The faster you run toward the thought, the more quickly it runs away. "Mother always said that Daddy proposed to her, and she didn't know what to do. She felt incredibly conflicted and wasn't sure if a life with him was the right choice. And then she came across a woman who gave her a wedding veil."

I could feel my brow furrow. It wasn't that great of a story when you got right down to it. And my mother was the world's best storyteller, so I had to be forgetting something.

"Why would a random woman give Gran a wedding veil?"

"A Russian woman," I added.

"How can I wear that wedding veil in good conscience one day without knowing its true origin? How can I walk down the aisle in this veil that has totally changed for me now?"

I sighed. "You're thinking of this all wrong. How can you not walk down the aisle in the stunning and blessed veil of your great-grandmother and *possibly* the Vanderbilts?"

A tiny smile played on her lips. "It's kind of cool, isn't it?" she whispered.

I said nothing, only smiled. I had no intention of ever getting rid of that veil that had become a symbol for my family of all we had been through, all we had fought for. It was a symbol of my parents' happy life that almost wasn't, my glorious years with my husband. There was something magical in that veil, something sacred. Something *ours*.

I thought of when I'd worn that veil to marry my dear departed Reid, of all the memories we'd made together. The births of our beautiful girls, saving and scrimping to buy our first house, our annual mountain trips, and the time we went to Morocco for a taste of another life. I loved him so much. But Reid could never come back to me.

Miles, on the other hand, was here. He was alive and well. And, though he hadn't said it in as many words, I knew he was offering me a shot at another love to carry me through until the end. There was, of course, always the chance that I would have to mourn his loss too. But I'd be mourning him whether we were together or not.

If I was honest, I had fled like my mother because Miles was getting too close. I had escaped to sort out in my head what my heart already knew.

"I think we need wine to really figure this out," Julia said, interrupting my thoughts.

As she walked into the tiny kitchen of the open-concept cabin Reid and I had enjoyed for so many years, I wondered: Would I never return to Miles? Or, like my mother, would our temporary separation reveal a deeper truth—that we were meant to be? I looked over at Julia. And what in the world would the future hold for her, the next generation?

"Hey, Babs?" she called from the kitchen.

She reappeared, handing me a glass of wine, and sat beside me on the sofa, curling her legs up under her again. "Do you remember that day I got in trouble in seventh grade, when Mom brought me over to do the dishes from your book club meeting as punishment?"

"Oh, you poor thing. All those china plates and crystal glasses. What did you do? I don't remember."

She crossed her arms. "It wasn't my fault, Babs. A friend asked me to pass a note to her boyfriend but I got caught with it, so I got detention."

I laughed at how incensed she was over the whole thing, even now.

"Mom didn't believe that it wasn't my note."

I squeezed her knee. "But I did. I believed you."

She nodded. "Do you remember what you did to cheer me up?"

I gasped, the day coming back to me. "I got the veil out of the closet and let you wear it with your rubber gloves!"

She nodded seriously. "It was the best day of my life."

She paused. "But wait. If you believed me about the note, why did I still have to wash the dishes?"

"Well, honey, good help is hard to find." I winked.

She looked down into her glass. "Babs, that veil had always been a symbol of the great love that was going to find me one day. And now that's all tainted."

I put my arm around her, gazing at the roaring fire, thinking of my mother holding me close when I was so very afraid of my own future. "Darling girl, it isn't tainted."

"No?"

I shook my head. "Don't you see? It's saved. You made the hardest decision of your life by walking away from Hayes. And, by doing so, you saved the veil. And I believe very much that your great love is still going to find you."

"You do?"

"Without a doubt."

Suddenly, I was swamped with sadness. I had found my great love and now he was gone. And, looking into the face of my granddaughter, I couldn't help but remember the day it felt like my life truly began.

My twenty-one-year-old self opened one eye and peered warily out the window as my stomach dropped from both the hairpin curve and the dizzying drop. We were running parallel to the French Broad River, on our way to the Grove Park Inn, and if Daddy steered our 1958 Ford even six inches too far, we would be over the side and in the river. I glanced at him, whistling in his short-sleeved, blue-and-white-striped button-down shirt and khaki pants. Not a care in the world.

I am a person who loves room for error. Planes with two engines, not one. Getting the paper written the week before the deadline in case of unexpected sickness, a sudden death in the family. This was a drive I did not like.

I closed my eyes again and, pretending I had a rosary in my hand, began to pray out loud, "Our Father, who art in heaven . . ." I would pray ten Hail Marys and one Glory Be, as I had been taught, right after. We weren't Catholic, but after twelve years at the all-girls Catholic school Mother had insisted I attend, the tenets of Catholicism had gotten in somewhere. Mother had believed that sending me to Catholic school would make me chaste, something I suspected she herself had not been.

It had almost worked.

As I began my second "Hail Mary, full of grace . . ." Mother chimed in from the back seat, "For heaven's sake, Barbara. Enough!"

Mother never rode in the back seat. But I got horrible carsickness and years of pulling over had taught her that giving up her seat was less of a sacrifice than the alternative.

She lit a cigarette, rolled down the window and, though I didn't look back to see, I was certain she had put her hand atop the yellow hat that matched her dress to keep it from blowing off. She added, "If we go over the side, someone grab the veil."

The veil. The sign my mother had been looking for, the one that had convinced her to take my father up on his offer of marriage. It was a veil that, she dictated, would be passed on to countless future generations of our family, that she would encourage friends to wear, cousins, anyone she trusted, really. All who wore it, according to my mother, would have long marriages and happy lives. So far, only Mother, her two sisters, and my cousin had worn it, but so far, so good. I'd take all the luck I could get. Already, the veil had become a legend in our family. And I loved the idea of having something special to pass on to future generations—assuming the veil didn't meet its demise in the French Broad now, of course.

My father laughed heartily from the driver's seat. "Yes, Gladys. Forget Barbara, but for God's sake save that precious veil." He reached behind him and squeezed my mother's knee, to which I squealed, "Daddy! Both hands on the wheel!"

"Barbara, have you ever been in any danger with me in the driver's seat? How many times have I killed you in a car crash?"

I swallowed the nausea that was growing and said, "It only takes once."

And then I saw it, the salvation my upset stomach couldn't have been more grateful for: the Grove Park Inn. We had made it.

I closed my eyes and could see myself playing rounds of golf with my father, jumping into the pool with my cousins, hitting tennis balls with my mother. I imagined the taste of the inn's famous French toast on my lips, the stone terrace high in the air, capturing the mountain breeze, cooling us to our cores after long days of sun and sweat.

This place had been my haven, my escape, for too many years to count. And now, in only three days, I'd make two more memories there. I would marry my Reid, the love of my life, the man who had changed everything. Then we'd stay for our honeymoon, to begin our lives as husband and wife. And, if the wedding veil had anything to say about it, we'd be happy forever.

And we were. It had worked. That heirloom that my mother had shared with me had done its job; Reid and I had had an undeniably successful marriage. Now, long after that happy day, my eighty-year-old self knew that life was full of questions, of uncertainties, of risks. Our veil was the one thing that had felt constant, safe; it had been something to cling to always, no matter what. Julia might think that, if she could indeed prove it was the Vanderbilts', we should give it back. But I wasn't going to let the wedding veil go without a fight.

Work and Creation

March 15, 1930

Cornelia yawned and stretched in her old bedroom at Biltmore House. Her eyes drew up to the brocade fabric of the canopy bed as her hands ran across the matching bedspread, thick and soft. She smiled at the pink molding that adorned the ceiling. She was in her childhood bedroom; she was safe. But was that a crack in the ceiling? Chipped paint on the molding? Was that dust congregating around the threadbare curtains?

It was only then that the sickness began to wash over her, the dread, the sadness that made her heart and her limbs feel stuck to this bed. *Her* bed.

This was the first night since their marriage—unless one of them was traveling—that Cornelia hadn't slept with Jack. She longed to lean over, to place her head on his strong chest, to be wrapped in his arms. She had meant, by sleeping in her childhood room, to punish him for making her open the house for the first time today. Now she realized she was punishing herself. And of everyone, the fault for this belonged the least to dear Jack.

But still, this was a sure sign of the end of an era. Opening the house back up for parties, which Cornelia had done with overwhelming regularity since it became hers on her twenty-fifth birthday—this was the Jazz Age, after all—had given her a sense of normalcy. Midnight buffets in the Tapestry Gallery, celebration dinners in the banquet hall, brunches by the pool. They were using Biltmore House in the manner in which it was intended. She had invested the majority of her fortune into shares of the Biltmore Company in an attempt to save this place. It was hers. She was going to enjoy it. Until the stock market crash a few months ago, of course. After that, everything had to be put on pause.

But now *this*. She had failed her father. And, furthermore, it seemed she had put all her chips on a losing bet.

There was a soft tap on her door, and she, wishing she could be eight years old again, nearly expected a maid to waltz in with breakfast in bed. But that was a fantasy. The staff who had stayed on at Biltmore after her father died had continued to shrink over the years and was now at a bare minimum. Her mother had absorbed her lady's maid and footman into her personal payroll to further reduce the cost to Biltmore. The few servants who remained had so many things to attend to that breakfast was now served buffet-style in the bachelors' wing. Jack had taken to calling it Biltless, which he found terribly funny. Sometimes Cornelia did too. But not today. Instead of a maid with breakfast, it was Jack who came through the door.

The Lord himself knew Jack was only trying to help. And how ungrateful she was being.

"I'm sorry, darling," she said. "I truly am."

Anyone who knew Cornelia knew she was a force of nature. She believed it was what Jack loved most about her—the combination of her mother's fire and her father's wanderlust. Jack was the calm and steady breeze that righted her ship time and time again. And he was the most wonderful father, far better a father than she could have ever dreamed of being a mother. He truly savored spending time with their young sons in a way that eluded her. And she, in many, many moments, knew that he understood her.

He understood her when he met her that fateful night in Washington, D.C. He understood her when he gave up city life and politics to move to Asheville. He understood her when he spent nights awake with her mother plotting how to turn the barely profitable dairy into the kind of business that could sustain their massive home's upkeep. He even understood her when she sat him down to explain numerology, to share her numbers and his, their compatibilities, strengths, and weaknesses as a couple.

"I know what great lengths you have gone to to save Biltmore for me, for our children. And if you think opening our home to the public is what we ought to do, it's what we will do."

He kissed her softly. "That's my girl."

Cornelia stepped into her bathroom and pulled her favorite skirt and blouse onto her lithe frame, draping an opera-length medallion necklace over her head and affixing a thick gold chain bracelet to her wrist. She sorted her short hair and took a deep breath. She was sad, yes. But she was American royalty. Her sons—who had both been born in the Louis XV suite, just as she had—would both be by her side to witness how their mother handled tough times. Rose and Cornelia's other dear friends of Biltmore, including the ones who had been fixtures of this estate far longer than she had, would all be there today supporting her. She would feel them rallying around her. And, when she really thought about it, she was doing this for them just as much as she was doing it for her family. She wasn't just saving her home. She was saving their livelihoods. That bolstered her spirits considerably, even made the smile she pinned on her face feel believable.

Besides, it was March 15—315—which was the number of letting go and moving forward. It almost always meant better times ahead. And it was the universe's way of saying there was something new and exciting to move toward. So maybe this was for the best. Maybe it was the only way. *The numbers never lie*, she reminded herself.

"Neely!" Jack called from the other side of the door. He opened it and peeked inside. "Ready?"

She smiled at him, cleaned and polished in his suit. Was it partially his mustache that reminded her of her father? Her father who had told her Biltmore was his legacy. *Their* legacy? What would her father have done in this situation? She took Jack's hand, which, despite her sulking and moodiness as of late, was outstretched to her all the same.

He opened his arms and she felt safe again as he wrapped her in them.

"You're beautiful," he said. "I'm proud of you."

"Mommy!" five-year-old George called to her. The nanny trailed behind holding William. Cornelia leaned down to kiss her older son and took her nineteen-month-old in her arms.

She smiled at her children and at Jack. She had somewhere she needed to be in these final moments before her home changed forever.

"Want to see something?" she asked George, who nodded effusively. Cornelia made her way down the long hall and pushed open the door to the Louis XV suite. It was, without a doubt, one of the most private places on the property, one of the most special and profound. For now, only downstairs would be open to the public, but there was already talk of which bedrooms could be restored enough to increase the scale of the tour—and perhaps the popularity if not the ticket price. Cornelia ran her hand along the velvet wallcovering, ignoring the bald spots and faded places. The mahogany bed was covered with sheets to protect it, and the drapes, worn and full of moth holes, were drawn to block out sunlight. Cornelia ran a finger across the wooden cradle, dust scattering. It was once swathed in the finest linens but now sat empty and austere. There was beauty in that too, though, Cornelia knew.

"This room is where Mama was born and where you were born," she said, ruffling George's hair. "And where you were born too," she said, touching the tip of William's nose.

"But it almost wasn't," Jack said, as she leaned into him. By the time William was born, modern women gave birth in hospitals, not at home. Hospitals were cleaner, safer. Cornelia had been set on it.

"You, William," Jack picked up, "were born in the middle of a terrible flood."

"What's a flood?" George asked.

As Jack explained, Cornelia could almost see herself in that bed. She remembered the rising water, how she was already in terrific pain, and how the change of plans, the lack of hospital, panicked her.

But her mother had said, "Darling girl, I gave birth to you in that room, and you gave birth to George. It is a room that protects us, that knows us. Daddy will be there with you and so will I."

Less than an hour later, William Amherst Vanderbilt Cecil made his way into the world, his cry strong and healthy, his mother safe and sound. As Cornelia held him in her arms, all, for the moment, felt perfect. She looked down into his bright blue eyes and that cherubic face that reminded her of Jack's, wondering what the future would hold for him, how he would grow up, how he would change—and how the world would change along with him. All was quiet; all was calm. "No matter what else happens in your life," Cornelia said to him softly, "you will always have a mother who thinks you hung the moon, who loves you more than all the stars."

Edith entered the room almost silently, and Cornelia couldn't think of anyone else she would want there quite so much. The pair sat in silence for a moment before Cornelia handed her new son to her mother. Her mother and her son. Three-and-a-half-year-old George burst in, his linen shirt askew and slightly untucked from its matching shorts. "I want to see the baby!" he proclaimed boldly. He climbed in bed beside his mother and Edith held out tiny William so that George could see.

"You're a big brother now, George," Edith said.

"Can he play tractors with me, Mama?" George questioned, peering at his mother.

She cocked her head as if she were considering this matter a great deal. "Maybe not quite yet. But soon."

George nodded. "Okay." Then, as if he'd finally made up his mind, he added, "I like my brother, Mama."

Cornelia's heart felt as though it truly swelled inside her chest and a contentment so pure filled every inch of her. She had never felt more complete or proud.

Now, less than two years later, Cornelia smiled at her sons again. She was still proud. But, much to her dismay, not as complete as she had once believed. She held her head up high, tears filling her eyes.

"Shall we?" Jack asked. They made their way, slowly, down the imposing staircase. As Jack led her out the front door of what, in moments, would no longer truly be her family home, Cornelia felt as if she were saying goodbye to her memories. *No*, she chided herself. Biltmore was still her home, the memories her own. It was still her name on the deed. She was simply sharing it.

Cornelia knew she'd never remember the speeches given to commemorate the opening of the home or the memorials raised that day to honor her father. When she handed William to Jack and stepped up to the microphone to speak to the press, to the townspeople, to the men and women who had been a part of Biltmore even longer than she had, she felt out of her body. "We both feel that in doing this," she heard herself say, "it is a fitting memorial to my father. After all, Biltmore was his life's work and creation."

Daddy's life's work and creation, she thought. *But what is mine?*

As she looked out into the faces of the crowd, Cornelia felt it was high time she figured out that very thing.

A Shock

Babs was in the kitchen of the mountain house prepping dinner and, as I finally unloaded our bags from our cars, my mind was in a million places. My parents had gone to retrieve my things from Hayes's and take them to Sarah's, where I would be going in a few days. We had always dreamed of living together, and even if I didn't get into school, Raleigh would be an easy place for me to find a job. I knew we would get along, and sharing a place would save me from going too much deeper in the hole on my student loans. My stomach flipped. This was it. It was just me on my own two feet now. No Hayes to fall back on.

The fact that I hadn't faced his texts—of which there were now at least ten—was clogging my consciousness. And then there was the wedding veil . . . This morning, Babs had been even more dismissive of my worries about it. And, well, she was probably right. I knew, when I really thought about it, that this was nothing more than a good way to get my mind off my real problems.

Even still, I had the urge to get in the car and drive to my parents', get the veil, and drive back to Biltmore to compare the two. But the original had been missing for decades. A few more weeks wouldn't hurt. I wondered if Mom had already had it preserved again in another one of the airtight sealed boxes it had been in when we first pulled it out after I got engaged. Suddenly, I was overcome with guilt. I had been engaged to Hayes, for heaven's sake. I owed him a phone call. I set the bags by the front door and, noticing that I had cell service outside the house, decided to bite the bullet.

I tapped HAYES and, on the third ring, almost hung up, hoping I could ignore him for one more day. But he answered.

"Are you avoiding me?" he asked, a smile lacing his voice.

I laughed nervously. "No, of course not. I've just been busy."

"Yoga teachers at island resorts *are* known for their busy schedules," he said sarcastically.

I rolled my eyes. "Ha-ha. Well, with the traveling and everything, there hasn't been a great time."

I sat down on the wooden porch bench by Babs's front door, the one that looked like it had been put together from raw tree branches. I was tempted to tell him I was in Asheville with Babs, but I didn't want to risk his taking a leap of faith and coming here. I was in a good place. I was convinced I had done the right thing. I didn't need him interfering with that.

"What's up with you?" he said breezily.

Ugh. I just wanted to get this over with. "I decided to go back to school," I said. "I'm going to finish."

"You can be an architect *now*, Julia. You have a degree. I don't get why you wouldn't just take the test and start working."

I was already irritated at him, and it had only been like thirty seconds. He was right. I had my bachelor's degree; I had completed my supervised hours. "Because I need to finish what I started, Hayes."

"Well, I have something I need to say . . ."

I steeled myself. At what point did I quit letting him down easy? At what point did I draw a hard line?

"Someone's moving in with me."

For a split second, I wondered why he felt it important to tell me that. Ben from work who had just gotten transferred? Alex from college who seemed destined for a life of couch surfing? Then, I felt all the blood rush to my head. "Someone?"

There was silence on the other line. "Another woman," he said quietly. "I know it's probably a shock. But I felt like I should tell you."

Probably a shock? Probably a shock? No. A shock is a shaved head. A shock is quitting your job on a whim. "Hayes, you were with me in the islands like a hot minute ago. You were begging me to take you back. How could you possibly have met someone new and gotten serious that quickly?" There was silence again on the other end of the line and then all the pieces suddenly came together. "Oh my God. Chrissy Matthews is moving in with you."

"Well . . ."

I couldn't breathe. The sadness of being away from Hayes came in waves every day. I knew it would take a long time for my heart to really heal. But this was a new feeling: Rage. Distress. Proof. He had lied to me. I had almost agreed to spend the rest of my life with him.

I scoffed, anger rising in me. "Wow. That's just. Wow." I didn't want him back, but I also couldn't believe he would so flagrantly disrespect me. It was shocking.

"Look, Jules, I don't want to dredge up old wounds—"

"Old wounds!" I spat. "Hayes, they're wounds from like a week ago. They don't even have scabs, for God's sake!"

"Well, you didn't seem to have too much trouble moving on," he said.

I was so shocked it took me a minute to figure out what he was talking about. "You mean Conner? The guy I made out with in the islands and will probably never see again? Yeah. I'll get you our Save the Date real soon."

I opened the email app on my phone—an almost unconscious but terrible multitasking habit I knew I needed to break—as Hayes was saying something that no longer seemed that interesting or important. Something like, "I'm sorry if this hurts you, but I can't stay stuck in the past."

I was getting ready to say "Thank God I didn't marry you," when I noticed an email from Conner.

Conner and I hadn't spoken since I'd left the islands, but we had had a brief email exchange. He had told me to send him the failed project, that architecture was often about making it work, not starting over, and he wanted to see if he could help. I had stayed up way too late the night before working on it. But, after not seeing it for months, coming back to my plans with fresh eyes gave me an entirely new perspective. I was proud of the changes I'd made, but I wanted another set of eyes on them before I presented them to the true judge and jury: Professor Winchester.

"Hayes, I have to go," I said.

"Julia!" he protested as I hung up. It was a poetic moment. I was hanging up on my past while opening an email that could define my future.

Jules, this is genius, the email from Conner read. I have a couple small tweaks, but your revisions are amazing. You've created something brilliant.

As I opened the new CAD files on my phone, glancing at the graduated living facility layout, I finally felt like I could exhale. Just a few tweaks to the "pod" living areas—mostly to get the nurses' stations up to Americans with Disabilities Act standards—and my plans would be ready.

I sat down, leaned my head back, and took a deep breath, trying to calm my racing heart. I was confident now that my plans were fresh and imaginative and, as I had learned we all must do every now and then, also followed the rules.

"Are you okay?" Babs asked, peering at me on the slate front stoop. I hadn't even heard her open the door.

I had a lot to tell her. She sat down beside me.

"Babs, I quit my program because I thought I was going to fail my final project."

She squinted at me but said nothing. I recapped my conversation with Conner and showed her my phone with his encouraging comments.

"I was too ashamed to risk failing and having to start over, so I quit instead. The professor made me feel . . . I don't know. Like I had chosen the wrong path. That I didn't have a right to be an architect. It's stupid, but it really messed me up."

She smiled at me. "Honey, that isn't stupid. That's life. We go to some great lengths to preserve ourselves. But sometimes it backfires and what you thought would help makes it a thousand times worse."

I nodded. "I know. I had just called my engagement off. And then this happened, and I just couldn't face it. I went back to Hayes, and I messed up everything."

Babs whistled. "Did you ever!"

I swatted her arm lightly.

"But it's time for me to stand on my own two feet now. I know I can. And, really, I have to." I paused. "No, I *want* to." Then I realized I had another piece of news to deliver. "Oh, and Hayes is moving in with Chrissy Matthews."

Babs had practically no reaction at all, her face as placid as it had been a moment earlier. "That doesn't surprise me in the least," she said. "Seems pretty typical Hayes if you ask me." Before I had a chance to respond, she said, "How do you feel about pork chops for dinner?"

I smirked at her. "Pork chops sound great. They'll be my last decent meal before I return to a life of ramen and instant oatmeal."

She made a horrified face. "I'd better pack you up some leftovers then." She got up and turned back to me. "Jules," she said, "I never doubted you for a minute. Not one."

I watched her walk back into the house, feeling a little teary-eyed. Hayes was in the past, and, no matter what Professor Winchester said, architecture was my future. I was going to go inside and celebrate with my grandmother. All was right with the world.

I typed a quick thank-you email to Conner. All I had wanted to do since I last saw him was call him. Well, no, all I had wanted to do was get on an airplane and fly to New York and surprise him at the door of his apartment wearing nothing but a trench coat.

I finished reading his email. I'm so proud of you. I hope you don't mind me sharing my thoughts. Your work is illuminating, and the world needs to see it. I want to see you more than anything, but I heard you on that boat. You aren't ready. In the meantime, I'll be waiting and working and dreaming about a beautiful yoga-doing, building-drawing heroine who makes great jokes about spaceships and has the most beautiful smile I've ever seen.

I felt so warm and tingly inside that I couldn't even muster up anger at Hayes anymore. Hayes was my past, my misspent youth. Conner could be my future. And so I typed back, I hope she ends up with a charming, handsome, and very generous architect who sweeps her off her feet completely. I can't wait for that day when I run into you on a street corner.

I held the phone to my chest, hugging it as if it were Conner himself. I knew if I called him, he would answer. But maybe he was right. Maybe I should honor what I needed before I jumped into another relationship.

I swiped to refresh my email and saw the perfect response: I can't wait for that wink.

I floated into the kitchen, where Babs was chopping okra. One look at my face and she laughed. "Oh, my darling girl, are we going to have cause to bring the wedding veil out again?"

I smiled. If we did determine that our veil was the Vanderbilts', the right thing to do was return it. But that wedding veil hadn't just brought my family love and luck. It had saved me. If it weren't for its weighty presence and meaning, I had no doubt I would have married

Hayes. I would have been his wife right now while he snuck out with Chrissy Matthews or, when he got bored, with whichever woman was next. What kind of life was that?

I walked up beside Babs and started chopping the onion on the cutting board. She nodded toward a pair of filled champagne flutes sitting on the counter, and I grabbed one and handed her the other.

We clinked our glasses. "To true love, in every form it takes," said Babs.

"To true love." Two months ago, "true love" would have meant Hayes, wedding vows, and a happily ever after. But, right now, I realized, I couldn't think of anyone I loved more truly than the woman standing right beside me.

A Rotten Egg

October 9, 1933

Rose's sitting room was one of Cornelia's favorite places in the world. It was cozy and homey, with dark wood and low ceilings, comfortable furniture, and today, as there was a bit of a nip in the air, a roaring fire.

"How do you do it?" Cornelia asked Rose. "How is it that you have always seemed so very content?"

Rose laughed, setting her coffee cup on the wooden end table. Her long-sleeved floral dress was simple but flattered the curves that four children had lent her five-foot-two-inch frame. Cornelia eclipsed her in height, but, she was realizing, maybe not in wisdom.

"It's just my nature, Nelly," she said. "I've never wanted much, and I've always felt happy."

Cornelia was bathing in shame now. "I'm sorry, Rose. What you must think of me. Poor little girl with the largest home in America, two healthy, beautiful sons, and a doting husband."

Rose laughed and leaned forward, her short hair, curled around her ears, staying put. "Nell, I know you better than most anyone, I'd daresay. You are a lovely person. Fun, vivacious, bright, outgoing—but you've never been one to feel terribly settled. You have a lot, but you haven't found what makes you happy. And that's okay. You're young. There's time. You don't need to worry about becoming the woman you were meant to be just yet."

Cornelia felt that Rose had hit the nail on the head. How she had tried. She had hoped marriage and children would make her happy like they had Rose. Then she had hoped that service to others would fill her cup, like it had for her mother. Or that throwing herself into the preservation of Biltmore would be the thing, like it was for Jack. Or maybe it was in big parties and good times, like it was for Bunchy. But, alas, Cornelia still hadn't found her place.

Why couldn't she just be happy?

Painting had helped over the last few years but maybe it wasn't quite right. "I hope I don't need to worry," Cornelia said. "But I hate to tell you: thirty-three isn't so young." She paused. "Did I tell you I've started writing?"

"You have?" Rose said. "Like, a journal? Or stories? Or what?"

"A story," Cornelia said. She didn't add that her quest to find a publisher wasn't going so well.

"Oh! Is that why you were in New York last week? Tell me all about it. Let me pretend I went with you."

"I wish you had. I stayed in the newly completed Waldorf Astoria. It was glorious." She took a sip of tea.

"Did I tell you Mother had leased our house in New York?"

Rose shook her head. Telling other friends these details might feel embarrassing. But Cornelia could always be honest with Rose. "And I finally rode down the 600 block of Fifth Avenue, where the Cornelius Vanderbilt II House used to be."

Rose's eyes went wide. "And it's gone? Leveled?"

Cornelia nodded. "The taxes were just too much." She shrugged. "Maybe it's for the best. People hate the rich so much now. Those monstrosities were simply taunting them. I think it's slightly better here, but I hate the idea of what people think about my family and me now."

"They don't even know you," Rose said. "If they don't like you, they have never met you and experienced your kindness for themselves."

Cornelia tried to let herself be cheered by her friend's statement. "Well, at any rate, the house wasn't ours. But it's sad to think of it being gone all the same."

"Just like all the grand estates in Britain that have been leveled to ashes—" Rose abruptly cut herself off.

Cornelia saw the flash in Rose's eyes that meant she wished she hadn't said that. Now they were both thinking of Biltmore.

"I'm proud of you, dear one," Rose said, changing the subject. "You have so much talent, and I know you'll find your happiness. Now, tell me more about all this time you've been spending in New York."

Looking around Rose's quaint and cozy home, life in New York seemed a world away. Cornelia shrugged, not wanting to seem like she preferred her life there to her life here. But did she? It was hard to tell. "I've been surrounding myself with the most incredible visionaries, Rose. Artists and painters, writers and sculptors, actors and playwrights. And you can't even imagine all I've learned about numerology." She paused and put her finger up. "I had a numerologist I met work up your numbers. It is a fascinating and telling report and so spot on, I think. You'll see."

Cornelia noticed the bewildered look on her friend's face and stopped talking. Of course, this was all a lot to take in. It was an entirely different world. Even still, Rose was always her safe place. Like coming home. "Remember those days when we used to run down to the creamery?" she asked, changing the subject. "When our biggest worry was choosing between peach and strawberry?"

Rose laughed. "You know what I think would be rather grand? If we went down to the creamery and got ice cream right now."

"That's the most fantastic idea I've heard in quite some time."

After a good afternoon with a lifelong friend—and a great cone of ice cream—Cornelia hoped she would feel cheered. And few things cleared her mind as much as her horse, but the ride from the creamery back home hadn't quite brought her peace. Instead, Cornelia felt restless as she wandered around the grounds of Biltmore. No, *restless* wasn't the right word for it. Panicked. Trapped. How was it that, surrounded by thousands of acres, one could feel trapped? How was it that a place she had once loved so fully could highlight everything that was suddenly wrong with her life?

Cornelia had hoped the visit with Rose and the ride would clear her head, but her humiliation from her trip to New York the week before kept popping up. Her story of an Elizabethan girl who ventures to North Carolina where she is inspired to take up the arts was a story that Cornelia could write. It was a story she knew. Painting perhaps hadn't panned out the way she thought it might, but that was okay. Because now she felt in her bones that she was destined to become a great writer, if only she could just break through the trouble she was having finding a publisher.

Her face went hot at the mere remembrance of what had transpired the week before. She had begged her mother to ask one of her oldest and dearest friends, Edith Wharton—one of the foremost women writers in the world, mind you—to help her. And Edith had delivered, procuring a meeting for Cornelia with J. W. Hiltman, the president of the newly merged Appleton-Century Company.

The architecture at 4 Bond Street, the building that housed Appleton-Century, was lovely, Cornelia had thought as she stood in front of the six-story building, with its mansard roof and cast iron façade. She knew from her schooling that it was Second Empire style, with a nod to the Baroque. She smiled, feeling pleased and proud that this, most surely, would be the home of her first published work. She took a deep breath and walked through the door that the doorman was holding open for her. She was guided to a shining brass bank of elevators and escorted to the office of Mr. Hiltman, the publisher. This was certainly treatment the publisher's newest talent would receive, right?

As she sat across the wide mahogany desk from Mr. Hiltman, looking over his shoulder out the long window at the bustling street she mused that New York really was marvelous. She had once preferred the quiet life of Biltmore, but lately, as a writer, an artist, this was where she felt she belonged. Sure, she hated being in the spotlight, in the papers. But perhaps if it was for her *work*, she would feel differently. She would have to, as Edith Wharton had told her. Publicity created book sales. She vowed to spend more time here, study writing. Painting too. She felt most herself, most alive, when she was engrossed in these pursuits.

"Your protagonist is well formed," Mr. Hiltman began, smoothing his hand from the knot in his tie to the top of his vest over and over again. Was he nervous? Did her literary prowess amaze him that much? "But, I'm afraid to say, Mrs. Cecil, I found—and my staff agrees—that her journey isn't quite the right fit. There's something forced about it. The ending lacks believability or, really, a true sense of finality for the reader."

"Shall I rewrite it with your suggestions?" Cornelia asked, still hopeful.

The look of pity in his eyes nearly broke her. "I don't think so, Mrs. Cecil."

Had he been mean to her, ridiculed her, she could have taken it. But nothing had ever wounded her pride quite as deeply as that pitying look.

Now, back at Biltmore, licking her wounds, Cornelia couldn't help but laugh at the irony of his words. Her journey hadn't felt quite right either. And perhaps she had been too concerned with creating an ending that she hoped for herself instead of an ending that felt right for her character. Or perhaps it simply wasn't realistic to feel properly creative when one's life was in such upheaval. Yes. That was it. She needed to go somewhere else.

She still hadn't gotten used to the hundreds of people traipsing through her house every day, but as Jack had told her, the income was helping with the day-to-day upkeep of the house. But still, she felt in the marrow of her bones that her home—the home they were trying so desperately to save—wasn't hers anymore. She had been spending more time in Manhattan, taking trips to Paris, anything to avoid the fact that her house had become something akin to cattle storage. Her recent travels were an excuse to escape. And maybe, she realized, to look for something that was all hers. Not her father's. Not her husband's. *Hers.*

Today, there were no tourists, only Cornelia and her family. As she arrived back to the main house she caught a glimpse of her boys tearing through a field—off to the creamery, no doubt—and felt such a surge of love for them that she knew she had to put her own concerns aside to find her roots here again, visitors or no. She *must* be the mother they deserved. As William called to George "Last one there is a rotten egg!," Cornelia felt as though her younger self were the one walking these grounds. She used to feel certain that of all the little girls in all the world, she must have been the luckiest.

Papa always told her she could live anywhere she chose. But she loved Biltmore. She couldn't have put it into words then, but it was her safety, her roots, her home. And, even as a child, she knew down to the very tips of her toes that she would never want to leave.

So why was it that now, all these years later, leaving was all she could think about?

Jack appeared at the crest of the hill then, and her heart surged with love for him, for the boys that looked so much like him. She was very blessed indeed, if only she'd take the time to remember it. Jack kissed her cheek, and Cornelia wrapped her arms around herself. They stood in silence for a minute or two before she said, "The boys love it here so much, don't they?"

Jack raised his eyebrow suspiciously. The proper schooling of their children was a primary concern these days. Jack had been sent off to school as a small boy, and he wanted the same thing for his own sons—something Cornelia was strictly opposed to. "Are you reminding me so that I don't bring up their going off to school again?"

Was she that transparent? "I just think fresh air and places to play are so good for them, Jack."

"I understand. I'm not forcing you into anything. I'm only saying that appropriate schooling—and the connections they will make—are paramount, and our personal feelings shouldn't stand in the way of what is best for their futures."

"Well of course not. Our personal feelings shouldn't matter. They're only *our* children."

Jack smiled good-naturedly. "We don't have to decide now. They can finish out the term and we'll see how their education is progressing."

Cornelia had to admit that, if the boys were gone, she could focus quite a bit more on what her own future held. She was considering sending them off more than she let on.

William, George behind him, ran to Cornelia with his ice-cream cone, shouting, "Mama! Mama!" The conversation was over—for now.

She knelt to catch him in her arms. "Hello, my precious boy." She pointed down at the old-timey milk tram at the bottom of the hill. "Do you want to know a secret?"

He nodded.

"Do you know why the horses that carry the milk tram are so quiet?"

He shook his head, staring at her, rapt with attention. "The horses wear rubber shoes instead of metal ones so they don't wake people up when they're clomping through town early in the morning."

He smiled.

"What flavor did you get?" Cornelia asked, but she knew already. William always got strawberry. He pointed the cone in her direction, and she took a bite despite having already had her own ice cream, the sweet, smooth flavor and texture filling her mouth. It really was the most spectacular ice cream she'd ever had, and she smiled thinking of the women who spent their days slicing thousands of strawberries and peaches to add to this divine marriage of cream and sugar. What if they advertised more, got more customers? Could the dairy ever be enough to sustain Biltmore?

She asked Jack that very thing.

"Dearest, we've been through this. The tenant farmers are barely producing enough to cover their rents and feed their families, as is. Expansion seems unlikely."

They had been through it all—Cornelia, Jack, Edith, and Judge Adams, sitting around the small family breakfast table, sharing numbers, projections. Even tourism at Biltmore was down as fewer people had two dollars to spare for admission.

She looked over at her husband, feeling resentful that they had become, so often, nothing short of business partners.

Cornelia sat down in the grass, pulling little William onto her lap, not even minding the sticky ice cream running down his arm and onto her. So often now she felt like giving up, throwing her hands up in the air, leaving Biltmore, never to return. She didn't feel like she belonged here. So where did she belong?

"Mommy," George said. "Can we live at Biltmore forever?" The boys always preferred life at Biltmore to that in Washington, but his question felt larger than usual, more laced with longing. She looked into his round eyes, the same eyes her father had had. How could she deny him anything?

"Of course. Biltmore will be yours one day. You can live here forever and ever."

Then, to her husband, she sighed. "You know best, Jack. You always have."

He squeezed his wife's hand, and both noticed the distance that had formed between them. Maybe it was the stress of the market crash, death and flooding, and the myriad problems they had faced together these past few years. Maybe it was because Cornelia's absences were becoming lengthier and more frequent than they had been before, and Jack, longing to keep her close, was holding on too tight. Maybe it was that while Cornelia's interests drew more and more toward her art and writing, Jack's were more steadfastly rooted in how to turn the estate into a thriving business—for his own edification, for his sons. But, most of all, for his wife. If he could hold on to Biltmore, he could hold on to Cornelia.

"Have you ever felt like this, Jack? Like I do?" Cornelia asked.

He smiled up at his young sons as the pair of boys took off over the hill again. Jack leaned back on his hands, his legs out in front of him. "I suppose I should ask you how precisely you feel, but I think I know."

Cornelia smiled. Then there was this. This man, these children, this life. It was what kept her here when she felt like she was drowning. She lay her head in his lap, enjoying the feel of the sun on her face.

"We all go through this, Connie," he said, looking down at his bride. "I think we all go through a period in our lives where we feel restless, when we begin to question what our purpose is and whether we've made the right decisions."

Yes. *That*. That was exactly how Cornelia felt. "I think I'm looking for meaning." She paused. "So what did you do, Jack? When you felt like this, how did you solve the problem?"

"Well, darling, I married you and I moved to Biltmore. We had our sons. There is no doubt that my life changed completely and, much to my surprise, it felt like the perfect fit."

She wished he had said something else because, truth be told, Cornelia had expected those things to solve her problems. Whenever she was feeling restless and searching in her early twenties, she had believed it was because she hadn't found her partner. Then, when the itch struck again, she thought having George would fix it. Then William. It was only now that she was realizing her problem might be bigger than all that. Well, not her problem. Maybe her passion, the life she felt she was supposed to lead.

She was entranced and spellbound by the people she was meeting in New York, their alternative view on life, where art—not things—was what mattered, the study of numerology. It made sense to her; the numbers made the pieces of her life add up. But it was more than that. These people understood her art and her writing, they understood her need to do something different with her life. But, then again, it seemed that her dear husband did too. Cornelia smiled as William practically flung himself at George and the two giggled, falling to the ground. Her heart swelled with love and pride for those precious children. And she remembered that she had a place here too.

"Jack, do you ever wish we could just sell it all? Sell Biltmore and walk away? Can you even imagine a life where we aren't weighed down by the constant struggle of keeping up this house, the grounds, the village? We would live like royalty anywhere else."

Jack smiled down at her. "I believe we live like royalty now."

Cornelia sighed. "You know what I mean, Jack. No panic about property taxes coming up again. No constant roof maintenance or leaks or peeling wallpaper. No moving money around to finance another disaster."

"I get it, but the woman I met was dead set on staying at Biltmore forever."

"The woman you met was a naive child!" Cornelia snapped back, suddenly infuriated that he expected her to always be the same, stay the same. "That woman had been handed everything on a silver platter. She had no idea the toll it would take to keep this ship afloat."

He rubbed her cheek. "Ah, yes. But I am committed now, I am afraid. As of now, my love, I must go down with the ship."

Cornelia let out a small laugh. Of course. And wasn't that what she wanted?

"I love you, Connie. From those first walks around Washington until forever. I will do anything I can to make you happy."

She brightened. "Even come to London to help me look for a publisher?" It was becoming clearer to Cornelia that the New York publishing scene wasn't going to be it for her. Her book was, after all, about an Elizabethan girl. London was a better fit for that story.

This was a common course of conversation between them. Cornelia couldn't understand. Wasn't it Jack who had been homesick for London for years? Why, now, could he not give in to her requests to spend time there—for her?

Instead of arguing, he just smiled. "We'll see, Neely. We'll see."

Like that little girl running wild and untethered through the vastness of this stunning estate, Cornelia knew what *we'll see* meant. For now, maybe forever, his answer was no.

Love Is Blind

I was too old to be afraid. And yet that's precisely what I was. As I packed my bags to get ready to go home, Julia lounging in my unmade bed going through my jewelry, I was scared. What would I say to Miles? It was all I could think about.

Julia held an earring up to her ear and got on her knees to examine it in the mirror hanging over the bed, her short exercise skirt falling into place as she did. Reid had hung that fifty-pound mirror with two hundred-pound hooks because he had been so terrified it would fall on us while we were sleeping. So far, so good.

I smiled at my granddaughter. "Those look good on you. You should keep them."

"I can't keep them, Babs. They're yours. Besides, where would I even wear them?"

"Everywhere." I winked at her. They were small clover studs that didn't look good on me anymore. No one told me that in the disastrous process of aging even my earlobes would begin to sag. It was very unfair.

Julia smiled. "No. I think you're going to have slightly more occasion to wear them than I am."

I rolled my eyes and, putting the last pair of pajamas in my suitcase, sat down on the bed. "Jules, I am an old lady. I was married to the love of my life. What am I even thinking? Maybe your mother is right. Maybe I am a little senile. I'm eighty years old. I can't *date*."

She put the earring back in my bag. "You know, Babs, I'm not an expert on love—which should be very, very clear by now. But what I am an expert on is how hard it is to find. And I have to think that once you've found it, once you've been given a second chance at something really remarkable, you shouldn't let it go. You deserve to be happy."

"How did you get so smart?" I asked, cupping her chin in my hand. Ah, that face. That milky, unlined skin. Those taut, fresh earlobes. The things you miss do surprise you.

"Good genes." She winked at me.

"My darling, I don't want to talk about things you'd rather avoid. But how are you feeling this morning? About Hayes and his news."

She shook her head and looked down at her hands. "I'm not going to tell Mom," she said, looking up at me with wide eyes.

I slid my finger over my mouth indicating that my lips were sealed.

"We were together for so long. I can't believe he'd just move on so quickly."

I believed the right answer was that he had moved on

about a million times while he was still with my grand-daughter, but I kept that unpleasantness to myself.

She shrugged and sat up straight. "But even though I'm surprised—and a little sad—I'm finished crying over him. I've done it for like half my life and I won't do it anymore. If he wants to make an ass out of himself, then great. Fine by me."

I nodded resolutely. "Good girl." I paused and added, "I'm proud of you."

She smiled. "You are?"

She couldn't hide the sadness in her eyes. In a world where people were supposed to materialize from the womb, life plans intact, I could only imagine how diffi-cult these last few months had been for her. "The things people want out of life evolve. It's necessary. It's natural. But I've seen more people than you can imagine stay the course instead of risking the discomfort of change. So, yes. I'm proud of you. You risked the change. It has already paid off, and I have to believe it will continue to do so."

Clasping my charm bracelet around her wrist and admiring it, she said, "Babs, it's okay for you to risk the discomfort of change too, you know."

I felt butterflies in my stomach at the mere thought of Miles. "In case no one has ever told you, everything becomes more uncomfortable the older you get."

We both laughed, and she removed the bracelet, put-ting it back inside the felt-lined jewelry bag the girls had gotten me for my birthday nearly twenty years ago.

"Sooo . . ." Julia said. "Not to bring up sore subjects, but . . ."

I raised my eyebrow. "We've covered Miles and Hayes. Do we have yet more sore subjects?"

"I have to go talk to my professor tomorrow. The one who told me I wasn't going to make it as an architect."

My stomach rolled for her.

"I'm kind of scared," she said.

Maybe I should have told her that I was scared too. But I didn't. Instead, I thought about the other times in my life I'd been afraid. Wondering if I was making the right decision by marrying Reid instead of pursuing my very real feelings for Miles. Coming home from the hospital with two babies, not one. Moving out of my beloved home and into a fresh start. But I had made it through each and every challenge. I had come through them better than the woman I had been on the other side. And so I said, "The greatest things that have ever happened to me have come when I have chosen to face my fear."

Julia zipped my jewelry bag shut. "Not true, Babs. I don't believe you have ever been afraid in your entire life."

Those words reverberated in my mind for hours after Julia and I parted, me heading back to the beach, her to Raleigh. I smiled thinking of Miles, of the way he held me close when we danced, of how his hand felt on the small of my back, at the silly way he grunted when he served on the tennis court. It was much too soon to call it love, but it was much too late in our lives to ignore it.

When I pulled back into my complex, I felt myself relax. As much as I wanted to pretend that nothing had changed, that long drive on the highway was getting harder. I was exhausted and shaken. As the stress of the drive wore off, I realized I had another thing to be nervous about: I had to talk to Miles. Who was I, at my age, to even pretend to have this sort of love affair? Did women my age get to feel these things again?

I was exhausted as I lay my small bag on my bed. I wanted nothing more than a cold drink and a hot bath. But I had always been one to unpack right away. I wouldn't want to do my chores tomorrow any more than I did today. And, being at Summer Acres, there were so few of them to do anyway.

When I unzipped my tote, the first thing on top was a postcard of Biltmore. I smiled at the sight of it. Julia must have slipped it in while she was putting my things in the car.

Dear Babs,

Thank you for encouraging me to live out my dream. I can't tell you what it means to me. I just want to make sure that you know it's okay to live out your next dream too, whatever—and with whomever—that might be. Mom and Alice love you so much that they will come around. And if they don't, I'll shame them into pretending that they have. Follow your heart. Be happy. It's what Pops would want. Love you from Asheville to Morehead City and back. (That's got to be farther than the moon, right?)

XO Julia

I smiled, held the card to my chest, and laughed at how similar we were. I'd snuck a card in her suitcase too. I hoped she would find it. I worried about her but reassured myself that her spirit was too abundant and wild to ever break.

I got up and, just as I was organizing my toiletries in the bathroom, heard a voice call "Barbara!" Those butterflies, the ones that had caused me to run off to Asheville in the first place, welled up. But then I felt myself smiling at the sound of Miles's voice. When I met him in the living room, the hug he wrapped me in, the kiss he placed on my lips, felt easy, natural, almost automatic.

When we pulled apart, I gasped and put my hand to my lips. How long had it been since a man had kissed them?

"I . . . I'm sorry," he fumbled. "I didn't even think. It was just my natural reaction."

"Mine too," I whispered. I was feeling so many emotions that I couldn't quite place them. But, no, perhaps I could. Relief was top of mind. It was like all that worry, all that stress, just melted away. I hadn't had to think about this big step, it just flowed; it was pure emotion and chemistry. To me, that was everything.

"That's good, right?"

"Our first kiss," I said, finally smiling now.

"No, no. Don't you remember? Our first kiss was more than sixty years ago."

I chuckled. "Of course. Of course it was." Somehow, the remembrance of that night on the riverbank as twenty-year-old camp counselors, fireworks bursting overhead, soothed the part of me that felt conflicted. This wasn't starting something new and scary, not really. It was falling back into something old and familiar. And old and familiar was what I craved right now. But old and familiar also meant truth. It also meant explanations.

I took his hand and led him to the couch. "You asked me a few days ago why I'd been so set on marrying Reid," I started, slowly.

His eyes were pinned on mine, searching my face.

"The world is a completely different place than it was when you and I were young. There's nothing that hasn't changed, but, even still, I feel a little ashamed . . ."

Miles squeezed my hand. "You should never have to feel ashamed of anything."

I smiled. "Well, I'm glad you feel that way, because the night you came to ask me to change my mind about marrying Reid, I didn't tell you the whole truth. The thing I didn't tell you, the line in the sand, was that I was pregnant."

His eyes widened and he leaned back. So I *had* shocked him, just like I had shocked myself all those years ago. I don't know why I'd slept with Reid in the first place. To celebrate our engagement, I suppose. But, deep down, I think it was an apology. Miles had part of my heart. I had to give my new fiancé something that was all his own, and my virginity seemed like a good start. Had we waited until our wedding night, as we had planned, my entire life could have been different.

Now, I plunged forward. "I need to be honest in that, pregnant or not, I believe I would have married Reid. We had been together for so long. He knew my heart so well, and everything with you was just so new. I still consider him to be the true love of my life." I paused and took a deep breath before I said, very slowly, "Reid is my one and only husband."

Miles nodded, taking it in, studying my face. "I understand that, Barbara." My heart raced at what he might say next. Was this too hard for him? Too much truth at once? "I don't *need* a new wife. I don't expect anything from you except for you to be your wonderful self."

He paused. "So, what if we don't worry so much

about what tomorrow holds and, tonight, I take you to dinner?"

I laughed. "Oh, um. Yes. But I need to unpack and freshen up."

Miles smiled. "You look lovely to me."

He had to have been lying. After driving all day, I was certain I looked like some unkempt creature the cat had dragged in. But the way he looked at me made me feel like the most beautiful woman in the world. "Well, love is blind," I said before I could stop myself. *Love.* I could feel the color rising to my cheeks. How mortifying. He surely didn't love me.

"Is it?" he asked. "Or is it through the lens of love that we finally begin to see clearly?"

I was grateful to him for covering for my gaffe. Now we had both said "love." I started to respond, but Miles interrupted.

"Barbara, in the name of transparency, there is something that is important to me." He stopped and looked at me seriously. My breath caught in my throat. "Even if you can't be my wife, could you still be my doubles partner?"

I put my hand over my heart with mock joy. "Oh, Miles! I thought you'd never ask."

He looked around, searching. "We need something to seal the deal."

I put my finger up and headed to my room. I opened the top drawer of the antique dresser that had belonged to my mother and would one day belong to my daughters. As I slid my hand inside to retrieve a small jewelry pouch, my fingers hit something smooth that seemed to be stuck to the underside of the top of the chest. I rescued it, surprised to see my mother's handwriting on the front of a letter that I had never seen before. It felt like a sign, like she was here with me. And, putting it back in the chest to save for later, I knew I would come back to read it to hear her voice.

Walking back to the living room, I held my hand out to Miles, along with the item I had gone to find. He took the object lying in my palm. "What is this rusty piece of tin?" He studied it, then laughed. "Is this my old fraternity pin?"

I nodded and smiled.

"You can't wear this faded old thing."

I shrugged. "The older I get, the more the faded things become my favorites."

Miles laughed and, with great pomp and circumstance, pinned the relic to my collar.

He held out his hand. I took it.

After I freshened up and got ready to go to dinner, Miles slid into the driver's seat of my golf cart. My *pink* golf cart. I gasped, suddenly remembering something. I pulled out my phone and texted my granddaughter. *We can't have the Vanderbilt veil! The hair of the woman who gave it to my mother was PINK. Cornelia would never.*

I set my phone in the cup holder and looked at the man who just kept surprising me. "I feel like walking. Do you?" I asked.

Miles wordlessly stepped out of the cart, and as we made our way down the gentle, winding sidewalk of Summer Acres, my legs stretching and my heart full, I wondered if, after all the life I had lived, love was even possible. But, for the first time since Reid had died, I felt like I was ready to find out.

The Helm

As Edith waited in the grand banquet hall for her daughter—and their meeting about Biltmore—it was the first time she noticed it: "The proportions of this table are absurd."

Jack laughed. "You think so?"

Of course, the room itself was ridiculous, and the table only matched its ludicrousness.

Judge Adams chimed in. "For a dinner party of sixty-seven, it feels right, cozy even."

They all laughed. For this small party of four, it felt mad. The space across the table was so large, the room so cavernous with its seventy-foot-high barrel ceiling, that even the giant tapestries and rugs were dwarfed by its enormous size. Even still, the acoustics were perfect. One of Bunchy and Cornelia's favorite activities as girls was to sit at either end of the mammoth table and hold a conversation in their normal voices. They could hear each other as well as if they were sitting side by side.

"We're glad you're here today," Judge Adams said warmly. Cornelia often complained of his chilliness to the staff, but Edith didn't see it.

For years, it had been Jack, Edith, and Judge Adams at the helm of this ship. Then Cornelia, when her time came, had taken charge, and, Edith, who had become president of the Women's Congressional Club, and who continued her vast volunteer and greater-good efforts—in addition to the entertaining that befit a senator's wife, of course—had stepped away from Biltmore. Truth be told, for years after that fateful night in the library, when she told George of her plans to remarry—the night she quit hearing his voice—returning to Biltmore had pained her. It had become easier over the years. If time didn't heal all wounds, it at least dulled them. But even when Edith most wanted to walk away from the estate, she didn't. She persevered for George's memory. For her daughter. For her grandsons' futures.

For the past several months, after what Edith gathered was a dreadful and slightly embarrassing meeting with a publisher in New York, Cornelia had been in a phase where she had thrust herself into Biltmore and its success, its care and keeping. She had gone so far as to personally help the maids and Mr. Noble repair upholstery, polish furniture, and procure replacement fabrics so that more rooms could be opened, more money made on tour tickets. She had accompanied Judge Adams on his rounds to the tenant farmers—something he'd hated so clearly that Edith had to hide her chuckles when he pretended to be delighted by it—and given them tips she had read about how to increase their yields and, thus, their profits. From any other lady of the house, this might have been met with eye rolls and sighs. But the farmers trusted Cornelia. They had grown up with her, counted on her, believed in her. They knew she had their best interests at heart.

Edith admired Cornelia's attention to the estate and all she was doing. "I'm very happy to be here," Edith said, glancing down at her watch. Where *was* her daughter? Edith still attended these meetings when she happened to be in Asheville, but Cornelia had asked them to gather today for some sort of announcement, she presumed about Biltmore. "So what do we think the lady of the manor has in store for us today?" Edith asked Jack, somewhat warily. He gave Edith a tight smile and shook his head.

"I haven't wanted to worry you . . ." he started, trailing off. That is perhaps the single phrase that makes a mother worry most. Edith's heart began to race. She hadn't seen her daughter in several months, but she had assumed that all was well. Or, at least, better.

"She might be in need of some psychiatric attendance." Judge Adams cleared his throat ominously.

Jack cut his eyes at the judge. "You could attempt to be less harsh. This is my wife we're talking about."

"And my daughter," Edith chimed in. "I thought she was doing so well!"

Edith had had a talk with her daughter three months ago over Christmas in which Cornelia had asked, "Mother, haven't you ever just wanted something more for yourself? Haven't you ever dreamed a bigger dream?"

Edith had been taken aback. "Well, yes, of course." She felt herself bristle. "In case you haven't noticed, I have dedicated my life to the service of others and raised a daughter to do much the same. Haven't I?"

Cornelia had sighed. "Sure, sure, Mother. And someone has to be the best dressed lady in Washington."

Edith had been proud of that nickname, but now the comment—in which Cornelia was clearly demeaning her mother's purpose—stung. Cornelia must have seen it in Edith's face. "I'm sorry, Mother. Yes. Yes, of course you have dedicated your life to service. It's just that Biltmore is Daddy's. You have your political life and all your causes. I want something to call my own."

Edith had wanted to protest that Cornelia had two of the most charming children she had ever met, that she had a husband who adored her, a mother who worshipped her, the grandest home in America. She had founded the first female polo league; she was a world-class sportswoman. She was admired locally for her art. What else did she need? It wasn't like Edith to back away from speaking the truth. But something told her that her words would be falling on deaf ears. How devastated poor George would be to know that his legacy felt like such a burden to his daughter.

"You've always reminded me of your father," Edith said. "You get your creativity from him. He felt such peace here at Biltmore and hoped you would too."

"I used to," Cornelia said. "But it's such a media circus now. It used to be my escape. Now it's just one more place the papers can find me, and people can judge us for being too rich."

Edith sighed. She couldn't change the way that, after the stock market crashed, the rich who had once been admired were now viewed with such disdain. But she did feel somewhat responsible for the media circus caused by opening the house: She had done everything humanly possible to maintain the estate when she was in charge, to keep it from swallowing them whole. Opening it to the public wouldn't have been her first choice. If she had known the toll it would take on Cornelia, she would take it back. She would take it all back. But then, these past few months, as Cornelia threw herself back into Biltmore, Edith felt like things had turned around.

Now, in this grand dining room that held her best memories, she waited anxiously for her daughter, her back to the doorway, Jack and Judge Adams sitting across the table. When they gasped in unison, she felt her heart stop.

She turned, hesitantly, as her daughter walked into the room. Her hair, her dark, sleek, shiny mane of glory, was now a glowing pink. Edith felt like she couldn't breathe. Her daughter—her nearly thirty-four-year-old daughter, no less—had dyed her hair. Pink. She wanted to say something, ask something, but her throat felt closed.

Cornelia took the seat they had left for her at the head of the table. This was, after all, her announcement. "Mother, Jack, Judge Adams," she began. "I have decided that the boys need to be in school in England, and I am going to accompany them."

Edith's first thought was that her grandsons were too small to be in boarding school. Jack had preached its virtues to her ad nauseum, but she felt sure that—after protests from Cornelia—Jack and Cornelia had decided to keep them home. Yes, of course, it was common for people of their set to send their children off when they were young, but it wasn't how George and Edith had raised Cornelia, so she had always just assumed . . . But, looking at her daughter, she realized that it was no longer safe to assume anything. She tried to catch Jack's eyes across the table, but they were fixed on his wife. Then again, she had to consider that perhaps this pink-haired mother of theirs was in no shape to raise them. Maybe they were better off abroad.

"Neely," Jack whispered. "Your hair."

"Well, I wouldn't expect *you* to understand it," she said pointedly. It caught Edith off guard. No one had been more understanding than Jack. It was an instance in which she believed Jack being quite a bit older than Cornelia helped tremendously. Everything Cornelia did, it seemed to Jack, was a youthful lark. But judging by the horrified expression on his face, it appeared the spell had been broken. Cornelia's tone softened, and she explained, "That is the other reason I have brought you here today. I am nearly thirty-four now, which is my age of becoming pragmatic about reaching my goals."

Now Edith had to speak up. "I'm sorry. It's what?"

"In numerology, Mother. Thirty-four is my year for that. And 1934 is also my year for exploring my creativity, talents, and life choices."

Jack met Edith's eyes now, both their faces alight with terror.

"And the pink hair?" Judge Adams chimed in.

"It's the color of my aura, of course," Cornelia said.

"Of course," he replied.

Edith wanted to smack him. Yes, Cornelia's interest in numerology and spirituality and her life path had grown even stronger as of late. But she hadn't gone to this extreme yet.

"It all makes sense now," Cornelia said. "My life-path number is twenty-two, which means that was the age I needed a partner's support most, the year I met Jack."

Edith knew from all Cornelia's obsessive chatter

about numerology that the life-path number—derived from a formula based on one's month, day, and year of birth—was the most important one. But it wasn't until this moment that she realized just how much her daughter was letting this nonsense control her life.

"And now, at almost thirty-four, you no longer need me, I assume," Jack chimed in. Edith could tell he was aiming for an angry tone but he barely managed sad—he sounded resigned. He had to be tired from facing down the hurricane that was her daughter day after day, explaining her absences to her children, running a behemoth of an estate with far too little staff.

"I need some time to pursue my goals," Cornelia said. "Not forever. But this is my year. It is my time."

"Cornelia—" Jack said.

Edith needed to say something, but she didn't know what, so she went with something simple. "Darling, you can't really believe that numbers define your fate. Are you okay?"

Cornelia sighed. "Yes, Mother. I do indeed believe that. Plus, I have spent my entire life surrounded by the press and prying eyes. I don't want the same for my children. This way, I can escape, just for a few months. I can work on my art; I can find my way."

"I know you weren't sure about boarding school. I didn't mean to push you into making a decision so quickly. I can keep the boys here while you work on your art, and plan what will be best for their education," Jack said. "You've been gone so much these past couple of years that we've managed quite well without you."

Edith waited for the hurt to register in her daughter's eyes. But it didn't. Perhaps because it was simply the truth.

"The schooling I received here wasn't adequate," said Cornelia. "I feel it has held me back. I'd like the boys to not face that same hurdle."

Edith could barely contain her scoff. Cornelia had had the most wonderful education at the village school, some of the best tutors in the world, and she would put the education at Miss Madeira's against any school anywhere. To blame her unhappiness on her education seemed off base. Edith wanted to scream at her daughter, shake her, tell her to snap out of it, grow up. But she was a lady, not to mention a mother who felt like her hands were tied.

Jack looked pleadingly at Edith. "Why don't we all go look at schools, make some decisions together?" she suggested. "Maybe even find something in America."

"I've already enrolled them," Cornelia said matter-of-factly.

Edith shared Jack's look of horror. Cornelia, as the mother, held all the legal rights, could make all the decisions about her children's lives without the input or permission of anyone else—including her husband and mother. And, with the way George had left his estate, it was Cornelia who held the purse strings. When George had planned for his eventual demise, neither he nor Edith could have imagined a scenario in which their bright, loving daughter wouldn't have been the best person to control her family's financial welfare. But they had clearly made a mistake. And now it was too late.

"Cornelia," Jack said, "you don't get to make decisions like this about our children without even consulting me. That isn't how this works." Edith could see how angry he was, how he was trying to hide it.

"Jack," Cornelia said. "I have enrolled them. There is nothing else to say. I thought *you* of all people would be thrilled. It was your idea in the first place."

"I think you know the boarding school part is not what I'm upset about. But, fine, fine, you win. Let's try it while you're on your journey. Then we can reassess." He cleared his throat and said firmly, "But the children will spend their summers at Biltmore."

Cornelia hesitated, but then agreed. "The children will spend their summers at Biltmore."

Edith felt sick at the idea of the boys going away. "Cornelia, I don't think you're being sensible. I understand that you need some time away. But the boys can stay here with us."

Cornelia gave her mother a look so cold it chilled her. "Mother, they are my children. I will do what I feel is best for them."

Her icy stare broke something inside Edith. When had this happened? When had her daughter, her best friend, begun to see her as a person whose opinion didn't count?

Edith took a deep breath. This was a fight she wasn't going to win. The boys were leaving. And, in all honesty, how often did she even see them now anyway? Three, four times a year? Plus, summer was right around the corner. If, God forbid, Cornelia didn't come back to Asheville, Edith could arrange to spend her summers at the Frith, her Asheville house, to help Jack and the nanny with the boys' care. The nanny was wonderful, of course, but Edith and George had both been close with their families and believed that familial influence was key.

She looked at her pink-haired daughter and soothed herself that Cornelia would probably change her mind shortly—perhaps before they even left. This was, she was sure, a phase. It would wear off. She would come back home.

"I'll go with you," Jack said. "To England, to drop them off."

"Or I can," Edith said.

"I think it will only make the separation harder for them," Cornelia said. "I can go alone."

"I'll go," Judge Adams said, shocking Edith. "I can help you find a new place to live and make sure the boys are seen to properly."

What shocked Edith more was when Cornelia replied, "Fine. That's just fine."

She didn't even *like* Judge Adams.

"All right, then," Cornelia said. "It's all settled. Should we move on to matters of the estate?"

But all Edith could think of while her daughter talked was that she had never imagined that the girl who loved Biltmore so much would leave it. She was sick with shock and worry, shaking with . . . Was it anger? Fear? Perhaps both. She couldn't bring herself to say a single word the rest of the meeting.

When Edith and Jack were finally alone in the banquet hall, after Cornelia and Judge Adams left to discuss matters of the move, Jack turned to her. "What do we do?"

Edith had been thinking the same thing. Her instinct was to tie Cornelia to a chair and never let her leave. But it wasn't realistic. And maybe it wasn't even right. As much as she would love to fight and protest, to take her grandsons away, that wasn't possible. She and Peter lived a life of constant travel; she couldn't spare the time she'd need to be at Biltmore. "How do you feel about the boys leaving?" she asked.

"While I wish I had been consulted on this, I do feel it's the right thing." He paused. "Not only for the education. For many reasons." Edith could tell he didn't want to say that her daughter's unstable habits and moods weren't the best thing for their children. But she already knew.

"Edith?"

"Yes?"

"I've tried so hard to make her happy. I need you to know that."

Edith smiled sadly at him. "I know, Jack. So have I. But I think we both know that happiness is something we have to find for ourselves." She took a deep breath. "If we love her, Jack, I think we have to let her go."

"I do love her," Jack whispered.

Edith took her son-in-law's hand. And she wondered how she could have had a daughter with dreams so big that even the whole of Biltmore Estate couldn't hold them.

Love and Luck

I studied myself in the mirror again. Black pants, white blouse, leopard flats, thin leather belt around my waist. Straight hair. No jewelry except the small clover studs that Babs had left on her dresser, pinned to a postcard that said, *These have always brought me luck. And the beautiful thing is, you don't even need it, my brilliant girl.*

I touched the earrings for courage and studied myself again. I wanted to look professional and grown up. No fuss, no frills. I thought I had pulled it off. Or maybe I looked like a restaurant hostess. I wasn't sure. Maybe that was better, though. I was about to stand off with my toughest adversary, something I'd had to do quite a few times during my college years with entitled customers demanding a table.

Sarah popped her head in. It was only seven in the

morning, but she was already up, showered, dressed, and ready.

"I thought you didn't have to be at work until nine," I said.

"I don't. But I'm going with you."

I laughed. "You are my best friend in the world, but you can't go with me."

She nodded. "I know I can't go *in* with you, but I'm going to wait outside. Then if you get nervous, you'll know I'm right there." She paused. "And if you change your mind and have to make a run for it, I'll be ready with the getaway car."

I wanted to protest. She was already working such long hours at her new law firm. I didn't want to add anything to her very full plate. But the thought of my best friend being right outside was too wonderful to turn down. And, well, it wouldn't be the first time in recent history I'd needed a quick getaway.

"How do I look?"

She studied me. "Like you're applying for a job at Outback."

"Perfect."

I grabbed my portfolio. I had printed out my plans complete with most of Conner's suggestions—but not all of them. It was still my project, after all.

Sarah dropped me off at the front door, and I took a deep breath as I walked up the steps into the imposing brick building of NC State's architecture school. Sun streamed through the glass panes in the ceiling, giving me a brief flashback to the moment at Biltmore, inside the conservatory, before my entire life had changed. But I steeled myself. My life was going to change again. This time for the better.

My flats tapped rhythmically as I walked down the hall, trying to avoid the fact that all that stood between me and my reentry to school was this meeting and Professor Winchester's approval. The door opened and there she was in her black pencil dress and spiky black heels, her black hair pulled into a severe bun. The precision of her took my breath away. She looked like one of the straight lines she loved so much. Suddenly, everything about me seemed wrong.

"Welcome back, Ms. Baxter," she said, gesturing for me to come in. I walked past her, gathering all my nerve, and slowly began taking my drawings out, one by one, and pinning them to the corkboard wall, which was completely empty.

When I finished, I turned to her.

"Might I ask you a question?" she asked, studying the board, her arms crossed.

"Anything."

"These drawings look familiar—you knew that I was going to fail this project before. Why not start over with something new? Why not play it a little safer? Why design an entire community when just a building would do?"

I could feel myself shrinking under her gaze, remembering that horrible day when I felt like my entire future had vanished right in front of me. "Well . . ." I hated how small my voice sounded. My heart was pounding, and suddenly, I felt like I had made the wrong choice. Why hadn't I undertaken something smaller? Something that didn't push the envelope quite so much?

"I'm just wondering why you would embark on something of this magnitude for your final project," Professor Winchester continued. "Why not stick to what you know?"

I would have said I didn't know the answer until I heard it come out of my mouth. "You taught me that in architecture we always have to push the envelope, to extend our boundaries, to test the limits. Affordable senior living is one of the most pressing issues facing our country today, and I think I can help solve some of its problems. I can't draw a community and plan a life around the ways we've always lived because that hasn't always worked. Plus, we can't know what the future holds."

I had proven that handily this year. I had ditched my career, abandoned my fiancé. My entire future that I had planned so seamlessly had fallen apart, burst at the seams. I had to build something new. I was determined. I might be blowing my shot at a second chance here, but I had told the truth. I had pursued my passion, and I was honoring what I wanted. The more I did it, the better I was becoming at it.

"All right then," she replied, smiling with a dazzling row of white teeth, which like her dress, were perfectly straight. "Let's see what you've done here."

I explained my senior living community model, which featured a health and rehabilitation facility at the center, and, around the edges, a robust fitness center, large community garden, three separate dining facilities, and a Google-style lounge for employees. In between, pods that each contained six bedrooms and bathrooms with a common living area, kitchen, and preparation space for one caregiver, who would be responsible for that pod's residents.

I paused. "Professor? I have a confession."

She moved her hand in a gesture that told me to proceed.

"I didn't fix this all on my own. I had a friend who's an architect help me." I smiled thinking of Conner, loving the way even the thought of his name sounded in my head. "I have detailed in an attachment which parts were his ideas in the name of transparency."

"Architecture is a team sport, Ms. Baxter. We have to be able to rely on each other at so many points along the way. Being able to work together is a fundamental strength. Not a weakness."

"Good to know." I pointed up and said, "You'll see on these revised plans how every ADA guideline has been met." I paused, deciding that a building should tell a story and so should I. "But, Professor, my grandmother, Babs, moved to a graduated living facility a month ago, similar to this one. And, well, I know a thing or two about southern ladies and how much they pride themselves on the aesthetics of their homes. So she and I put our heads together to make some of these features a little more pleasing to the eye."

"When in doubt, ask the client." She paused, pointing. "Tell me about these choices for the common spaces."

And so I did, noting the focus on utilizing technology to increase self-reliance. As I'd learned in my research, the over-sixty-five age group is largely willing to adapt to new technology.

An hour later, I could feel myself starting to sweat. I had truly enjoyed presenting my project, but Professor Winchester was impossible to read. Now the verdict would be laid down. "Ms. Baxter," she began, "it's clear that you have worked very, very hard on these drawings, that you have not only studied but also put your heart into them." She crossed her arms, a smile playing on her lips. "I knew you were up to the challenge. I have to admit, when you didn't come back right away, I felt like perhaps I'd been too harsh on you."

I laughed. "So . . ."

"So I think we are going to have a very productive semester." She held her hand out, and I shook it. "Welcome back, Ms. Baxter. I trust that you will leave my care ready for any firm you choose."

I wanted to hug her, but she didn't seem like a hugger. So, instead, I said, "Thank you, Professor. This time I won't let you down. I promise."

She shrugged. "This isn't a contract with me, Ms. Baxter. It's one with yourself."

She was right. I knew that now. As I left, I was floating on air. I had been intimidated by this legend of a woman. But I also felt proud because I had faced my fear. Again. In so many ways, I realized that, perhaps, that was what Professor Winchester had wanted me to do the entire time.

As I headed out to meet Sarah, I realized I had failed in two of the biggest ways I could have imagined this year. But that was okay. That was life. And, as I stepped outside into the cool, crisp air, I thought that maybe Babs was right. Maybe my failures hadn't actually ended anything. Maybe they were teaching me how to get back up and move forward in a better direction, toward the life I imagined.

I had reinstated my rightful place in architecture school. Instead of going deeper into student loan debt—and with Hayes's blessing—I had sold my engagement ring to pay for my last semester and some of my existing loan. I had celebrated with my friends. I couldn't procrastinate anymore. I had to go see my parents and apologize for ruining the wedding that wasn't.

I had asked Babs to come too. I knew it was a lot to ask her to come to Raleigh, but she'd argued that we could all do with a nice lunch and visit.

As I pulled up our road, my family's pretty two-story brick house gave me its usual homey feeling, followed immediately by an uneasy one. Sometimes I thought that maybe that was a little bit dramatic. But, then again, sometimes I felt like it wasn't dramatic enough. I sat for a moment in my car, admiring the way the trees framed the house from the street. The landscaping was always perfectly manicured thanks to Dad. (I assumed he spent a lot of time in the yard to keep from fighting with Mom.) Boxwoods framed either side of the small front stoop and little flowers lined the brick walk.

It looked like the perfect home, and in so many ways it was. We had been a strong family unit, Mom, Dad, and me. I had been so happy—right up until the time I turned eight and started to realize that *I* was happy. And my house seemed happy. But my parents weren't happy. At least, not together. The first separation came right before my thirteenth birthday, and honestly, I was relieved. When they got back together six months later, I thought things were better—until the summer I turned seventeen and they split up again. By the time they got back together the second time, this house had quit being a safe space for me. Instead, it was a place of instability.

A tap on my passenger-side window made me jump. I smiled, unlocked the door, and Babs slid in, wearing a tailored yellow pantsuit, her hair freshly combed. "You ready?"

I nodded. Then I told her what I had been thinking. "You know, Babs, I would never blame any of my life decisions on my parents. But there's a small part of me that thinks maybe that's why Hayes and that can't-live-with-you, can't-live-without-you thing was so appealing for so long. It was what I knew. And it was exciting."

She nodded. "It makes your heart race, all right. But I have to think it also makes for a difficult life."

"Are we going to tell Mom? About the veil looking like Cornelia's?"

Babs pursed her lips. "We know now that Mother couldn't have gotten it from the Vanderbilts."

For some reason, I still wasn't convinced. Or maybe I was just looking for a reason to break free of the thing. "Well, maybe it would be nice to see it anyway."

We walked slowly up the brick walk. "Was Miles excited to have you back?"

She tried not to, but she smiled. "This day is about you, Jules. We'll worry about all that later."

That was a big yes.

When I opened the front door, my dad was walking through the dim foyer in a pair of khakis and a polo, golf bag strapped to his back.

"Jules!" he said, engulfing me in a hug. "Isn't this a great surprise?"

"Surprise?" I asked as Mom appeared and hugged me and then Babs.

"Oh, I didn't tell you she was coming?" Mom said. "It must have slipped my mind."

Things definitely weren't going well if she hadn't told Dad I was coming. I turned and raised my eyebrows at her. "Dad, do you have time to sit down for a second before you leave? There's something I want to talk to you and Mom about."

He looked down at his watch. "Want me to cancel my tee time? I certainly would have had I known you were coming." There was a sharpness at the end of his sentence as he glared at Mom.

"No," I said quickly. "This will only take a minute." Thirty seconds in and I was already trying to soothe, to fix. Maybe that's who I was. A fixer. But now, I realized proudly, I was fixing myself.

We all followed Mom into the formal living room off to the left, which felt wrong because no one ever sat in there. She looked thinner than usual, and I wondered if that was from the stress of my calling off the wedding. I felt guiltier, if that was even possible.

The living room still had the same pink and green drapes with the swooping valances that had been the height of sophistication when I was a kid, and which now desperately needed to be replaced. The worn velvet on what had been my great-grandmother's chair was still soft, but I could feel every spring underneath me. As if I wasn't uncomfortable enough.

"I just wanted to apologize," I said.

"There's no need—" Dad started.

But Mom cut him off. "Actually, there really is."

I nodded. "I wanted to apologize for running off the way I did, for ruining the wedding, and for wasting all the money I know you worked so hard to save for that day." It made me a little sick to think about all the food and the band and the rentals and the flowers that we didn't use. Mom and I had tried to keep the number of guests down and make substitutions for lower-priced choices when we could, but any way you sliced it, it was an expensive day. And, looking around, I knew that money could have been used for some much-needed improvements around here.

"It *was* a lot of money," Mom said.

"I don't know how, but I promise I'll pay you back."

"Honey," Dad interjected, "I don't care what it cost. There is no price too large to pay for your daughter's happiness."

I still felt ashamed. I wanted to say more, but it felt like he had brought an end to the conversation.

"Thank you for saying that," I said finally.

"I agree with your father," Babs said. "An unhappy marriage makes for a long life."

On that note, Dad stood up, kissed me quickly, kissed Babs, and was gone.

"Play well!" I called after him while noticing that he didn't kiss Mom.

"Well," Mom said, "let's put that ugliness behind us and go get some lunch. Where do you want to go?"

Babs and I shared a glance.

Mom sighed. "What now? What else could possibly go wrong?" She was in a *mood*.

"Can we see the wedding veil?" I asked sheepishly, just as a voice called, "Hello! I'm here!" and the storm door slammed.

"Hi, Aunt Alice!" I called.

Mom didn't say a word. She just crossed her arms. "I knew it. I knew that we would be right back here, you wanting to marry Hayes and having to start this whole ridiculous thing over again." She sighed again. "You could have said so before your father left for the golf course."

Alice stood in the doorway, purse on her arm, and beamed. "The wedding is back on?"

"Meredith, calm down," Babs said. "You too, Alice. She just wants to see the veil; she isn't getting back together with Hayes."

"I just have this weird feeling," I began, taking a breath, "that our wedding veil is actually the long-lost Vanderbilt veil."

Mom and Aunt Alice burst out laughing.

"Julia, you and your imagination," Alice teased. "That's the funniest thing I've heard all week."

"I do not share Julia's feeling," Babs picked up, making an exaggerated nod toward me, "but *someone* is having a guilty conscience about keeping it after seeing how similar it looks to Cornelia Vanderbilt's, which is absurd because I'm certain my mother told me a Russian woman with pink hair gave it to her."

Babs filled Alice and Mom in on all the details.

"I thought Gran found the veil on a tree," Aunt Alice said, sitting down beside Babs on the sofa.

"A tree!" Mom said, laughing. "Not a tree. It was a *train*."

"Oh no," Alice said sadly. "I'd had this vision my entire life of Gran running away from her marriage proposal into a tree, the veil draped elegantly in its branches, blowing in the wind, stopping her in her tracks."

We all laughed.

"What's this about pink hair?" Mom asked when we composed ourselves.

Alice cocked her head to the side, looking thoughtful. "You know . . . I think Cornelia Vanderbilt dyed her hair pink in her thirties, right before she fled Biltmore."

Mom shook her head. "I'm sorry. What now?"

"Seriously?" I asked. "With what? You could dye your hair pink in the 1930s?" That hadn't even occurred to me, or I would have looked into it as soon as Babs texted me.

Alice nodded authoritatively, and the beating in my chest became very loud. "When you've done as many weddings at Biltmore as I have, you learn a thing or two about the family."

"See!" I said to Babs. "I told you I had a feeling."

Babs raised an eyebrow. "It's a little strange; I'll give you that. But it isn't *proof*."

Mom got up and I heard her footsteps on each stair as she made her way into her bedroom, into her closet, to retrieve the heirloom.

She returned with it draped over her arms like she was holding a precious baby. I got up and studied the Juliet cap, the lace around the edges. Babs did the same. She shrugged at me. "I don't know how we'll ever know. It's not like we can take it to Biltmore, compare the two, and casually leave."

Our eyes locked, and Babs said, "I can just see my mother curled up on the sofa, telling me the story of running away from Daddy, while he was still down on one knee—without so much as a suitcase—and meeting a pink-haired Russian woman on a train who promised her that this veil would bring love and luck to all who wore it." She looked so wistful as she spoke. She was appealing to my emotions. "It meant so much to her. It means so much to *me*."

I laughed. "Okay, Babs, fine. If you want to keep the veil, you keep it. But I'd like to hear you say it."

She looked me dead in the eye. "Fine. I guess it's *possible* it's the veil." She lifted her head higher. "But I'm still not giving it back."

"Wait just a minute," Mom said. "You were thinking about giving this veil back? Are you kidding me? This is our family veil. It's a symbol of good luck, hope, and eternity. Do you know what I have been through so as not to tarnish this veil's peerless reputation? It has guided more than a few decisions about my marriage."

In an instant, Babs went from haughty to heartbroken.

I had grown up hearing the tale of the great family wedding veil and the beautiful love stories it had cemented. I had imagined it as the key to happiness.

But seeing my family's tortured expressions, I realized that maybe this veil, this family symbol of good luck and great love, didn't mean as much to me as it did to them. Maybe I wasn't the one who had the say in whether we kept it or not. Then and there, I decided to wash my hands of that decision. I wanted to do the right thing. But I wanted the women I loved most to be happy even more.

"I'm starved," Mom said. I assumed that meant we were shelving the conversation.

I wasn't sure why, but as they discussed the pros and cons of local eateries, I flipped the Juliet cap over in my hand, running my finger around the seamless silk. There was no doubt about it: this was a perfectly constructed garment. My finger caught on a loose corner, and I lifted it curiously. Then I jumped up out of my chair. "Oh my gosh! Oh. My. Gosh."

"What?" Alice asked.

"Initials. There are initials under this piece of silk. It just lifts right out and there they are!"

"There are not," Babs said. "I don't believe you."

"Well, what are they?" Mom asked at the same time.

I squinted to read the two sets I recognized. "EDV and CVC. Edith Dresser Vanderbilt and Cornelia Vanderbilt Cecil."

"Well, I'll be damned," Babs said under her breath, looking over my shoulder. "What are the others?"

"NDB," I said. Then I looked at Mom. "Someone needs to be googling Edith's family!" My voice was much more high-pitched and frantic than I had meant it to be. I paused while my mom typed on her phone. "Natalie Dresser Brown!" she called.

"PDM," I said. "Pauline Dresser Merrill," Mom and Aunt Alice exclaimed simultaneously.

I looked up. "This is so fun! SDD."

"Susan Dresser D'Osmoy!" Aunt Alice exclaimed, butchering her last name, I felt certain.

"SLD?" I asked questioningly.

We were all silent for a moment.

"Well, that would be Edith's mother, right?" Mom picked up. "Her married last name would have been Dresser?"

I grinned at Babs, a shiver of excitement running through me. This was, in fact, the missing Vanderbilt veil!

"All right," she said. "You don't have to gloat so openly. Fine. We have the Vanderbilt veil."

"Now what?" Alice asked.

"Lunch!" Babs said. "I am positively starving."

Suddenly I was too. "You guys, we are in possession of a real piece of American history."

Mom scrunched her nose. "It probably doesn't belong under a bed in a storage box, huh?"

"Hmmm . . ." Aunt Alice added.

Babs crossed her arms.

I looked over at her. "It's up to you, Babs. Your veil, your rules."

She stood up. "I can't possibly make a decision like this on an empty stomach."

As we reached the entrance hall, Aunt Alice stopped. "Wait," she said. "Mom, did you say the woman who gave Gran the veil was Russian?"

Babs nodded.

"Was her name by any chance Nilcha?"

I watched as a wave of recognition passed over Babs's face. I didn't know why that was significant, but even if it wasn't, I was confident that we had solved the mystery of the wedding veil. And now we had to figure out what to do about it.

The Feminine Divine

March 30, 1934

On the train from Asheville to New York, Cornelia knew she looked positively mad holding her wedding veil on her lap. Her life-path number, twenty-two, indicated that insanity was likely a part of her journey. So maybe this *was* insane. Fleeing her home for England with one trunk and one suitcase of personal belongings? It did give her pause.

But perhaps *fleeing* wasn't the right word for it. Judge Adams had—much to her chagrin—come along to help her get the boys settled in school. *As if I need his help*, she'd fumed. But when choosing between Jack, her mother, and the judge, he seemed the easiest, least emotional choice. And it was nice that he had taken the boys to meet the conductor to show them the inner workings of the train. She missed them already. But luckily, she had the long boat journey from New York to London with them.

Even still, sending her off with a chaperone as though she wasn't a proper mother was just one more piece of proof that Jack didn't understand her anymore. He didn't understand why she needed to eat pink grapefruit every morning because it was her cleansing food. He didn't understand that she needed to dance nude in the rain to regenerate her positive aura. He didn't understand that she *had* to dye her hair pink to balance her hormones, reset her internal clock, and get some sleep. Oh, dear sleep. Yes, she needed some of that.

Cornelia sighed, leaning her head back on the seat as the train stopped. Yes. It had been a hard few years, as Jack had said. But what he didn't understand was that this was her life. Everywhere she went, people knew her, the press followed her. Asheville had been her only safe place. But now, all the speculation about why they had opened the house to the public, whether she'd lost all her money—whether it had been immoral to have so much to begin with—and, worst of all, whether her father's dream was destroyed, was more than she could take. *George Vanderbilt is dead. The dream is dust and ashes.* Damn that *Kansas City Star*.

"Cornelia, why would you do that to me?" Jack had asked after her mother and Judge Adams left, the day she'd announced her decision to take the boys to England. He rarely called her by her full name, so she knew he was upset. "That was a conversation we should have had alone, something we should have decided together."

She obviously knew that. But she felt that he was less likely to make a scene in front of the others and, thus, she'd have a better chance of getting what she wanted.

"You're the one who wanted the boys to go off to school!" she protested, knowing in her heart that Jack wasn't disagreeing with that part of the plan.

"Yes, fine. Great," he said. "But my wife moving to England was never quite a part of it."

"But won't it make you feel better if I'm close to them? If I can get to them at a moment's notice?"

Jack looked dubious.

"I just need to disappear for a while," she continued.

"Disappear?" he asked.

She nodded. "I need to be somewhere where the press doesn't know me, where I can be alone."

"There's a lot to do here," he said. "But I can make a trip happen. I can go with you."

This was the hard part. How could she make him understand that she was on a personal spiritual journey and the road she was walking she had to walk alone? Well, maybe he had been understanding of that. He had been understanding when she had fallen apart after every editor she heard back from told her her book wasn't fit for publication. And he had been understanding when she had said she needed to study art again, to find a way to express her emotions in a way that wasn't writing. Writing was so . . . constricting. She was free with her brush in her hand.

"I know you have most of the power here," Jack said. "I'm not stupid. But, Nelly, we have to make these decisions together. I can't be told what the rest of my life will be like. I can't be told I can't see my children."

Something broke inside Cornelia when he said that, the idea of actually being separated from her children searing through her. But this was just a test run, she reasoned. And she believed with all her heart that she had been given every advantage on earth, and she should pass every advantage along to her children. People in their world sent their sons to the finest schools. She could certainly afford to do it. And she would.

That was what she told herself. But somewhere, deep down, she knew she simply needed to be free from all the trappings and stresses of her life. She needed to be alone.

"I will not take them away from you, Jack. I promise. You are a wonderful father. They need you. But we've talked about this before. I know you must agree that they deserve the best."

He nodded and, for a few moments, was silent. "Nelly, I get that you're going through something here, and I have tried to help. I really have. But if you are leaving me, could you please just tell me?"

Something caught in Cornelia's throat. *Leaving him.* That was what she was doing, wasn't it? She had realized she was leaving the United States. She had realized she was leaving her family home and all it had meant to her. She had hoped that, by being away, she could escape from the mounting and unrelenting pressure of keeping up this boulder of a house that had turned her life into a daily avalanche. But had she really meant to leave Jack? She gazed at his handsome face, his groomed mustache, his spotless suit. There was no doubt Jack was part of a past Cornelia was moving away from. He didn't fit into the world she imagined for herself, the world of freedom and happiness, art and humanity. But leaving him was a big decision. "Jack, I'm not leaving you. I'm leaving me." Concern passed across his face, but she liked the way it sounded.

"I have worked too hard here. Your mother and I have," he said. "I cannot leave Biltmore for good. I won't."

"No one would ever ask you to leave Biltmore," she said.

Jack and her mother. Were they the solution? Or had they been the problem? Had they kept her locked tight in this massive cage originally constructed by her father? She would find out, she guessed. That was what this journey was all about.

Her pink hair matted against the train seat, *Leaving me, leaving me* bounced around in her head as she closed her eyes. She could see why Jack would be concerned, but Cornelia didn't want to die. No. Quite the contrary. She wanted to live.

The seat jostled, and she opened her eyes hesitantly to see a rather unfashionable woman sit down in the seat across from her. "This sure is a full train," she said.

Her irritation immediately turned to joy at having someone to share the journey with. Sharing this earthly journey. Wasn't that what she was trying to do?

"Hello," she said, "I'm Nilcha." Cornelia's numerologist had long tried to persuade her to change her name, but it hadn't felt right until this exact moment. At home, she was Cornelia of Biltmore. On this train, she was Nilcha of Nowhere.

"I'm Gladys," the woman replied. "How do you do?"

Cornelia smiled kindly.

"Are you getting married?"

Cornelia looked down at her lap and realized she was petting the yards and yards of crumpled tulle like a lapdog. "No," she said. "Far from it. I got married long ago." She couldn't say why she had brought the veil, why, out of the few possessions she had gathered for this trip, she'd packed something so useless. But it was a symbol of her mother and grandmother, her aunts, the feminine divine from which she had come. She wanted to hold that close, had needed its power to walk out the door, to find her truth, to create a path and a way forward that hadn't been available to the other women in her family.

"My sweetheart proposed," Gladys said conspiratorially. "But I just don't know what to say. I can't say no. It would break his heart. But can I say yes?"

"I'm not sure," Cornelia said. "Is he your truth?"

Gladys looked at Cornelia sideways. "If you mean do I truly love him, then yes, I think I do. But I've seen people be unhappy for all their lives. It seems like a big risk to take."

"Everything is a risk, Gladys. Everything."

She looked confused again. But Cornelia was feeling less so by the minute. A risk. That's what she was taking here. A risk to find herself again, to right her place in the universe. Maybe she would go back to Biltmore. Maybe she would find an answer in England of how to fix the problem of the house. Maybe she could restore it to its former glory. Just maybe.

But, then again, didn't growth require separation? What was keeping Cornelia tethered to the past? What was tying her there and causing all this anxiety? She looked down at her lap. This veil, for one thing. Yes, it was a symbol of the women in her family whom she admired. But it was also a symbol of this great love between her parents that she could never live up to. It was a visible sign that she was failing at marriage. It was a sign that she was failing Jack. Failing the legacy she'd inherited. Feeling strong and brave, feeling the need to break free from all the chains of the past, Cornelia smiled at Gladys and handed her what was arguably her most priceless possession.

"You want me to hold this for you or something?" Gladys asked.

"No, no. I want you to have it. I want you to put it on and see if it resonates with you. Put it on and see if you feel the way you're supposed to feel about this man you might want to marry."

"Right now?" Gladys whispered, looking around.

Cornelia laughed heartily. "No, not right now," she whispered back. "Or right now if you want. It's your life. You should live it."

She was losing Gladys again. She could tell from her confused expression. "It's a gift, dear friend," she clarified. "From me to you, the stranger you met on a train. Our paths crossed for a reason, and maybe one day we will know what that reason was. If not, I'm still happy we met." She paused, and, knowing she was lying, continued. "This veil is a symbol of good luck in my family. Now, it will be good luck in yours. May all who wear it have long, happy lives and marriages."

Gladys was speechless but managed a small "Thank you. Thank you so much."

"Now, I am very tired and I think I'll take a nap."

Gladys nodded, her eyes wide.

When Cornelia woke, Gladys was gone. The veil was gone. And, instead of feeling a sense of loss, she felt like she had shed a heavy second skin that she had been wearing for far too long. Without her name, her appearance, and her house, Cornelia was free. She was her own woman. And she was ready to take on the world.

Between Two Worlds

E dith had defended Cornelia through everything. Through her obsession with numerology. Through her fascination with her aura and Edith's aura and Jack's aura and the children's auras. She would have loved her through anything and everything because she was her daughter. She was her remaining connection to her dear George. She was half of herself. She was the bright light of her life that would never go out.

Here, now, in the library at Biltmore, only days after her last conversation with her daughter, the house suddenly felt indescribably quiet. Empty. Lonely. The house, like Edith, was bereft. Cornelia was gone. The children were gone. George was gone.

Jack entered the room. "Well," he said softly, "they're really gone."

Edith was supposed to be on the campaign trail with

Peter right now, was supposed to be making a speech to a group of Portuguese immigrants. But she couldn't bring herself to leave Biltmore. Not yet.

Instead, she nodded. "The irony that I am supposed to be speaking to America's newest, poorest, most downtrodden citizens—inspiring hope in them—when instead I am here, attempting yet again to save this impractical and maybe even unconscionable home, is not lost on me."

Jack sat down in the red chair across from Edith. Edith and Jack had become partners in crime these past few years, bonding over the dairy, the land, the creation of Biltmore Forest. Edith had counted on Jack for a great deal, but she believed that not only was he a man who could be counted on, he was a man who enjoyed being counted on. Both Edith and Jack had hoped that Cornelia would change her mind, that she would stay. But she did not. Edith's stomach dropped at the realization that everything was different now.

"She isn't coming back," Jack said. There they were, two people at a loss, drowning in their grief. How could you miss a person so fiercely who was still living? George was truly gone. Cornelia would simply be across the ocean.

"Did she say that?" Edith asked, her heart racing with an alarm that surprised her. They'd all known this was coming, hadn't they? Edith had wanted to fix this for her, this restlessness, the way that mothers always want to. But she didn't know exactly what needed fixing. Cornelia simply wanted a different life. If her two beautiful, bright sons couldn't keep her tethered to Biltmore, her mother certainly couldn't. Edith knew Cornelia would never abandon her children. But she hadn't predicted that she would simply take them with her when she decided to leave everything else behind. Edith took a deep breath.

"She never said it, Edith," Jack said, "but I think we both know that was what she meant at that meeting."

"Well, that isn't what I heard. I heard she was thirty-four and it was 1934 and some nonsense about her path. It won't be 1934 forever, you know."

Edith wished, in this moment, that she still smoked—or, at the very least, that it was the appropriate hour for a cocktail. Neither was the case. So, instead, she allowed her heart to break into a million pieces as she thought of her little girl, happy and free at Biltmore, the way she would practically run to school in the village, cheeks pink, smile wide. Would her grandsons learn more about art history and Parliament at a school in London? Perhaps. But what could be a happier childhood than roaming free on acres of your own against an inspiring mountain backdrop?

"George's dream is here, Jack—it was never Cornelia's," she said sadly. "This was George's dream and, in the end, it didn't make his daughter happy. And now here we are."

Jack looked down at his hands and laughed ironically. "She felt trapped in the largest home in America."

Edith couldn't imagine how terrible it must be to feel trapped in a life that had been predetermined for you. Because, yes, Edith's life had been difficult, but it had also been filled with bright, blazing moments of glory. It had been unpredictable, but she had become her own woman, a woman strong and fiercely independent, capable and wise. Now, her daughter was at that crossroads, and Edith had tried to fix it. But it wasn't up to her. It was up to her daughter.

"If she doesn't come back in a few months, I can go after her," Edith said. "I can make her come home." Edith wanted to weep. Cornelia had been her best friend since she was a child, her most likely companion. They were almost one person. And then, fiercely, abruptly, they had become two, divided. Her grandmother had been right all those years ago. They were no longer united. The house had fallen.

"Edith," Jack replied, sounding much older than he was. "I think we both know that no one can make Cornelia Vanderbilt do anything she doesn't want to."

Edith knew. All that was left to do now was let her go.

"Are you going to divorce her?" Edith asked, stupidly. How could he not? Cornelia had abandoned him. More than once, really.

"I'll leave that up to her," he said. "I don't want to cause her any more coverage in the press than necessary. If she wants to divorce me, she can announce it herself. Until then, I'll wait and hope that whatever she's going through is a phase, that she'll miss me, Biltmore, our life. That she'll come back home."

It struck Edith then that this was a great love, the one her son-in-law had for her daughter. She couldn't imagine many men who would resist the urge to get the last word in, who would protect her daughter even at the worst.

Edith didn't respond, as she was trying to regain her composure.

"But Edith," he said, this next part clearly paining him, "the mistress of Biltmore is still gone. There's the house. And the farm. And . . ."

"Jack, you know as well as I that the house belongs to Cornelia. It's up to her. But, if she asks, it's my opinion that you should stay here as long as you like, as long as you feel comfortable. You have been invaluable to me, Jack, to this family. It will be the boys' one day, and they might as well enjoy it as much as they can." In spite of everything, George's legacy would live on for another generation. She smiled with pride at the thought. The house that the Vanderbilts had ridiculed, George's Folly, was one of the only Vanderbilt mansions left standing.

"No matter what happens with you and Cornelia, George and William will bond us forever. As will Biltmore."

Jack stood and smiled sadly at his mother-in-law. "Well, there is work to be done." He paused. "Will you stay tonight?"

Looking around the library, all Edith saw was George, even though she had a life now with Peter. She and Peter were politically aligned, and he believed as strongly as she did in the women's movement, in equality, in helping the less fortunate with real change. But no, she would admit, Peter was not her great love. That space would always be reserved for George.

Edith was about to say that she would stay at the Frith that night, the house she shared with Peter. But then *Thank you, dear Edi* rushed through her mind. With no warning whatsoever, the voice that had been lost to her returned.

"You know, Jack," she said, "I think staying would be very nice."

When she was alone again, Edith confessed, "George, for all this time, I have been a woman caught between two worlds."

She wasn't sure if his spirit was really there, but in her heart, Edith knew George would know what she meant. Edith was a woman of a bygone era, fighting to keep a house that was nothing more than a relic now, a woman who had given so much of herself and her life to preserving the memory of a man. But then, also, she was a woman on the forefront of a revolution that would change the trajectory of America, making the past she was so desperately trying to preserve irrelevant. She thought of her daughter, and she understood a little more how you could be two people at once.

You aren't caught between two worlds right now, Edith, the voice replied simply. *Right now, you are home.*

Edith smiled, closing her eyes, remembering her mother's proclamation to her six-year-old self. She would be a princess; she would live in a castle. For a time, she had. It had all come true. She could almost see Biltmore as it had been. The dozens of servants bustling about, mending, cleaning, serving, cooking, entertaining as gaily and brightly as had ever been seen in this country. The thousands of acres where children roamed, gentlemen hunted, and ladies fished in clear flowing streams. The bright sunny porches where books were read and great thoughts formed, plans discussed and futures melded.

She imagined herself in her palace fit for a queen, where breakfast, instead of being eaten in bed, was served in the oak-paneled parlor between her bedroom and George's so that his was the first face she saw in the morning. So many nights she had fallen asleep next to him, with the light of the moon, which always shone brighter in Asheville, filling the dark corners of her favorite place. The wind would rustle through the trees, singing a lullaby sweeter than any voice, and with her beloved beside her, her baby down the hall, Edith would sleep peacefully, not a worry in the world.

For once, Edith was where she should be. The smell of honeysuckle in the air and the fresh breeze blowing through the open windows made Edith, for a time, no longer a Gerry. She was a Vanderbilt once again.

Time would pass, the world would continue to change. But one thing remained true. Edith opened her eyes and said, softly, "As long as Biltmore stands, George, I will have a piece of you and you will have a piece of me."

And even when it doesn't, George replied, *I will love you still.*

Edith closed her eyes again, tears spilling down her cheeks. Somewhere, lost in time and space and memory, the pealing laughter of Tarheel Nell would fill empty halls, and celebrations with friends would soothe broken hearts. Edith's dream. George's dream. It had not died. It could not die. No, as long as Edith was here, as long as Biltmore stood proud, her perfect family, those idyllic days, would continue to exist. George's dream would live on.

It's You

It had taken six months. Six months for everything, really. Six months for me to walk across a stage and receive a diploma that I knew I had really, truly earned. Six months for Babs and me to decide, once and for all, that we must dispose of the Vanderbilt veil in the proper way. (What that was, we weren't sure. It wasn't like an American flag, where the protocol was stipulated.) And six months—along with his engagement to the woman he'd cheated on me with—for me to truly accept, deep down, that Hayes was not the one for me. When the habit of leaning on him had faded, I realized that I was finally standing on my own two feet. The thing that scared me most was that now, months later, I barely thought of him. I didn't hate him, didn't miss him. He simply did not occur to me. What a terrible thing to think . . . But it was the truth. My truth. It had taken separating myself from Hayes, walking away, to discover what that was.

Now, my butterflies had butterflies. I had just had my very first New York City job interview. It was at the same firm I had interned at, so I felt comfortable if not totally confident. I had carried a folded-up postcard inside the breast pocket of my suit for good luck. It—comically— had a picture of Garrison Towers, the building that had made Conner famous, on the front of it. The back read:

Darling Julia,
    Look at you! Look AT YOU! You have done it. You have fought through so many hard things to get this dream. You have gone through so much to create this life for yourself. You are an inspiration to me, and you will be an inspiration to many. No matter what your future holds from here, please remember how very proud I am of all you are and all you do.

All my love,
Babs

As I put my hand to my pocket, I had a flashback of standing with Sarah in the airport bathroom, removing my wedding gown, of her telling me I deserved someone who wrote me love letters. I realized now that I had had that all along.

As I rode the elevator down to the first floor, I marveled at the idea that I might get to work in this big city with these huge buildings all around me, that I might get to learn from the greats. Jumping off this ledge all alone was a little scary, of course. But I had prepared for this. I was ready.

I walked across the marble floor and out the revolving door. I was looking down at my feet—revolving doors always made me a little nervous—and, as I stepped out onto the sidewalk, I almost ran right smack into a man.

"Oh, I'm so sorry," I said, looking up. Then I laughed, my nerves from the interview floating away, the sheer absurdity of this moment not quite taking hold yet. "It's you," I said.

"It's you," he responded, grinning at me.

I stood quietly for a moment, letting the serendipity of it all, the glow of standing in the presence of Conner Howard, wash over me. "How did you know I would be here?!" I exclaimed.

He laughed. "Well, I received a postcard at my office with very specific instructions from someone named—"

"Babs?"

He nodded.

"My grandmother," I said. Why was I not surprised? She was the very best kind of meddler.

"You hungry?"

"Starved."

"Your grandmother said I should take you to Sarabeth's because you really like their pancakes. And she made sure to mention that she'd like you to bring a bottle or two of syrup back home to her."

I laughed. Oh, Babs. "I can't bring syrup in my carry-on," I said.

"Then you'd better mail it," Conner said, wide-eyed. "I don't know this woman, but I can assure you I don't want to cross her."

Conner reached his hand out to me. I took it, and we started walking in the direction of Central Park—and Sarabeth's. We stopped briefly in front of the Pulitzer statue across from the Plaza. The bronze nude of Pomona, the goddess of abundance, was located in perhaps one of the most bustling areas of New York. I wondered how many times people walked past her in a day, never realizing that they were passing in front of the work of one of the world's greatest sculptors, Karl Bitter.

"Have you ever been to Biltmore Estate?" I asked Conner.

He shook his head.

"There are several Bitter pieces there," I said, thinking of *Boy Stealing Geese* and the *Fashionable Romance* exhibit that day with Babs when I remembered how strong I could be, when I realized that if my grandmother could move forward in her life so could I.

"Did you know that it was actually Konti who finished this sculpture, not Bitter?" Conner asked.

I shook my head.

"Karl Bitter was killed the night he finished the plaster mold of this statue. He pushed his wife, his great love, out of the way of an oncoming car, and he was crushed by it."

It made me cringe. "How awful," I said. "I had no idea. But just think of that, of your legacy standing tall and proud in the center of the greatest city in the world, of being immortalized in that way." I gasped. "Like you, Conner. You have created something lasting and real, something that will stand in this city forever."

He nodded. "Well, maybe not forever . . . But I bet if you asked Karl Bitter what was the most lasting, the most real—his work in this city, his work at Biltmore, or his life with the woman he loved—I bet he'd choose her."

I thought back to the boat and our proclamation of how we'd meet again. Of how we'd signal to each other that it was time, that we were ready. Was I ready? Was this it? As if he were reading my mind, Conner winked.

He winked. He remembered. And, just like that, the racing thoughts in my head stopped. He smiled. I locked eyes with Conner. I felt like that gaze conveyed everything I wanted to tell him, everything I needed to say. In that glance was all the nights I'd lain awake longing to feel his lips on mine, to hear his laugh, every morning I'd wanted to call him just to listen to the smooth, calm cadence of his voice telling me it was going to be okay.

It was barely even a choice: I winked back.

It was a perfect moment, a movie moment, and when he touched my cheek, leaned down, and kissed me, it felt so right. A part of me had worried that our romance was just a side effect of being in one of the most beautiful and ethereal places in the world. But here, in this noisy city full of cabs and strangers, cement and grime, I realized that no matter where we were, being with Conner felt perfect.

He took my hand again, and we strolled toward Sarabeth's for pancakes—and syrup. But I'm pretty sure my feet never touched the ground.

Maybe Conner was right. Maybe the only thing better than discovering what you should do with your life is finding the person you want to spend it with. For me, maybe that was Conner. Maybe it wasn't. But in life, as in architecture, a little trial and error never hurts.

Companions to the Death

March 31, 1934

Cornelia felt a slight pang when she realized that Gladys and the veil were gone—but of guilt, not loss. She had portrayed the veil as a talisman, an offer of good luck and a bright future. But she knew that it was far from that. Maybe it wasn't the veil that was ill-fated, though. Maybe it was the life she had tried to live; the life she had been part of. She wished she could blame Jack, but it was she who had fought so hard for a life at Biltmore for so long.

She could feel, even now, how it—along with the impossible, unwavering scrutiny of a public that wanted to know everything about a woman who wanted nothing more than to slip off into the shadows—had driven her to her breaking point, how it had pushed her to the point of madness.

She knew her mother would be devastated if she

stayed in England, but Edith had Jack to help her save the estate—a place that had once felt like a beautiful home but had now become a reminder of all her failures.

It was too much for one person to take. And her attempt to disappear was working already. That woman, that stranger? She didn't recognize Cornelia Vanderbilt, who was, most certainly, one of the country's most recognizable women.

Footsteps rang through the train car, and she smiled to see her little loves, George and William, running to her. She gathered them up in her arms, kissing their sweaty foreheads. "Did you have quite the adventure?" she asked.

As they answered excitedly, talking over each other, she remembered her father telling her to have as many adventures as she could. Now she was. This year would be an adventure. A new school for the boys would be one too.

As the train pulled into the station, she smiled animatedly at her children. "Boys, you can't even believe how marvelous this ship is going to be. I bet we could even eat dinner with the captain one night. Would you like that?"

William and George enthusiastically expressed their agreement, but Cornelia's mind was already somewhere else. She had failed. Failed herself, failed her father.

No, Cornelia decided again as she took her boys' hands and walked out into the day, her legs feeling stiff and tired but lightening with every step. A new world was out here waiting for her to turn into the woman she was meant to be, a woman her father would be proud of.

For days on the ship to England, Cornelia and her boys ate their meals together, played cards and squash on the deck, swam during the day and listened to the orchestra at night. And what would happen once they arrived at their destination finally sank in: there would be no more breakfasts together and silly jokes. Had she made the right choice? Only time would tell.

It seemed like only a moment later that a porter was unloading the boys' trunks at the ancient, imposing school, the headmaster there to meet them.

"Are you ready for this?" Judge Adams asked Cornelia.

"I assure you, Mrs. Cecil," the headmaster said, "your fine young gentlemen will receive the best schooling and the best care available."

She smiled, looking braver than she felt. "Yes. That's what my dear husband assures me. And we will be checking in often to be certain of it." She liked the way it sounded, how she could put it off on Jack, like she was the doting mother who could scarcely bear to part with her children.

Cornelia held her boys close to her and then knelt down, kissing them. "This is going to be an adventure, my darlings," she said. She was shocked at how stoic her children were as she kissed them again. "Goodbye, Mama," they said.

She took a deep breath as she turned from them, tears filling her eyes.

"You're doing the right thing," Judge Adams confirmed as they got back in the car and pulled away down the school's long driveway. Cornelia dared not look back lest she lose her nerve and call the whole thing off.

"I know," she whispered, unable to keep the tears from rolling down her cheeks.

Jack and Judge Adams thought her children would have a better education here, but Cornelia wanted her children in London for a different reason. She never

wanted her boys to feel the burden that she had, the glare
of being in the public eye like she did. Here, she could
keep them safe. Here, she could tuck them away and let
them grow into the men they were already becoming.

The first step was always the hardest.

She and Judge Adams parted ways, her heart feeling
heavy at the separation from her children, but lighter
at the idea that she was protecting them. And, with
the man she felt lukewarm about at best gone, she was
free. Really, truly free, to soar higher and dream bigger, to uncover the path that the stars had been leading
her toward since she was a child with her father in the
observatory at Biltmore, when she contemplated how
numbers governed the universe for the very first time.

She slipped into a table at the first café she saw, fully
intent on ordering bread and cheese, wine and choco-
late, until she soothed this very uneasy feeling inside her
stomach. As she sat inside this old place that felt very
new to her, she realized that Cornelia Vanderbilt—and
all her disappointment—was gone.

She thought back to the letter she had left for Jack,
her once love. Maybe her always love:

Dearest Jack,

*I was thinking this evening about the first note
you ever wrote me. It is the only personal paper I
haven't burned. I keep it close to my heart, folded in
the tiniest parcel inside the locket I sometimes wear
around my neck. I think you must feel what I feel—
that we have somewhat grown apart. And I do hope
that you can forgive me for having to leave you, for
having to leave Biltmore, that we can be friendly in
the sharing of our beloved sons.*

I know that sometimes, in the deepest parts of your soul, you have wanted to return to England, and that it was for me you stayed. The irony that I am leaving to find a new life there can't be overstated. But I feel as though abroad I will be less of a spectacle. I will be less of the disgraced heiress who couldn't hold on to her father's dearest possession and more of a new artist who happens to be philanthropic. Can you ever understand that?

Please do not feel like you need to stay at Biltmore. You have given it more time and attention than anyone could ever ask for, and I am most grateful to you. I know you must long to return home, and when you do, I hope that I will see you on the sidewalks, that we will smile at each other. Perhaps my book will be published in England. Maybe you could come celebrate?

You have been as kind and generous a man as I could have ever hoped to know, but the life we led wasn't the life that was meant for me. I hope you can understand.

With deepest gratitude and affection,
Cornelia

If he had ever sent it, Cornelia would have read Jack's reply:

My dearest Nell,
You are right. I have pined for my home country more times in more ways than I can ever say. But now, it is only for you I long in the very depths of my soul. That first night I laid eyes on you, something changed in me, something shifted.

*And you became the purpose in my life; you
became the reason for living. I feel as though you
are going through a stage, my darling, much as
our boys do, and I have to think that you will snap
out of it. When you do, I will be here waiting, at
the place you love most, protecting your legacy
and enacting your will. And if you do not return,
it is still here that I will always be waiting, for it is
here that I can be with you, even if you are gone.
I meant what I wrote all those years ago. In my
mind, in my memory, I am still Mark Antony. You
are Cleopatra. And the two of us are, forever and
always, Companions to the Death.*

*All my love, devotion, and fidelity forever,
Jack*

Maybe that reply would have changed something.
Maybe not. But, either way, now Nilcha ran her hand
through her newly pink hair and took a deep breath, lilt-
ing her order in a southern accent that contrasted starkly
from its British counterpart. Across the café, she met the
eye of a man who smiled, one who didn't know she was
Cornelia Vanderbilt, one who had never seen her in the
papers, had never heard of Tarheel Nell. Remembering,
she got the slightest pang for her old life, could smell the
magnolia tree that was hers, the one that was planted in
her honor in earth that bore secrets and lies, truths and,
for some, the freedom that Nilcha never seemed to find.
She could always go back if she wanted, she told herself,
even though she knew it was impossible.

As the moon started to rise in the still-blue sky, she,
beginning to feel guilty about simply abandoning the

place that had meant so much to her father, said, aloud, "We're still under the same moon, Daddy. Always. But I need a fresh start."

Here, now, in this café in London, she could be anyone she wanted to, someone of her own making, free of the pressures and confines of her previous life. What's more, she had broken her children free, prevented them from feeling the suffocating weight of saving a home that was perhaps beyond saving. She pushed away the thought of all the pain she had caused her mother, her husband, her sons. She caught the eye of the man again. All she could think of now was a fresh start. Nilcha, in spite of herself, smiled.

A Sky Full of Stars

If a few months ago we had been fugitives, now Julia and I were a couple of bandits.

"You know, Babs, we could just explain to one of the curators what happened and turn the veil over."

I stopped the car in the parking lot outside Biltmore and looked at her in disgust. "Julia, who raised you, child? Where is your sense of adventure? What fun would that be?"

She laughed. "You're right. You're totally right." Then she added under her breath, "Breaking into Biltmore at night seems like a much safer plan."

"Safe is for the birds!" I trilled, musing at how the woman I had become was so different from the one I had been when I was young, who had craved safety at all costs, who had pinned her entire life on it. "And if we

get caught?" I asked, not as a question but to confirm
she understood the facts.

"I start speaking Spanish, you start speaking French.
Very loud and very fast and at the same time."

I nodded. "Good girl." We had left Miles at the house,
cell phone by his side, in case we needed someone to get
us out of jail. First rule of law-breaking: Always know
who has the bail money. That he didn't argue with this
spoke volumes about our future.

"Are you sure about returning the veil?" Julia asked.
"I feel like I've pushed you into this. We can change our
minds. We haven't done anything yet."

"Well, let's see," I said, counting on my fingers. "Edith
Vanderbilt's grandfather battled dementia for decades,
her grandmother lost her daughter and her husband—
who left four orphans, Edith's first husband died way
too young, as did her sister Natalie's, Cornelia was so
unhappy she fled her life never to return, and she pawned
this damn thing off on my poor, unsuspecting mother."

"I think we're lucky to have avoided its curse!" Julia
said, laughing.

What I didn't add was that this godforsaken veil had
contributed to my poor daughter fighting her entire life
to stay with a man she wasn't happy with. Because of a
veil. Well, maybe it was more than that. But it had contributed. That moment in her living room, feeling the
tension between her and Allen, seeing the way her face
looked, had made me realize that the veil was a piece
of history and it should stay that way. Signs could be
great, yes. But when they overruled our happiness, they
needed to be gone.

Julia laughed and held up part of the veil with two
fingers, as if it was terribly soiled laundry. "This thing

is a curse, not a blessing!" She paused. "But you and Pops?"

I smiled, warmth flooding over me at the mere mention of my beloved husband. "Pops and I were perfect." But I didn't want to give the child unrealistic expectations of marriage. "No, actually. We weren't perfect. I'd get PMS, and he'd sulk when UNC lost a basketball game. Taking care of my parents was a terrific nightmare when they got older, and we fought mightily about whether we should sell the mountain house to ease the financial strain." I paused. "I won, by the way." I took her hand in mine. "But that is marriage, my love. Real partners fight and forgive. It is the only way to truly be equals, to find the kind of happiness that I hope and pray you will."

She smiled. "So at least one victory for the veil?"

"Absolutely."

As she folded the massive veil as best she could, I began to feel a little nostalgic. But, well, I had come to terms with letting go of it. Besides, I had discovered something vastly more important in my drawer that night I was searching for Miles's fraternity pin: a letter from my mother that went along with our beloved veil, one that I had never read, one that was almost lost to time. I had read the letter probably a dozen times since finding it, and, well, I am somewhat embarrassed to say, still fought against my determined granddaughter's quest to find the truth even after. But sometimes the past is difficult to part with, no matter how it has changed.

My dear Barbara:

It is an odd sort of thing to write to you, knowing that if you're reading this, it means I am gone. While

I do wish that you had brothers and sisters to share this time with, the glory of having an only child is that it makes the logistics quite a bit easier. What's mine is yours—my possessions, and, what's more, my stories.

There is one I haven't told you, wasn't sure if I should, a secret of sorts that I have kept not for myself but for a woman I did not know at all, one I met in passing but who, nonetheless, changed my life. The woman who gave me the wedding veil on the train, the one that's become our family's dearest treasure, was, I knew then just as I know now—and despite her pink hair and new name of Nilcha—Cornelia Vanderbilt. She was one of the most recognizable women of my day, with her height, beauty, and that distinctive mark of wealth all about her.

Of course, history had not been written yet then. What Cornelia Vanderbilt would ultimately do hadn't been set in stone. But I could see in her face that day that she was leaving her life behind. Normally, I would have argued when she handed me that veil, something so intensely valuable. Not only did it seem like the sign I had been waiting for, but I also felt strongly that she needed to let go. Handing over that veil to me was an outward and physical sign of the metaphorical things she had to leave behind to move forward. Why I kept it a secret I cannot say, only that it was one of the most intimate experiences of my life, and I felt that she had handed me a burden, a secret one, that was entirely too personal to share, even with you, my love. That is our sometimes unhappy—but wholly necessary—task in life: Sometimes we must take on another woman's burdens, even if we can't imagine her having any at all.

It was a lesson for me then. It is a lesson I have carried through the rest of my life. We spend so much time thinking of what more we need, what we will do next, what we can have that will make us happy, fill our dark places with light. But, as I've come to find, so often it isn't what we hold on to that moves us onto the right path. It's what we let go of.

You, my love, will have to let go of me now, and while I know it is hard to lose the ones we love, I have to ask: What will letting go allow you to move into? Knowing you, it will be bright and beautiful, big, and glorious.

We have always said that the wedding veil connects us to each other, to the women in our family. But, my girl, I have to think that maybe we are bigger than that, greater than that. We are connected not only by blood but by history, a life we have led together, woven into a tapestry of the finest cloth. We shared so many experiences. I shared but one with Cornelia Vanderbilt, and I only tell you now because I find that, as I reach the end of my life, the truth seems to matter more and more. Knowing now what the Vanderbilt legacy means to our country, I wonder if perhaps I should turn the veil in. But, knowing what this veil means to our family's legacy, I find that I cannot.

So, my darling, I leave it in your capable hands. Do what you will, what you must. And know that, no matter what decision you make, I support you wholeheartedly.

Goodbye, my dearest—not forever, but for now. You are my greatest achievement, my greatest love,

*whom I have found I could not, cannot, and will not
ever let go of. Those are the things—and the people—
that mean the very most.*

*All my love,
Mama*

That veil, as it turns out, was the one thing I could
not let go of. Until now, at least. I finally knew what my
mother meant. I had to let go of this tangible, outward
thing to move forward, just as Cornelia had. And I was
certain that my daughter and granddaughter needed to let
go of it as well. It was the only way for them to forge ahead.

A part of me wondered if I should tell them about
the letter. But I decided not to. Maybe it was selfish, but
my mother had been gone for decades. The opportunity to have a secret all our own, after all this time, was
too wonderful not to take. I would leave the letter in my
things and, one day, after I was gone, the women in my
family would know the secret too.

Julia zipped the veil into a backpack, at which I
began hysterically laughing. This entire operation was
ridiculous. And I knew I would remember it for the rest
of my life.

"Your mother would be just thrilled if she knew we
were doing this," I said sarcastically.

But I smiled all the same. Meredith, Alice, Miles, and
I had had the most wonderful dinner the week before.
I had almost wanted to stand on the chair and sing—
if I could have actually gotten up there, that is, which
seemed doubtful. Miles was so charming. He said all the
right things, dodged all the backhanded compliments
and questionable comments. And, after dinner, Mere-

dith pulled me aside and said, "Mom, we see why you love Miles. We might not ever get used to seeing you with someone who isn't Daddy, but we are going to try."

That assurance had meant the world to me. Miles had slept over that night, and for the first time in almost two years, I hadn't woken up a single time to the panic that there was a dead man in my bed.

"Okay," I said. "We sneak through the woods, pray there aren't laser beam alarms, and leave the veil."

Julia nodded, got out of the car, and strapped the backpack on her back. We locked eyes and pulled our neck gaiters up over our mouths. We couldn't have looked more suspicious if we tried, but we could always say we were cold, which wasn't completely untrue. It was cold here. And since we'd be saying it in French and Spanish, respectively, it would probably work.

Julia pulled my arm through hers and clasped my hand, supporting me as we trekked down the asphalt road, through the dark woods, and into a wide, grassy field that led to the right side of Biltmore. My eyes soon adjusted to the light and, after a trip on Julia's part, several bouts of uncontrollable laughter, and, fortunately, no police, we made it to the house. Summoning all our courage, we snuck around to the front steps of the glittering limestone palace that seemed to be the stuff dreams were made of, but really, was no more a symbol of hope and prosperity than the veil. In fact, maybe both were nothing more than relics of a time gone by.

Julia silently dropped the backpack on the front steps and we both stood there.

"This isn't right," I whispered.

"I agree," she said, leaning over and unzipping the backpack.

She grasped the point lace cap and we both gently pulled until the veil was laid out, in all its glory—perhaps a full third of the length of those gigantic limestone stairs—underneath a sky full of stars.

"It is beautiful, isn't it?" I asked.

She nodded. "It doesn't feel right to just leave it here."

"Darling girl," I said in a pinched tone, "I am an eighty-one-year-old woman who just braved the forest in the middle of the night in a mask. We're leaving the veil."

She laughed quietly. "No, I mean, it's like we should say a few words or something."

I nodded. "Ah. Well, you're the one who wanted to give it back. You do it."

She looked down at the veil and said, "Thank you for being, in our family, a symbol of hope. Thank you for being the thing that brought my great-grandparents together, the thing that brought my grandparents so much happiness, and maybe even for keeping my parents fighting for a marriage that could have easily ended long ago." She took a deep breath. "But, most of all, thank you for being so weighty and important that you kept me from marrying that asshat Hayes."

"Amen!" I said, a little too loudly.

I took Julia's hand. "That was lovely." I paused, feeling, in the eerie light of the moon, less a need to escape and more a need to unburden myself. "Julesy, I need to tell you something."

"Oh no," she said, downtrodden. "You and Pops weren't that happy either?"

I laughed. "No, no. We were terribly happy." I bit my lip and swallowed. I didn't want to say it. I never wanted to tell her. But in the dark of night with one of the grandest symbols of our family tradition and unity before me, how could I not? There shouldn't be big secrets among family, should there? "I'm the one who texted out that video at the bridesmaids' luncheon."

Julia's eyes went wide. "Wait. What? No you didn't."

She was mad. Well, of course she was mad.

She shook her head. "You would have told me alone, not sent it to all my friends and family."

Very softly and calmly I said, "Someone sent the video to Sarah, and we knew if we just showed it to you that you would reason that it didn't matter. But I needed all the most important women in your life fighting you on your decision, not just me. I couldn't be solely responsible for your making a huge mistake."

Julia nodded. She crossed her arms. "Who sent it to Sarah?"

I paused, deciding whether I wanted to keep something else from my granddaughter. But the truth was that Therese—Hayes's mom—had sent it. She didn't want to blow up her son's life yet again, but she also couldn't in good conscience let my granddaughter marry him without knowing who he was. She had sworn us to secrecy. I respected her for making what had to have been an impossible decision. And, from one mother to another, I decided, in that split second, that I couldn't betray her trust. It wasn't important now anyway.

"Oh, I have no idea," I said. "Sarah didn't know the person." I could tell Julia was fuming, so I continued, trying to make it better. "But I wanted you to know how it was going to feel. That man wasn't going to change and there was going to come a day in your life when he did something big and public and embarrassing and everyone around you was going to know about it." I paused. "Maybe even your own children."

I braced myself for what she would say.

"Babs, you ruined my wedding," she said solemnly. Then she repeated, her tone changing, "Babs, you *ruined* my wedding."

Julia was quiet for a long moment, and my heart was racing. I had hoped that her anger and hurt might not feel so fresh, that she would be so relieved she hadn't married Hayes she would feel grateful. I did what I had to do because I loved her. And, truly, I hadn't known for sure she would even call the wedding off. But I had hoped . . .

Then, as if she had decided something, Julia burst out into free, unquiet, non-sneaky laughter. She put her hand up, trying to compose herself. "Wait, do you mean to tell me that my tiny grandmother figured out how to group text everyone at my bridesmaids' luncheon— including my fiancé—and ruin my wedding day?"

I let out an annoyed, breathy sigh. "I'm eighty-one. I'm not dead. It's not that hard to send a group text. I'm a little offended that you would even suggest I couldn't do it." So, yes, maybe I had had Brian at the senior center practice with me over and over on something he called a burner phone, and he even helped me create a group so I didn't have to add anyone and couldn't mess it up. But Julia didn't have to know that.

She reached over and wrapped me in a hug. "You really are one of a kind, Babs. You really are."

"So you aren't mad?"

"Mad! I'm impressed. I'm grateful. I'm going to have the single best story to tell at parties for the rest of my life. I've won the game of dinner party guest for all eternity. Mad? I'm thrilled!"

All that worry for months and it led to this. Maybe time really could heal all wounds. I thought of Reid, of my wound. Then again, maybe not all wounds could be healed completely. My only hope was that my granddaughter would find a love just like that.

"You're sure you won't want to wear the veil on your wedding day?" I asked. "Last chance to change your mind."

She shook her head. "It's too much for a boat in the BVIs."

I raised my eyebrow questioningly, and she grinned from ear to ear. "Maybe it won't be Conner," she said, shrugging. She looked down at the steps. "But I kind of think it is. And I don't need a wedding veil to tell me whether we'll be happy forever."

I laughed. "Well, three cheers for that."

"We should go," Julia whispered. "I think we're tempting fate."

I took her hand as we stared for a final moment down at a family heirloom that was no longer ours. We both blew kisses into the wind and said goodbye to the wedding veil. And, as we walked arm in arm back around to the side yard, I almost felt the women who had lived in this house, who had worn the veil before me. Brave women, strong women, trailblazers and leaders who fought against oppression and adversity, who bore unthinkable tragedy and disaster, and who came out on the other side better and stronger for it.

In our family, that wedding veil had been a sign of union, a symbol of bonding together. But it was only now that I realized that, maybe, it hadn't been a talisman of good luck and strong marriages with faithful husbands. No, the wedding veil was never about the men. It wasn't even about the marriages. It was about the women who wore it, the connection, the insatiable lust for life—for adventure, for meaning, for *everything*. To some, it was just a little piece of lace. But to us, it was so much more.

I almost looked back, to see its glorious tulle blowing in the wind one last time. But the women who wore that veil? We weren't the kind to look back. No. We kept moving forward, pressing into the future, into the unknown, into an endless night and a sky bursting with stars, full of nothing but possibility.

AUTHOR'S NOTE

My cousin Sidney Patton got married in 2019, and I, her matron of honor, stood with her in a bridal suite in Cashiers, North Carolina, in those final moments before she had a new last name. As I placed the mantilla that had been in my husband's family for generations on her head, I was struck, as I often am, with a book idea. The next day I called my agent and told her I wanted to write a novel about a fictional family wedding veil and the stories of all the women who had worn it. I would call it, simply, *The Wedding Veil*.

She loved the idea but asked, "What if you wrote about a real, historical veil?"

I remember pushing the idea aside because what were the chances I could find a real, historical wedding veil owned by a woman so interesting to me that I wanted to spend a year researching her life? A few months later, unable to sleep one night, I got up and got on Google. I remember where I was sitting, on a barstool at a house we were renting while our home was in month eight of renovations from damage caused by Hurricane Florence. When my family had evacuated for the storm, we left the coast for Asheville, North Carolina, only a few hours from where I grew up.

My husband and I wanted to take our son to Biltmore Estate, and, though I had been many times before, I had never once considered until that trip that George Vanderbilt died too early, leaving behind a young widow, a thirteen-year-old daughter, and America's largest home. I had never before wondered how this woman, in a time when women couldn't even vote, managed to hold on to this expansive property with its unimaginable upkeep. I knew then that, one day, I wanted to tell her story.

So, that night as I sat awake, considering crumbling 120-year-old molding and mold-covered furniture, feeling downtrodden that the historic home we had completely restored not six years earlier was having to be redone all over again, I decided to focus on my next book. On a whim, I googled "Edith Vanderbilt wedding veil."

What I found was a flurry of articles about the creation of a reproduction of the Vanderbilt veil. The original was worn by Edith Vanderbilt, her mother, her sisters, and her daughter, Cornelia—and then disappeared.

I sent a link to my agent with the heading: Sometimes the Stories Write Themselves.

As a contemporary fiction author, I knew I wanted to write a present-day storyline alongside the tale of two remarkable Vanderbilt women who saved America's largest home against incredible odds. The veil became a touchstone that connected four generations of women—and a physical symbol in the novel of letting go of expectations, something that I had to do many times while writing this book.

When I decided to dive into this story in early 2020, I had visions of driving across the state, burning up my Biltmore Annual Pass with tour after tour, interviewing guides and experts on-site and rummaging through library documents to glean all the details about Edith and Cornelia Vanderbilt. I don't think I need to tell you what happened next, but, just in case, only two months later, the world as we knew it shut down. Life was canceled; my book deadline was not.

And so, I decided to power through with the help of some truly amazing librarians, former and current Biltmore staff—most notably Will Morgan and Michelle Kreitman—my newspaper.com account, the Biltmore blog, every single book I could find that so much as mentioned the name "Vanderbilt," and even a few sources who asked not to be named. I was drowning in details and brimming with stories. *The Wedding Veil* was born. (So many thank-yous to all who helped! Your knowledge was invaluable—and all mistakes are mine alone!)

I had been taught how to research in journalism school and had learned that primary sources are the ones that matter. But, wow, did I have a rude awakening. One of the first newspaper articles I was so excited to find—one that talked about Cornelia Vanderbilt's time at my alma mater, the University of North Carolina at Chapel Hill—quoted her father talking about his pride in his daughter. At the time the article was published, George Vanderbilt had been dead for almost seven years, making a quote from him . . . *unlikely*. And, after some very deep digging by UNC staff, no one could find any evidence of Cornelia ever actually attending the school.

This is a small example, but an example all the same, of what it was like to research two women whose lives were intimately covered in the media, often by gossip columnists or sources who, needless to say, weren't fact-checking. Quite often, I found, in writing, sources that confirmed two very disparate ideas: On Edith's wedding day, for example, some newspaper and magazine articles waxed poetic about her dripping jewels, gifts from George. Other sources were firm that she wore no jewelry at all. Similarly, sources differ widely about whether Cornelia first moved to England, France, or Switzerland after leaving Biltmore.

I'll be honest: when in doubt, I went with the source that fit my novel best, and, quite often, relied on a story from a Biltmore guide, even if I didn't have proof in print. Oral history has been so important to North Carolina's preservation that it seemed necessary to honor that. But despite my research, this is, through and through, a work of fiction, and much of the story that I couldn't find I dreamed up as best I could. How Peter Gerry and Edith Vanderbilt began their courtship, for example, is a detail I could never confirm. But the Helen Keller speech in Washington, D.C., where I placed them, was real, and is an event that would have been reasonable for either of them to attend.

No one seemed able to confirm exactly how Cornelia and John Cecil met, but the Vanderbilts' fancy dress balls were legendary, and, while I have no proof that Cornelia ever dressed as Cleopatra, I know Edith did. And since her dressing as the Queen of the Nile didn't have a place in my story, this is a nod. Jack's proposal on the day of her father's death? True—and, in my opinion, so lovely.

I also took a few liberties: The flag in the Biltmore Banquet Hall wasn't commissioned until 1920, but I wanted the ladies to see it as a visual reminder of what they were fighting for back home in 1918. Believe it or not—and this one shocked me—no one knows which bedroom belonged to Cornelia Vanderbilt in her childhood, before her father's death, so I have guessed.

If you want to know more about these remarkable women, this extraordinary family, and what remains America's largest privately owned home, I recommend *The Last Castle*, *Fortune's Children*, *Images of America: Biltmore Estate*, *Lady on the Hill*, *Biltmore: An American Masterpiece*, and *The Vanderbilts*. And, just for fun, *Specialties of the House*—which I relied on for several food-related bits and pieces—is a great look at the Vanderbilt menus. And check out some of the many ghost stories about Biltmore that, if you've already read this book, you'll see inspired one of its storylines.

Oh! And since I have been asked several times already, it is true that *All Men Are Ghosts* is the last work of fiction George Vanderbilt read before his death, according to his reading journal. Again, sometimes the stories write themselves.

All of this to say, Edith and Cornelia's rarefied world is one that, against all odds, we still have a true glimpse into, and re-creating what might have happened inside of it was one of the most fun writing experiences I've ever had. When I was almost finished with this novel, I began to have a scary thought: Who was *I* to tell these women's stories?

That night, as I was perusing Instagram, I came across a piece of jewelry. A signet pinky ring, bearing the initials E.D., just like the one Edith received on the day of Cornelia's baptism. Maybe it was a coincidence. But I took it as a sign, one of many that came during this process.

I worked my very hardest to tell these incredible women's stories with creativity, insight and, most of all, compassion. We might truly never know their inner lives at this point, but I hope this novel gave you a glimpse behind the curtain—and perhaps even inspired your first or next visit to Biltmore Estate, the lady on the hill that, with any luck, thanks to the tireless efforts of Edith Vanderbilt among many, many others, will stand tall among the mountains of the beautiful Blue Ridge for generations to come.

ACKNOWLEDGMENTS

I have always felt an indescribable connection to the women in my family, both the ones who have formed the fabric of my life with memories and the ones who came before who I never had the pleasure of knowing. I think, at its core, that is what this novel is about: the connection we can feel to people we have never met— whether through a shared history, or, perhaps, a family heirloom.

So it would make sense to thank, first, the women in my family: my sister-in-law, Dorothy Coleman, who passed along her family veil to me; my cousin Sidney Patton, who I passed it onto next; my cousin Catherine Adcox, who, being the perfect three years older than I am, taught me pretty much everything I needed to know about life; my aunts, Cathy Singer, Anne O'Berry, and Nancy Sanders, who showed me what sisterhood means and who are my A+ editorial team; my grandmother Ola Rutledge, who lives her life with heart, humor, compassion, and tradition, and is everything a matriarch should be; and my grandmother Hazel Woodson, who I knew for only a short time, but who, in leaving me her treasured pearls, proved the power of a family heirloom. My mom, Beth Woodson, gets her own lines of thanks because she is not just my mother; she's my business partner, my biggest cheerleader, and my inspiration, the perfect example of how to never stop growing, taking risks, and learning new things.

My friends have to hear a *lot* about any and everything I'm writing and offer their opinions, so love and gratitude to Millie Warren, Lee Taylor, Kate McDermott, Jessica Wilder, Booth Parker, Shelley Smith, Leeanne Walker, Kate Denierio, Drew Beall, and so many others who probably feel like they've already read this book as much as I've talked about it.

My *Friends & Fiction* partners in crime, Mary Kay Andrews/Kathy Trocheck, Patti Callahan Henry, and Kristin Harmel: This book would not exist without you and our morning writing sprints during the darkest, deepest early days of the COVID-19 shutdown. Thanks for your guidance, your support, and for never letting me miss my word count! Speaking of *Friends & Fiction*, Meg Walker, friend and brilliant managing director, Ron Block, genius librarian and rock star podcast host, Lisa Harrison and Brenda Gardner, peanut butter and jelly and loveliest book club hosts, Annissa Armstrong, launch day love lender and head cheerleader, and Shaun Hettinger, tech genius and five-star cabana boy—you guys add so much light and love to my world, and I am so grateful!

I met Michelle Kreitman at a literary luncheon where

I just happened to mention that I was working on a story about Edith and Cornelia Vanderbilt. Michelle, I don't know what magical inner workings of fate brought us together, but I can't thank you enough for all your help! I am eternally grateful for your advice and support.

My team at Gallery Books wows me each and every day. Thanks to Molly Gregory for picking up this book midstream and wading through the depths of it with me. I can't thank you enough for your dedication to making this story the best it could be—and for always doing it with a big smile! Bianca Salvant, thanks for being a never-ending font of fabulous ideas and implementing them so (seemingly!) effortlessly. Jennifer Bergstrom, Aimee Bell, Jennifer Long, and Abby Zidle—endless gratitude for continuing to let me do what I love so very, very much. Gabrielle Audet and Sarah Lieberman from Simon & Schuster Audio: Thank you for always bringing my novels to life in a new way so gloriously. I wait with bated breath for each audiobook to experience my novels in a brand-new way.

Elisabeth Weed, this book would not exist without you for a million reasons. Thank you for suggesting a "real wedding veil." I can't imagine this book any other way! Olivia Blaustein, you're the greatest, and I'm so grateful for you.

Kathie Bennett, Roy Bennett, Susan Zurenda, and everyone at Magic Time Literary: I know these past few years have been different to say the least, but you have risen to each and every challenge with grace. Thanks for making so many incredible things happen for me year after year!

I would not be here after nine novels were it not for the selfless and lovely support of the Bookstagram, blogging,

418s

418   Acknowledgments

library, and independent bookstore communities. To all of you who share my work: Thank you. Thank you. Thank you. Kristy Barrett, Stephanie Gray, Andrea Katz, Dallas Straun, Susan Roberts, Susan Peterson, Ashley Bellman, Susan McBeth, Zibby Owens, Judy Collins, Hanna Shields, Courtney Marzilli, Jennifer Clayton, Chase Waskey, and Randi Burton, your love for this book humbles me, and I can't thank you enough. And Meagan Briggs and Ashley Hayes of Uplit Reads, you guys are amazing!

Tamara Welch, I can't believe how many books we've brought to life together now. You are the glue that holds this all together! Ashley Edmondson, thanks for being such an important part of our family. What would we do without you? And many thanks for introducing me to Sam Douglas, who was invaluable in answering my NC State Architecture questions!

Speaking of family, the ladies got love at the top, but I certainly need to thank my dad, Paul Woodson, who has always believed in *all* my dreams, no matter how big. The only person who quite possibly believed in me even more was my grandfather, Joe Rutledge, who I was blessed enough to get to have for thirty-four whole years—and who I miss every day. I guess it's no coincidence that I married a man much like my dad and granddad, someone who always jumps at the chance to help, whether that means fact-checking part of a book, driving me on tour, taking on extra dad duty, or helping me unpack a business problem. Thanks, Will, for thinking I can do anything even when I forget. My son, Will, can catch any fish, anywhere, has the absolute greatest dance moves, and cracks me up every day. He's also an amazing writer, but I'm not getting my hopes up . . . I love you guys so, so much.

So, these acknowledgments end much as they began, with my family. This book is, more than anything, and maybe as usual, about family. How it shapes us, creates us, how we fight for those who went before us and long to change the world for those who are to come. Maybe that's why we're here; maybe that's what matters. Maybe we'll never know. But, in the meantime, I hope this story encourages each of you to draw close to the ones you love, to reach out a hand to someone who needs you, to fight for your dream even when it's hard—maybe *because* it's hard.

Edith did it. So did Cornelia. And I know you can too.

The
Wedding Veil

Kristy Woodson
Harvey

This reading group guide for The Wedding Veil *includes an introduction, discussion questions, and ideas for enhancing your book club. The suggested questions are intended to help your reading group find new and interesting angles and topics for your discussion. We hope that these ideas will enrich your conversation and increase your enjoyment of the book.*

Introduction

Four women. One family heirloom. A secret connection that will change their lives—and history as they know it.

Present Day: Julia Baxter's wedding veil, bequeathed to her great-grandmother by a mysterious woman on a train in the 1930s, has passed through generations of her family as a symbol of a happy marriage. But on the morning of her wedding day, something tells her that even the veil's good luck isn't enough to make her marriage last forever. Overwhelmed and panicked, she escapes to the Virgin Islands to clear her head. Meanwhile, her grandmother Babs is also feeling shaken. Still grieving the death of her beloved husband, she decides to move out of the house they once shared and into a retirement community. Though she hopes it's a new beginning, she does not expect to run into an old flame, dredging up the same complicated emotions she felt a lifetime ago.

1914: Socialite Edith Vanderbilt is struggling to manage the luxurious Biltmore Estate after the untimely death of her cherished husband. With 250 rooms to oversee and an entire village dependent on her family to stay afloat, Edith is determined to uphold the Vanderbilt legacy—and prepare her free-spirited daughter, Cornelia, to inherit it—in spite of her family's deteriorating financial situation. But Cornelia has dreams of her own. Asheville, North Carolina, has always been her safe haven away from the prying eyes of the press, but as she explores more of the rapidly changing world around her, she's torn between upholding tradition and pursuing the exciting future that lies beyond Biltmore's gilded gates.

In the vein of Therese Anne Fowler's *A Well-Behaved Woman* and Jennifer Robson's *The Gown*, *The Wedding Veil* brings to vivid life a group of remarkable women forging their own paths—and explores the mystery of a national heirloom lost to time.

Topics & Questions
for Discussion

1. When we first meet Julia at her bridesmaids' luncheon the day before her wedding, she experiences a moment of panic about getting married. She soothes her nerves by thinking *"Follow the rules. Follow the rules"* (pg. 9). How do each of the narrators "follow the rules"? Do they ever decide not to follow the rules? Discuss how Julia's mother, Meredith, *did* follow the rules, and how it affected her life and marriage.

2. The wedding veil is what weaves the characters and their stories together in the book. Discuss how it impacts each person who wears it. What does it represent for each of them?

3. Throughout the book we see characters creating second chances for themselves: Julia by making the decision to leave Hayes, forge her own path, and go back to school; Babs and Edith by allowing themselves to find love again; and Cornelia by leaving the life she knows and searching for her own happiness.

Have you ever had a second chance at something? Do you wish you had?

4. Edith and Cornelia recognize their privilege and feel a strong sense of social responsibility, often lending a helping hand within their community. Was this common at that time? How do they compare to today's very wealthy class in this regard?

5. When Julia returns from St. Thomas, she and Babs visit Biltmore Estate. While admiring the beauty and extravagance of it, Julia also acknowledges the "impracticality and inefficiency" of it (pg. 277). She thinks to herself, "that was part of being an architect—creating structures that fit the times" (pg. 277). How do Julia's reflections on architecture also apply to her feelings about her own life and the choices she has to make?

6. Discuss how the family traditions of the characters bring them closer to the people in their lives. Does tradition ever create unfair expectations?

7. In the last chapter of the book, Babs confesses to Julia that she was the one who anonymously texted the video of Hayes with another woman to the bridesmaids' group the day before Julia's wedding. How do you think Babs handled this situation?

8. Cornelia Vanderbilt grew up in the limelight. How do you think this affected her mental health and the decision she ultimately makes to leave her home, her marriage, and her life to move to England to

find her calling? Were there other contributing factors?

9. When Babs's mother is reflecting on the moment she received the wedding veil on the train, she remembers experiencing uncertainty about marrying Babs's father. When Cornelia hands her the veil, she tells her, "What you need is a sign" (pg. 260). What other "signs" do the characters use throughout the book to help them make decisions?

10. Although Julia loves Hayes, she never feels completely confident that being with him is the right decision; still, she sometimes finds it easier to make decisions based on safety and comfort vs. being true to her own feelings. Discuss how some characters find comfort in playing it safe while others find it restricting.

11. Moving on is an inevitable part of everyone's lives. How does Edith handle George's death and moving on with her life? How does Babs handle moving on from Reid? And how does Julia handle moving forward from her relationship with Hayes?

12. After Babs moves to Summer Acres she immediately reconnects with Miles. She feels conflicted, as if she is betraying her late husband. She understands that she will always mourn Reid and that there is a possibility she will mourn the loss of Miles one day too, but realizes it would perhaps be worst of all to mourn a relationship that was never given a chance. Do any other characters in the book come to this realization too? How so?

13. The four narrators are from different times and up-bringings. Discuss what they have in common. How are they different?

14. Throughout the story, we see different women moving through different phases of their lives. How does what they want in life change as they move through these different phases?

15. In the chapter "Mistress of Biltmore" (pg. 241), George tells a young Cornelia, "Writing and art are what we use to make sense of our lives. But it is science and math that truly govern them. The words might lead you astray, but the numbers are fixed, unchanging" (pg. 242). What role do you think this plays in Cornelia's fascination with and dependence on numerology?

Enhance Your Book Club

1. Imagine Cornelia as a young woman today. How might her life path be shaped by the presence of social media?

2. Does your family have any heirlooms? Share with the group and discuss their significance to your family.

3. Research a local place of historical significance. How did this place, and the people surrounding it, help shape your community as it is today? Perhaps you can plan a group trip to explore it.

4. Think about something you have always wanted to do (learn to paint, take a language class, etc.) but never felt was attainable. Discuss this with the group and strategize about how you can take the next step toward this goal.

5. Cornelia married John Cecil in 1924. What dishes and beverages were popular among the upper class during this time? Create a menu for their wedding.

Don't miss the next novel from *New York Times*

bestselling author Kristy Woodson Harvey

A Happier Life

Coming soon from Gallery Books!

Keep reading for a sneak peek . . .

Prologue

....

The House on Sunset Lane: Pioneers

Houses outlive the people they love. When my fellow clapboard houses on Sunset Lane in Beaufort and I were being built by shipbuilders just discovering this port, proud and young and new, we had no idea what our futures would hold. How could we? In 1769, we were the first houses on this street, as much pioneers as the fishermen, whalers, and shipping merchants, like the Saint James family—my family—who made us their homes.

But what we understood immediately was that it was our job to care for the families who lived within our wooden walls—often repurposed from the ships they came in on—who loved us, who filled us with furniture and bedding, crotchety aging grandparents, and howling, beloved infants. It was our job to remember every word spoken, every breath breathed, to store their secrets and successes, heart-breaks and joys, and keep them safe.

Here, on Seven Sunset Lane, the sun still glints on water that slowly, patiently laps the sandy shore. People marvel at us, these structures that have been here since before America was America.

But I alone hold the distinction of still, two hundred fifty-four years after I was first built, being the Saint James House. Other houses on this street have changed hands, been sold, filled with fresh wallpaper, trendy paint colors, and new people who don't care quite so much about the stories their houses hold. That I have been owned by one family should be a point of pride. Only, it has been nearly fifty years since anyone has lived inside of me, since I have swayed with voices singing Christmas carols, vibrated with dog paws speeding down my halls, and cheered with friends blowing out birthday candles. But those aren't the moments I miss most. What I long for is the sound of my door swinging open, the rush of sea breeze through cracked windows, my kitchen filled with the scents of cakes and cookies, roasts and chickens, the simple laughter of ordinary days.

I loved all the families who brought those days to me. But my happiest years, my best times, were with Becks and Townsend Saint James and their children, Lon and Virginia. Sometimes, when I miss them most, I cling to the specks of sand between my floorboards, reminders of when the children tore inside with such jubilance that I would have cried if I had tears. Their mother, Becks, instead of scolding them, wrapped them in towels and kisses and fed them homemade strawberry ice cream on my wide, spacious front porch. I kept them cool in the summer and warm in the winter, a product of facing perfectly south, to the credit of my savvy builders.

I once believed, foolishly, that the parties and dinners, friends and fun—and, most of all, great love of this family, love so big and so pulsating that I could feel it down into my very foundation— would stay forever. For years I have hoped, prayed, wished that they would return, ever since Rebecca and Townsend Saint James unexpectedly met their demise on August 28, 1976. I alone know the real story, have held the truth right here all this time, if anyone had bothered to uncover it.

But that is the plight of old houses. At some point in our seemingly infinite lives, we may be forgotten. And so, we must cling to the joys and secrets forever stored within our walls, until we are remembered again.

Keaton

....

All (Are Not) Welcome

I will get this promotion *or something better*," I whisper as I walk down the gleaming, glass-walled hall of All Welcome, the lifestyle brand I have been working for since I was a college intern twelve years ago. Allison, our CEO—and, well, my hero—is big on the phrase. She claims she has used it to manifest her massive success over the last thirteen years, when she started this brand as a recent college grad. Who am I to doubt her? If I'm going to manifest something, now seems like a good time to start.

Casey, one of our interns, winks at me as she passes me in the hallway and crosses her fingers. Her encouragement boosts me as my stomach rolls with the reminder that Jonathan, the head of HR and my ex, is going to be in this meeting about my "future with All Welcome" too. We broke up about a month ago, after eighteen months of dating, but I still haven't told my family. I can almost hear my mother's voice in my head: *I don't like to interfere, but, darling, the man still works for his ex-wife's company. And you work for him. It is unsavory at best, a recipe for disaster at worst.*

Despite my mother's concerns, I had always felt proud that Jonathan—who was *not* my superior when we started dating, I might add—Allison, and I have always been able to work together so seamlessly. Allison and Jonathan used to say it was because their relationship was ancient history. And now, so was ours. Because after we moved in together six months ago, Jonathan and I realized that the single thing we had in common was work. Now the three of us are back to being just coworkers. Coworkers with weird personal histories, to be sure, but just coworkers all the same.

I walk to the end of the hall to the smallest conference room. It is the only one that has solid, soundproof walls instead of glass, so it's the most private. And it's where most promotion meetings take place.

Allison is already there, as I assumed she would be. Punctuality is one of her core values. The others, as I well know, are transparency, honesty, innovation, and excellence. She is a motivational speaker who gets paid in the high five digits each time she flies off to inspire companies and their employees to reach their full potential. She has a huge conference—All-Fest—each year that literally fills an arena, a line of journals and goal-setting notebooks, and has penned four *New York Times* bestsellers. We even decided to publish her last book in-house. We were nervous, but it went so well that we're publishing a handful of other meaningful titles this year by other authors in the space.

It's very exciting. It is also very on-brand for Allison, someone who many, many women aspire to be like. As I open the door, I see that right now—aspirationally—she is walking on the quiet, non-motorized treadmill in the corner of the room. She has exercise equipment in every conference room and her office because she doesn't have time for regular workouts, but this ensures she can still honor her body and spirit each day—her words, not mine. She is *such* a badass. I feel the tiniest twinge of guilt that I can't remember the last time I actually exercised myself.

"Oh, hi!" I say as I spot Jonathan shifting a stack of papers at the head of the table. I thought the breakup would be harder, but since we have had to work together every day since, it already sort of feels like we're back to just coworkers. Even at thirty-seven, he still has ashy blond hair and big puppy-dog brown eyes. He's a good guy. Not *my* guy anymore. But a good guy all the same. He has been letting me stay in the town house we shared while I frantically look for another apartment. Something decent in my price range in New York City is, evidently, hard to come by. And our breakup made me realize I don't have so much as a friend's couch to crash on. My parents' place is a last resort that I hope I don't need.

A glass of water is in front of the seat next to

him, so I figure it is mine. I take my seat and am shocked when Allison quits walking. She usually keeps working out, getting progressively more breathless as a meeting goes on. Usually, by the end of an hour, I'm translating because I'm the only one who can understand her. Curiously, though, the woman never sweats.

"Keaton, Keaton, Keaton," she says as she sits down. "Our girl wonder."

I sit on the edge of my seat, keeping my fingers crossed under the table. "I brought you here today to tell you that I'm pregnant."

That's not what I'm expecting to hear, but, still, I gasp and clap my hands. I would know if she was seriously dating someone, so I wonder if she has done in vitro or, knowing Allison, has engineered some new pregnancy procedure that doesn't involve sperm at all. A woman-only pregnancy. She'd be really into that. It would also be great for our brand. I briefly wonder how on earth she's going to take care of a child when she works absolutely nonstop. All that aside, she's obviously telling me I'm promoted because she can't take on anything else in her state.

"That is great news, Allison," I chime in. "And I'd like you to know I'm here for anything you need."

She smiles with an ethereal glow and reaches across the table to take my hand. "I am so glad to hear you say that because there *is* something I need from you."

I feel a grin spread across my face, and I glance briefly at Jonathan. He looks kind of . . . constipated. Which I know he never is because we shared a bathroom in his two-bedroom town house. Maybe he's worried about what Allison's pregnancy is going to mean for his job, which I totally get. But now he'll have me—with my corner office and big, fat salary—to lighten his workload. I try to convey that with my glance, but he doesn't seem to notice.

Then Allison says, with a light squeeze of my palm, "I'm going to need you to move out of the town house."

I look at Jonathan again, not quite comprehending. "Well, I'm looking for a new place, but . . ." I trail off. Some fuzzy atoms are connecting in my brain.

I remove my clammy hand and take a sip of water just as Allison lets out a breathy little laugh. "Oh my gosh. Pregnancy brain. The baby is Jonathan's, and I am going to move back into the house y'all have been living in. My apartment is too small."

I honestly don't mean to, but I choke and spit the water out, spraying it all over Jonathan. He barely moves to wipe himself off; he only looks really apologetic. And kind of sick.

"*My* Jonathan?" I squeak.

Allison smiles in a way that feels very condescending. "Well, mine," she says as she rubs her impossibly flat stomach.

Jonathan barely pipes up. "Well, actually, Allison, I'm not sure I would say I *belong* to you."

She smiles at him in a way that conveys, *Oh, but don't you?*

"I. What? No. You can't. It doesn't . . ." I'm obviously having some trouble with my words.

"Don't worry," Allison says. "We'll have someone

pack up all your things and get them moved wherever you go next."

"That is literally the last thing I am worried about." I turn to Jonathan, doing the math in my head. We've only been broken up for four weeks. "How long has this been going on?"

"Well, I'm twelve weeks along," Allison says, batting her eyes at Jonathan.

"What?" I practically scream, realizing *this* is why I'm in the soundproof conference room. I turn to Jonathan. "Are you insane? We only moved in together like six months ago! You're the one who talked me into getting rid of my apartment!"

"I'm really sorry," Jonathan says. "It was so obvious things weren't going to work out with us that I just . . . moved on before it was official. It didn't mean anything at first."

"But then we realized we were still in love," Allison says. "That we wanted to start a family. I truly hope this doesn't hurt you, Keaton, but Jonathan and I think consciously recoupling is the right thing for us."

Consciously recoupling. This can't be real. Anger, which I am usually good at controlling, rises in me. The hypocrisy is too much for me to take. "Do you believe your own psychobabble bullshit?" I ask her, my face turning red. "I mean, do you hear yourself? Oh, *honesty and transparency are my core values*," I say in a singsong voice.

"I'm sorry you feel that way," she says, "because we were here to offer you a promotion to director of marketing. But if you aren't committed to the brand then—"

"You were going to offer me a promotion?" I practically spit. "A *promotion*? So we can work more closely while you and your ex remarry and start a family?"

"Oh, we won't remarry," Allison says. "Marriage feels so archaic and confining now. But we assumed if the two of us could work so well together after a divorce that surely you could manage . . ."

That's when I know I'm going to cry, and that's the last thing in the world I want to do. I *want* to be archaic and confined. I want to be *married*. I don't want to be married to Jonathan. But the fact that he cheated on me really stings. And, well, explains why he's been so nice about letting me stay in the town house. Guilt is powerful.

"Jonathan, how could you do this to me? All that time we were planning our future together, and you were screwing your ex-wife?" *And I had no idea?*

"I'm sorry, Keaton. I really am."

"You should never be sorry about living your authentic path, Jonathan," Allison interjects.

I take a long look at Allison, and I can't believe that I was so enamored with her for so long. Yes, she's beautiful in this bird-boned, hippie-at-Woodstock kind of way. And she has this soft voice that you have to lean forward to hear, that makes you want to listen. But she's also selfish. It's always about her. I know this, and yet I've always forgiven her for it because I believed she was a good person deep down.

When I got my internship the summer after my junior year at our shared alma mater, UNC–Chapel Hill, I felt like I had won the lottery. Allison and I together felt like kismet. It was clear I would come work for her after graduation. I knew she was going to change the world. And, well, she has. And so that's why it's so hard for me to say, "Why did I buy into this for so long? I did your program to the letter for years, and it's just now occurring to me that I'm not any better, any more enlightened, than I was when I started."

"What do you mean *did*?" Allison asks.

I squint at her. "*Did*. Now, a lot of mornings, I don't even make my bed." *I don't have time since I'm basically running your company*, I add, only in my head.

Allison gasps. "Making your bed is a Vision One, Track One foundation habit. Are you even drinking your eight glasses of water? Moving your thirty minutes?"

"Nope!" I say, crossing my arms, feeling childish. I know she is going to be offended by this admission.

"The foundation habits aren't really that difficult if you're committed," she says. "Keaton, maybe you and I should dive into why you're letting yourself stay stuck."

"Because your entire company is crap, Allison, based on making women feel like they aren't good enough if they aren't as perfect and motivated and successful as you." I know I've gone too far. All Welcome's whole premise is that everyone can find their happiness if they make the time to do what inspires them. And Allison has helped people do that. Even still, I can't help but hit her where it hurts most.

She smiles sadly at me, and I'm torn between

regret and hatred. "Keaton, I'm sorry to say, but I think your journey here at All Welcome is coming to an end. I can overlook a spiritually unenlightened reaction in a moment of turmoil, but I can't have people who don't believe in the process be a part of this company."

Jonathan finally speaks up. "Well, maybe it isn't fair to fire her . . ."

I know he's thinking it isn't fair to fire me because in what world am I *not* going to sue the hell out of this company for wrongful termination? "Nope!" I say. "I'm fired."

"Maybe we can discuss a severance package that feels right?" Jonathan says, hesitantly, still trying to smooth over something that has already gotten out of hand.

"Well," Allison says, still with that slick calm voice of hers, "I feel that giving Keaton severance is offensive; it's like saying we don't believe in her or her ability to begin anew. And that simply isn't true. I do believe in Keaton and the power and beauty of her dreams."

I am too nauseated to respond.

"Okay," Jonathan says, standing up. "Allison, we might be making some hasty decisions here."

No severance, bigger lawsuit. For all her preaching, Allison isn't a very good businesswoman. Which is why she needed me. Well, that, and the fact that my role as marketing coordinator had morphed really far from my job description. In addition to handling marketing strategies—like advertising, paid editorial placement, and merchandise—I also oversaw all of All Welcome's social media (which is technically a different department), scheduled all of Allison's podcast guests, the launches for the four books a year (and growing!) the company is now publishing through its publishing arm, sat in on practically every meeting, and on and on and on.

Allison and I worked together nonstop. We laughed together. We dreamed together. I couldn't imagine that it could come to this. And I had no idea what she would do without me. It looks like she's about to find out.

I stand up. "You heard her. I'm fired. No severance. I want all my stuff returned to my parents' place right away. And you damn well better bring my dog."

I'm not moving there, I tell myself. Just staying until I find a new apartment. I have some money saved, and besides, I can always go live with my brother for a while instead.

Only, as I storm out of the building and call said brother to tell him what happened and ask him if I can stay, he flat-out says, "No, Keaton. You cannot come live with me."

I am aghast. "Harris! Are you kidding me? Why can't I live with you for just a little bit? I'm looking really hard for an apartment." I pause, putting the pieces together. My brother is my best friend. There is only one reason he wouldn't want me to live with him. "You have some rando woman living with you, don't you? And you haven't even told Mom and Dad. Or me. What is wrong with you?"

"Well, you won't approve," he says.

"She's like twenty-three, isn't she?"

"Thereabouts."

"Harris! Get your shit together. Break up with her and choose your sister for once in your freaking life."

"I'm not not choosing you, Keat. I love you. But just think about it. How cool would it be to use your severance to get away for a while?"

"I didn't get severance," I say. "Allison feels that would send the message that she doesn't believe in my ability to begin anew."

"O-kay," Harris says. "Well, you still can't live here, but I am hiring you a lawyer."

I enter the code in the keypad to Mom and Dad's building, which is an easy couple blocks' walk from my office—well, it *was* anyway—and swing open the door. "Mom told me not to move in with him," I say out loud as I step into the elevator, more to myself than to Harris. "If I had listened to her, maybe I wouldn't be in this mess."

"Oh, Keat. I'm sorry. But, look, I'll help you find a place to live. We'll figure it out."

"Okay," I whisper. "Can you help find me a job, too? *Oh my gosh I don't have a job!*" I am filled with dread. "I have to go." Tears puddle in my eyes, and I literally have to sit on the elevator floor since my legs won't hold me up any longer. I realize that I have given every single part of myself to this job that I just walked away from. I don't have hobbies. I don't volunteer. All my meals are either from a frozen meal delivery service or DoorDash because who has time to cook? I barely have friends because when would I see them? My social life consisted of Jonathan and Allison and my colleagues and now it's all just . . . . gone.

The elevator opens, and a woman pushes her walker through. "Hi, Mrs. Ellis," I say with zero enthusiasm.

She starts. "Oh dear. What are you doing on the floor?"

"Bad day," I say.

"Well, a bad day is always a good time to visit one's parents."

I nod, but then another sick feeling washes over me: Worse than getting dumped, worse than getting fired, I'm going to have to tell my mother she was right.